A GENTLEMAN'S MURDER

CHRISTOPHER HUANG

Published by Inkshares, Inc., Oakland, California
www.inkshares.com

Cover design by Oliver Munday
Edited by Matt Harry, Adam Gomolin & Barnaby Conrad
Interior design by Kevin G. Summers

ISBN: 9781942645955
e-ISBN: 9781947848030
LCCN: 2017955468

Second edition

Printed in the United States of America

"Crime is terribly revealing. Try and vary your methods as you will, your tastes, your habits, your attitude of mind, and your soul is revealed by your actions."

—Agatha Christie

"We are the Dead. Short days ago
We lived, felt dawn, saw sunset glow,
Loved and were loved, and now we lie."

—John McCrae, "In Flanders Fields"

"No Chinaman must figure in the story. Why this should be so I do not know, unless we can find a reason for it in our western habit of assuming that the Celestial is over-equipped in the matter of brains, and under-equipped in the matter of morals. I only offer it as a fact of observation that, if you are turning over the pages of a book and come across some mention of "the slit-like eyes of Chin Loo," you had best put it down at once; it is bad."

—Ronald Knox, *Best Detective Stories*, 1928

"I can make a lord, but only God can make a gentleman."

—King James I

RULE, BRITANNIA

THE BRITANNIA CLUB stood on King Street, a respectable limestone facade among respectable limestone facades, with a brass plaque that nobody had looked at in decades; if you had to stop to check the address, you were clearly in the wrong place.

This was St. James. "Clubland."

The men traversing these streets walked with that air of self-assurance that comes from belonging to a privileged set. In bookish Bloomsbury, the Londoners drifted around the British Museum in the wake of literary romance. In the working-class areas of the East End, such as Limehouse or Whitechapel, they trudged with a grim determination, playing the cards they'd been dealt. South of the Thames, in Battersea, where in 1913 John Archer became the first black man elected as borough mayor, they simmered after a better tomorrow. But in affluent St. James, they simply knew that they *were* the Empire.

Here, for instance, was Lieutenant Eric Peterkin, late of the Royal Fusiliers. He was buttoned up against the October chill in a double-breasted greatcoat of military cut. His homburg was tilted at just enough of an angle to be rakish without being disreputable. His suit was pressed, his collar was starched, and his gait was brisk. His companion, Avery Ferrett, was more unconventionally dressed in a shapeless overcoat and a beret; and though much taller, Avery had to trot to keep up with Eric.

"It's the only way to kill someone," Eric was saying. The good people of London, well bred as they were, pretended not to hear. "Most people would go to pieces if they had to do it up close, with a knife or a bludgeon, or something of the sort." He nodded sagely. "Guns and poisons, Avery. That's the way to do it."

"Well, I think it's ghastly," said Avery. "You read too many of these murder mysteries, Eric."

"It's what I'm paid to do." Eric had a job evaluating manuscripts for publication, and lately, most seemed to be about mysterious deaths behind locked doors.

"You don't have to take such ghoulish enjoyment out of it. Honestly, Eric, I'm surprised at you. After the War, I'd have thought you'd had your fill of death."

Eric came to a stop. One never quite forgot the War, however one tried. "That's different. Death in the War was . . . just death, nothing personal about it. But this"—he held up the envelope containing his next assignment—"this is murder. Do you understand? It's personal. It's intimate. You know the poor bugger who gets stabbed in the locked room. The killer and the victim were probably friendly once upon a time. And it puts a sort of meaning on death, which makes it manageable, like a puzzle to be solved rather than a thing you just endure. Do you see?" Eric wasn't sure if he did. Avery had spent the entirety of the War in Buenos Aires for his health.

Avery just shook his head. "I still think it's an inhuman business whatever the case. You always leave something of your humanity behind in a murder. I could never do it."

"Something of your humanity . . . well, yes. That's what makes it personal, and what gives it meaning. You see the murderer's soul reflected in all the little details surrounding the crime, and that puts a human face on Death. Death becomes a thing you can understand because of . . . of the residue of humanity left behind."

"No, no. What I mean is, you're never a whole person again afterwards." Avery paused and added, "Sometimes I wonder if anyone is a whole person anymore."

"That's the price of our present, Avery. The War was a terrible thing, but the great thing is that nothing approaching that scale will ever happen again, because no one wants to go back to the trenches. There's some sense being made out of all the killing, if you like."

Indeed, in that year of 1924, the world preferred not to dwell on the past. It looked outside and to the future, and in Eric's opinion, that was not a bad thing at all.

They were now passing the St. James Theatre, with its posters advertising the current play. Eric considered this production a very poor copy of the previous year's *The Green Goddess*, but it featured even more exotic fare, with a "menacing Mandarin" villain straight out of a Sax Rohmer novel. No matter how distasteful Eric found this current fashion for Oriental villains, there was no denying that it illustrated his point. They were headed towards a more cosmopolitan world, even if some aspects of the road getting there set his teeth on edge. One looked outwards.

Over at Wembley Park was the ongoing exhibition for the British Empire in all her glory, with pavilions and displays representing every corner of the world where the rule of His Majesty King George V was law. And just a few months ago, the Paris Olympics brought all the world to the French capital just across the Channel. Women were allowed to fence at the Olympics for the first time that year, and Eric had gone to see them. His sister, Penny, had gone for a glimpse of her personal hero, equestrian Philip Bowden-Smith. And Avery had gone for the French chocolates.

Along with looking outwards, one also looked forwards: simply being alive in the here and now was a cause for celebration. The stodgy Victorian and Georgian architecture found on King Street—the St. James Theatre, the Golden Lion pub, the Britannia Club itself—was giving way elsewhere to the clean, angular lines of Egyptian-inspired art deco and the broad white expanses of modernism. Electric lights were the rule now rather than the exception; they blinked from the marquees of theatres and shone from the windows of houses, lighting up the night the way gas lamps never had. Motorcars had superseded horse-drawn carriages in the streets, changing the very sound and smell of London: for better or for worse, brass horns and chemical exhaust had taken the place of hoofbeats and horse sweat. Hot dance music—what the Americans called "jazz"—had begun to fill the nightclubs, and the advent of the wireless and the newly minted British Broadcasting Company meant it might very well begin to fill the parlours and drawing rooms of British homes as well.

"Penny for the Guy, sir?"

Eric and Avery looked down as a pair of ragged urchins brought them back to the reality of King Street, London. Oh yes, the fifth of November, Bonfire Night, would be in just another couple of weeks, wouldn't it? Enterprising young urchins were already plying the streets with wagons and barrows loaded up with artful effigies of Guy Fawkes. This one was stuffed with rags, with a head like a boiled pudding and a long, curling moustache drawn on in ink.

"Now that is what I call a nice Guy," Eric said, tossing tuppence into the barrow. "And what a fine, villainous moustache he has too!"

The urchins behind the barrow just stared at him. Avery chuckled. "You're frightening the young'uns," he said. He dropped his own penny into the barrow, and the urchins raced off to present their Guy to the next man on the street.

Avery turned to Eric and said, "Your club's probably got a vastly superior Guy in a vastly superior wagon just waiting in the wings, I'll wager. All you toffs tossing in sovereigns instead of pennies, I should expect some jolly impressive fireworks."

It wasn't the done thing to bring up money in conversation, but Avery never seemed to care. Eric had known him long enough to forgive the odd gaucherie. "We don't much care for fireworks, actually," Eric said as they crossed the street to the Britannia Club itself. "Reminds some people too much of the trenches, I think. They'd rather stay home than risk the streets, so the place is always empty on Bonfire Night."

The Britannia Club had but one requirement for membership, aside from being a gentleman: experience on the battlefield in the service of the Empire. Eric qualified with a year in the trenches, whereas Avery, thanks to his extended Argentinian tour, did not.

"I always wonder what goes on behind those doors," Avery remarked, gazing up at the neoclassical facade. The oak doors were enormous, and the great brass knockers didn't look as though they'd ever been lifted. "One of these days, Eric, you will have to bring me in as a guest."

"It's just a lot of men sitting around and smoking, Avery. Nothing you don't see yourself every day at the Arabica."

The Arabica was a coffeehouse just off Soho Square where Avery could usually be found poring over a Tarot spread as a cloud of clove cigarette smoke gathered around his head.

"And yet you maintain your membership," Avery replied.

"It's a family tradition," Eric said, shoulders drawing back as he drew himself up. "Like going into the Army. It's bad enough that I didn't make a career of it after I was demobbed. I don't know what Dad would say if I gave up my membership here as well."

"I could ask."

"Don't you dare. Anyway, it's . . . convenient."

"So's the Arabica, and that doesn't cost me more than a shilling for coffee." Avery looked up at the club's front doors again, then turned to his friend with a sly, playful smile. "I can only conclude that there must be something nefarious afoot."

"Nefarious!"

"Yes, nefarious! My friend, the villain. Tell me, is there a murder every week, and a dastardly plan to rule the Empire from the shadows?"

Eric laughed. "Get on with you! I'd hardly tell you if that were so!"

Avery let out an exaggerated sigh. "Then I shall leave you to your scheming. Just be sure to give me some kind of warning before you set your plan for world domination in motion, or I shall be quite upset."

Eric laughed again and waved his friend off. Avery responded with a jaunty tip of his beret, and headed off in the direction of St.

James's Square. Eric watched him go, then trotted up the steps to the club. One door opened just wide enough to let him through, then swung silently shut behind him.

Eric hadn't been entirely truthful, even to himself, when he said the Britannia was only "convenient" to his purposes. If he had, he might have realised what Avery already knew: Membership in the Britannia Club was more than simply convenient, or even a home away from home. It was the imprimatur of his very identity as a Peterkin.

Eric's flat was a cosy but cramped corner of London that Avery described as "a claustrophobic little hole." Eric thought it decent enough, but he wasn't too fond of solitude, and so he spent most of his waking hours at his club.

Silence closed in all around as soon as the great front door clicked softly shut behind him. The entry vestibule was an austere marble hall, a buffer between the bustle of London and the comfort of the club. One wall was entirely taken up by a roster of men who'd lost their lives in the Great War. Sobering as this reminder was, it was still "the war to end all wars," and there was at least some comfort in knowing that the opposite wall would never be filled in the same way. Eric took a moment to pick out the Peterkins among them, then proceeded through to the warmth of the walnut-panelled lobby, where sunlight from a skylight two floors above illuminated the marble floor tiles, discreetly patterned and polished to a mirror shine. The silence was barely broken by the clink of silverware coming from the adjacent dining room.

The front desk opposite was a dark polished walnut, like the panelling on the walls. Eric's heels tapped across the floor as he approached the desk to sign the register.

"Morning, Cully," he said to the porter stationed behind the front desk.

"Morning, Lieutenant Peterkin, sir." The porter's name was Ted Cully, though Eric and the other members generally referred to him

as "Old Faithful" behind his back. He was a short, squarely built
fellow with twinkling blue eyes who'd recently been persuaded that
his age more than warranted the growth of a short salt-and-pepper
beard. He addressed most members by both name and rank, the
result of a lifelong attachment to all things military. Eric knew that
he'd lied about his age to enlist, and that his military career had
taken him all over the world, from New Zealand to Africa; but even
a lifetime of world travel and regimental spit-and-polish couldn't
iron out the musical Irish lilt from his speech.

The same might be said about the Britannia Club. It didn't
Old Faithful was the first person Eric had met at the Britannia
Club. That seemed like almost another time, in another world; Eric
had been only a boy of ten, not yet a lieutenant except in his games,
here for his first Christmas outside of India and deeply curious
about the man with the twinkling blue eyes behind the big walnut
desk. Old Faithful had barely changed since then, and it seemed
unlikely that he ever would.

The same might be said about the Britannia Club. It didn't
change. The men were gentlemen, the conversation was civilised,
the attendants were invisible until you wanted them, and the toast
was, unfortunately, burnt. Much like a warm blanket on a winter's
day, this changeless certainty insulated and comforted; it offered an
escape from the chaotic hubbub of the London streets.

On the first-floor landing hung a massive oil painting, a
pre-Raphaelite depiction of King Arthur's knights around the
Round Table. There had always been Peterkins at the Britannia:
one of Eric's ancestors had been a founding member, and his like-
ness was immortalised in this painting as a white-whiskered King
Pellinore. There were the distinctively heavy Peterkin eyebrows, the
only physical feature Eric had inherited from his father. Eric felt
more family pride here than he was willing to admit. He always
stopped to give old Pellinore-Peterkin a nod of recognition on his
way up to the lounge. But his attention was just as often drawn to
another figure in the painting: Sir Palomides, King Arthur's Saracen
knight, the one dark, non-European face among the pale Britons
who made up the rest of the cohort.

Eric remembered that he'd spent much of that first English Christmas standing here, trying to identify everyone from the legends. Sir Palomides had, of course, been the easiest to recognise. Then as now, Eric felt a special sympathy for him. Alone in a crowd, he mused. Surrounded by the bright pageantry of Camelot, yet still quite on his own. Poor fellow.

And the rest of the knights represented the body of the Britannia's membership, of course. It was not that the club members were truly perfect paragons of virtue; twenty-six years as an outsider and twelve months in the trenches of Flanders had taught Eric better than to expect that. None of the Arthurian Knights really were, excepting perhaps the impossibly perfect Grail Knights. But each member here had made the choice to put up his life in the service of his country, and that, to Eric, made them noble.

Eric continued into the lounge, where soft carpets muffled his footsteps and blazing fires crackled in the fireplaces. His Usual Armchair was waiting for him, a high-backed affair with wings against which one might lean one's head for a nap. The fireplace nearby was excellent for toasting one's toes when the weather got grim.

Yes, he was far from the muck and cold and death of Flanders.

Elsewhere in the room, armchairs and low tables were organised in a scattering of little groups both discreet and discrete. Tall curtained windows overlooked King Street. And there was the bar, also nearby, just a little battered from that one time fifty years ago when Eric's grandfather threw the then-reigning club president over it in a brawl.

Eric had ensconced himself in his Usual Armchair almost every day since he'd first got the job evaluating manuscripts for a small publisher. He had more than once been glad of the bar, when he needed to salve his brain with good whisky after a particularly bad manuscript. He rather hoped the new manuscript he had in his hands would want no such solution.

The Case of the Jade Butterfly, he read. Another Far East mystery. His employers seemed to think he was very good with those.

Perhaps, he thought as he glanced at the wall of text on the first page, a preemptive measure of whisky and soda would be a very good idea.

Standing at the bar with a tumbler of whisky was Edward Aldershott. The Britannia Club was run by an elected board of five officers, and Aldershott was the stiff-backed, stony-faced club president. Tall, prematurely grey, and with a habit of standing perfectly still, he looked like a bespectacled stone lion. But his starched collar failed to hide the boil scars of a run-in with mustard gas in the War; he was still flesh and blood, for all he pretended not to be.

Aldershott's work outside the club revolved around advising others on how best to manage their investments—or how to best let him manage their investments, as the case might be. Most of his clients were members of the club. He often conducted his business from the club president's office, which explained his presence here on a workday morning.

"Morning, Aldershott," Eric said politely, sliding up to the bar to place his order.

The granite-grey head didn't move, but even in the soft lighting of the club lounge, the spectacles glinted like diamonds: hard, cold, and unwelcoming. Abruptly, Aldershott swallowed the remainder of his whisky and moved deliberately away to strike up a conversation with a bearded club member at the other end of the bar.

Eric's lips settled into a hard line, and he ordered his whisky and soda somewhat more brusquely than usual.

There had always been Peterkins at the Britannia, and the Britannia was a nonnegotiable fixture in Eric's life. But there was a reason he'd always felt that kinship with poor old Sir Palomides at the Round Table. This latest slight was hardly an isolated incident, and Eric had got to the point where he found it deeply annoying rather than truly mortifying.

What would Sir Palomides do?

What would any Knight of the Round Table do? Obviously, he'd take up his lance to set things right . . . Eric shook his head. He was being fanciful. The Britannia Club was not Camelot. It was . . .

civilised. Safe. Untouched and untouchable. And Flanders, too, was far away, never to return. Whatever else happened in the world outside, the Britannia was proof against it. A bastion. No, Eric thought as he turned back to his assigned manuscript. Nothing unseemly could ever happen at the Britannia.

Little did he know, twenty-four hours would change everything.

THE KNIGHT ERRANT

THE LATE-OCTOBER AFTERNOON turned to dusk, and dusk to evening. Light dimmed to darkness outside the windows of the Britannia Club lounge, and flared up again with the fog-fuzzed glow of the streetlamps. Sunset came noticeably earlier now, with October beginning to fade into the expectation of November. The season of fog was upon London: yellow-grey curls of moisture seeped up from the grates to climb the iron lampposts and wilt the starch of one's collar. Inside, shadows gathered at the corners, and lamplight further isolated the groupings of armchairs into islands of discretion.

Eric was still in his Usual Armchair, warm with the cheerful flames of the nearby fireplace. He was quite recovered by now from Aldershott's earlier snub, and he'd taken a break to dine on an excellent curried pheasant in the dining room downstairs. The Britannia was proof against the clammy chill of October, and all was well with the world once again.

All except, perhaps, for the manuscript he was supposed to be reading. Eric frowned down at it and shifted uncomfortably. The trouble was that, halfway in, he already knew the identity of the murderer, and all the tension was gone. He desperately hoped that some twist would prove him wrong, but it was looking very much as though the clues from which he'd derived his conclusion were quite inescapable.

There was a creak from the armchair across from him. Mortimer Wolfe—sleek, dapper, and elegant, hair slicked down and gleaming like mahogany—had dropped into it with his usual careless grace. He was just a year or two past thirty; he'd been that age his entire adult life, and careful polish would keep him there until the end of time. As one of the five men on the Britannia Club's governing board of officers, he was insufferable.

"Feet on the floor, Peterkin. Are we six years old?"

Eric had his stockinged feet curled up under him as he sat. "Sod off, Wolfe. I'm comfortable this way."

Glancing at the manuscript in Eric's hands, Wolfe said, "My goodness, is it really very bad? Your moustache is drooping dreadfully."

Wolfe's own moustache was a pair of perfectly symmetrical triangles; they might have been printed on his upper lip with a stencil. Eric hurried to tweak his moustache back into shape and said, "Not quite. This fellow writes like an angel. The problem is, he doesn't seem to have quite managed a watertight plot . . . I'm not sure he really knows what he's on about."

"And you know better, I suppose? Is it because of the inscrutable wisdom of the Chinese ancients, passed down to you from your most honourable ancestors?"

For some people, a Chinese mother was simply a mother like any other. Wolfe was not one of those people. If Aldershott preferred to ignore him, Wolfe made it a sport to twit Eric on his heritage whenever he could. "No," said Eric, "only a matter of common sense. And for what it's worth, I do know a thing or two about the exotic settings this fellow's chosen to write about."

"If you're such an expert," Wolfe replied, "I know a fellow in Churston who's looking for someone to go hunt down Chinese antiques for his collection. That might be more your cup of tea than reviewing manuscripts."

The one thing Eric missed about the War was that one had slightly more pressing things to worry about than blood heritage. The respect he'd received from his comrades had not been immediate, but after enough shells and sorties and gas attacks, no one cared anymore who your grandparents were—as long as you did your job well and kept your men alive. He was simply Lieutenant Peterkin.

"I've promised to finish reviewing this one, at least. Perhaps after it's done, I'll go look up this antique collector friend of yours."

"Suit yourself," Wolfe said with a shrug. "I merely thought you wanted a distraction, and I was feeling a trifle bored. What would you say to a game of cribbage, then? We can make it interesting with a shilling a point."

"You must be mad." Cards with Wolfe was a sure way of losing one's shirt. Eric had never known him to lose. Then again, if the alternative was to keep reading this manuscript . . . "Sixpence a point, no more. I think I can afford to lose a crown or two."

Wolfe smirked. "If you think that, Peterkin, then I've already won."

A cribbage board appeared on the table between them as if by magic. Wolfe, with a magician's dexterous fingers, shuffled the cards and dealt them out. As they settled into the game, Wolfe said, "You know, Peterkin, a good man is so hard to find these days. A good gentleman's gentleman, especially. The world really needs more valets, Peterkin. You simply have no idea."

Eric had been wondering when Wolfe would get around to the all-important subject of Wolfe. The man went through his valets as a compulsive smoker went through matchsticks: burning them out in quick succession and discarding them with nary a thought. Eric could never quite picture Wolfe in Flanders, knee-deep in the mud and filth that he himself had grown to loathe even in his short service. He supposed that Wolfe must have somehow commandeered the entire British supply of soap and hot water for the duration of the War.

Captain Mortimer Wolfe wasn't quite the useless dandy he presented, however. Wolfe had led countless strikes against the enemy—not all of them sanctioned—and been captured at least three times. Countless retellings of his exploits blurred the line between fact and legend, but all agreed that he'd always escaped in under a day. Wolfe himself pretended not to care, but he certainly made no effort to curtail the telling of tales.

As one irrepressible wag had said, he was "more fox than Wolfe, all slippery-sly in his perfect little black socks." And Eric respected his resourcefulness, even if he didn't care for his superior attitude.

"Such a tiresome business," Wolfe said with a sigh, when Eric failed to shut him up immediately. "You simply cannot get a good man these days. Not that I shouldn't have seen it coming, what with the War and all. I've had to settle now on a fellow with no references whatsoever. I suppose I'll have to train him and not expect too much. It will be just the same as the raw, rotten batmen I had in Flanders. I suffer, Peterkin; decidedly, I suffer."

Eric hid a smirk behind his cards. Wolfe was one of the few Army officers who habitually spoke of his batmen in the plural; he'd gone through them the same way he went through his valets now. The position of batman was normally an enviable one: a comparably soft job with all the benefits of being close to one's superior. Wolfe's men actively feigned incompetence to avoid it.

"Speaking of batmen, servants, and the like . . ." Wolfe nodded in the direction of the bar, and Eric turned to see a tall, rather lumpish-looking individual whom he did not recognise, deep in conversation with Edward Aldershott.

The stranger's straw-coloured hair flopped loosely across his forehead, and his tie was crooked—a distinct contrast to the primly buttoned-up Aldershott and the sleekly polished Wolfe. His face was bland, and he was looking around with vaguely bovine interest. Eric wondered who he was. He turned back to Wolfe. "An old batman of yours, is he?"

"Not quite. I met him at the hospital where I was warded, near the end of the War, though I remember very little of it. He was an orderly there. Name's . . . Benson, I believe. Yes. Albert Benson. And he's a conscientious objector." Wolfe paused to grin at Eric's startled reaction. The Britannia Club took in men who'd fought for the Empire; what was someone who'd refused to fight doing in their midst? "Curious, isn't it? We had a meeting all about it earlier. Saxon spoke up quite well for him, which was a surprise, and not just because Saxon's a disagreeable blighter who's chummy with no one. As far as I know, Saxon's the only one of us to have nothing to do with Sotheby Manor."

"Sotheby Manor?" Eric glanced at Wolfe as he pegged his score on the board, before scanning the bar again for Saxon. There he was, in a shadowy corner, munching on an apple and staring off into space. Every so often, he'd come back to the present and glare around as if daring anyone to come close.

Oliver Saxon was something of an oddity, a brooding, unshaven figure who haunted the club at all hours with his shirttails hanging halfway to his knees, picking apples off the centrepiece displays in the dining room and leaving their cores in the oddest places. Eric recalled having once found a rotting specimen wedged behind the frame of the Arthurian Knights painting down on the staircase landing. Saxon never really seemed to notice, and in any case, he made no apologies for any of it, nor for anything else; he was the son of the Earl of Bufferin, one of the oldest houses in England, and he could afford to be as absentminded as he liked. He had the right to call himself Lord Saxon, but there he went against convention by eschewing the courtesy title.

He worked for a living, too, as an exports manager for Saxon's Hard Cider—a family concern—which was unheard of for one who was Lord Saxon . . . but perhaps not so much for one who preferred to be only Mr. Saxon.

Focused as he was on Saxon's situation, Eric nearly missed Wolfe's reply: "Sotheby Manor was the war hospital where I was warded, Peterkin. Lovely place on the Sussex Downs, lorded over by a baronet with pretensions of being a medical doctor of some sort. Do try to keep up."

Eric ignored the barb and focused instead on Benson. "But if he never fought, then how is he here at all? Is it only on Saxon's say-so?"

"Well, we'll let anyone in nowadays, won't we? Ever since we opened up to the Chinese Labour Corps, as you know better than anyone."

The legendary Peterkin eyebrows crashed together into a frown. The Chinese Labour Corps was a noncombat unit, and the pride of Lieutenant Eric Peterkin, late of the Royal Fusiliers, was stung. "I wasn't with the Chinese Labour Corps," he said. "I was with—"

"I never said you were." But the malicious glint in Wolfe's eye betrayed him: Eric had taken the bait after all. Wolfe continued as if nothing had happened. "I don't know how Saxon came to know Benson. I barely remember the great oaf at all. But then, you tend not to remember a face when you've only met it through a haze of morphine. And . . . a hundred and twenty-one," he said, moving his peg on the cribbage board. "You owe me seven bob and sixpence."

Eric gathered the cards to one side of the board and dug out the price of entertainment.

Over at the bar, Aldershott had taken off his spectacles and was pinching the bridge of his nose. Behind him, Saxon dropped the remains of his apple into an empty beer mug and extracted another apple from the recesses of his jacket. Benson's gawking, meanwhile, finally settled on Eric himself, and he was now openly staring. Eric stared right back.

Aldershott, replacing his spectacles, followed the line of Benson's gaze and caught Eric's eye. His lips twitched—was it relief?—and then he tugged on Benson's sleeve to draw his attention back to the here and now.

"Peterkin!" Aldershott said, approaching them with a smile as genuine as paste. "And Wolfe. May I introduce Mr. Albert Benson, our newest member? Benson, Wolfe here is one of our governing board of officers, and the Peterkin clan has been at the Britannia since practically before the Magna Carta. Why don't I leave you in their capable hands for now, and they can show you any ropes I've missed?" The spectacles flashed meaningfully at Wolfe, who pretended to examine his nails. "I can count on you, can't I, boys?"

"Oh, absolutely," Wolfe replied without looking up from his nails. But Benson just grabbed Wolfe's hand and shook it, earning a very annoyed look that was quite lost on him as he turned to do the same with Eric. Aldershott was gone by the time the usual greetings were exchanged, and Benson pulled up another armchair to the fire. His blond hair fell loosely across his forehead as he sat down; Eric was put in mind of an ungainly sheepdog padding about among sleek greyhounds.

There was a certain degree of scruff, too: Benson's cuffs and collar showed signs of wear, and his trousers appeared to have been taken in at some point; but his jacket was both new and expensive. Eric glanced down at his left hand and noticed a faint greenish tinge on the skin around Benson's wedding band. Here's a fellow who's had to practice economy for a while, Eric thought. He must have come into money quite recently.

"I don't know if you remember me, Mr. Wolfe," Benson was saying, "but I certainly remember you. Lot of familiar faces around here, I must say."

"Indeed," said Wolfe, engrossed in his cuticles.

"And I'm quite sure I've not met you before, Mr. Peterkin," Benson continued, turning to Eric. "Though I'm quite pleased to meet you now." There was a brief, awkward pause. "So . . . where are you from?"

"Barsetshire." Eric had no taste for delving into the story of his ancestry and antecedents at the moment. These queries happened with distressing frequency, and Eric was sure he'd met his quota for the month. "Wolfe mentioned that he met you at the Sotheby Manor war hospital," he hurried on, ignoring Wolfe's icy glare.

Benson just grinned. "Oh yes. Half-dead from Flanders, and he wanted a shave and a haircut. Our friend here's got a proper set of nerves, I'll say—two days in, and you'd wonder if he'd even seen a picture of the trenches."

"It's not my call what God chooses to bestow upon me from His bounty," Wolfe drawled. "Though I daresay I could have stayed home had I wanted to; heaven knows, many men did."

Benson didn't seem to register this as a barb, only saying, "Well, Flanders was a rotten place to be. I was there for a year, and you couldn't pay me to go back. I wonder that anyone volunteered."

There for a year? But hadn't Wolfe said that Benson was a conscientious objector who'd served his duty as a hospital orderly? Benson elaborated: "I was a stretcher-bearer, one of the first to get out there. But a shell knocked me out—my memory's not too clear—and put me in a cast. They decided I'd be better off serving back home in England after that. Lucky for me, eh? But having been out there, I reckon I knew better than most at the hospital what all those men were going through."

"And now, here you are," said Wolfe. "Isn't it amazing what a year in hell can do for one! I must confess I am quite surprised to see you here among us bloodthirsty war hounds. I'd have thought you'd give us all the widest berth possible."

Benson was beginning to relax. He signalled to an attendant for a drink, then said, "I had a certain change in circumstances. Mr. Saxon suggested that, now I could afford it, I consider joining his club, because it's the sort of thing a fellow in my position ought to do. So here I am." Eric noticed him unconsciously fidgeting with the band on his left hand. Had he recently married into money, then?

"These clubs always looked so imposing from the outside," Benson continued. "I've no idea what to do or where to begin."

"Well, for starters," said Wolfe, eyeing the untidy knot of Benson's tie, "I know you can tie a better knot than that. Did they teach you nothing at the hospital aside from how to make a bed while someone is still in it?"

"It's hardly a requirement," Eric said. He'd remained silent for too long, and Wolfe clearly had no intention of making things any easier for Benson. "You could loosen it a bit, if you like. Saxon even takes his off entirely."

"And what a shining example he is," Wolfe said. "I can't think why more of us don't follow in his hallowed footsteps."

Eric forced himself to ignore Wolfe's sarcasm. "Most of us come here to unwind after a day's work. Play a game of billiards, perhaps, or cards. But I'd avoid cards with Wolfe." Eric indicated the cribbage board on the table. "He'll let you win a few hands for sport, and then he'll fleece you utterly."

"Oh, I know." Benson grinned suddenly. "There wasn't much else to do in the convalescing ward aside from read and play cards, and word gets around. It's all right, though, so long as you shuffle the cards under the table."

Eric darted a glance at Wolfe, who looked merely annoyed—but it was Wolfe's way to never appear shaken by anything less than the Second Coming. The charge of cheating at anything was a serious matter among gentlemen, but Benson continued, too cheerfully for this to be meant as anything more than a wry observation: "He's got an amazingly quick eye. They say he can track an ace through seven shuffles of a deck, just by watching." Turning to Wolfe, he said, "You got out of Jerry's hands once by challenging their commanding officer to a few rounds of pinochle, didn't you? Won the uniform right off his back, and nearly got his medals, too. That's the story I heard."

"People will insist on spreading the most outlandish tales," Wolfe said. A smirk pulled at the corner of his mouth. "We were playing cribbage."

It was, of course, a signal that Wolfe was ready to "reluctantly" divulge the details of his escapades, which in turn meant that there was no point in trying to read anything. Eric tucked his manuscript behind a cushion and went up to the bar to order a few drinks for their little group.

Saxon was still at the end of the bar, munching on an apple. Eric began to feel a little bad for him: it was never very pleasant to be left out of things, and if Saxon were Benson's sponsor into the club, it seemed hard that he should be left out of this. As the bartender prepared the drinks, Eric turned to Saxon and said, "Your friend Benson seems like a jolly chap. Will you join us, Saxon? There's plenty of room by the fire for another chair."

But Saxon, momentarily startled into the present, just glared. Eric saw, half hidden under the edge of the bar, a book lying open in Saxon's lap. It was entirely in Greek and spotted all over with doodles, underlinings, and notes. "I didn't come here to talk," Saxon snapped, and turned back to the book. Eyes down, he absently deposited the remains of his apple into a nearby mug of beer—one still in use, unfortunately—and extracted another apple from the recesses of his rumpled jacket.

Shrugging, Eric returned to the fire, where Wolfe had begun once again to complain about the lack of qualified valets in post-War England.

THE GAUNTLET

THE KEY WAS small and flat, with sharp, triangular teeth. It was untagged, but it was unmistakably one for a safe-deposit box down in the club's vault.

The conversation had turned to the amenities afforded to the club members, and Benson, admitting that he'd already availed himself of one such amenity, had taken the key out to show them.

"Lucky of you," Eric said. "I wanted to get a box earlier today, to keep this manuscript in—better than carrying it home and here every day—but the vault was full at the time."

"Old Faithful just didn't trust you with a key," Wolfe replied.

Eric thought it highly unlikely, but Benson, seemingly oblivious, carried on. "Mr. Aldershott showed me how it all worked—how to choose a box and all that. It seemed easier to just hand everything to the porter and let him do the rest. Either way, Mr. Aldershott said it's safer than the Bank of England."

Looking around, Eric saw Aldershott had returned to the bar, just within earshot. Eric guessed that he was actively listening in on their conversation. Insufferable as Wolfe could be, he was also an excellent storyteller . . . as long as he didn't realise you were part of his audience. The only other club officer about was Saxon, still doodling notes into his Greek text at the far end of the bar. He hadn't moved since they'd spoken earlier, though he mercifully seemed to have exhausted his supply of apples.

Wolfe, meanwhile, was eyeing Benson speculatively. "Aldershott thinks that, does he? I'll wager ten shillings that whatever you've got squirreled away there, I could have it out of the vault and on this very table by this time tomorrow."

"You're having me on! I've seen the vault. You can't get in without the combination, and then there are all the keys—"

"Is it a bet, then?"

"What? No!"

Eric nodded his approval of Benson's refusal. "I've learnt the hard way not to take up wagers with Wolfe unless you're prepared to lose. Wolfe never makes a bet on his own exploits without first carefully considering how he might pull it off."

Wolfe raised an eyebrow. "Are you suggesting our new friend here doesn't have ten shillings to put on the table, Peterkin?"

"Not in the least. I'm suggesting that you're taking advantage of the poor fellow."

That might have been the end of it, if Aldershott had not decided to jump in.

"I thought I heard my name taken in vain." He chuckled. "Is this another of your silly wagers, Wolfe? I think you may have bitten off more than you can chew this time."

"You'll take it, then? Our lily-livered friend here won't."

"Certainly. Ten shillings against your ability to sneak into the vaults and lift just one item from a safe-deposit box—whose number, by the way, Benson here is not going to tell you." Aldershott gave Benson a wink. "Nor is he going to tell you what's inside. Is it agreed?"

"I never agreed—" Benson began, but Wolfe laughed.

"Just one item? Child's play! Make it a whole pound, and I'll have the mystery prize on this table before noon."

As Benson hesitated in bemusement, Aldershott slapped him on the shoulder and said, "Come on, be a sport! It's all in good fun, and no harm done. It'll be a fine way of testing the club's security."

"I've no choice in the matter, have I?" Benson said, looking from one officer to the other. He seemed, on the one hand, eager for a bit of a lark with his new club mates, but uncomfortable with the very idea of letting someone break into his private possessions. For a moment, Eric thought he'd caught a fleeting glimpse of something calculative in Benson's expression, but it was quickly overridden by anxiety. Benson closed his eyes, took a deep breath, and came to a decision. "Very well, then. I'm in." He didn't sound entirely certain about it.

"That's the spirit!" Aldershott shook hands with Benson, and then with Wolfe. "We'll have no brutality, of course: no broken windows or anything of the sort. I know you, Wolfe, and I know you'd rather die than leave a mess behind, but it still bears saying. Peterkin here will act as referee, of course?"

Was it a ploy to make him look foolish? Wolfe specialised at that sort of thing, after all, and Aldershott knew it. You're just being ridiculous, Eric admonished himself. What would your father say?

"Of course. I'll be here at noon tomorrow, and if Wolfe hasn't made good on his claim by then, the two of you win. Benson, in the interest of fairness, I think I had better have a look at what you've got in there—just so I know what Wolfe's meant to find."

"A wise decision, Peterkin. I was about to suggest something along those lines myself." Aldershott clapped Eric on the back, and Benson stood to lead the way down to the vault.

Behind them, Eric observed Wolfe leaning back in his chair and lighting a cigarette, supremely sure of himself. Eric was glad he had not been talked into the wager. Aldershott, meanwhile, appeared to be in an uncommonly good mood.

Eric wondered which of the two would still be in such a good mood when the clock struck noon on the next day.

They descended to the lobby, passing the Arthurian Knights, then walked down the corridor past the club president's office and the porter's office. Near the end of the corridor was a nondescript wooden door. At their request, Old Faithful opened it and led them down a narrow staircase to a windowless antechamber, where both members were advised to stand back while Old Faithful busied himself with the combination lock on the steel door of the vault. This door finally swung inwards, triggering the illumination of a single bare bulb overhead.

Eric didn't know what use this room had seen before it was appropriated for the club's vault. Its walls were whitewashed concrete, blinding in the electric light, and its floor was picked out in mosaic, blue grey and cream, more intricate than was right for a room so rarely seen. There was an antiseptic hush as they crossed the threshold into the room. *Dulce et decorum est pro patria mori,* the old Latin phrase of Horace's, ran right across the middle of the floor: "It is sweet and honourable to die for one's country." Once, perhaps, it was a source of pride to the warlike, patriotic members of the club; but the Wilfred Owen poem "Dulce et Decorum Est" made that motto something of a bitter joke these days. A plain wooden table was positioned over it in some attempt to pretend it didn't exist.

A bank of deposit boxes lined the far wall, an array of steel doors set into a solid frame of yet more steel. Benson walked around the table to the bank of doors, tracing his fingers over them until he found the one he wanted: number 13. He unlocked this door, withdrew the snugly fitted box from behind it, and set the box on the table.

Upstairs in the lounge, Benson had given every impression of being just a little simple, but there was a subtle change in his manner now. The softly rounded shoulders squared themselves, and the once-slack jaw seemed to set itself into something closer to the concrete and steel surrounding them. The man who looked at Eric from the other side of the table was not a village idiot but a knight errant, and Eric had an idea that it wasn't cowardice that had kept Benson from fighting in the trenches.

Eric looked inside the box. There was a hypodermic kit containing a well-kept hypodermic syringe and a few needles. Its lid was engraved with a stylised letter *S*. There was a pair of surgical scissors, the sort with long, slim handles and sharply pointed blades. There was a photograph of a very pretty dark-haired woman in the uniform of the Voluntary Aid Detachment, smiling over a birthday cake. A few other VAD nurses were gathered around her, and a number of patients as well. And at the bottom of the box was a manila folder containing a medical report for one Horatio Parker, who'd apparently received a nasty cut to the face and required stitches.

Eric had expected valuables, or private papers, or even a war souvenir or two. He could think of no earthly reason why anyone would want to keep this rubbish under lock and key. Or could he? It was a puzzle, and Eric's brain began churning over possible ways in which these pieces could fit together. Meanwhile, Benson the knight errant was watching Eric like a hawk. Eric said, as mildly as he could, "Are these things very important, somehow?"

"Taken together," Benson said, "I expect these things to right a great wrong from the past. Oh, I don't mind Wolfe getting at them—it's not Wolfe I'm afraid of. But there are a few people around here who could stand a bit of shaking up." He added, under his breath, "I just worry we're going a bit too quickly."

Eric looked back down into the box and frowned. If he had to guess, he'd say these were the detritus of a temporary war hospital, now returned to civilian use. The photograph had found its way into his hands, and he studied the face of the nurse who was its main subject. There was a luminous, Madonna-like quality to its oval shape. "Do I know this woman?" he wondered out loud. "I rather wish I did."

"That's my wife, Helen," Benson said mildly. "I doubt you've met."

"Oh." Eric turned his attention to the surrounding faces. They were strangers, most of them, but wasn't that . . . yes, that was Aldershott in the background, wasn't it? Not one of the patients, no; but unmistakably Captain Edward Aldershott in his uniform, holding himself as stiff as ever while a pair of pretty nurses laughed from either side of him.

"Is this something to do with Aldershott?" Eric asked.

But Benson only smiled and plucked the photograph out of Eric's hands to return it to the box.

"You know," Eric remarked, "you don't strike me as the sort who'd just skive off his duty to his king and country. Why didn't you join the Army like everyone else?"

Benson's smile faltered, and a muscle twitched under one eye. No doubt he'd had to defend himself to countless others before Eric. Turning away, Benson busied himself with replacing his box in its compartment, and said, "It's the 'conscientious' part of 'conscientious objector,' Peterkin. I refused to fight because I believed the War was wrong. You were there, yes? Can you think back on all those years of carnage and tell me that it was good and just? I did my part when I volunteered as a stretcher-bearer, bringing the dead and wounded back from the field. That means going out into a battle-field without so much as a knife for self-defence. And mark this, Peterkin: conscription didn't start until 1916, which means I was out there in Flanders well before His Majesty's government made me go."

"And now here you are."

"Here I am." Benson's face turned grim. "It's a grand honour." But there was a twist of irony in his tone that made Eric wonder. And before Eric could make any further remark on it, the lock of straw-coloured hair fell into Benson's eyes again. The grimness faded away, the blandness returned, and Benson was once again the oafish lump who needed things explained extra slowly.

Saxon was scowling from his end of the bar when Eric and Benson made it back up to the club lounge. The Greek text was on the bar behind him with a beer coaster shoved between its pages. He'd got wind of the wager, of course, and he looked none too happy about it. "So," he growled, fixing his glare on Benson, "you've gone and got yourself caught up in one of Wolfe's ridiculous little productions. And on your first day, too. Peterkin, I'm holding you responsible."

"Me? I told him it was a bad idea!"

"You should have told him harder!"

Benson, looking sheepish, rubbed the back of his head. "Well, it's too late now. Or is it? D'you think I should tell Mr. Wolfe the bet is off?"

Eric glanced over to the fireplace, but Wolfe was no longer there. Saxon said, "Try it, and he'll ruin you. Especially now that Aldershott's involved as well." He let out a gusty sigh and heaved himself from his barstool. "Forget it. Let's just go home."

The pair of them had just reached the lounge doors when said doors were flung open by Edward Aldershott's wife, Martha, who was emphatically not supposed to be here. Club attendants hastened from the shadows to halt her progress, but she would have none of it. She'd been a military nurse before her marriage, and she strode past the attendants with the same air of brisk purpose with which she must have handled life and death on the field, an effect only heightened by the military cut of her double-breasted tunic dress and the spit-shine of her boots. Her posture made her seem taller and more formidable than she was, and her blond hair was cut into a severe Dutch bob that seemed to have more to do with workplace functionality than fashion.

"Martha!" Saxon barked. "You're not supposed to be here."

That arrested her progress. Mrs. Aldershott was also Oliver Saxon's cousin, and the bonds of family could slow her even if they could not stop her entirely. The cousins looked little alike: Mrs. Aldershott kept herself impeccably dressed, and as neatly turned out as a disinfected hospital ward, whereas Saxon shaved roughly once a week if he remembered. But one thing they did have in common was a seeming disregard for the rules of conventional society.

"Hullo, Oliver," she said, flinging one end of a fox fur stole over her shoulder. "I hope you don't plan on being ridiculous. I certainly don't plan on staying longer than I can help." She wrinkled her nose. "Those foul cigars you men insist on smoking—it's enough to ruin one's dinner. I'm just here for that husband of mine . . . Where is he? Hiding, I suppose. Well, he can't hide forever. And who's this, then?"

"Albert Benson. You remember, I—"

"Benson? Oh, Benson!" Mrs. Aldershott's face lit up with delight. "I remember now. Emily wrote to me about you quite often. It's a pleasure to finally meet you face-to-face. Listen, we simply must have you over to dinner at your earliest convenience."

Meanwhile, Benson's ears had gone quite pink at the mention of this Emily, and Eric, watching unobtrusively from one side, felt a spark of curiosity. Hadn't Benson said his wife's name was Helen? Who was this Emily, then? A mistress, perhaps?

Before anything more could be said, Aldershott emerged from one of the lamplit armchair groupings and hurried over. Before his wife, he looked more like a naughty schoolboy than the stiff-backed martinet he normally pretended to be. "Martha," he was saying, "you know the club rules prohibit—"

"Oliver's already reminded me. Is there some reason you have not deigned to return home for dinner?"

"I mean, look, I'm dreadfully sorry, but something's come up and . . ."

Behind them, Saxon just shook his head and turned to go, dragging Benson along with him. Eric decided to take his cue from them and picked up his manuscript from where he'd left it. Amusing as it was to see Aldershott being taken down a peg by his wife, the night outside the Britannia wasn't getting any clearer, and Eric wanted to be home before the rising fog turned the journey into something unpleasant.

THE BROKEN LANCE

ERIC SET OUT for the Britannia just a little later than his usual time the next day. His dreams had been filled with Chinese antiquities: terracotta warriors, porcelain urns, scrolls painted with yellow-robed monkeys wielding iron cudgels. These images felt to him both familiar and alien, like a well-loved book written in another language.

There was no hint of the light fog that had risen the evening before as he trotted down St. James's Street to the corner of King Street. The fogs of London could, on occasion, last into the afternoon, growing denser in the sunlight rather than dissipating; but today promised to be clear and windy. It would be a marvelous day for flying kites, and Eric caught a glimpse of two or three brightly coloured lozenge shapes ducking and weaving over the skyline to the south. That would be St. James's Park, he thought, craning his neck for another glimpse before turning into King Street. The wind hastened his pace, right past the posters for the play at the St. James Theatre.

He breakfasted in the club's dining room and sat down in his Usual Armchair with his reading. He was thinking, mostly, about the contents of Benson's box. What could those disparate objects add up to? Perhaps it would all become clear once Wolfe fulfilled his part of the bet. Wolfe had to know already that he was capable of the task, which made it almost certain that he'd emerge the victor. Still, there was always a first time for everything. Eric found himself rather hoping that, for once, Wolfe would fall a few inches short of his claim, and that he'd have a good view of Wolfe's face when it happened.

At a quarter to twelve, Eric put aside his reading and contemplated the possibility of shepherd's pie. Oh yes, tender chunks of lamb under a warm layer of mash delicately crisped on top . . . the Britannia's kitchen added a sprinkling of grated cheddar and parsley over the top of its shepherd's pie. Eric considered that most things were improved tenfold with the addition of cheese, and shepherd's pie was no exception.

Eric looked up to see Jacob Bradshaw approaching the fireplace with a copy of the *Times* under one arm. "Hullo, Peterkin," he said, smiling warmly behind his snow-white beard as he settled into an armchair. "Aldershott told me about this newest wager of Wolfe's and suggested I drop by. Club security, you know."

Bradshaw was the club secretary, another of the club's board officers, and the longest-serving officer of the lot. He'd been club secretary when Eric first joined, and it looked very much as though he'd continue for several years yet, whatever happened to the rest of the board. It was simply that he Got Things Done: he was efficient, remarkably so, and over the course of his career, he'd collected a network of contacts stretching twice around the Empire. Anything you needed done, they said, Bradshaw knew a man to do it. Eric always thought Bradshaw looked more than a bit like Father Christmas, and it was hard to imagine him as company sergeant major at the Sussex training camp where he'd served. CSMs, in Eric's experience, tended to be a queer combination of fatherly—which Bradshaw had down pat—and nightmarishly tough. But Bradshaw never seemed to raise his voice, and always seemed to have a kind word for everyone.

"Who do you expect will win the bet?" Eric asked, putting his manuscript aside. "I've learnt not to underestimate Wolfe, but you never know."

"He isn't here yet, is he?" Here, Bradshaw cast a glance at the clock. "And neither are Aldershott and Benson. I know Aldershott, at least, wouldn't want to miss this. Perhaps his work is keeping him. I don't know about Benson."

"I got the impression he was staying the night with Saxon. He'll have to hop to Saxon's schedule."

"I wonder how he and Saxon came to be friendly," Bradshaw said. "I admit I was surprised, pleasantly so, when Saxon proposed him as a member and spoke up for his service as a stretcher-bearer. I was more than happy to have him—it's no secret I think these membership restrictions just a little too restrictive—but talking Aldershott around took some doing. In the end, we put it to a vote, and Wolfe was the only holdout. And as you know, it takes two officers to block or boot a member. Wolfe was furious, though heaven knows why. I know a little of what Benson went through, and he deserves his place here as much as anyone else."

Eric nodded. He still remembered what Benson had told him the night before about the perils of being on the battlefield in a noncombat capacity. "I expect this whole wager was Wolfe's way of getting back at Benson, then. Make him look a bit of a fool."

"I don't doubt it."

Aldershott strode up to them as they both looked up at the clock. It was five minutes to the hour. "Are neither Wolfe nor Benson here yet?" he said, frowning. "It's nearly time."

Eric replied, "I expect Wolfe to sweep in with fifteen seconds to spare, deposit the prize on the table, and then calmly sit back and light a cigarette while the rest of us squawk in wonder and consternation."

"That does rather seem like his style," Bradshaw said, and let out a low chuckle.

They turned to watch the clock, Aldershott tapping his foot impatiently. Outside, a particularly fierce gust of wind rattled the windows. As the second hand of the clock swept past the nine, the lounge doors swung open to admit Mortimer Wolfe. He had a Cheshire cat smile on his face, and a small linen-wrapped bundle tucked carelessly under one arm. He swaggered up to the gathered men, dropped the bundle unceremoniously on the table, and threw himself into an armchair. "Benson not here yet?" he drawled as he lit up a cigarette. "That does rather spoil the effect."

Aldershott eyed the bundle and said, "I suppose I owe you a quid. Unless Peterkin here can swear that this is not one of the items from Benson's safe-deposit box. Peterkin?"

"Let's wait for Benson." It was only fair, though Eric could tell from the shape of the bundle that it was probably the pair of surgical scissors. An odd choice, Eric thought, but either way, it looked as though Wolfe had made good on the wager. Waiting for Benson was a mere formality.

"Bother Benson," said Aldershott. "It's past noon, and I'm fairly certain that nobody ever said anything about everyone having to be in attendance for the grand unveiling. Wolfe, let's see what you've got there."

"As you wish." Wolfe stood up and whipped off the linen wrapping with a flourish to reveal the pair of surgical scissors, as Eric had expected, glinting in the light. All eyes turned to Eric for confirmation.

"That looks like one of Benson's prizes," Eric said. He turned to Wolfe. "I'd have taken the photograph, personally, as being more distinctive and easier to carry around than the medical report, but, unless you've gone and picked this up from Harrods, this looks about right."

Wolfe frowned. "I don't know what you mean about any photograph or medical report. That box just held this and an old hypodermic kit. And I don't like your tone, Peterkin. If you want to see if I'd really taken this from Benson's box, you have only to go look at it yourself: you'll find only the hypodermic kit there, where I left it. As it so happens, I did choose this because it was easier to tuck into a pocket without leaving an unsightly bulge, but perhaps I'd have done better to take the kit instead. It had a nicely distinctive monogram engraved on its lid, as I recall."

"No one's doubting you," Bradshaw said, but Eric was uneasy. Benson had said that those four items should right some great wrong, and Wolfe's claim that only two of the four were in the box suggested nothing good. And where was Benson?

Eric stood up. "I think we should inspect the box," he said, earning a hard glare from Wolfe. "If there's a master key for the boxes—"

"No need for that," Wolfe snapped, also standing. "I left the box conveniently open on the table so everyone could see just how shoddy the security around here really is." He shot Eric a hostile glare. "Honestly, Peterkin, you people have no shame. I've never been so insulted in my life."

Eric ignored him. He was already on his way to the lounge doors, and the others, swept up in the moment, followed behind him. They grabbed Old Faithful as they passed the reception desk in the lobby, and the group of them—Eric in the lead, followed by Old Faithful, Aldershott, Bradshaw, and Wolfe—trooped down to the vault's antechamber.

It was deathly still. Some of the fog had got in from the night before and never left; Eric could smell a faint tinge of sulphur in the air, and . . . copper? The uneasiness he'd felt earlier redoubled as Old Faithful, asking no questions, began dutifully turning the wheel of the vault door. A moment later, the door swung open, and a hush fell on the assembly.

Albert Benson lay crumpled on the floor, half under the table in the vault. He was barefoot; his shirt and trousers appeared to have been thrown on in haste, and his braces hung loose at his sides. His head was turned just so, and he was looking right at Eric.

And for a moment, Lieutenant Eric Peterkin was not in the vault of the Britannia, staring into the eyes of Albert Benson. Instead it was his first day in Flanders, and he was looking out across the wire to no-man's-land, right into the eye of a corpse not ten feet away. Mud and rot rendered the body the same colour as the field in which it lay, but that eye was still a startling pale blue that pierced his very soul—much as Benson's pale blue eyes now did.

Protruding from the side of Benson's neck was the decorative handle of a small knife. Too fancy for Flanders, Eric found himself thinking. There was something familiar about it, and with a start, Eric recognised it for the letter opener that normally sat on the desk of Aldershott's office upstairs.

Blood had splashed a good distance out from Benson's wound, in a fountain spray across the mosaic motto on the floor. It seeped into the grout, *decorum est* now outlined in Benson's cruor.

It is honourable . . .

Above, the clinical white glare of the electric light bathed the room in contrasts. The clean white walls, the polished steel, the gleaming tiles—these things were a mercifully far cry from the murky, muddy shadows of the trenches.

Beside him, the others began to stir.

Old Faithful took a step forward, but Wolfe pulled him back. "Don't. Don't bother; he's clearly beyond help. Call the police."

THE INSPECTOR

OLD FAITHFUL PUSHED past to hurry up the stairs, and Aldershott, spreading his arms, drove the other men out of the vault. Both he and Bradshaw had slipped back into their old Army mindsets: Aldershott's expression was even stonier than usual, and Bradshaw had lost his affability. This was, of course, a crisis, and each and every one of them had been taught to deal with a crisis in terse, impersonal terms.

"That's your letter opener," Bradshaw told Aldershott, with a nod towards the knife handle. His voice was unusually steady. "Better check your office."

"In good time, Mr. Bradshaw," Aldershott snapped back. Eric had never heard Aldershott address Bradshaw as "Mister" before.

Meanwhile, Wolfe had turned around and begun to climb the stairs.

"Captain Wolfe!" Aldershott barked. "You are not to leave the premises! Return at once!"

Wolfe stopped at the top of the stairs and only half turned back towards the club president. His face was white and his voice was almost a caricature of its usual smug, superior tone. "You're not my commanding officer, *Mr.* Aldershott. I know perfectly well how this looks now, and how much worse it would look if I were to run. But

I refuse to spend the next hour standing about in that filthy little room with a body rotting not five feet away. If you need me, I will be in the lounge."

And with that: exit Wolfe, stage right.

Eric glanced around at the other two men. Bradshaw's beard was beginning to quiver with uncertainty as the man recalled the complications of dealing with civilian crime. Aldershott looked determined to stand here until he was relieved, whenever that might be.

"Wolfe is right," Eric said. "There's no sense in waiting around down here. We'd better wait for the police up in the lounge. And tell the attendants not to let anyone leave the building."

Aldershott rounded on him as though this were all his fault. "Don't presume to tell me how to run my club, Peterkin," he snapped. He made an inarticulate sound of frustration, then brusquely gestured to Bradshaw to proceed.

Bradshaw gave Eric a curt nod, then hurried up the stairs to call the police and make sure no one left the building. Not that it would do much good, Eric thought, his mind already working through the facts of this very real murder mystery. If he had to guess, he'd say Benson was killed several hours ago, certainly before Old Faithful came on duty and the Britannia began to wake up. Someone would have seen Benson coming down from his room otherwise. Whoever the killer was, he would have had ample time to make his escape, and might be halfway to the Hebrides by now, for all they knew.

Unless it was Wolfe. But would Wolfe's excessive pride allow him to leave such a messy crime scene? Even if the encounter had occurred on the spur of the moment, Wolfe was sure to have found a way to keep it tidy.

The office of the club president was no more than five feet from the door to the vault stairwell. Aldershott paid Eric no mind as he ascended the stairs and made straight for the office door, then uttered an oath when he found it unlocked. No, not unlocked, but forced: someone had taken a fireplace poker to it and cracked the frame. The poker itself lay discarded in a corner of the office, while all the drawers of Aldershott's desk had been pulled out and rummaged through. The floor and desktop were littered with papers, which Aldershott, after letting out a grunt of frustration, began sorting into tidy little piles.

Eric pulled to a halt at the doorway and said, "Aldershott! What are you doing? You shouldn't touch anything!"

"Shut it, Peterkin."

"But the police will want to look at this. Whatever's happened here has to be connected to what's happened downstairs. I mean, the letter opener—"

"I told you to leave things to your betters," Aldershott snarled, shaking a handful of papers at Eric. "Previous presidents may have used this room as a place in which to nap, but I use it for important business! These documents represent interests in a hundred different investments related to the members of the club. Not that I expect you to know anything about such things." Aldershott shoved the handful of papers into one drawer and slammed it shut. "If the police want anything, the poker's right there, and I can tell them where my letter opener's usually kept: right here on top of my desk blotter. There is nothing, Peterkin, to be gained from leaving sensitive documents lying about for all to see."

Eric briefly considered wrestling Aldershott away from the room, or calling for someone to help him do so, but reflected that this would only further disturb the scene. If he couldn't stop Aldershott from cleaning up the office, he could at least take a minute to study it before it got completely ruined.

The passage of past presidents, each with his own peculiarities, had left its imprint here: there were cheap prints pulled from art folios, newspaper clippings of forgotten exploits, a dead fern that had yet to be thrown out, and a rather alarming African mask. The wallpaper was a patchwork of faded rectangles where pictures had been put up and taken down again. Through the window, one could look out onto the utility court that ran along the side of the building and the bare brick wall opposite; Eric could see the catch on the window casement was in the locked position, and nothing there appeared to have been touched. The transom pane above was wide open, letting the cold air in, but climbing in and out through it seemed like an unlikely prospect.

By the desk, a wastepaper basket contained a few torn envelopes and some brown paper, the remnants of yesterday's post. An ashtray had been knocked from the desk, scattering a full complement of cigarette stubs and ash over the floor. A table in the corner held a decanter of brandy, and here Eric noticed a slight grease stain on the lip of two of the glasses beside it.

"Hello," he said, "it looks like someone's been at the brandy. You'll want to not touch those. There'll be fingerprints—"

"Of course someone's been at the brandy! It's my office, so who do you think that might be?"

Eric gave the room another look around—nothing in the fireplace grate, nothing out of place except for the poker and the papers thrown haphazardly from the drawers of the desk. He'd seen, perhaps, everything there was to see. It was time to make a retreat, before Aldershott really got upset.

He bumped into Bradshaw a few steps down the corridor. Behind him, Aldershott had gone back to tidying up his office, cursing all the way.

"The police should be here very shortly," Bradshaw said. "Aldershott will want to know."

"You'd better be the one to tell him," Eric replied. "He isn't too happy with me right this minute. You'd better tell him to leave off cleaning his office, too. Someone ransacked it last night, and the police will want to look at it."

Bradshaw nodded and ambled past Eric to give Aldershott the word. Eric noted that Aldershott seemed far more amenable to Bradshaw's persuasion: the sound of rustling papers and slamming drawers ceased, to be replaced by a whispered discussion between the two men. But perhaps it was only that they'd worked together before and knew each other better. Or so Eric told himself.

Back in the lounge, Wolfe had secluded himself in a corner of the bar and was nursing a drink with every appearance of normalcy. It wasn't in Wolfe to let on that anything was amiss: if his upper lip were any stiffer, he'd need surgery to eat his dinner. There were very few other club members in the lounge at the moment, thankfully, and a handful more in the dining room downstairs. They all seemed quite oblivious to the crisis as yet, but Eric took the precaution of noting who was here, just in case.

Was it just half an hour ago that he'd been thinking of a nice helping of shepherd's pie for his dinner? The thought of food right now made him . . . not precisely ill, because he was almost never ill, but certainly unsettled. The sense of unease that had begun with Wolfe's unveiling of his prize hadn't left him, even after the discovery of Benson's corpse.

Corpse.

That word belonged out in the trenches of Flanders, not within the comforting confines of the Britannia Club. A corpse was a thing rotting in front of the trenches, half sunk into the mud, too close to ignore but too far away to do anything about. A corpse was a limp, gas-drowned body—certainly not your mate of five minutes ago—flung into the back of a wagon. A corpse was not a thing found within the polished, hallowed halls of the Britannia Club. If you threw someone over the club bar in a brawl, it was supposed to end with the both of you uproariously drunk and sworn to be brothers in arms forever. Not with one of you bleeding out on the floor with a knife in your neck.

This wasn't how the world of the Britannia Club was supposed to work.

Turning on his heel, Eric strode out onto the landing overlooking the lobby downstairs. Up above, clouds raced across the face of the sun, and the skylight showered the marble floor with intermittent bursts of sunlight and shadow. He could just see Old Faithful pacing agitatedly behind the front desk. People had to know, from the fellow's behaviour, that something was up. Aldershott had finally gone to Bradshaw's office to wait for the police, and Bradshaw was with him—hopefully keeping him out of trouble.

Eric frowned. Given the way Benson was dressed when they found him, he must have spent the night here after all, instead of at Saxon's. He looked as though he'd come down in a hurry, barely bothering to do up his trousers . . . could he have left his door unlocked behind him? When did the custodial staff set about cleaning those rooms, anyway?

It took Eric a moment to remember Old Faithful's real name. "Cully!" he called. "I say, Cully! No, wait right there; I'll come down to you."

Eric made his way down the stairs and over to the front desk. "Benson spent the night here, didn't he? Which room was he in? We can't let anyone in there until the police get here."

Old Faithful's eyes went wide. "You're right, sir! I never thought of that. Come with me, sir."

They hurried up the main staircase to the first floor, and then up a smaller set of stairs to the second. "Here we are, sir." Old Faithful stopped in front of a door and opened it. "I should have known there was something amiss when I found it open this morning, but it looked like he'd only stepped out for a moment, maybe to use the facilities. I just closed the door without locking it. I'm quite sure nobody else has been in there yet."

Eric knew better than to enter a room that the police might want to examine, but from his vantage point he could see quite a good deal. He'd nearly forgotten how windy the day was: the window was open, and some soot and detritus had blown in. That window overlooked the utility court beside the building, and all the sounds below came funneling up and echoing back against the hard brick of the building opposite.

Old Faithful shifted nervously from one foot to the other, and Eric said to him, "Benson wanted this room last minute, did he? I thought he had other arrangements planned for last night."

"I reckon he did, sir. It was quite late—nearly ten o'clock—when he rang me bell and said he was going to be spending the night after all. Not but it hasn't happened before, with other gentlemen. Things happen of a sudden, and then plans have to be changed, and what can you do?" The old man fidgeted again, and went on, more anxiously: "This . . . this murder, though—it's murder, isn't it? Man doesn't stab himself in the neck, either on purpose or on accident. Never seen the like of it, sir, not in all the time I've been here. And I never saw nor heard nothing. I waited downstairs until half eleven in case any other gentlemen decided they were in no fit state to go home to the missus after last call at the pubs, and then I went back to me own little flat, upstairs from the staff room, and went to bed. The night attendants will vouch for me, sir."

"No one's accusing you of anything, Cully."

It seemed ridiculous to think of Old Faithful as a suspect in a murder, but then it had seemed ridiculous to think of the Britannia as the scene of a murder, too. Unwilling as he was to consider it, Eric had to admit that Old Faithful was a suspect . . . unless the night attendants really could supply him with an airtight alibi. And why on earth would Old Faithful, permanent fixture as he was, want to injure a member of the club to which he'd devoted his life?

"I think it's only a matter of time, sir," Old Faithful went on, his voice dropping to an anxious whisper. "They'll know I've been down in the vault, too; my fingerprints will be on the vault door. And nobody touches that door but me." The poor fellow had no idea about the bet.

"But turning that wheel is your job," Eric said. "Everyone knows that. I'd be more worried if your fingerprints weren't on it. If they're there, it's really more a sign you've got nothing to fear."

"You think so, sir?"

Eric nodded, and felt the tension ease out of the man beside him. Old Faithful had always treated him as a proper member, he thought, never as an interloper. It was something Eric had grown to take for granted, and he reminded himself now to be grateful for the old man's service.

The lodging rooms of the Britannia were fairly spartan, each containing a single bed, a washstand, a chest of drawers, and a single chair that had probably seen long years of service in the public rooms below before being retired to the lodging rooms above. Benson's room had an armchair similar to those in the lounge, though considerably more threadbare; his jacket and waistcoat were flung carelessly over its back, and his necktie lay on the floor beside it. His hat, a grey felt cap better suited to the countryside than to the city, had fallen from the hook behind the door and now lay on the floor against the corner of the door. The bed itself, positioned lengthwise about a foot from the window, was a similarly untidy situation: its covers were heaped up on the near side and practically spilling over onto the floor, as if violently cast aside.

Eric's attention was arrested by a photograph lying on top of Benson's chest of drawers, among the toiletries. This one was a studio portrait of a young woman, a different one from the nurse who'd been the subject of the now-missing photograph from the vault. There was no mistaking the eyes, the cheekbones, or the nose . . . Eric wanted to say she was Chinese, if only because his mother had been, but she could easily have been Japanese or any of the Far Eastern races. Who was she, and why did Benson have a picture of her on his chest of drawers? Wasn't he supposed to be married to the "Helen" of the other photograph?

Could this be the Emily whom Mrs. Aldershott had referred to last night?

"Peterkin!"

The hearty slap to the back nearly sent Eric tumbling headlong into the very room he was trying to keep people out of. He caught himself just in time and turned around. "Norris," he said, recognising the man who was now grinning mischievously at him—and wearing nothing but a towel. Evidently, Patrick Norris had spent the night here too, and had only just stepped out of the bath.

"Lieutenant Norris, sir!" Old Faithful exclaimed. "You're not decent!"

"I don't think I ever was," Norris replied with a laugh. "What? We're all men here; I'm sure you've seen worse in the barracks. I know I have."

"You'll catch your death of cold!"

"Certainly, if you insist on leaving that door open. There's a nasty draught . . . Oh, someone's left the window open, has he? In October, no less . . ." Here, Norris attempted to enter the room, and both Eric and Old Faithful hauled him back out. Norris turned to them in surprise. "I say! What's got into the two of you? Such grim expressions you've got! You'd think someone died."

"There's been a murder, sir!" Old Faithful burst out.

Norris's eyebrows shot up into his damp-tousled curls, and he turned to Eric for confirmation.

"Albert Benson," Eric clarified. "He was found in the vault not half an hour ago with a knife in his throat."

"I see. Well, that's one way to ruin a weekend." Norris's tone was light, but his expression was anything but. "I reckon I'd better get dressed in a hurry, then. Wouldn't do to meet the bobbies in the altogether."

Eric motioned to Old Faithful to stand guard, and followed Norris as the latter trotted down the corridor to his room. "I take it you spent the night as well, then?" he said, more as a way to tag along than to confirm what he already suspected.

"I'm between lodgings at the moment. Rather bad luck: it's no fun being woken up at all hours by people knocking over dustbins outside your window, but this time I've got a quiet room, at least."

Patrick Norris was the last of the five board officers after Aldershott, Bradshaw, Saxon, and Wolfe. He was a wiry little ter-rier of a man built on much the same lines as Eric himself, and with similarly dark colouring. But Norris was of unquestionably Anglo-Saxon descent, and he had the roguish, scruffy charm of an unrepentant ne'er-do-well. This was a different sort of scruffiness from Saxon's: where Saxon looked as if he simply didn't care what you or anyone else thought, Norris looked as though he was just so happy to see you that he couldn't be bothered to quite finish knotting his tie before taking you out for a night on the town.

"Damned shame about Benson," Norris muttered as he rubbed his towel vigorously over his wet hair and then carelessly cast it aside. "We were just discussing the fellow's membership yesterday morning. I've been meaning to talk to you as well. I'd like to pick your brains about what it's like as a . . . well, you know, living in two worlds as you do. For this stage production I'm collaborating on." Norris made his living as a musical composer and had garnered a moderate degree of success. His work was largely for the stage, and he often had as much interest in the play itself as in the musical accompaniment. The fashionably Oriental villain of his last collaboration had been suspiciously Eric-like.

"I'm here nearly every day," Eric said. "Now seems like an odd time to bring it up."

"I know, I know, but I actually just met with my playwright friend yesterday afternoon. This next production is going to be a full-blown opera, Peterkin." Norris gave a proud wave to the music score pages scattered around the armchair, and promptly lost his cufflinks. "This murder, though. Terrible," he went on, opting to roll his sleeves up over his forearms instead of hunting under the bed for the missing cufflinks. "Do we know who did it? No? I heard about that bet poor Benson had with Wolfe and Aldershott . . . I reckon that means Wolfe will be the prime suspect. I wouldn't want to be in his shoes. Should I shave?"

"I don't think there's any hot water in the jug," Eric said, peering at the washstand. "And the police will be here by the time you've had an attendant fetch some . . . or fetched some yourself."

Norris set his razor aside with an air of regret. "I reckon you're right. And I reckon a man's got a right to a certain amount of stubble on a Saturday. Don't tell Wolfe I said that." He rummaged around in his chest of drawers and emerged with a silver cigarette case. "I think I'm as presentable now as I need to be. Cigarette?"

Eric accepted the proffered cigarette, lit it, and, occupied as he was, promptly forgot about it. "Wolfe was with us when we found the body. He seemed as surprised as we were. I don't know if he's so good an actor, or if he has quite the bloody cheek to stick around after doing the deed."

Norris blew out a smoke ring. "Wolfe's got plenty of cheek. That's what I like about the fellow. But I don't see him doing a murder, not if it means getting blood on his precious shirt cuffs. Depend upon it—it'll be some burglar whom Benson caught unawares. The blighter struck back, killed him, got cold feet, and did a flit."

"How'd he get in the vault, then? We're supposed to be proof against that sort of thing."

"Wolfe found a way. And that, by the way, is a waste of a perfectly good cigarette."

Eric looked down in surprise at the tower of ash extending from the filter between his fingers, and quickly disposed of it. Meanwhile, Norris went to open the door, and the soundproofed silence was broken by the tramp of heavy footsteps coming up the stairs.

"Here's the police," Norris said, "right on schedule. And it looks like we're in luck. That's Detective Inspector Horatio Parker himself. They say he's an absolute wizard at the Yard. Aldershott's been trying to get him to join since the dawn of time—he's a Victoria Cross, you know, and Aldershott positively worships that sort of thing—though maybe it's just as well Parker never took up the offer . . . Would be a conflict of interest otherwise, wouldn't you say? Mark my words, with Parker in charge, this whole thing will be over and done in an hour, tops."

Horatio Parker?

Wasn't that the name on the medical report that had gone missing from Benson's box?

The first thing one noticed about Detective Inspector Horatio Parker was the scar that went from cheekbone to temple on the left side of his face, pulling the flesh towards it and shining like silver in the light. Another inch up and it would have blinded him. Eric imagined it might have been a duelling scar, left a little too long before being given medical attention.

Parker himself was slightly built, his whipcord-thin body lost under the layered fabric of his trench coat and suit, and his untidy dark hair was shot through with grey. Eric guessed him to be just past thirty-five, though there was a haggardness about his cheeks that suggested a much older man. He works too hard, Eric thought. That much was obvious.

He'd seemed much younger in the now-missing photograph from Benson's box. Oh yes, Eric recognised him now as one of the patients crowding around the nurse whose birthday it was, though the scar hadn't been present then.

Funny that both articles referencing the inspector directly should be the ones to go missing first. Eric had an idea that Detective Inspector Horatio Parker was the last person who should be handling this murder inquiry.

The inspector pulled out a pocket watch to check the time. The dull brass gleamed like an echo of the scar on his cheek. "Mr. Cully here," he said, "says it was your idea to guard the dead man's room and see that no one got in." Hard eyes scanned Eric from head to toe before boring into his eyes. "Good thinking," he barked suddenly, in much the same tone as one might say, "Go to hell," just as Eric opened his mouth to inform him that he might be an interested party.

"I'll want to take your statement later," the inspector said. "For now, I must ask you to wait." He looked down the corridor to the doors of all the club's lodging rooms. "Alone, if you don't mind. It reduces the potential for collusion."

He suspects me, Eric thought, and why am I not surprised?

Not that there was much choice about it. Without waiting for a response, the inspector had turned to enter Benson's room, and Old Faithful was now apologetically tugging at Eric's arm to take him to the nearest lodging room. Norris had long since retreated to his own room and locked the door.

A loud crash from the stairwell interrupted them. It was followed by sounds of a struggle, and a stream of bitter invective. Old Faithful dropped Eric's arm to stare down the corridor. Eric turned around to address the inspector, but stopped.

Inside Benson's room, Inspector Parker had picked up the photograph from Benson's chest of drawers—the portrait of the Chinese woman—and folded it into quarters.

He tucked it into his inside jacket pocket.

Before Eric could say a word, a pair of constables erupted into the corridor with Oliver Saxon, snarling like a savage animal, held tightly between them. Saxon stopped abruptly as Inspector Parker stepped out of Benson's room and fixed him with a stern glare.

"We caught this one sneaking in from the back entrance," one of the constables announced. "Mighty suspicious, wouldn't you say?"

Saxon glared back at the inspector and spat on the carpet. "You," he growled. "I might have known it would be you."

INTERROGATION

DETECTIVE INSPECTOR HORATIO PARKER quickly determined who all the main players in the drama were, and they were shuffled separately into empty lodging rooms to await their turn to speak with him. Not everyone took this well: Aldershott was very vocal about the indignity of it all, and Saxon's mood grew blacker than Eric thought possible. Wolfe, accosted in the lounge, simply picked up a magazine and sauntered upstairs with an injunction that they try not to bore him too much.

Eric was in one of the front rooms, overlooking King Street and the St. James Theatre opposite. The wind hadn't abated since this morning. Overhead, kites leapt like anxious dogs on long leads at the clouds racing by, while down on street level, the wind plucked at the posters of the St. James Theatre and sent at least one hat scuttering across the pavement. Eric wanted to lean his head out of the window and hold his face against the fresh blast of air, but found that this window was painted shut. He could only stand in the stifling stillness and watch the restlessness outside, through ancient glass whose slight distortions turned smooth movements into a vaguely drunken weave.

The leering yellow face on the theatrical posters filled Eric with unease. English society liked to paint the Celestial as subtle, treacherous, and too clever for his own good. It was not a character-isation Eric had to think about much, but now it seemed painfully relevant to his situation. He had no doubt that he'd be the last suspect to be interviewed, if only so Parker could have everyone else's statements on hand to catch Eric out in a lie.

I'll simply have to be very sure of my facts, he thought.

He cast his mind back to the image of Albert Benson lying dead on the vault floor, and tried to fix in his mind where everything had been.

The table had been bare but for Benson's vault box, he remembered, and the box had been empty. Yes, he was very sure of that. And the little door to its compartment had been open, revealing an empty space within. The murderer must have taken the remaining contents of the box away with him. That would be the hypodermic kit, if Wolfe was to be believed. But why would the murderer want that?

It didn't look as if the murder had been premeditated. Benson wasn't even supposed to have been in the club that night: he was supposed to have spent the night as Saxon's house guest. There were few signs of a struggle, though, implying that the killer had caught Benson by surprise—from behind, no doubt—and the position of the wound therefore indicated a right-handed blow.

The letter opener had severed at least one of the major blood vessels to the brain, if the spray of blood was any indication. Eric had seen enough to know this. Was it luck or skill? Eric imagined stabbing someone as the murderer must have stabbed Benson. He'd get blood on himself, surely. But it was late October, and he could pull on a coat over his bloody clothes; people on the street might not notice anything at all. Once home, he'd only have to burn the clothes and take a bath . . .

A key turned in the lock of the door. It was Old Faithful. "The inspector will see you now, sir."

So soon? "Has he spoken to everyone else already?"

Old Faithful shook his head. "He spoke to me and to the two attendants who were up last night, but you're the first of the gentlemen he's wanted."

Jacob Bradshaw had been club secretary for longer than anyone cared to remember, and over the years had impressed the stamp of his personality on his office in a way that Aldershott, president for only half a year, had not. It was comfortable, cosy, and quite overcome with tortoises. They peered out from pictures and prints, and porcelain specimens sat atop stacks of meticulously sorted correspondence.

Visible through the window was the narrow passage leading to the back door in the utility court behind, and the brick wall of the next building; but sunlight came through it to gleam on the sides of a chipped teapot and a teacup commemorating the coronation of Edward VII in 1902.

Inspector Parker sat behind Bradshaw's desk, looking very un-tortoise-like. Another policeman stood in the corner by the window, notebook in hand. Behind him, in a watercolour print from some children's storybook, a tortoise wobbled down a country lane on a battered blue bicycle. Parker's expression, by contrast, was grim and businesslike, accentuated by the disfiguring scar on his cheek. He checked a dull brass pocket watch and gestured to Eric to take a seat. Another policeman came in to take Eric's fingerprints, and then, as Eric struggled to wipe the ink from his fingertips, the inspector began with a few standard questions about Eric himself and his movements over the past twenty-four hours.

Eric repeated to the inspector the events of the previous night: how Wolfe had proposed the bet to Benson, and how Aldershott had taken it up. He told the inspector what Benson had said about the items in his box contributing towards the righting of a "great wrong," and what he'd seen of them.

"One of them was a medical report," Eric said, with a sideways glance at the policeman taking notes. He wondered how they'd take this. "Your name was on it."

Parker's expression didn't change. "You don't say. Can you give any further details?"

"I saw that it was about a facial wound that wanted stitches," Eric said. He wasn't sure, but he thought he saw the scar twitch, ever so slightly. "There was also a photograph of a nurse having a birthday party, and you were in it."

"You think I'm an interested party."

The statement was a challenge, and Eric nodded. In his corner, the note-taking policeman had raised his head to look questioningly at the inspector. Parker, meanwhile, remained impassive and expressionless; he might have been carved out of wood for all the human emotion he showed.

"Can anyone else corroborate your statement?" the inspector asked.

"One of the attendants, perhaps? Benson had left it to them to put those things away. Whoever served him must surely know. Wolfe said he found only the scissors and the hypodermic kit in the box, not the photograph or the medical report."

The inspector nodded. "If what you say is true, Mr. Peterkin, my handling of this case will be mercifully short." He checked his pocket watch again, then called for another policeman to fetch him the register for the vault boxes.

It hadn't occurred to Eric that they had a register for the vault boxes.

"According to your porter," the inspector said, "they take careful note of the items received from members when they're tasked to handle the boxes themselves. If Mr. Benson handed these objects over to be put away for him, there will be a record." It was only a minute before the policeman returned with the requested vault register.

The entry for Benson's box listed only a pair of scissors and a hypodermic kit. There was no mention of either of the items implicating Inspector Parker.

"But this is all in pencil," Eric protested. "Someone's rubbed out the other two things from the list. If you look really closely at the paper—"

Parker's face, if anything, grew grimmer. "That's quite enough, Mr. Peterkin. I don't know what your game is, but making a false statement to the police—fabricating evidence—is a very serious offence. I could have you charged with perverting the course of justice."

"I know what I saw!"

"I'm sure you do." Inspector Parker got up and went to open the door. "If that is the extent of your assistance, I believe we're done. You're free to go."

Was that it? Eric stood and eyed the inspector, uncertain. Somehow, he thought he'd have a much harder time of it, and he wasn't sure whether he should be relieved or disappointed.

"What about the others?"

"They're not your business," the inspector said. "When I say you're free to go, I mean it. Go home, and stay out of our way. If we need you, we'll know where to find you."

He was being summarily dismissed. Far from being a focus of suspicion, he was being cut out altogether.

Eric hesitated at the threshold, then turned to face the inspector. "I saw you remove something from Benson's room just now, when you thought no one was watching. It was a photograph of a Chinese woman. Who was she?"

Surprise registered only fleetingly on Parker's face, and then it closed off again behind narrowed eyes and lowered brows. Over in his corner, the inspector's assistant stood with his arms folded, not even bothering to write down the details of this particular interaction. The inspector took a step forward, forcing Eric back against the doorframe. He smelled of strong coffee and stale sweat.

"Don't ask stupid questions," the inspector said, his voice a steely whisper, too low for his assistant to hear. "And stay out of my way."

Abruptly, he shifted his position and shoved Eric bodily through the open door. Eric sprawled over the floor of the corridor, and a pair of policemen popped their heads out of the next office—Aldershott's, where they'd been busy with fingerprint powder and brushes—to see what had happened.

"Perverting the course of justice," Parker said, loud enough for everyone to hear. "Interference. Wasting police time. Count yourself lucky I don't arrest you on the spot. Good day, and go home." Turning, he shouted for someone to fetch him Mortimer Wolfe, then slammed the office door shut.

THE VIGIL

"THERE'S NO PLEASING YOU, IS THERE?" Penny Peterkin shook her head in exasperation. "First, you're miserable because you think the police will suspect you, and now you're miserable because they don't. I do wish you'd make up your mind."

Eric had taken Parker's instruction to heart and retreated all the way back to the Peterkin family home in Barchester. This was a long, low-slung structure with the characteristic half-timbering ascribed to Tudor architecture and more gables and dormers than was wise. Ivy and honeysuckle competed for supremacy over its walls and roofs, and a six-foot-high hedge hid it from the road. With Eric now permanently established in London, it was perhaps a little too big for its occupants; but Penny's passion for horses made it the unofficial meeting place of the local hunt club, and her hunt club friends threatened to blow out the diamond-paned windows with their laughter.

Eric, sunk into an overstuffed armchair by the fire, just shrugged. "There's something rotten at the heart of all this. I feel as though I've been shut out of it just so people can twist things to their own ends with no one the wiser."

"Most people would be pleased as punch to be shut out of a murder inquiry."

"Well, I'm not most people."

"No. You're more infuriating." Penny threw herself into the opposite chair and regarded him with a mixture of sisterly devotion and annoyance. She was younger than him by three years, but taller by half a head, having inherited their father's powerful build and most of his features. This enabled her to pass for an Anglo-Saxon thoroughbred most of the time, whereas Eric struggled to convince people that he was not, in fact, adopted. Eric often wondered if some of their mutual friends had accepted him only because they'd unwittingly accepted her first.

Penny was well respected in the community as a young woman of uncommonly good sense. Both the house and the household finances were well maintained, and she often effected minor repairs on her own; but she always seemed to regress into something much younger when her brother was about. Coming in the gate this evening, Eric had caught her on the roof, wearing an old cast-off pair of their father's trousers as she replaced the storm-damaged shingles. She seemed quite peeved at having her self-sufficiency found out.

"Let me see if I understand this," she said. "Someone got into the Britannia Club, despite it being all locked up for the night, and did a murder. And you think it might have been the police inspector himself, because he's definitely mixed up in this somehow. Am I right so far?"

Eric nodded. "Parker removed a photograph from Benson's room. That's tampering with the evidence, Penny."

"Have you tried speaking to someone at Scotland Yard?"

"Yes. Parker's apparently their most hardworking detective; it's my word against his, and he's a VC."

Eric crossed his arms and glowered into the fire. More thoughtfully, he continued: "Old Faithful and the night attendants vouched for each other. This seems too much of a mess for Wolfe. Norris had no way of getting rid of any bloodied clothing—he was locked in as much as everyone else was locked out. And it seems unusually foolish of Saxon to have come in by the back way and let on that he had his own key if he'd done it." Eric paused. "I wonder how Wolfe got in."

"Eric."

"What is it?"

Penny was staring at him with something bordering on horror. "I know that look on your face. It's the same look you get when you're opening Christmas presents. You think this is just a jolly good game."

"No, I don't!"

"I don't believe you. Ever since you came back from the War . . . I think you left a piece of your soul behind after shooting at all those Germans. You've no feeling left. Everything's just a puzzle for your own amusement, and don't tell me that's not the real reason you review only murder mysteries these days. There's a man dead—"

"Do you think I don't know that?" Eric snapped.

Penny studied him for a long minute, then looked away. "I wonder what Daddy would say."

There was another minute of silence before Eric replied. "I could ask."

Eric turned off his electric torch as he passed through the lychgate into the churchyard of St. Tobias. His father had found the concept of battery-powered anything, torches in particular, immensely fascinating; but now seemed to be a time for darkness.

The church caught the moonlight with its ancient grey stone. It had stood here since at least two centuries before the Reformation, and it had no plans of ever changing. Tobias, an Old Testament hero, might never have been a proper saint in the usual sense of the word, and the Church of England might have relegated the Book of Tobit to the no-man's-land of the Apocrypha, but every school-child in the parish knew the story. It was told in the stained-glass windows: Tobias, son of Tobit, journeyed with the angel Raphael, rescued the lovely Sarah from a demon, cured his father's blindness, and lived happily ever after.

Eric loved the story. But his father often pointed to its comparatively dull first chapter—Tobias's father, Tobit, working tirelessly to give decent burials to the destitute dead, people he never knew in life—as the book's true lesson. "A gentleman does what he does," he'd said, "not because he'll win the hand of the princess, or because he has an angel of God in his corner, but because people deserve justice and respect."

It was especially quiet in here. Yew trees, that favourite of churchyards everywhere, leaned over the walls with twisted trunks and tightly furled foliage to shade the monuments and resting places gathered below, shielding them from the general flow of village life. In the section reserved for the Peterkin family, many of the monuments had been erected in memory of men lost in foreign lands, enough that they almost equalled the Peterkins who'd actually been buried there.

Eric's fingertips brushed over the smooth marble of angel wings as he found his way to the graves he sought. Magdalen Peterkin's headstone featured a phoenix rather than an angel. It was the only indication that she had been born to an Eastern culture. She'd died young—Eric had been twelve at the time, and his sister only nine—and people, more charitable to her in death than in life, whispered that it had been a sin to uproot her from her homeland and bring her here to the comparatively cold and dismal England.

Not to Colonel Berkeley Peterkin's face, though. Never to his face.

Nights in the country were different from nights in London. One forgot how the lights and noise of the city intruded on one's consciousness until one got away from it all. Then the silence and darkness were startling in their depth. In the sky, the bright constellations in their slow celestial dance made one stop to stare in awestruck wonder. October meant harvests and plentiful larders, and the smoky scent in the air of burning leaves. It also meant a gathering chill, mist on one's breath, and the coming death of the year. Eric paused to absorb the stillness, then sat down beside the Colonel's plain rectangular slab. The damp grass soaked into his trousers, but he didn't much care about that.

"Hi, Mum. Hi, Dad. I've missed you."

There wasn't a lot of difference between the Chinese devotion to one's ancestors and the Christian communion of saints, or so Eric often thought. Certainly, it had been his mother's favourite tenet of Christianity after her conversion, and Eric had an idea that religion in the Peterkin household had got a touch more High Church afterwards as well.

Moonlight slanted through the trees to pick out the sharp lettering cut into the marble. Magdalen Peterkin's headstone bore an inscription from John 6:37: *Him that cometh to me I will in no wise cast out.* The Colonel's headstone bore only the chapter and verse reference for Matthew 10:39.

"There's been a bit of a mess at the club," Eric began, brushing away a few fallen leaves. "I wonder what you'd make of it."

It was easy to talk to the Colonel. It always had been. The old man never interrupted, and he always seemed to understand exactly what you meant. Even as Eric poured out his account of the past two days, he could imagine his father sitting back in his armchair under a shaft of warm sunlight, those famously thick Peterkin brows half shading half-closed eyes. Eric would come to the end of his story, and there'd be a pause as he wondered if his father had in fact fallen asleep. Then the Colonel would suddenly come up with something seemingly beside the point but curiously insightful all the same.

What would the Colonel say?

Eric shifted his position to lean back on the cold marble headstone. Gazing up into the stars, he let his mind drift back to his father's funeral service. That had been two years ago now—1922. Eric remembered a day with too much sun and too little warmth, and the smell of lilies over the strange, sickly sweet odour of embalming work.

There'd been a surprisingly large crowd in attendance. Penny, supported by a pair of old school friends, had wept discreetly into a handkerchief, keeping her emotions respectably in check. Eric himself hadn't shed a tear; he'd calmly busied himself with arranging the funeral, dealing with the lawyers, and playing host to the mourners who'd travelled some distance to be there. The undertaker tried to cheat them of seven shillings, and Eric had to have a few firm words with him behind the church.

Tonight hadn't been the first time Penny accused Eric of a lack of feeling. But then, as now, as it always had been, it was the only way to stay sane.

Jacob Bradshaw, the eternal club secretary, had been there, along with the then-officers of the Britannia Club and a strangely emotional Old Faithful. Eric had just come around from behind the church when he met Bradshaw in the shade of a spreading hawthorn by a quiet corner of the churchyard.

"I'm glad to see you're holding up," Bradshaw said. A cautious smile twitched up behind his Father Christmas beard, gaining confidence as Eric smiled back.

"Life goes on," Eric replied. "One has to move forward somehow."

Bradshaw nodded and came to the point. "I wanted to talk to you about your membership, Peterkin." Bradshaw had never called him Peterkin before. He'd always been Eric. Eric swallowed, realising the implications of the change. Bradshaw continued. "You know there have always been Peterkins at the Britannia Club, and your father would have liked you to carry on the tradition."

"I've been at Oxford," Eric replied, glancing over at the monuments to the Peterkin cousins who'd fallen in the War. He hadn't considered what it meant to be the last male representative of the family. "It wasn't practical while I was still neck-deep in books and lecture notes. Now that I'm done, a club in London would be a very fine thing; but . . . well, Dad always said he'd sponsor me, and that seems quite out of the question under the circumstances."

"Not entirely." Bradshaw pulled a set of folded documents from his pocket. They were the application forms for membership at the Britannia Club. "Your father signed these before he died, and of course the rest of the board signed them as well—we're doing things backwards, but it's your father's final wish, after all." He held out a fountain pen. "The only signature missing is yours."

Eric took the fountain pen and looked over the forms with just a touch of wonder. He'd always loved visiting the Britannia Club, those times he met with his father in London. There really was no question about it. Eric signed the papers and handed them back, and in that instant, he belonged.

Bradshaw tucked the papers away with a genial smile. "Your father would be proud of you."

Would he really?

They'd stopped on the outskirts of the Peterkin section of the churchyard. The mourners had moved on, but a pair of gravediggers were carefully filling in the Colonel's grave. Bradshaw gestured to another gravestone, one of Eric's ancestors, and said, "There's old Fitzwilliam Peterkin. He was a founding member of the Britannia Club, you know, and a fine gentleman by all accounts. There's a painting at the club, in which he sat as a model for one of the figures."

"The Knights of the Round Table. Yes, I know all about it."

"I think Fitzwilliam Peterkin's the last founding member to still have family in the club."

Eric blinked, coming abruptly back to the present. Nighttime, 1924, damp grass soaking the seat of his trousers. Somewhere, an owl let out a forlorn hoot.

There had always been Peterkins at the Britannia, and Eric was the last. A Peterkin had been a founding member of the Britannia. The Britannia was fundamentally a Peterkin concern: what happened to the club, happened to the Peterkins. Why, then, was he being shut out of things? His inclusion as a referee for Wolfe's wager with Benson had been a pleasant surprise, but perhaps it was really because he was the only person in the group to not be involved—included!—in the bet. He'd been dismissed as a suspect, and his concerns about Parker had been similarly dismissed, because he lacked credibility in the eyes of those around him.

And what was he being shut out of? His mind went back to Benson, standing over his vault box with the determined look of a knight on the eve of a battle. Benson might not have fought, but there was no doubt in Eric's mind that it was not for lack of courage; he was a gentleman, and he deserved better than to be swept under the carpet. The key to what had happened lay in the four items in Benson's box, which were as mysterious to Eric as the items paraded before Sir Percival in the hall of the Fisher King. Eric couldn't let that go either. Benson had been trying to correct some past injustice, and Eric was damned if he let that quest die along with the man.

All right, then. He owed it to Benson to finish what he'd started, and he owed it to himself to prove his worth. He'd do this thing, and present the authorities with such a good, clear-cut case that they couldn't dismiss him again if they wanted to.

Eric stood up, brushed off his trousers, and said, "Thanks, Dad."

He glanced over at his mother's headstone. *Him that cometh to me I will in no wise cast out.* Yes, that was strangely appropriate. "Thanks, Mum," he added, before turning back to his father's headstone and its inscription. Matthew 10:39 . . . What was that passage? He couldn't remember. He'd have to look it up sometime. But for now, he had work to do.

Eric drove back to London the next day in the family motorcar—a Vauxhall D-Type originally intended for the Army as a staff car. The vehicle was generally more useful to Penny in the country, but Eric had an idea that he might want a more personal means of transport than the trains for his upcoming investigations.

Penny didn't mind. She was to spend the next weekend visiting with some old school friends out in Cambridge, but she could take the train. "You'll owe me a favour," she said. "A night out, at least. I'll be stopping into London on the way, and you've got to promise me something a little better than two hours of watching Avery see doom and destruction in our tea leaves. I simply won't allow you to spend your every waking minute sunk into this . . . this *quest* you seem so set on. That will be Thursday evening—what's the play at the St. James this season?"

Eric had no intention of taking his sister to the disaster on the St. James Theatre stage, and as far as he knew, every theatre in London was playing something with a similarly menacing Mandarin. "I'm sure I'll find something suitable for Thursday," he said. One of these days, he thought. One of these days, someone would have to write a story, perhaps even a detective story, featuring a Chinese hero. The world needed this as much as a house needed a key.

"Ask around at the club," Penny told him. "Didn't you say that this Patrick Norris was a musician? Musicians always know the best entertainment in town. Besides, what's the point of having a club if you can't ask your fellow club members for help?"

What indeed. Well, there was probably no harm in it . . . as long as Norris didn't decide to join them wearing nothing but a towel.

SOTHEBY MANOR

CONVINCING AVERY TO JOIN HIM, Eric found, was startlingly easy. But what with having to explain the situation twice over and suffer through a vastly pointless Tarot reading, it wasn't until the next morning, Monday, that they actually set out on their quest.

They were driving down the country roads of Sussex. They'd just passed through Bruton Wood and were now emerging onto the downs. The Vauxhall kicked up fallen leaves in its wake, leaving behind a plume of swirling gold. Above, the sky was a clear, shocking blue, and the rolling downs were like waves of green velvet. This was England at her finest, and Eric was glad to have ditched his manuscript in favour of a country drive.

Flanders had never been anything like this, Eric thought as he leaned to catch the full blast of the cold, clean air in his face. The battlefields had been an abomination, but this! This was the world as it was meant to be. This was what he'd fought for and prayed nightly to come home to. A flock of migrating long-tailed ducks soared overhead; fields and hedgerows whipped by as he drove, and the chill of late October invigorated him.

Avery huddled in his seat with his scarf wrapped tightly around himself, trying to avoid the draught from the car's open top. He would have preferred, Eric knew, to remain in London and spend the day curled up in the back of the Arabica with an endless supply of coffee.

Pulling down his beret, Avery said, "All right, then, just so I'm clear: You have one fellow who was actually in the club at the time, one fellow who found a way to break in with no one the wiser, and one more who has a key to the back door. So, instead of looking at them, you're choosing to focus your attention on the police inspector who's investigating the case. Makes perfect sense. When's this Inspector Parker's birthday, do you know?"

Avery often declared that there was nothing in the newspapers that he could not divine himself from the stars. Since leaving the Arabica, he'd asked after the birthdays of each and every one of the personages introduced in Eric's account of the murder, and Eric rather irritably replied, for the seventh time, that he had no idea, before ploughing on. "Benson had proof of something involving Inspector Parker, and now that proof is gone. He removed something from Benson's room, and I wouldn't be surprised if he had a hand in lifting the contents of Benson's box as well. I don't know how, but it stands to reason."

"He does sound like a thoroughly bad hat, and that Victoria Cross was probably never meant to be his to begin with. But he's in London, so tell me again why we're heading into the rural wastelands of Sussex?"

The Vauxhall plunged into one of those narrow stretches of road where the tall hedges on either side came practically onto the road itself, and the overarching trees blocked all but a few intermittent flashes of blue sky. The light dappled the road and flashed over their heads, and every so often, the seemingly solid hedges would break to reveal a gate with a house standing amid surprisingly well-tended lawns beyond. The scent of freshly mown grass blended with the smoke of burning leaves. They might have been in an underground tunnel between discrete pocket worlds, and Eric slowed down lest he run over some traveller.

"We're driving into Sussex," he said, "because Benson used to work as an orderly at a war hospital around here. Sotheby Manor,

according to Wolfe. It won't be a hospital now, of course, but someone there might know something. Inspector Parker was hospitalised
there, and I'm guessing all the items from Benson's box originated
there as well. Ten to one, the key to the mystery lies in Sotheby
Manor."

"It seems to me like you're expending an awful lot of energy for a
fellow you knew all of one day." The car shot out from the tree cover
into the bright sunlight, and Avery, groaning, pulled his battered
old beret over his eyes. "I honestly don't see why this is any concern of yours. Aren't your gentlemen's clubs supposed to be hotbeds
of dreadful conspiracies? As long as this Parker doesn't decide that
you're the guilty party, I don't see why you should care."

Eric gave Avery as much of a disapproving glance as he could
without losing sight of the road. "You know, you could probably
walk home from here, if you wish. I'm certainly not turning back,
but if you'd really prefer to have no part in this, I won't stop you
from getting out now. The journey on foot shouldn't take you more
than a day."

"Fine, fine. Have it your way, Sir Palomides. In the end, it may
just turn out that there is no mystery, and that the butler did it."

"The Britannia doesn't have a butler." They did have attendants, though, and there was Old Faithful; but, as Eric had already
explained, all of them had vouched for one another.

"You know," said Avery after a while, "I could simply do a Tarot
reading for you and find your murderer that way. I have my cards in
my pocket right now."

Eric rolled his eyes. "Thank you, Avery, but I think I'd much
prefer to rely on cold, hard logic."

"Your cold, hard loss."

"I'm sure I'll survive." Eric brought the car to a sudden halt.
"And, incidentally, here we are. The village of Wexford Crossing.
Sotheby Manor should be somewhere close by."

Avery sat up, pulled back his beret, and peered around at the
squat, flint-walled buildings gathered about the crossroads. There
was a quaint little church, a public house, and a post office; ivy grew

thick on their walls, and curled up the church steeple to grasp at the cross above. The village green, its grass short and well tended, occupied the fourth quadrant; a willow arched over a duck pond in one corner, and there was already a cleared circle in its middle where a bonfire might be lit for Bonfire Night. A sign by the post office gave the departure times of the motor coach service running to Chichester, the nearest large town. Around the green, the thatch-roofed cottages of the local residents could be made out, discreetly tucked away behind their garden hedges. It all seemed quite idyllic, but Avery said, "Are you sure this miserable little huddle of houses qualifies as a village?"

Eric ignored him, studying his road map.

"We could ask for directions," Avery continued hopefully. "But I expect you'd prefer to solve the mystery of this manor house's location by yourself."

"I would. Especially as the old gentleman in front of the pub has been giving us the evil eye ever since you called this place a 'miserable little huddle of houses.' Your voice does rather carry, you know."

Avery swivelled around in his seat and doffed his beret apologetically. The old gentleman in question sniffed and looked away. Meanwhile, Eric, having found his bearings, started the car up again and set off in the direction of Sotheby Manor.

Sotheby Manor was a rambling Georgian structure in red brick, with white limestone quoins and the occasional Greek Revival element for accent. Like many such mansions, it rambled in a symmetrical fashion, and Eric could make out a pair of lesser wings to the main house beyond the screen of poplars, one to either side, and connected by means of a single-storey passage. Both wings were boarded up. The overgrown front drive and a network of scaffolding over one side of the main house rather spoiled what was otherwise a grand approach. In the distance, beyond a line of trees, the rolling South Downs extended onwards to the silver-grey ribbon of the English Channel.

Eric pulled up before the Greek columns of the front portico, leapt out of the car, and hauled at the bell pull. The door was answered a few minutes later by an elderly maid, who afforded Eric barely a glance before turning her attention to Avery. Clearly, she took Eric for Avery's valet. Eric quickly introduced himself before Avery could spoil anything. He'd had a glance at the baronetage before making the journey, and he knew whom to ask for. "Is Sir Andrew Sotheby available?"

The maid's already stony expression grew stonier still, and she continued to address her words to Avery. "Sir Andrew is unlikely to be available before the last trump."

"I'm sorry to hear that." Apparently, his copy of the baronetage was a little out of date. There hadn't been a Lady Sotheby since before the War, but Eric seemed to recall mention of a daughter . . . "Is Miss Sotheby available, then?"

"Yes. Miss Sotheby is at home." There was a peculiar emphasis on "Miss," and the maid continued to address herself to Avery. "Who shall I say is calling?"

Eric handed her his card. "Eric Peterkin. From the Britannia Club."

The maid took the card and briskly led Eric and Avery through the entrance hall to a sitting room, there to wait while she went to fetch her mistress. This was a gracious chamber with white-painted wainscoting and wallpaper striped in shades of yellow and golden brown. Tall windows looked out to the gravel front drive over misshapen bushes, and a pair of sofas and a low table were gathered beneath them. The intention was a light cheeriness, but, with the windows shut tight against October, the room felt empty rather than airy. Compared to the tighter living arrangements in the city, the proportions were almost majestic, and the spartan furnishings made it seem larger still. One's footsteps echoed on the parquet flooring; Avery moved instinctively to the carpet, while Eric went to explore the framed photographs ranged across the mantel of the unlit fireplace.

"Someone's been letting the dog onto the furniture," Avery remarked. He wrinkled his nose and picked a hair off a sofa cushion. "Or else the staff has been getting slack. Or both."

"I fancy this room doesn't see much use," Eric said mildly, "and I'm not sure the Sothebys keep as many servants now as before the War. They've probably economised a great deal." His interest was fully focused on the framed photographs. Most of them had been taken during the house's stint as a war hospital: groups of wounded soldiers, attended by nurses, smiled up from them. The nurse from the birthday party photograph in Benson's vault box was in constant evidence, more than any of the others. There was a gap in the arrangement too, where it appeared that a picture might have been removed: if, as Eric suspected, this was where Benson had obtained that birthday party photograph, he must have been here recently.

Another framed photograph caught his eye, and he took it down for a closer look. This was a group of men, several of them in casts, on a lawn with Sotheby Manor in the background. Benson himself was among them, leaning on a crutch; this must have been immediately after his return from Flanders and before he'd been officially posted here as an orderly. But what was most interesting was the woman standing next to him: it was the same Chinese woman whose portrait he'd had in his room, and which Inspector Parker had so surreptitiously removed.

A loud bark interrupted his thoughts, and he turned to see the very same woman from that birthday party photograph, now in a black crepe dress that might have belonged to her mother. Benson had identified her as his wife, Helen, Eric remembered, and one assumed, under the circumstances, that she was also the Sotheby daughter whom the maid had gone to fetch.

Helen Benson had grown only more attractive over the years since that photograph was first taken, Eric thought. Her dark hair, which had been long and pinned up in the photograph, was now fashionably bobbed and parted to one side, with a sinuous, curling wave weaving over her forehead. It sat oddly with the old-fashioned dress, but there was a regal dignity to her posture that Eric hadn't noticed from the photograph. A hint of red about her eyes and a dusting of fresh talcum powder on her nose suggested that she had been crying just minutes before.

A white bull terrier with a brown patch over one eye stood close beside her, its tail whipping against the fabric of her skirt. It let out another bark. Helen Benson gave it a nudge with her calf, and held out her hand to Avery. "Mr. Peterkin, I presume?"

"Oh, I'm not Mr. Peterkin," Avery said, taking a wary step away from the bull terrier. "My name is Ferrett—Avery Ferrett. Eric Peterkin's my friend here. You must be Miss Sotheby."

"Mrs. Benson." She eyed Eric with some curiosity. "My maid told me . . . I mean . . ."

Eric smiled wryly. "It isn't the first time someone's made that mistake."

"My apologies, then." Mrs. Benson sat down on the sofa and gestured to the chairs across from her. The bull terrier leapt up into the cushions beside her and curled up with its nose in her lap and a wary eye on the two men. "You don't mind dogs, I hope? Glatisant is more Albert's dog than mine, but under the circumstances . . ."

Eric and Glatisant peered at each other until the latter decided the former was of no interest after all, and snuggled closer to his mistress.

Avery remarked, "Glatisant. What a curious name!"

"From the Beast Glatisant, the Questing Beast of Arthurian legend," Mrs. Benson told him. "Because he's a beast who won't do as he's told for love or money or even soup bones." Glatisant let out a loud sigh, and his belly gave an even louder rumble. "And because he will insist on making the most awkward noises in polite company. Honestly, it's as though we starve him, and he's fat enough as it is." She shook her head indulgently, then turned to her guests. "You mentioned you were both from the Britannia Club? Oh, just you? I wasn't aware . . . I mean, were you with the Chinese Labour Corps?"

"I wasn't—" Eric began, then bit back his usual retort. It wouldn't do to blow up at the young widow, not if he wanted any answers.

More calmly, he told her his regiment, mentioned his father, and confirmed that he was indeed here from the Britannia Club.

It did occur to Eric that if Benson had been admitted on the strength of his service as a stretcher-bearer, then there ought not to be any objection to the noncombatant Chinese Labour Corps, either.

The maid returned to set a tea tray on the low table before them, a little too brusquely it seemed to Eric, and Mrs. Benson began to pour. "I suppose Mr. Bradshaw must have sent you," she said, handing the teacups to her guests. "It really wasn't necessary. When we met on Sunday, I thought we'd said everything we needed to say. We've had some recent business dealings with Mr. Aldershott; I expect it was his influence that gave Albert the idea of joining the club."

Aldershott was doing business with Benson? That was news. "I'm here as a private individual," Eric said, wondering how to turn the conversation around to his questions, now he knew he was also dealing with a grieving widow. "And I would like to offer my condolences, of course."

"And to ask a few questions," Avery broke in. "My esteemed colleague fancies himself a detective, you see; and this, of course, is a mystery."

Eric winced. Trust Avery to step in with no tact whatsoever! Mrs. Benson's brow furrowed, and her expression grew guarded. She put down her teacup and folded her hands primly on her lap. "You're not with the police, are you? I've already spoken to the Scotland Yard man, and I've nothing to add."

"Ah, the Scotland Yard man." Here was an opening, and Eric seized it. "You remember him, of course? He was a patient here during the War, I think."

"A lot of men were. We were a war hospital—my father's contribution to the war effort—and we took all the overflow from Graylingwell Hospital in Chichester." When Eric expressed surprise, she explained, "Graylingwell may be a mental asylum now, but it was the primary military hospital around these parts during the War."

Eric nodded. "But you do remember Horatio Parker?"

Mrs. Benson nodded, albeit reluctantly. "Yes, I remember him. He got the Victoria Cross afterwards, didn't he? That sort of thing makes one sit up and take notice. I remember him as a bit of a Byronic figure: very intense, very inclined to brood." She paused in thought, then said, "Mr. Peterkin, I think it's clear from your questions that you didn't come here to offer your condolences, as you claim, and that you really do fancy yourself some kind of amateur sleuth. I think this is in very bad taste."

"Mrs. Benson—"

"Did you even know my husband at all?"

"Before he died, your husband confided something in me. He had a box of four items with him, items that he said were some sort of evidence in a past crime—"

"Oh, that!" Mrs. Benson huffed in exasperation and got to her feet. Glatisant, displaced from her lap, sat up with an air of curiosity. "Of course he'd confide in *you*." Something in her manner changed, and she said, "*Four* items? What did he tell you, exactly?"

Eric repeated to her what Benson had said to him in the vault. Then he described in detail the contents of his box: the medical report, the photograph, the surgical scissors, and the hypodermic kit with its identifying monogram. "He told me they were to right a great wrong. Obviously, that's gone undone, and will likely remain so unless someone takes up the torch again, as it were. Is there anything you could tell me about what this 'great wrong' might be?"

Mrs. Benson considered Eric for a long time, then sat down again and said, "Before my husband married me, he had an obsession with a Chinese maid here, an Emily Ang. Well, Emily up and disappeared one fine day, and Albert was heartbroken. That was six years ago, and I thought he'd got over it. He married *me*, after all. But then, I don't know, suddenly he took it into his head that he needed to get to the bottom of her disappearance, as if it weren't over and done with already, ancient history. Emily ran away, very suddenly, without a word to anyone, and without even stopping to collect her things. I don't mean to cast aspersions on an entire race of human beings, but I think it's unrealistic to assume that we, as decent Englishmen and -women, could understand how someone of *her* background would think. Very likely, it made perfect sense in her mind." Mrs. Benson paused as both Eric and Avery stared back at her. "You must know how it is," she added, appealing to Eric.

"I'm sure I don't," Eric said at last, taken aback by this sudden outpouring of information.

The tears had started up in Mrs. Benson's eyes. She dashed them away with her handkerchief before taking up her teacup again. "Albert said it was about Emily," she said, "and that it was something he had to do or he would never be able to sleep again. That's all I know."

"You seemed surprised when I mentioned the number of items in his box."

"Obviously he didn't tell me everything . . . the sentimental idiot."

Her hand trembled ever so slightly, but the rim of a teacup made a convenient mask for her emotions. Perhaps sensing his mistress's distress, Glatisant tried to climb fully into her lap, and Mrs. Benson nearly spilled her tea pushing him off.

"It must all be connected," Avery piped up. "I'll wager anything that whatever caused this Emily Ang's disappearance is also the root cause of Benson's murder. Are we in a Sax Rohmer story, Eric? I don't want to infiltrate any opium dens in the Limehouse district if I can help it. Such nasty places, opium dens!"

Mrs. Benson's knuckle tightened on the handle of her teacup. The glare she shot Avery might have killed him if he weren't so thoroughly armoured in sheer obliviousness.

Eric said, "Avery, it occurs to me that the servants must know something about this. Why don't you go speak to them? Or better yet, give them a Tarot reading; you've always said you could learn so much more that way. They might have coffee, too."

Avery took the hint. "As you wish, oh great commander." He finished his tea and, tipping his beret to Mrs. Benson, lurched out of the room.

Once he was gone, Mrs. Benson said, "I realise he's your friend, Mr. Peterkin, but Mr. Ferrett strikes me as a rather insufferable sort, and now you've set him loose on my household. Not that I don't appreciate the gesture, of course."

"I admit he takes a little getting used to," Eric replied, "but he means well. I'm sure he'll be doing his fortune teller act in the kitchen to everyone's entertainment. He does raise a good point, though: your husband's recent interest in this missing maid could be relevant to his murder. Did you speak of it to Inspector Parker?"

Mrs. Benson shook her head. "A woman doesn't like to think her old rival still has any sort of hold over her husband, Mr. Peterkin. Most women don't like to think of their old rivals at all, unless it's to gloat. I fancy it's much the same with men. Why? Should I have?"

"I doubt if it would have made much difference," Eric said. "I saw Parker removing evidence from your husband's room at the club. I'm sure he's an interested party, and we're not likely to get justice for your husband if we depend upon him. I just need to know *how* he's an interested party. Was he here when Emily Ang disappeared?"

"I don't remember," Mrs. Benson replied, somewhat shocked. "But . . . Scotland Yard! If you saw something, why not bring it up with Scotland Yard?"

"It's just my word against his, isn't it?"

"Yes. Your word against his. And he's a decorated war hero, a Victoria Cross." After a moment's thought, she said, "If you want to know anything about Parker's stay here, it will be in his patient records. I had better show you. And I expect you'll want to see what we have on Emily, too."

Mrs. Benson got up to lead the way. As they drew closer to each other to pass through the door, she stopped and turned to Eric, saying, "Mr. Bradshaw mentioned you to me, you know, when I went up to London after getting the news. They wouldn't let me see Albert—I expect they thought it'd be too much for my fragile nerves—but Mr. Bradshaw told me about the bet he had with the other members, and how you were acting referee. He told me you were there when they found him."

"Yes. Yes, I was."

"They told me he'd been stabbed. They wouldn't say how or where. They just assured me that he must not have suffered. I was a nurse, Mr. Peterkin; I ought to be able to judge for myself if he suffered or not."

"He was stabbed in the neck," Eric told her, albeit reluctantly. He indicated on his own neck where he'd seen the handle of Aldershott's letter opener protruding.

"The carotid artery," Mrs. Benson murmured, touching the spot on Eric's neck. "If he suffered, it would not have been for long." She paused. "Did he remind you of the comrades you'd lost in the War, and is that why you're so interested?" There was a strange intensity, a combination of pity and eagerness, in the look she gave him.

She must be thinking of when Benson was alive, Eric thought. "I respected his courage. Being a stretcher-bearer wasn't much safer than fighting."

Some of the intensity faded from Mrs. Benson's eyes. That hadn't been what she meant. She turned away. "Follow me. I'll show you the office Albert was using." Passing through into the hall, Mrs. Benson shut the door on the bright light pouring through the windows of the reception room behind them.

With Glatisant padding along behind, they proceeded through the hall and down one passage to the eastern wing of the house. The rooms here were bare, nearly everything presumably having been moved into storage. Any remaining furniture was cloaked in dust sheets, and only an empty gun cabinet in one room gave evidence to its former use. The past had been swept away. Pencil marks on the walls hinted at a promised future that had yet to manifest itself.

Mrs. Benson explained: "You'll have to excuse the mess. My father died of the Spanish flu almost as soon as the War ended. It was a difficult time, and there didn't seem to be much point in keeping the place up. Such an awfully large place for a woman on her own. The Sothebys have been here for a long time, and it's a lot of pressure to suddenly discover you might as well be the local Member of Parliament as far as the villagers are concerned. And of course, it turned out there wasn't quite enough money after all to keep the place running. I couldn't exactly marry a wealthy American heiress, as many in other families have done."

"You married Benson instead." Eric wondered what the late Sir Andrew Sotheby would have thought of the match.

"A little under a year ago now. Father wouldn't have approved, but I'd always been fond of Albert, from the time he first came here with a broken leg and that lost-puppy look in his eyes. He was supposed to be sent back to Flanders after his recovery, but you could see he was too gentle for that sort of thing. And he was making himself so useful around here anyway. Father spoke to someone at the Chichester camp who knew the right people and had Albert permanently reassigned here."

Bradshaw, Eric thought.

"After we were married," Mrs. Benson continued, "Albert and I occupied just a small portion of the house and managed with just the one maid. But we started on some renovations last month, and Albert took over what used to be Father's office when this place was a hospital."

She opened a door, and Eric found himself looking into a room lined with filing cabinets on one side and bookshelves on the other. The boards had been taken down from the one window, and sunlight spilled over a wide mahogany desk. He had expected the room to be dusty, but it was spotlessly clean. A cushioned basket lay in one corner, and Glatisant went to sit in it, still keeping an eye on Eric.

Mrs. Benson said, "Turning the house into a military hospital meant turning everything upside down. But . . . I'd never known the house quite so full of life as when the rooms were filled with convalescing soldiers. Albert and I had the same idea, to go back to *that* part of its history, not the idle mansion it was before."

Eric turned to her in surprise. "A hospital? You were going to turn this place into a hospital again?"

"Not quite a medical hospital. More of a . . . a rest home. An asylum for sufferers of addiction. A place for people who need help, but a more gentle sort of help than they'd get at Graylingwell. The air out here on the downs is wonderful, and with the proper staff . . ." She stopped, and the life drained away. "It's all moot now that Albert's gone. I just don't know what to do."

Eric, in the meantime, had begun exploring the room. The bookshelves were full of learned works of medical literature. The desk was bare, and its blotter unblemished; Benson might have chosen to use this room as his study, but it seemed he still conducted most of his work and correspondence elsewhere. The filing cabinets looked more promising. Mrs. Benson indicated the one where her father had kept the hospital's personnel records. "Anything you might want to know about Emily would be in there," she said.

"With the hospital personnel?" Eric remarked. "I thought you said she was a maid." Emily Ang's file was the first alphabetically, and Eric pulled it from its drawer. A few scraps of notepaper had been tucked into it as bookmarks, pushed so deep that he almost missed them. Opening to the first of these, Eric realised that Emily Ang had not, in fact, been a household maid but a qualified hospital nurse. "She seems," he said, "rather overqualified for a maid."

It must have been quite the slap to the face, and Eric sympathised. He himself had expected a posting to military intelligence when he first volunteered, only to find that no such position was in store. At least, he reflected, his expectations hadn't been based on paper qualifications, as Emily Ang's had.

"She came to us as a maid," Mrs. Benson insisted. "She was a lady's maid to Martha Saxon—you probably know her as Mrs. Edward Aldershott, but this was before her marriage. Martha was a military nurse, and when she was posted to Flanders, she left Emily with us. One does not bring one's maids and valets into a battlefield, after all."

Of course. Mrs. Aldershott had spoken of Emily that night at the club. Had Eric known that the Emily mentioned then was the very centre of the mystery that led to Benson's murder, he might have begun by speaking with Mrs. Aldershott instead.

"Even so, the documents here say she was fully qualified as a hospital nurse, trained at Netley Hospital and registered with the Royal British Nurses' Association." Netley Hospital was a military institution; as Eric understood it, training there meant Emily Ang was qualified as a military nurse and could have gone to Flanders with Mrs. Aldershott if she so desired.

Mrs. Benson shrugged. "I don't know anything about that. Perhaps my father didn't think she was up to the exacting standards of an English nurse. She did as much nursing work as anyone else, when it came down to that, and she was lodged with the nurses too. She was a nurse in all but name, now I think about it."

Or perhaps, Eric thought, your father didn't fancy seeing his precious daughter take orders from a Chinese upstart.

Eric thought he knew something about the hierarchy within the nursing profession, and he suspected it could get as sticky as the rank structure in the Army. A woman who was only unofficially a nurse might have a pretty poor lookout among the official ones.

"You know," Mrs. Benson added, "I was only unofficially a nurse, too. The military nurses didn't think much of us VADs when we first started working together. They wouldn't say it to your face, of course, but I've overheard at least one of them describe us as 'rich girls playing at nurses.' They warmed to us eventually, but that was a respect we had to earn."

Glatisant had come out of his basket and was now nosing about Eric's shoes, his tail whipping against the side of the cabinet. Eric gave up trying to push him away, and finally sat down on the desk with Emily's file wide open beside him.

The only reprimand was for "carelessness" in losing her hypo-dermic kit a few days before her disappearance, but the kit was her own and hadn't actually been issued by the hospital. It made Eric think of the kit from Benson's box, but the monogram there had been an *S*, not one of Emily's initials. Aside from that, her service was exemplary. The bookmarks indicated the key points, but Eric was more interested in the end of it.

She'd had her day off on the twentieth of July 1918, a Saturday; she had been expected to report for work the next day, Sunday, but she never appeared. Sir Andrew had initially assumed truancy, and written a sharply worded note to that effect in her file. When she failed to appear for dinner or tea, a search was made of the hospital and grounds, to no avail. The police were alerted the following day—Monday, the twenty-second of July—but very little came of it. Sir Andrew's final note in her file was that he'd thought her more reliable than that, but "it just goes to show."

Just what it went to show, Eric didn't know. He suspected he would not have got on at all well with the late Sir Andrew Sotheby. As for the police inquiry, Sir Andrew was of the opinion that, given their reduced manpower due to the War, they had little hope of tracking her down.

Eric shook his head. The thing he'd come to find was Horatio Parker's connection to Benson. In the rush of new information, he'd almost forgotten, but here were cabinets full of the hospital's records for everyone who'd passed through the place during the War. If there were any sort of hint of Parker's involvement in the disappearance of Emily Ang, it would be here.

Eric found Parker's file very quickly. He sat down again on the desk and opened the file in eager anticipation.

Here were the details of his admission. He'd been at the Graylingwell war hospital for his physical injuries before being transferred here for the remainder of his convalescence. There was a note that he was suffering from shell shock and needed rest.

But this couldn't be right. "Horatio Parker was discharged from here on the twelfth of July? A full week before Emily's disappearance?"

"If that's what it says," Mrs. Benson said, "then that's what happened. My father was quite meticulous about his records. I think he found his true calling when he opened up the house to the wounded soldiers. They still think quite highly of him both at the Royal West Sussex Hospital and at Graylingwell."

That's torn it, Eric thought, closing Parker's file. If Parker had left the hospital before Emily's disappearance, then there was hardly any chance at all that he could have been involved in it. Eric had been so sure that this disappearance was the thing at the bottom of Benson's murder. It was Emily's portrait that Parker had removed from his room, after all, and Mrs. Benson had said that the missing objects from Benson's box were related to her disappearance. It all added up to a concerted effort to stifle the investigation of Emily Ang, and if Parker were not involved . . .

Eric's eye fell on the bookmarks sticking out of Emily's file. Pulling them out, he laid them side by side on the desk. They were, in fact, a single sheet of hotel notepaper torn into three long pieces. The address of the Butterworth Arms hotel in Chichester was printed in one corner. Written across the reconstituted notepaper were three separate attempts at beginning a letter. *Sir,* it began, in an attractive schoolroom cursive. *Go to hell! If you think I'm giv—* This line was scored out in favour of a more polite opening, which was again scored out in favour of a third attempt: *I will return tomorrow as instruc—* And here it seemed that the author had given up on writing anything. No doubt they'd realised that if they were "returning tomorrow," they might as well deliver their message in person.

There was a date, too: the twentieth of July 1918—the very day before Emily's disappearance was first noted, and probably the very day she'd actually disappeared.

"Have you found something?" Mrs. Benson asked, watching Eric curiously.

"Yes, I think I have." Eric looked up from the notepaper. "Did your father allow many people access to these files?"

Mrs. Benson shook her head. Everything here was meant to be confidential.

"Someone else has been into Emily's file," Eric said. He considered the notepaper scraps and began to think out loud. "I doubt if these were left by your father; they've been placed to draw attention to Emily's achievements, which is rather an odd thing for him to do. The fact that it's hotel notepaper indicates someone who'd been staying at the hotel, which again is rather odd for a man whose own home is only a stone's throw away. I doubt if Benson left these either; the creases have been pressed flat after years between the pages, so they're not recent enough. The few lines we do see indicate a person who's away from his post—not a policeman investigating Emily's disappearance, then. It must be some stranger, but not someone who found his way here in secret, or he'd have been careful not to leave traces of his passing. It's someone with enough weight to convince your father to let him into the files—someone he feared or respected . . . but probably not a friend, or he'd have stayed here instead of at the hotel."

Mrs. Benson stared at him. "I can't think of any such person . . . and you got all of that from just those scraps of paper?"

Eric didn't look up. He was still considering the paper. "This isn't a finished letter," he continued. "It's rubbish, so why is it here? Why wasn't it crumpled up and dropped into a wastepaper basket at the Butterworth Arms? Perhaps it wasn't in the writer's nature to go hunting about for somewhere to toss his rubbish . . . We're looking for someone who's careless about his personal effects. He knows he shouldn't leave rubbish lying about, so he tucks it into the nearest convenient receptacle—in this case, his pocket. That classic schoolroom handwriting, though . . . this is someone who's also paid scrupulous attention to his lessons. A careful intellect with careless habits. Very likely, a member of the upper classes, someone who grew up under the tutelage of a strict governess, with servants to pick up after him."

An image came to Eric of Oliver Saxon tucking an apple core into the frame of a nearby painting . . . Oliver Saxon with a classical Greek text open on his lap, and doodling notes all over it. Eric hadn't been close enough that night to take note of Saxon's handwriting, though, and there were probably thousands of other men and women who might fit the profile.

"Someone," he mused, "was interested in Emily. Not in her disappearance, or there'd be bookmarks later in her file, but in her professional standing. This suggests that the visit took place before her disappearance became known. And the date on the letter suggests that it might actually have taken place on the day itself. I wonder if the Butterworth Arms still has its register from six years ago."

"The Butterworth Arms closed down very soon after the War. The owners lost interest when their son and heir returned from the front only to die from the Spanish flu. I remember it quite well—the funeral was only the day after my father's."

Glatisant, who had been nosing about Eric's shoes as he sat against the edge of the desk, leapt up now to brace his paws on Eric's lap and grin up at him. "Oof!" Eric cried in surprise.

Mrs. Benson laughed. It seemed that the combination of Glatisant's antics and Eric's investigations had served to make her forget her grief, at least for a little while. "I think he likes you, Mr. Peterkin. He doesn't usually take well to strangers."

Eric shoved the dog off his lap, leapt off the desk, and hastened to return the files to their cabinets. "Perhaps I'm just not strange enough," he said. "Stop following me, you daft dog. The Beast Glatisant is meant to *be* pursued, not to pursue!"

Glatisant let out a bark and sat grinning with his tongue hanging out like the roguish monster he was. Mrs. Benson said, "Or perhaps you're just strange enough to be more curiosity than threat. That moustache of yours, now . . . I doubt I've ever seen one that long on an Englishman."

Eric's hand went protectively to his upper lip. "I saw several specimens just like it when I was in Paris to see the Olympic Games," he protested.

"Foreigners with foreign moustaches! Respectable Englishmen don't permit that sort of length on their moustaches, I don't think. Well, you know what I mean."

"I need all the help I can get to pass as a respectable Englishman?"

Mrs. Benson blushed a bright red, and Eric grinned playfully at her. She replied, "I think we're simply too accustomed to seeing long moustaches like that on caricatures of Guy Fawkes, who was neither respectable nor English."

"Perhaps." Eric picked up the scraps of notepaper. "You won't mind if I hold on to these, will you? I think they might be important."

"Be my guest."

The smile she gave him was genuine, and Eric found himself smiling right back.

Abashed, Eric stepped away and said, "I think I had better go see what Avery's got up to."

THE VEIL OF VERONICA

IF ERIC HAD A FAULT, it was his tendency to run off after every interesting object that caught his eye. He'd started out in an earnest attempt to locate his friend, but he was wandering alone in a strange house, rendered stranger by its arrested transition from manor to rest home. And there was the lingering evidence, too, of its history as a war hospital. As Eric went from room to room, he couldn't help but notice the stains on the floor where things had been spilled, or marks where beds had once been packed, sardine-close, into what might otherwise have been a generous space.

Here, for instance, was the dining room. It had been a truly grand space once, with three gracious French doors opening onto a wide stone terrace. The floor was an intricate parquet, and the panelling below the rust-red Victorian wallpaper was elaborate. A pair of chandeliers still descended from the plaster medallions in the ceiling, but they were dusty now, and Eric doubted whether they still worked.

Before the War, there would have been a long table down the middle, covered over with a snow-white tablecloth. Eric imagined the Edwardian gentry trooping in—gentlemen in dinner jackets escorting ladies in evening gowns, in order of precedence as dictated by social etiquette and understood by the lady of the house. Footmen as silent and deferential as the attendants at the Britannia would glide around the table with serving dishes of fragrant meats and soups while the guests made polite conversation about the weather. They'd have stayed the night, because one generally didn't travel all the way into the country for a single evening, and repeat the whole process the next evening.

It was still done elsewhere, Eric knew, and often enough; but it was not being done here. The War threw out the table and filled the room with cheap metal beds that scored scratches across the parquetry and chipped the wall panelling. The same gentlemen might have lain in those beds, attended by the same ladies, now in VAD nursing uniforms. The smell of savoury herbs would have been replaced by the sharp tang of disinfectant. Perhaps they still discussed the weather, if only to stay sane.

The Bensons must have carved out some other part of the house for their domestic use. An apartment upstairs, perhaps. They certainly didn't use this room for dining now. The chandeliers, hanging a trifle lower than might be comfortable for someone to walk under, were Eric's only clue that this might have once been the old dining room. Taking a deep breath, one smelled nothing at all.

Avery would have insisted he felt a ghostly presence, and demanded to hold a séance.

The passage from the dining room to the west wing of the house had been stripped of decoration, and the floors were bare. Only the windows facing the front drive had been boarded up: the back windows were clear to let in the muted north light. Outside, unpruned yew hedges closed in to scratch the glass with their branches. They were an additional barrier, cutting one off from the sunlight on the open green lawn.

The air was still and carried a faintly unclean odour, but there was less dust than he'd expected. The passage was still in use but on a reduced scale. He pictured Mrs. Benson rustling down the shadowy corridor to whatever lay at its far end, a stranger in her own ancestral home. If his understanding of country house architecture was correct, this would have been the servants' territory; even Mrs. Benson's parents would have been counted outsiders here.

The old barriers weren't so much being broken down as allowed to rot away, even as other barriers grew up, unbidden, to take their place.

Eric's footsteps echoed into the dead silence and shadows, a stalker following just behind, just outside one's field of vision. None of the bright sunlight on the lawn seemed to penetrate into the passage. The fine parquetry of the dining room had given way to terracotta tile; to reduce the unsettling echo, Eric found himself tip-toeing as softly as he could between the twin tracks of scratch marks where, once, something heavy had been repeatedly dragged back and forth. The thought of it screeching across the tile set Eric's teeth on edge.

The door to the kitchen was locked, but the next door opened into a simple white-tiled room. Here, Eric found the metal frame of a little cot pushed up under one of those inspirational posters of the war: a sailor-suited girl in a rowboat, with the slogan, *Every girl pulling for victory*. A small battered desk was in the opposite corner, and Eric guessed that this room had barely changed at all since the end of the War. Eric took a peek inside the desk's lone drawer and found it empty. What could this room have been used for? It looked like the sick bay from his old school: there was Matron's desk, and there was the cot where one could lie down until one felt well enough to return to one's lessons. Eric concluded that the nurses must have used it in much the same way, as a place to get a bit of respite from the demands of the hospital. The poster, of course, was to remind them to return to their duty.

Perhaps, before the War, this had been a serving pantry. In place of the cot and the desk would have been a sideboard with a row of chafing dishes where the food prepared in the kitchen would wait until the guests in the dining room were ready for them. He could picture the kitchen staff bustling out of the kitchen with their dishes to set down, and the footmen from the dining room bustling in to pick them up. And then, during the War, a nurse sitting down to rest while another stood to begin her shift.

By now, he'd forgotten that he was meant to be searching for Avery at all. Surely Mrs. Benson must have already found Avery in the servants' hall, telling fortunes to whoever would listen. For the moment, however, there was still too much to see.

Indeed.

After the little nurses' station was a square vestibule with a door to an outside yard and an archway into some sort of storage room. There was also a sturdy oak door directly across from the nurses' station, and Eric passed through this into a large sun-drenched, white-washed room crowded with painted canvases. The smell of oil paint and mineral spirits assaulted his nostrils. The room went right up to the rafters, and a cupola skylight allowed diffused sunlight to filter down from above. There were wide mullioned windows on three sides of the room, none of them boarded up. Through the north windows, Eric could see the edge of the back lawn and the wind chasing fallen leaves over it; grassy waves undulated in the bright sunlight beyond the shadow of the roofline, and beyond the lawn were the woods. White curtains shielded the windows on the other two walls, blending the light into a uniform glow that reflected off the white walls and terracotta floor tiles.

Near the door were an easel, a paint-spattered cabinet, and a divan heaped with soft flannel blankets. Eric's curiosity was piqued; this room, unlike the others he'd seen so far, clearly saw extended personal use. Someone in this house was an artist, that much was obvious, though Eric didn't recall noticing if either of the Bensons had the telltale paint scrapes under their fingernails. Then again, the easel was bare; it might have been a while since they'd taken up a brush.

The divan had been recently used, though. There was a sort of warm muskiness about the blankets, and their arrangement suggested that someone had very recently been wrapped up in them. The strand of dark finger-curled hair caught in the upholstery confirmed Eric's suspicions: Mrs. Benson had been here. And so had Glatisant, judging by the dog hairs.

Eric paused. Why would Mrs. Benson be napping here, if she weren't working on a canvas? Had she, in fact, slept the night here?

Grief did things to a person, he thought uncomfortably. It had dawned on him that he'd intruded into the lady's private sanctum, and the right thing to do would be to leave.

He couldn't avoid hazarding a glance at the paintings that filled the rest of the room, though, and that nearly undid him.

Here was a man, a soldier, staring out of the canvas with his head held high. It took half a moment to realise that his right sleeve was empty, and his left hand was a misshapen stump.

Here was another man, reclining in a chair, sun shining on the prosthetic leg cradled in his half lap. No blankets hid the stump of his left thigh, and behind him were the bright summer-green fields of the English countryside, through which he'd never run again.

Another man, bare chested and pale, sat with his head bowed. A deep gash in his side, infected, wept pus onto the hands of unseen attendants as they changed his bandages.

There was a full-figure nude: the shrapnel-twisted torso was a mockery of classical antiquity's clean, athletic forms, and the face was so badly mangled, you only recognised the bright green eyes staring back into your soul.

Next was a mustard gas survivor, a vision of melting flesh, red, raw, and gleaming. The face was barely human, and Eric had to look away . . . but there was nowhere else to look. Everywhere, he saw—immortalised in oils and watercolours, in various stages between study, sketch, and finish—the broken men and open wounds of the War. Impressionistic colours, bloodred and bile yellow, drew the eye and emphasised that which in real life might have only been flat detail.

Eric remembered them. He remembered them rotting on the parapets, the ones who hadn't lived. Benson's killing wound had been comparatively clean, and the mustard scars discreetly hidden under Aldershott's collar were comparatively mild.

You knew they existed, of course, these maimed survivors of the War. You remembered the dead and you supposed the survivors were the lucky ones. You saw the ones who came out whole, and you focused on them instead, the majority who could go back to civvy street with little to mark them but a few stories to tell their future grandchildren. The maimed were relegated to a sort of no-man's-land beyond one's consciousness, to be conveniently forgotten.

Looking around here, the situation was taken to the opposite extreme. One might suppose that no one at all had come back whole.

"You know, this room is supposed to be private."

Mrs. Benson stood in the doorway, her black dress a sharp contrast with the bright, colour-filled room. She didn't seem at all upset by the intrusion, however. Hastily, Eric put down the brushes that he only now realised he'd picked up in the course of examining the room.

"I was just admiring these paintings," he said, affecting a light tone to mask his discomfiture. "Are they all your work?"

"Yes." Mrs. Benson quietly shut the door behind her and walked forward. She'd relaxed somewhat over the course of their conversation in Benson's office, and she relaxed further still in the presence of her paintings. The light caught the reds and yellows and reflected colour onto her pale cheeks, even as her gaze went lovingly from painting to painting. She seemed lost in fond memory, and her voice softened. "I'd always had a talent for it, and I'd had a bit of training. I painted a bit during the War, but there wasn't much time for it then." Here, she indicated some of the rougher studies and a series of watercolours. "And after the War . . . there didn't seem to be much else to do."

"Not much else to do! But—"

"I daresay you had plenty to do. It was different for me. I'd put so much of myself into my VAD work, I felt lost without it. So I took to painting. I looked up some of the men who'd been here, and I visited the hospitals where Father's friends worked, and I painted what I saw."

"You could have picked a cheerier subject, I think." There was something unquestionably morbid about these paintings. Eric had always chosen to dwell on life—the wholesome life of a home worth fighting for. What possessed anyone to focus instead on this . . . this unpleasantness?

"You can't just look away from someone because his injuries are unpleasant," Mrs. Benson said gently. Her fingers brushed across the canvas of the mustard gas victim. "Please. Take a look around, and tell me what you think."

Eric looked again at the armless, the legless, and the cruelly disfigured. It was somehow easier in the trenches, where your concern was for immediate survival. Seeing these open wounds in the aftermath made the bile rise in his throat. "It's the price of war, isn't it?" he said, and swallowed. "People still have to live with the pain and suffering, even now that we have peace."

"Pain and suffering, Mr. Peterkin? Is that all?"

What did she want him to see? Eric turned to the first painting he'd seen, the armless soldier. He swallowed again, and stared into its painted eyes for a good long minute. They seemed sad, he concluded, but not despairing. It was that faraway, romantic sadness of a noble hero looking back over his journey. The buttons on the man's uniform gleamed, and he held himself in a way that radiated pride and dignity. Mrs. Benson had painted the light striking his jawline at just the right angle to emphasise its strength.

Turning around, Eric spotted a gold band gleaming from the shrapnel-scarred nude's ring finger. The green eyes above were taunting, he realised, and the jaw was held in an attitude of challenge. And the expression on the mustard gas survivor was one of laughter in the face of loss. It was the survival of spirit, pure and simple.

Mrs. Benson nodded. "You can't tell a man to run at a line of rifles and then throw him away because a bullet's taken off half his face. I wanted people to see. I wanted these men to know that they were still worth something. Some of them needed to be reminded. We didn't get the difficult surgical work here, Mr. Peterkin—those men all went to Graylingwell first. The men who came here came to recuperate after they'd already been patched up and were quite sure they weren't going to die tomorrow. And once you're over that great anxiety, once you know you're going to live, you start to wonder what your life is worth, without an arm, without a leg . . . without a face. People look at you, and that's all they see. It didn't seem fair."

Eric was studying the paintings with more of his usual curiosity. The pain and suffering were still there, but there was something more behind them. A hero did what was right, he thought, whatever the cost to himself.

Looking further, he caught sight of a familiar face: Patrick Norris, grinning from another canvas. Norris's teeth were whiter than in reality, and springtime glowed from the fields in the background. Mrs. Benson had captured quite accurately the essence of his laughter and love of life.

"Here's someone without a scar," Eric said, picking the painting up. It was dated just earlier that year, in May.

Mrs. Benson only laughed softly. "Some scars aren't visible, Mr. Peterkin." She stopped just a foot away from Eric. Their eyes met. "You must know that," she whispered. "Nobody comes out of a war unchanged."

"I'm just as I was before."

"Are you really?"

"Of course I am." But even as he said it, a vision of no-man's-land swam before his eyes, and the paintings around him faded into a reality of broken men, scattered by an exploding mine. He blinked to snap himself out of it.

Mrs. Benson's hand went up to his cheek, and Eric, afterwards, would wonder why he didn't flinch at the familiarity.

"I'd like to paint you, I think. You're . . . not exactly handsome, no, but unusual. I saw the way you were looking at the photographs in the reception room and all these paintings here. You had this expression of such rapt fascination. I don't know how that boyish fascination with the world survived Flanders, but it did, and . . . yes. I'd like to paint you."

"Mrs. Benson—"

"Helen."

"I'm not sure this is appropriate."

Mrs. Benson—Helen—didn't seem to hear him. She said, "I always wondered what Albert saw in Emily. The lure of the exotic, I expect." Her expression hardened. "Albert had no business running off, trying to play the hero to her memory. I thought he'd forgotten about her by now. It wasn't fair." Tears sprang up in her eyes, and Eric guessed they were as much from anger as from grief.

They were standing so close to each other now that he could smell the same warm muskiness he'd detected on the divan blankets. Helen's hand had fallen to his collar, and now burnt against the pulsing artery in his neck. Norris's portrait was all that stood between them. Cautiously, Eric lowered the portrait, then reached up to catch Helen's hand and hold it away. Her hand twisted in his to clasp it and pull it towards herself. Eric felt reluctant to let go, though he felt sure it would be wrong to take advantage of her in her current weakness. She was a new widow: there was Benson's memory to consider, and Eric understood very well how the pain of loss could lead one to seek comfort from regrettable sources.

The soft crepe fabric of Helen's black dress rustled against the stiff, starched front of his shirt. She moved to rest her head on his shoulder.

Eric wasn't sure what he'd have done if Avery hadn't come barging in right that minute.

"There you are," Avery cried. "I wondered where you'd gone. The housemaid was just showing me around. There's a cottage out that way, which she says used to be the groundskeeper's cottage until this place became a hospital."

The spell was broken. Helen was Mrs. Benson again; she stepped away from Eric and said, a little too brightly to be natural, "Yes, the nurses were lodged there, including Emily. Women only, of course. They'd come up to the house by the path and come in through the west wing vestibule. This room here became the quarantine ward, for patients with contagious diseases. Before the War, it was the dairy; but of course, we don't make our own butter and cheese anymore."

Leading them back out into the vestibule, she pointed out the adjacent dispensary, where the drugs were kept. It had whitewashed walls and a terracotta tiled floor, and its small square windows were positioned high and out of reach. The smell of disinfectant still lingered in the corners of the now-empty cabinet.

They trooped back through the little room with the desk and the cot, which had been, as Eric suspected earlier, the nurses' station and resting room, then continued back down the passage to the main house. They'd all slipped into pretending that nothing had happened in the studio—what had once been the quarantine ward—and that Mrs. Benson had only been giving Eric a tour of the house.

Glancing back at his friend, Eric was sure that, for all his usual obliviousness, Avery hadn't been fooled one bit.

RETURN TO LONDON

AS THE VILLAGE OF WEXFORD CROSSING slipped out of view behind them, Avery slid down in his seat and braced his knees against the dashboard, making himself comfortable. The air had crossed the line from merely brisk to distinctly chilly, and he wrapped his scarf around himself a few more times. Meanwhile, Eric was enjoying the cold blast of air over his head, which was boiling over with new ideas. The touch of Mrs. Benson's—Helen's—hand on his cheek still burnt, and he wanted more than anything to have the feeling blow away in the wind.

"I hope you're happy with the outing," Avery said. "I can't say I enjoyed it all that much, but I expect you've solved the whole mystery based only on what Mrs. Benson told you."

"And what I found in the old office at the manor. Yes, Avery, the things in Benson's box must have all come from here. The medical report came from Parker's file, the photograph came from Mrs. Benson's mantelpiece, and both the scissors and the hypodermic kit were probably leftovers from the hospital. I don't know what happened to them, though. That's as much a mystery as anything."

"So where does that leave us?" Avery asked.

"The disappearance of Emily Ang," Eric replied. "Benson talked about righting some great wrong, and Mrs. Benson said her disappearance was the thing occupying his mind. If we know what happened to Miss Ang, we'll know what happened to Benson." He paused, thinking. "She can't have got far, I don't think. A Chinese woman out here in the English countryside would have stood out something awful."

"You don't think she just ran off on her own, then."

Eric shook his head. "No. That wouldn't make sense. So if she did disappear, it would have to be foul play: kidnapping or murder."

"Is it still white slavery if she isn't white?"

"Avery!"

"I'm only joking." But Eric shot him a glare to show he was serious, and Avery hastily apologised.

"If it were white slavery," Eric said, "she can't have been the only one. There'd be other reports of missing women around the area. And if it were murder, someone might have found the body, though it wouldn't have been identified. That's the sort of thing that gets reported in the news. Avery, first thing tomorrow morning, we've got to visit the British Museum and search the newspapers. We're looking for reports of missing persons and unidentified bodies discovered in the south of England. That should be good enough to be starting with."

"Oh, research," said Avery dully. "My favourite. I don't know why you bother. You knew this woman even less than you knew Benson. And speaking of Benson, I honestly think he was just asking for it."

"What do you mean?" Irrationally, Eric wondered if Helen— Mrs. Benson—had something to do with it.

"His box, Eric. Box 13. An unlucky number, and it's hardly a surprise what came of it. Frankly, if I were him, I'd have insisted on changing boxes immediately, and none of this would have happened."

"He didn't have much choice. The vault was full—" Eric stopped. Wolfe knew that the vault was full.

"What?"

"Wolfe could have forced Benson to take whatever box he wanted by taking the last box and vacating it at the last minute! No, that doesn't make sense unless he knew Benson would be wanting a box that evening, and could prepare for it." The next mile was spent lost in thought, and then Eric said, "I have it. Benson said it was Aldershott who showed him how the vault worked. Perhaps box 13 was Aldershott's, which he gave up to Benson because . . . oh, call it hospitality. A favour for the new boy. Whatever the reason, Wolfe guessed that the only person likely to have vacated a box for Benson would be the one who was actually showing him the boxes. And if he knew which box was Aldershott's, he'd know which box Benson had." Eric felt quite pleased with himself.

"That's one mystery solved, then. Don't say I'm of no help to you. And how do you reckon Inspector Parker got in, or did Wolfe let him in after his own spot of burglary?"

"Mrs. Benson's scuttled my ideas about Inspector Parker," Eric said, frowning in consternation. Parker's leaving when he did meant he wasn't involved in Emily Ang's disappearance; but Parker's removing her photograph meant he was connected to it somehow. It really was quite vexing. Eric did have one concrete lead, though, such as it was: the notepaper scraps from the Butterworth Arms in Chichester. If it came down to a matter of handwriting, the simplest thing to do would be to compare the note against written entries in the register at the Britannia. Everything else would have to depend on what he and Avery found in the newspaper archives, and what they said about Emily Ang.

"You know, I don't think I like her very much," said Avery, interrupting Eric's train of thought.

"You never even met her, Avery!"

"Not Emily. Mrs. Benson."

Eric fell silent. "War does things to people, Avery."

"That's no excuse! If it brought out the ghoul in her, then that ghoul was always there to begin with. All those mutilated people! It was horrifying. And you! You were completely taken in by her. I expect she fed you some romantic twaddle about noble heroism, and you believed her."

There's still a certain nobility in smiling through the pain, Eric thought. But Avery seemed to have slipped into a foul mood, and nothing Eric could say would rouse him out of it.

Eric left a brooding Avery Ferrett at the Arabica before proceeding back to the Britannia Club. The last time he'd been there was Saturday, when they'd found Benson's body. The police inquiry under Inspector Parker had just begun, and a general state of discomfiture was spreading through the air. He remembered that, coming out from his interview, he'd found the dining room empty and lifeless. Far from remaining silent in the background, a couple of attendants were whispering anxiously in one corner about the recent developments. Those who could leave had left, and those who could not didn't seem to know what to do with themselves.

None of that had quite departed from the Britannia in the time since.

The soft clink of silverware was still missing. There were no diners tonight, and the smell emanating from the dining room was not of meat and gravy but of lye and disinfectant. Someone must have decided that Benson's murder rendered the premises unclean, and ordered a thorough scouring of the public rooms. Perhaps it was simply for want of something to do. The waiters right now were lounging about, looking as much at a loss as the attendants that other day.

Peering down the corridor to the vault stairwell, Eric caught sight of the cleaning staff—characters one generally never actually saw—scrubbing away at the wainscoting in Aldershott's office. Ugly black marks blotted various surfaces, and Eric at first wondered if the fireplace had exploded and deposited soot everywhere. He soon realised, however, that this was in fact fingerprint powder. The police had gone over every inch of Aldershott's office with the stuff, and the rest of the corridor appeared much the same. One often read of fingerprint powder, but no one ever told you how tiresome it must be to remove it afterwards. Eric could only imagine what the scene must be like down in the vault itself, or up in Benson's room.

Even Old Faithful, still behind the front desk, seemed a little more on edge than usual. "You're a sight for sore eyes, sir," he said as Eric came to sign the register. "I doubt we had more than a handful of gentlemen come in here today. No one rightly knows what to do, now there's been a murder."

"It'll come right again, Cully. It's just been too soon, that's all."

"I hope you're right, sir." Old Faithful heaved a sigh, then brightened up again. "Oh, and there's a letter here for you, sir! From Captain Aldershott himself."

Eric took the cream-coloured envelope from Old Faithful with some surprise. The thick, smooth card paper was luxurious under his fingertips—too fine an article to be wasted on ordinary notes and memoranda. Eric guessed a polite social engagement was in the offing, and tore it open to see.

Mr. and Mrs. Edward Aldershott
cordially request the company of
Mr. Eric Peterkin
for dinner on
Friday, the 31st of October,
8:00 P.M.

The address was in Mayfair, not far from Marble Arch and Hyde Park. Eric noted that, whereas his own name and the date and time of the event were handwritten onto blank spaces, as might be expected with an invitation card bought at the stationer's, the Aldershotts' names and address were printed along with the rest of the card. Evidently the Aldershotts gave dinners often enough to want a set of personalised invitation cards prepared.

But why was Aldershott extending the hand of friendship to Eric now? No doubt it was something of a response to the recent upheaval. Eric looked around again at the listless waiters just visible through the doorways of the dining room, and the corridor blackened with fingerprint powder. Perhaps it was even something of an apology for words exchanged in the heat of the moment. Aldershott must surely have realised by now how right Eric had been in warning him against tidying up his ransacked office.

Whatever the reason, Eric was happy to accept.

He glanced up at the grand staircase and the painting of the Arthurian Knights on the landing. The lights were dim, and he couldn't see his usual touchstones, King Pellinore and Sir Palomides. There really is nothing quite like a crisis to spark camaraderie, he mused. When the shelling begins, you don't care who or what the next soldier is, as long as he's watching your back.

And speaking of shoving things about, here was a torn envelope shoved between the pages of the register. It looked identical to the one Eric himself had just ripped open, and it was addressed to Oliver Saxon.

"Begging your pardon, sir, I should have caught that." Old Faithful took both torn envelopes from Eric and deposited them in a nearby wastepaper basket. "Lieutenant Saxon does tend to leave things lying around when he doesn't want them. Half the books in the reading room have his scraps tucked in them for bookmarks."

But Eric was looking at the entry right at the bottom of the previous page. *Mr. Oliver Saxon,* written in a textbook-perfect cursive, but for the curiously formed lower-case *r* in Oliver. Funny that such a slovenly individual should have such fine penmanship, but it was a perfect match for the notepaper Eric had found in the Sotheby Manor office. He took out the scraps of paper and laid them atop the register to confirm it. Yes, the handwriting was identical.

Saxon, who supposedly had no personal connection to Sotheby Manor, had been there at some point on or after the twentieth of July 1918, with a special interest in Emily Ang.

Eric remembered Saxon being manhandled up the stairs, and how the tension thickened the air when his eyes met Parker's. Saxon had a key to the club's back door and could come and go as he wished. There wasn't any question, with him, of how he got in or how he might have disposed of any bloodied clothing. And Saxon was the only one with a reason to know that Benson might be found at the club that night. Why had Benson decided, at the last minute, to spend the night at the club rather than at Saxon's? One assumed concerns over Wolfe's proposed burglary, but what if it were really about Saxon?

Perhaps, Eric thought, perhaps he'd read this from the wrong side around. Perhaps Parker had been a secret ally of Benson's, and the two had followed the trail to Saxon. Who better to enlist in an investigation, after all, than a police detective?

THE LONDON PAPERS

THE GRAND ENTRANCE of the British Museum stretched across Great Russell Street, almost all the way from Bloomsbury Street in the west to Montague Street in the east. An Ionic colonnade reached around a wide plaza from a central neoclassical Greek portico; the pediment above, with its carved figures representing the progress of civilisation, proclaimed the institution's position as a temple of learning. It was early in the morning, and harried academics—shabby, clumsy, and giving the impression of having just fallen out of bed—hurried up the front steps to claim a desk in the great circular Reading Room at the heart of the museum. A few early tourists in sturdy walking shoes were drifting in to see, perhaps, the Elgin Marbles, or the Egyptian exhibits, or any number of other relics of antiquity—and stopping just as much to see the museum itself. All of them looked a little lost and insignificant between the towering columns.

Eric and Avery paused only a moment to observe this dawn of regular activity before continuing on to Montague Street. Their goal was the Newspaper Reading Room, at the extreme eastern end of the building. It thrust out among the houses of Montague Street, smooth stone beside the brown brick, far more modest than the portico and plaza on Great Russell Street. One might never know, without rounding the corner, that the buildings were one and the same. Climbing the steps to the side door, one felt less like a supplicant at the temple of knowledge and more like an everyday bureaucrat going in to work.

Perhaps it was simply this reduced scale, but Eric sensed a more relaxed atmosphere here: the academics were generally less anxious, and the tourists were nonexistent. The room itself was long, as high ceilinged as the rest of the museum rooms, and filled with academic clutter. Three of its tall windows faced northeast onto Montague Street, and the crisp grey morning light flooded in over the desks and reading stands. There was the subdued rustle of broadsheet pages being turned, and the musty smell of old newsprint. Elderly eccentrics in threadbare jackets and with unruly grey beards barely looked up from their perusal of the most recent newspapers, which they preferred not to purchase for themselves. Others were harder to place: students of more recent history, perhaps, tracing obscure threads through the past few decades; or novelists anxious to avoid an anachronism. Perhaps one or two were amateur sleuths researching a forgotten crime for some connection to the present.

The simple fact was that if one wanted to know about anything that had happened in the world in the past hundred years, one began with newspaper reports; and that meant a tedious and meticulous search through the British Museum's collection. Every issue of London's various newspapers since the 1820s had a copy kept here.

Eric set Avery to reading backwards from the present day, while he himself began ploughing forwards from the day of Emily Ang's disappearance. "Remember," he said, "we're looking for reports of unidentified bodies and the like. We also want every report of a missing person, whether it's a man or a woman. It might be that one of the unidentified bodies can be matched up to another missing person, and we'll know then that it's not Emily Ang. And we want those missing persons for another reason: a spate of disappearances could mean a gang of white slavers, and that she'd been abducted by them." His brow furrowed in concern. "I just hope it'll all be in the London papers."

Avery looked up sharply. "Oh?"

"This thing happened in Sussex, Avery, so of course it'd be reported in the Sussex papers; but not everything in the Sussex papers gets repeated in the London papers. And if it's not in the London papers, we'll have to order the Sussex papers down specially from the repository in Colindale. I think the next delivery will be in three days from now."

"Oh, I do say." Avery huffed in annoyance. "Why don't you do that, then, and come back in three days? Instead of dragging me down here at too-early o'clock today to look for something you're not sure is here?"

"Because we can't order down six years' worth of newspapers, that's why. Even if we don't find what we want, the London papers might give us an idea of where to look. And we'd better get it right the first time around, because these deliveries from Colindale are only done once a week and we'd have to wait that long again. Oh, chin up, Avery: maybe we'll find everything we need today after all, and it'll save us all that bother."

Still grumbling at what he considered a fool's errand at an ungodly hour, Avery buried his nose in his paper. He was not a man who suffered mornings gladly.

The light intensified with the afternoon, shifting as it did into a more indirect glow and trading contrast for brightness. The threadbare eccentrics shuffled off in search of other entertainment. Other readers took their place. The researchers and academics came and went, but Eric and Avery ploughed on. Evening fell, and the glare of electric lights overhead replaced the daylight from the windows. At their elbows, their research notes grew and shrank as hopeful leads were found and answered, until they finally met over the *Times* of the second of February 1921.

It was dark outside now. All but one of the researchers had gone, and this last one seemed desperate to fill up his notebook before being kicked out. The fellow in charge of shutting up the Newspaper Reading Room for the night was hovering in a corner, giving all of them the evil eye. There were still fifteen minutes on the clock before the official closing time, but he'd already shut off most of the electric lights and left half the reading desks in shadow. The subdued library hush had turned into a dead silence.

Eric sat next to Avery and said, "I'm going to assume, from your lack of excitement, that you didn't find anything definitive."

"I think it was a rotten trick to make me go backwards from today. Anything you wanted about Emily Ang would almost certainly have been much earlier."

"You don't know that. And anyway, I didn't find much that might be definitive, either. I reckon we really will have to order in the Sussex papers after all."

Avery let out a long-suffering groan. Over in his corner, the museum employee cleared his throat and glanced meaningfully at the clock.

Eric pulled over his notebook and the four newspapers he'd saved over the course of his search. "I'll go first, shall I?"

"Please do." Avery lit up a clove cigarette, and the smoke coiled around them like incense, shielding them from the museum employee's malevolent glare and the last researcher's growing desperation. The silence deepened.

26 November 1918: Miss Jane Harris, 27, was reported missing yesterday from St. Catherine's, a girls' boarding school near Petersfield where she taught mathematics and history. Miss Harris, an alumna of the school, was last seen departing for the weekend on Friday the 22nd, supposedly to visit her aunt, Miss Gladys Atkinson, in Ashford, Kent. Miss Atkinson admits no knowledge of any planned visit.

"Jane's been a bit queer since her young man was killed in the fighting over in France," says Miss Atkinson. "She told me once that she blamed herself, as he wouldn't have gone but for her making him. I hope she hasn't gone and done anything foolish."

"That sounds promising," Avery said, and Eric nodded in response.

"Aside from the suggestion of her having 'done something foolish,' the details sound rather like what Mrs. Benson told us about Emily's disappearance."

> **10 April 1919:** Yesterday evening, Miss Angelica Truelove, 23, was abducted by persons unknown from outside the Monkey's Paw pub in Southampton, where she worked as a barmaid. Witnesses describe a black Vauxhall tourer driven by an unsavoury foreigner with a sinister beard . . .

"It's always an unsavoury foreigner with a sinister beard," Eric remarked, "unless it's a sinister foreigner with an unsavoury beard. I doubt that the description is accurate, but here's an actual abduction, with witnesses."

But Avery said, "Angelica Truelove! What a name! Wait . . . yes . . . isn't that Lady Felton's maiden name? I remember now, Lord Hadley Felton eloped with her to America, and there was a great to-do because she was only a . . . a chorus girl's the most common story, but I've also heard she was a shopgirl or a barmaid. Everyone who wasn't a Felton thought it too romantic for words, but the family was desperate to hush it all up."

Eric sighed and struck a line through Angelica Truelove's name.

> **3 September 1920:** The body of a young woman was washed up on the beach near Bognor Regis earlier today. Police are seeking the public's aid in identifying the woman. She was between 5'1" and 5'4" in height, with black hair. The cause of death is believed to have been an accidental drowning . . .

"Oh, I say!" Avery exclaimed. "That does sound right. Eric, you could have told me you'd found her, and saved me a long afternoon of slogging through all those papers."

"I didn't want to jump to any conclusions, Avery. This might easily be someone else."

"I don't see how. Bognor Regis is just a short jaunt from Chichester and that dreadful village we were in, and this was only two years after the disappearance—"

Eric gave a start. "Two years! I'd missed that. After two years in the water, how on earth would there have been enough left for anyone to know so easily that she was a woman with black hair? No, this body must have gone into the water much later, long after Emily disappeared."

"Oh." Avery looked crestfallen. "Perhaps she wasn't killed until much later?"

"It's possible," Eric replied slowly, "but it seems unlikely. If she wasn't killed immediately, then we're back to the question of it having been a kidnapping first. And unless there are more reports of missing women in the Sussex papers, it's looking more and more unlikely that she was the victim of white slavers."

25 January 1921: Police are seeking the whereabouts of Mr. Robert Unwin, 32, who was last seen departing his house in Petworth, Sussex, on Sunday for a walk. He is described as about 5′6″, weighing approximately 11 stone, with a persistent cough due to lung damage sustained in the War. He had just undergone retraining as an accounts clerk, as this lung damage had rendered him unfit for his pre-War occupation in farm labour. He was to begin work within the week with the Walton-Gale Shipping Company in London.

Friends and neighbours describe Mr. Unwin as a quiet, unassuming individual with a deep love of the countryside. "He didn't like the idea of moving to London," one friend says, "but he knew how lucky he was. Not everyone gets these opportunities, and it was better pay than he ever got before. We all reckoned things were on the up and up for old Robbie Unwin."

"I know the answer to that one," Avery said, digging out the last page of his own notes.

4 April 1921: The body of Mr. Robert Unwin, 32, of Petworth, Sussex, was recovered from the River Rother on Saturday afternoon by Boy Scouts exploring the local flora. Unwin, an ex-serviceman with an unblemished record, is believed to have shot himself with a pistol he'd taken as a souvenir of the War.

Mr. Unwin was fond of long walks along the Rother, and friends describe him as a great lover of the English countryside. The suggestion of suicide has been called into question by the fact that Mr. Unwin had been looking forward to a new job with a shipping company in London. "He had everything to live for," say friends. "He knew how lucky he was."

A coroner's inquest is to be called for a closer examination of the facts.

"Shot himself," commented Avery. "At least he knew what he was doing, if he really did shoot himself . . . I seem to have come across a rather awful lot of stories about ex-servicemen accidentally shooting themselves while cleaning their guns. You'd think a soldier would know to be careful."

Eric nodded slowly. He'd seen a few of those as well. He knew enough to know that these were probably suicides disguised as accidents, but the sheer number of them was unsettling. It made him wonder about the men he'd had under his command. They'd drifted apart after five years, and many were never the sort to write, but still . . . they were his responsibility once.

They'd reached the end of what Eric considered plausible or relevant. He'd found and discarded several other stories that had clearly nothing to do with Emily Ang. They turned now to Avery's stack of notes.

15 February 1924: Police are seeking the identity of a young woman whose body was discovered in an abandoned cottage outside Basingstoke on Wednesday. Her estimated age is between 18 and 30, and she is believed to have been a victim of murder. The woman's hands and feet had been bound with rough hemp, and her face mutilated with a sharp, heavy implement, possibly a machete . . .

"I reckon we can put this aside for the same reason as the Bognor Regis woman?" Avery asked. "I really don't want to read any more of it, not again. I don't know, but I get the idea that she hadn't only been murdered."

Eric nodded. "It reminds me of another story, actually. The exact same thing happened to another woman in Reading this last May. That time, the murderer was caught almost immediately, and I wonder if he did this murder too. As I recall, he'd been an inmate of a hospital somewhere, being treated for shell shock, until about two years ago." The gentlemen of the Britannia had been strangely interested in the story, though no one seemed to want to talk about it.

Avery asked, "Do you think he could have murdered Emily Ang in the same way?"

"I'll have to find the story again to be sure, but I think he was already locked away in a hospital by then." A glance up at the clock told them that they should have left the Newspaper Reading Room five minutes ago. The museum employee glowering at them had let them stay on only because of a hefty bribe from the other researcher to keep the room open a little longer, and no amount of money would induce him to let them seek out another newspaper to confirm their theories.

"Let's carry on," Eric said. "What else have you got?"

> 10 August 1923: Skeletal remains, believed to be that of a woman, were discovered in a shallow pond near Wilmington, within sight of the Long Man. Police are seeking aid in identifying these remains. While nearly all articles of clothing have since rotted away, the skeleton was wearing a ring bearing an unusual crest . . .

"Here's a picture of the ring," Avery said. "Does it look at all familiar?"

Eric examined the picture and nodded. "Yes. I recognise it. It's the school crest for St. Catherine's, the girls' boarding school that Miss Jane Harris disappeared from back in 1918. There was picture of it with the story." Going back to his own notes, he scored a line through Jane Harris's name. "And that's one mystery solved, though unfortunately it's not ours."

It looked as though Emily Ang was now the only undiscovered missing woman of 1918.

> 6 February 1923: Mr. Joseph Davis, 39, of Horsham, Sussex, was reported missing yesterday morning when he failed to report to work at the solicitor's firm where he had only just been named a partner. Foul play is suspected.
>
> Mr. Davis was last seen drinking heavily at his London club, in celebration of his promotion. He is thought to have retired to one of the club's lodging rooms afterwards, though there was no sign of him in the morning. It was believed that Mr. Davis had risen early and left before the day's staff came on duty. According to the club's porter, this was not at all unusual for Mr. Davis, and in fact it was more expected than not.

"Stop right there," Eric said. "I know that one. Davis was a member of the Britannia Club. I know I've seen his obituary, too. Are you sure you didn't see any other news about him? The discovery of his body, perhaps?"

"If I had, I'd have written it down, just in case you found the missing person report first. You know, just as I did for Robert Unwin. There wasn't anything. Do you know what happened to him in the end, then?"

"He's supposed to have fallen off the pier while on a day trip to Eastbourne," Eric said. "An accident." But was it?

"I've got one last grisly discovery," Avery said, interrupting Eric's thoughts.

> 17 May 1922: A skeleton was unearthed from a shallow grave in Bruton Wood on the afternoon of the 15th. It is believed to be that of a young woman, aged between 16 and 28. Police are making inquiries.

"Is that all?" Eric asked, flipping through the copy of the *Times* where Avery had found the article.

"No," said Avery, shaking his head, "that's all I found. I very nearly missed it, in fact."

Eric wanted to be excited, but caution reined him in, and he was still feeling some lingering unease from having been inundated all day with stories of untimely death. On the whole, he had more unidentified bodies than missing persons: some disappearances must have gone unreported, and this skeleton, the Bruton Wood skeleton, might have been an unreported disappearance as well. He'd have to know more, and that meant ordering the Sussex newspapers from the time around 15 to 17 May 1922.

There was no ignoring the time any longer. Eric and Avery bundled out into the darkness of Montague Street, the museum employee practically snapping at their heels to hasten them on their way. They'd spent the whole day there, and Eric was suddenly aware of a gnawing hunger in his belly. "It's been a good day's work, I think," he said, his breath misting in the sudden outdoor chill. "Tell you what, Avery: Why don't I take you out to tea? My way of saying thanks."

"Tea . . . at the Britannia Club?"

Eric hesitated. "I was thinking of the Shafi, actually. What do you think?"

The Shafi on Gerrard Street catered to an Indian palate and was Eric's favourite restaurant. It was Avery who'd introduced Eric to it back in 1920 when it first opened, but Avery was in no mood for it tonight. "I'm still trying to wash the curry stains from our last visit out of my handkerchief," he said. "It's yellow splotches all over."

"That would be the turmeric. Turmeric never washes out."

"Then I reckon you owe me a new handkerchief in addition to tea."

The two men turned the corner into Great Russell Street. The plaza of the British Museum was empty, and the Ionic colonnade was dark. A lighted window here and there indicated a curator working late, but the harried academics and eager-eyed tourists of that morning had gone, no doubt to get their own tea. Light and life had moved to the other side of the street, where movement in the windows of the venerable terraced townhouses showed residents settling in for the evening. Listening carefully, one could hear whispers of modern dance music: someone was having a party, and getting more unpopular with their neighbours by the minute. But on the street below, as on the museum plaza, all was quiet.

The news stories had got Eric to thinking about his men. Collins, he remembered, had been convinced to volunteer by his girl, just as Jane Harris had convinced her young man. One hoped that had ended in significantly less tragedy. Jenks had gone to Canada. Eric frowned. Forrester had dropped their correspondence rather too suddenly, now that he thought about it. He'd have to find out what happened.

Avery said, "This is all very well, Eric, but shouldn't we have started by looking up Emily Ang's actual disappearance? I hope you did that, at least!"

That brought Eric back to the here and now. "Oh, I did. Of course I did. But here's the thing, Avery: there wasn't anything in the London papers about it. Not one word at all."

"How curious! Do you know, Eric, I could barely find a word about that new murder at your club, either? I went looking for it when we got back from Sussex yesterday, and all I found was a single paragraph in the *Times*, saying that a Mr. Benson had been found dead in his London club, and that police were making routine inquiries. I wouldn't have known it was the Britannia Club, or even that it was murder, if you hadn't told me. Do you suppose someone was trying to keep that quiet too?"

A RICHER DUST
CONCEALED

THURSDAY MORNING. The little church in Wexford Crossing was called St. Julian's, after St. Julian the Hospitaller—patron of innkeepers and repentant murderers. Its exterior was faced with flint: jagged black and bone white, like broken seashells sunk into mortar. Inside, the walls were smooth plaster. Stained-glass windows over the sanctuary, depicting the crucifixion, the resurrection, and the final judgement, cast coloured light down onto the simple casket containing Albert Kenneth Benson, late of the Britannia Club. The rest of the windows were tall lancets of clear diamond-paned glass; through them, you could just see the tops of the churchyard yews swaying in the wind. Above them, fleecy white clouds sped across a bright blue sky.

It was a modest country church, boasting perhaps twenty ancient pews polished smooth by generations of worshippers, but it was barely a quarter filled. Benson didn't have much in the way of family. There was, apparently, a sister in America, who could not reasonably be expected to make the journey in time. She'd telegraphed, instead, instructions for the ordering of an especially elaborate funeral wreath, and that was the extent to which she was allowed to convey her grief.

The Britannia Club was represented by just Wolfe, Saxon, and Eric himself.

Some of the local villagers made an appearance, more for his widow's sake than for Benson himself. Eric got the impression that most of them regarded Benson as an interloper at "the big house," though none were so crass as to speak ill of the dead. Mrs. Benson, pale as alabaster and straight-backed in her mother's black dress, simply stood alone in the front pew throughout the service, a respectful distance between her and everyone else. No one expected her to speak, and she said nothing. There was no eulogy.

The funeral was part of a requiem service. Mrs. Benson had insisted on it, even though it appeared that Benson himself had been a Quaker. That meant the sacrament of Holy Communion, and Eric came forward dutifully to receive it. Wolfe and Saxon followed, the first studiously expressionless and the second with his head deeply bowed. Turning to return to his pew, Eric caught sight of a figure at the back of the church, half hidden behind a column: Inspector Parker, on his knees, watching the proceedings with beady eyes. Light from the clear lancet window above made his scar shine like a thunderbolt on his cheek. He did not rise to receive Communion. Perhaps he was only here on duty, but if so, why kneel when he could sit?

Saxon, Eric noticed, remained on his knees until the end of the service when everyone rose for the interment.

There was a blast of light and wind as they opened the doors to the churchyard and carried the casket through. The wind had grown significantly stronger while they'd been inside at the service. It tore at the vicar's vestments and whipped swirls of autumn leaves through the mourners. The sky overhead was still a bright blue, but there was a line of slate grey in the clouds speeding in from over the Channel, turning steadily blacker as it approached.

Eric found Saxon and Wolfe afterwards, standing by the front doors of the church. They were partly sheltered by the steeple. Ivy crawled up the flint beside them and trembled against the gath~~ing wind. Most of the village mourners had already departed for the public house across the village green.

"I'm surprised Bradshaw didn't come," Eric remarked. He was equally surprised that Wolfe and Saxon should be the ones to make an appearance, though he did not say so.

"Bradshaw's a busy man, Peterkin." Wolfe lit up a cigarette and blew a smoke ring into the air. The wind shattered it immediately. "Far too busy to attend the funeral of every club member with the bad taste to drop dead on his watch."

"He came to my father's funeral."

"Ah, well, that was the passing of an era: your father was the last of the Peterkins."

Eric swallowed the temptation to punch Wolfe's smirking face into the rough flint wall of the church. Wolfe just grinned and took a long drag on his cigarette.

Saxon, focused on devouring an apple, seemed not to notice.

"What about Aldershott?" Eric asked, pretending not to grit his teeth. "As the club president, you'd think it would be his responsibility to make an appearance."

"Aldershott's responsibility is to the living," Saxon remarked. He was still munching on his apple, and gave no indication of being part of the conversation at all. Eric wasn't sure if he meant it as an excuse, that Aldershott was busy with the still-living members of the club, or as a criticism, that Aldershott really ought to be here to support Mrs. Benson in her grief. Hadn't Mrs. Benson said that they had a business relationship outside of the club?

"And then there's Norris."

Here, Wolfe gave a bark of laughter, and Saxon looked around. "God forbid Norris see anything so unpleasant as death," Wolfe said. "I don't know how the little bounder survived the trenches. By playing the clown, no doubt. There isn't a responsible bone in his body."

"That's not quite fair," Saxon rumbled, frowning.

"Oh, isn't it? Don't forget, dear Saxon, that the first thing he did after we were elected to the board was to do a flit . . . to Italy, as I understand it. 'For his muse.' Bradshaw had to cover his duties for the next three months while he 'amused' himself."

"What exactly are the duties of the board of officers?" Eric asked, curious.

"Never you mind!"

Saxon stuck the remains of his apple into the ivy covering the church wall. "I think we're done here," he said. "Are the two of you staying around much longer?"

"I think I'd better have a word with Mrs. Benson," Eric said.

"Ever the respectful gentleman," said Wolfe. "Suit yourself. I see the motor coach approaching, but if you'd prefer to wait for the next one, be my guest."

"I can give you a ride to Chichester," said Saxon, indicating the green Crossley he'd motored down in. "But you'll want the train if you're going back to London. I've got some business to take care of in Southampton."

"And sit among all your rotting apple cores, in seats sticky with spilled lemonade? Thank you, but I'd rather suffer the smell of the provincial motor coach." Wolfe strode swiftly off to where the coach was waiting, and in another minute, he was gone.

Saxon shrugged, and trudged off to get into his motorcar. It coughed, backfired once, then zoomed off down the country roads with a little more speed than was wise.

Mrs. Benson was standing alone in the churchyard, watching the gravediggers from a distance as they finished filling in her husband's grave. Black was the expected colour among mourners, but Mrs. Benson still seemed out of place in the bright sunlight, with a carpet of golden autumn leaves underfoot. The black fabric of her skirt flapped as more of the red and gold leaves danced in the wind. She looked up at Eric's approach, and a small smile flickered across her pale features.

"Mr. Peterkin. This doesn't paint too unpleasant a picture for you, I hope."

"Not at all. I'm sorry for your loss."

"Everybody's 'sorry for my loss.' I don't know if Albert was ever really mine to lose."

This was awkward. Eric changed the subject. "I thought Aldershott would be here," he said. "I thought you had some business dealings with him outside of the club."

"Yes. He was renting the old groundskeeper's cottage from us, and . . . well, it's not important."

Ask no further, in other words.

"I wasn't expecting to see him," she continued, "so you can rest easy on that score. It was only business: impersonal and terribly mercenary. Though he did give us the idea of what to do with the house, for what it's worth now. I wonder if I should continue. It won't be easy for a woman on her own."

Aldershott was the reason the Bensons were able to afford those renovations, Eric realised. He said, "This idea of a rest home, is it what you want?"

She didn't have to say anything. There was a resolute set to her shoulders that hadn't been there two days ago.

They turned to walk back together to the churchyard's lychgate. The other mourners had all gone: the villagers back to their daily work, and the very few outsiders, like Saxon and Wolfe, home by whatever means they had at their disposal.

"You won't have much time for your painting," Eric remarked.

"It might be worth it to be part of things again. I know Albert would have agreed." She was silent a moment, then said, "I've been thinking, you know, about our last conversation. I said then that Albert shouldn't have run off to chase after whatever happened to Emily, but he thought it was the right thing to do, and . . . I think perhaps it was. And now you've taken it on yourself to finish what he started, haven't you?"

"I've been looking into things, yes."

"I hope you find the truth, Mr. Peterkin. About Albert . . . and about Emily, too. Mr. Bradshaw's been very helpful about keeping things discreet and respectable, but I'm not sure anymore if that's what I want. We can't close our eyes to unpleasantness if it means living with lies. And I'll admit there's a far less noble part of me that simply wants to see someone pay for what they've done."

The sky to the south and southeast was a roiling darkness, though the churchyard was still bathed in bright sunlight. They were just rounding the back of the church now. Overhead was one of the sanctuary's stained-glass windows, and Eric thought it must be the one depicting the crucifixion. It occurred to him that the scene was more terrible than anything Mrs. Benson had put on canvas, though centuries of familiarity had blunted its visceral impact.

"We are alike in this respect, I think. We both need to finish something that Albert began. I need to finish what Albert started at the house, and you need to finish what he started at the club. I don't know why it had to be you, specifically, but I'm glad somebody's taken up the torch, as it were."

"This business with the house . . . I hope it's not only because Benson wanted it."

Mrs. Benson shook her head.

They continued on in silence until they reached the lychgate. Stopping in its shelter, Mrs. Benson suddenly turned to Eric. The low lychgate roof made it dark, and the bright daylight outside made it seem darker still. Mrs. Benson's black dress and finger-curled hair melted into the shadows, turning the pallor of her face into a white blaze.

Eric remembered the rustle of her crepe dress against his shirt front, and he took a step back.

"You've been very kind, Mr. Peterkin," she said. "And I really would like to paint you one day. Promise me you'll call . . . not today, perhaps; I—" She glanced, searchingly, over Eric's shoulder to the green outside the church, then turned back to him. "Soon. Not too long from now."

Her fingertips, cold from the October wind, brushed lightly against Eric's jaw and touched his neck. Then Mrs. Benson turned and hurried away.

The daylight was fading quickly with the approaching storm clouds. A drop of rain hit Eric as he emerged from the lychgate, and then another. He had better hurry to put the top up on the Vauxhall, he thought, or motoring back to London would be a miserable experience indeed.

Looking around, Eric realised that not all of the mourners had departed after all. Inspector Parker was watching from the shade of a nearby tree, his scar rendering his expression unreadable. Before Eric could hail him, the inspector's eyes dropped to check his pocket watch, and then the man strode away to his own waiting vehicle.

BROLLY'S

ERIC DIDN'T REALLY want to spend Thursday evening out on the town with his sister. Mrs. Benson's continued desire to paint him, and the intensity with which she expressed that desire, had an unsettling effect. That Parker had been watching them unsettled him still more. Regardless of Parker's motivations and Eric's own intent, any appearance of intimacy with the new widow could be seen as indicative of motive. After whetting his appetite on the London newspapers, it was the most irritating thing in the world to wait for the Sussex papers to be delivered. He didn't feel he could sit down long enough to enjoy a night's entertainment in the meantime.

He applied to Patrick Norris for help in finding that entertainment, and Norris, on hearing that the outing would involve Penny, was more than happy to oblige. "I'll help anyone into their cups," he said, "but getting out again will be your own problem. And I know just the place for you: Brolly's. It's a music hall, and I promise you it's the most fun you could have without a one-way ticket to Bow Street and gaol. Bradshaw goes there all the time—it reminds him of the way things were done when he was a boy. Say what you like about this modern age, sometimes it's the older generation that knew how to live."

That did sound promising. Norris insisted on joining them, and Eric felt relieved to have him: Norris, he thought, would distract

Penny and allow him to mull over what he'd learnt so far about Benson's murder and the disappearance of Emily Ang.

Brolly's had an unassuming entrance on a fairly quiet street that didn't especially inspire confidence, but the lobby inside was much closer to what one expected. It had plush carpeting and velvet hangings, and there were posters for all the current acts attractively plastered across the walls. The auditorium was up a flight of stairs and consisted of a high-ceilinged space with a stage at one end and stairs up to a shallow gallery above. The floor was crowded with tiny tables and bistro chairs, which seemed like a novelty. The last time Eric had been to a music hall, it had been set up with stalls like a regular theatre; but Norris assured him that the setup at Brolly's was how music halls were done in "the good old days."

"Well," said Penny, "I know exactly which table I want." She pointed to a table right by the stage and a little to the left. "It's absolutely meant to be ours."

"You'll be heckled by all the comedians," Eric warned, "and every magician will want you for their assistant."

"Isn't that the whole point of a music hall?"

Norris laughed and elbowed Eric. "That's the spirit! I say, Peterkin, your sister really is a sport. I think I'd like to keep her for myself."

"Please do," Eric replied, still taking in his surroundings. "She's an unholy little terror."

From their table, Eric noticed a set of swinging doors in the shadow of the gallery. A waiter in a black tailcoat had just gone in, and another similarly dressed man had come out with a tray of glasses. No doubt those doors led back to wherever the alcohol was stored and prepared. Alcohol had supposedly been banned from the London music hall auditorium, and knowing this gave the whole experience a certain added spice.

"What're you having, Peterkin?"

"What?" Eric looked back down, and found Norris looking at him expectantly. One of the tailcoated waiters was standing at his elbow.

"I'm having a gin and tonic," Penny said. "I expect you're having the same?"

"You know me too well." Eric laughed. A fig for the police, he thought. If they were going to pay this place a visit, he planned on being properly fortified against it.

Norris ordered a beer, and the waiter moved on to the next table.

"I say, this is exciting," said Penny, watching the waiter. "I feel like I'm in one of those American speakeasies, and that at any moment a gang of toughs is going to walk in and start threatening people with tommy guns."

"It sounds romantic until it actually happens," Eric replied, pretending he wasn't thinking the exact same thing. "It's more likely your gang of toughs will turn out to be a squad of bobbies."

"No fear of that," said Norris. "Bradshaw's friendly with the manager, and Bradshaw takes care of his friends."

Bradshaw's connections smoothed the way for many things at the Britannia Club, that was true; it stood to reason that they smoothed the way for others as well.

Their drinks arrived. Norris took a long pull of his beer and turned to Penny. "It's a pleasure to finally make your acquaintance, Miss Peterkin. Your brother, that great stick-in-the-mud, speaks of you frequently. It's good to see someone in the family's got a sense of humor."

"Idle gossip," said Eric to Penny. "Nothing that's actually true."

He could see Norris shifting into a more playful, less formal approach. "Then we'll all have fun discovering things about one another. Has Peterkin warned you about me yet?"

Penny smiled. "He tells me you're an incorrigible liar."

"Oh, well, that's true. Creative types generally are. But your brother knows all about that: he's one of the big, bad men enthroned on high, ruthlessly ripping our life's work to shreds. You should hear him, Penny: 'Away with this drivel! It is unworthy!'"

Penny laughed. She did not seem to notice or mind that Norris had so quickly fallen into the familiarity of her first name.

"Eric's been quite distracted by this murder at the club," she told Norris. "Haven't you, Eric? I'll bet you've been too busy making inquiries to even look at the manuscript you're paid to read."

"Inquiries?" said Norris, looking around at Eric. "Do you fancy yourself an amateur sleuth, then? Something akin to another Lord Peter Wimsey?"

"You should see him tear a puzzle apart, Mr. Norris! He should have gone into military intelligence, but of course they won't trust half-castes like us with top secret anything."

"Penny!" Eric chided his sister. "You don't know that."

"You could investigate and find out the truth," Norris said, "once you're done with this present inquiry."

"Yes," said Penny. "How is it going, Eric?"

"Oh, it's just been a lot of running around and asking questions. I was down at Sotheby Manor on Tuesday—that's the place where Benson was a hospital orderly during the War—and it turned out that he was also married to the lady of the house."

"And you two hit it off right away, I'm guessing. Was she very pretty?"

"I remember her quite well," Norris said. "And yes, she's very pretty."

The two of them grinned at Eric. "Get on with you!" he said. "The poor woman's been a widow less than a week! She's just been . . . very helpful, that's all. She showed me Benson's office, and all the files from when the place was a war hospital. If I go back, it'll be to look up those files because I'm quite sure I've not found everything yet. And if she helps me, it'll be because she wants justice for her husband—she said as much when we met at the funeral earlier today—not because she has any interest in me. She's been through a hell of a time, and I wouldn't push her to try to remember much more of whatever Benson's told her until she's ready."

"But she does have some interest in you, doesn't she?" Penny asked.

"She seems quite intent on painting me," Eric admitted, "and I don't know what I'm to do about that."

Norris winked. "Just lie back and think of England, Peterkin."

The appearance of the master of ceremonies onstage signalled the end of their small talk. Eric settled back with some relief, as Penny and Norris turned their attention to the show. The first act was a pretty songstress with an old, oft-adapted song.

"Courage, boys, it's one to ten,
But we'll return as gentlemen;
All gentlemen as well as they,
Over the hills and far away."

The audience joined in the chorus, but Eric was far away himself, reflecting on what he'd learnt so far.

It did seem odd that there hadn't been anything in the London newspapers about Emily Ang's disappearance. A Chinese woman disappearing from an English estate . . . one would think there'd be some ghoulish interest there, if only for the "exotic" flavour. Eric wondered if someone had hushed up the matter and prevented it from extending outside of Sussex, assuming the Sussex papers had carried the story at all. He'd find that out tomorrow.

He'd gone back to the British Museum earlier today to be doubly sure of his facts. In the process, he'd had another look at the articles surrounding Joseph Davis, the club member who'd supposedly fallen off the pier at Eastbourne. No one would have reported him missing if he'd only gone to Eastbourne for a bit of a holiday, Eric thought. But for that, everything about his death was clear and above board: there was the obituary, and presumably there'd been a funeral as well. The police seemed satisfied, but Eric now felt less so. It felt as though all the follow-up news had been suppressed somehow.

Of course, the news about Benson's murder had been suppressed as well, but that was to be expected. A club like the Britannia demanded its discretion, and Bradshaw ensured that they got it.

Onstage, a trio of young ladies meant to represent the three main political parties of the United Kingdom began to tear the clothes off one another in a simulated spat. Eric would have laughed but for the sudden realisation that this was, perhaps, not the sort of entertainment one wanted to expose one's darling little sister to.

Stealing a glance at Penny, he noted that, far from being shocked, she was taking it all in good fun. In fact, she and Norris seemed to be lacing the onstage satire with satirical commentary of their own. Thank heaven for that: Penny really was quite a sensible girl. And how would Helen take this entertainment, Eric wondered. She seemed rather serious in outlook, but that could simply be because of her recent bereavement. He remembered the way her face seemed to blaze, white-hot, in the shadow of the lychgate.

Mrs. Benson, Eric reminded himself. Not Helen. She was *Mrs. Benson*.

Over Penny's shoulder, Eric caught sight of a familiar white-bearded figure slipping behind the tables to the swinging doors. It was Bradshaw, and he was glancing around as if on the lookout for witnesses. Norris had mentioned that Bradshaw had an interest in this place, hadn't he?

Eric frowned. Bradshaw?

Davis had been a member of the Britannia. Bradshaw had to have known him. If Bradshaw had hushed up the news around Benson's death, he might have done the same for Davis. Had he done so for anyone else? Obviously not for that poor chap, Robert Unwin, who'd shot himself out of doors and been found in the river by Boy Scouts three months afterwards.

Around him, the audience burst into applause, and the three young allegories for political infighting, wearing somewhat less than was decent, curtseyed prettily. Eric stood with everyone else to applaud. Ordinarily, he'd have done so wholeheartedly, but he was beginning to wonder at the real extent of Bradshaw's influence and what he did with it.

"Now that's a body politic I prefer." Norris chuckled.

"I think I saw Bradshaw back there," Eric said, affecting a casual tone. "He's not here for the show, it looks like. I wonder what he's up to."

To this, Norris replied, "Oh yes, the old man never stops to watch the show. He visits to talk politics with Breuleux, the manager. Dreadfully boring stuff; I don't see why a music hall manager would bother with politics when he's drowning in actresses."

"Perhaps he's trying to impress a politically minded actress," suggested Penny.

"Then they're both idiots. Me, I'm quite happy leaving politics to someone else. I wouldn't even have had to vote at all if the Britannia hadn't gone and made a gentleman out of me." It wasn't strictly true; as of 1918, all Englishmen over the age of twenty-one were eligible to vote. But Norris wasn't one to let the truth get in the way of a good retort.

Eric watched the swinging doors for a moment, then whispered to Penny, "Keep Norris occupied. I'm going to see what Bradshaw's up to."

Excusing himself, Eric made his way, as unobtrusively as possible, to the swinging doors. Glancing back, he saw Penny engaging Norris in a spirited discussion—Penny, bless her, had a lot more in her head than she at first let on. Norris would have his hands full trying to keep up.

Beyond the swinging doors was a corridor. Eric could hear the clink of bottles and glasses from an open archway at one end; at the other end was a flight of stairs leading up. Midway down the corridor and a few steps from the auditorium doors was a plain wooden door with the word "Manager" stenciled across it. Eric sidled over to the door. He could hear voices coming from beyond, and he tried to adopt a careless, idle air as he leaned against the wall outside and listened. As far as any observer was concerned, he hoped, he was just someone waiting to have a word with Mr. Breuleux.

"It's a great relief," said a lightly accented voice, which Eric assumed must be that of the manager, Mr. Breuleux. "I don't know what I'd do without you, Jacob."

Familiar enough for first names, Eric observed.

"Think nothing of it, Johnny." That was unquestionably Bradshaw: genial, expansive, fatherly. "You know the last thing I want is to see this place shut down by an overzealous policeman. The fellow owes me a debt of gratitude, and he'll stay out of your business if he knows what's good for him."

"Hey!" A huge paw landed on Eric's shoulder and spun him around. A hand closed tightly over his throat, thrusting him forcefully against the wall and startling him clean out of his wits. The sudden realisation of acute, physical danger sent his mind skittering off into a realm of pure instinct, and he reacted by driving his knee up into his assailant's midsection.

No-man's-land. Creeping mist the colour of mildewed wallpaper enclosed him and cut him off from his mates, wherever they were. The isolation set Lieutenant Peterkin's heart racing with anxiety, more than the fact that Jerry—faceless, malevolent Jerry—was struggling to pin him down. Lieutenant Peterkin was damned if he was going to let himself be taken so easily. He smashed his forehead into Jerry's nose, and warm blood burst across his temple.

Eric dropped painfully to the hard wooden floor as the bruiser who'd set upon him stumbled backwards. A moment's confusion: for some reason, Eric had expected mud. Instead, he saw mildewed wallpaper the colour of creeping mist and badly worn floorboards. Eric shook his head to clear it, and the bruiser pounced. Instinct took control once more. Lieutenant Peterkin seized hold of his assailant, using his momentum to roll them both around. Now he was on top, straddling Jerry's chest—

"Peterkin!"

Hands gripped Eric by the shoulders and pulled him to his feet. Eric shook them off, and blinked away the unbidden memories. He fumbled for a handkerchief to wipe his forehead.

Bradshaw, radiating concern, stared back at him. Behind Bradshaw stood a dark-haired man with a pink bow tie and the sort of whiskers one normally associated with bad Chinese caricatures, though the man himself was unquestionably European. Eric's opponent, a husky bear of a man nearly twice Eric's size, was scrambling to his feet with a bloody nose and a surly expression.

"Bugger went mad on me," the bruiser growled, applying a dirty handkerchief to his bloody nose. Curious waiters had gathered at the archway farther down, and the man in the pink bow tie waved them away. This had to be Breuleux, the manager of Brolly's, which was a music hall in London, England, in the year 1924. Yes. Eric knew exactly where he was. Didn't he?

"Caught him listening at the door," the bruiser told Breuleux. "Why don't you ask him what he was about, eh?"

But Breuleux was eyeing Eric with mounting excitement. "You're here to, ah, audition for the upstairs room, yes? Now is a very bad time."

Bradshaw affected a good-natured chuckle, though the eyes he fixed on Eric were sober. "I don't think Peterkin's here to audition for anything. He's a member of my club in St. James, and probably came to speak to me. Right, Lieutenant?"

Breuleux's face fell. Eric eyed the bruiser, who was clenching and unclenching his fists and eyeing him right back. "Yes, that's it exactly. I saw Bradshaw and came to say hello, and your fellow there surprised me," Eric said, hoping he wouldn't have to explain the rather distressing memories that had overcome him as his fighting instincts took over. "I . . . lost my head."

"Lost his head, he says!" The bruiser let out a harsh bark of laughter. "Reckon he's more *off* his head than lost it!"

"That's enough, Frye," said Breuleux. "The back stairs aren't going to guard themselves."

Frye muttered something impolite and lumbered down the corridor. Breuleux watched him go, then turned to Bradshaw. "This is the second time in a week I've had someone from that snobby club of yours coming around after you. Can't they just find you there, or have you finally given up your office?"

"I don't believe that first one was a member of the Britannia," Bradshaw replied.

"Who was this person?" asked Eric. "I mean, I might recognise the name or the description."

Breuleux looked doubtful, but said, "He was a tall blond man; pink in the face and stupid looking, like a fat pig. He said his name was Rex Pellinore."

The physical description matched a good many men at the club, but the last name was unusual. Pellinore . . . as in King Pellinore, the Arthurian Knight who'd dedicated his life to pursuing the Questing Beast—the Beast Glatisant. Eric thought of Glatisant, Benson's bull terrier back at Sotheby Manor, and felt quite sure he knew exactly who this Rex Pellinore actually was.

Bradshaw only shrugged helplessly at the description. "The world knows I don't hold myself aloof from anyone, Breuleux. It was probably nothing."

Eric wanted to know what information Benson—if it had been Benson—had wanted from Breuleux, but Breuleux was in no mood to repeat anything he'd already told Bradshaw, especially not to someone who had just assaulted one of his men. He retreated back into his office with a final thank-you to Bradshaw for services unde-scribed, and shut the door.

There was no sense speaking on their way through the audito-rium, not with the current act trying to be heard over the rolling hubbub of drinking patrons. Eric just walked with Bradshaw until they emerged into the front lobby.

Benson might have been interested in how Bradshaw was able to make the police look the other way, Eric thought. Come to that, Eric was interested too. He'd got used to thinking of Bradshaw as a benign, fatherly presence, but there was clearly more to him than that. There was the tough-as-nails drill sergeant, for one thing, that everyone knew about but very few ever saw. Was there anything else? Eric considered the white-bearded figure with the gentle eyes and the rosy cheeks, and tried to imagine him stern as a drill ser-geant, perhaps, or crafty as a broker of favours. Once one recognised that Bradshaw had more than one face, one began to wonder what other faces existed.

"Is there something on my nose, Peterkin?"

"What? Oh! No, I was thinking of something else." Eric blinked, looked away, and said, "I came across an old news story the other day, about a former club member, Joseph Davis, who'd gone missing. But I'm sure I remember there being no mystery at all about him disappearing, which itself seems a bit of a mystery. I wondered if you knew anything about it."

"Joseph Davis?" It took Bradshaw a moment. "Oh yes. I remember now. He was supposed to have accidentally drowned himself at Eastbourne, wasn't he? I'm afraid there was nothing accidental about it. His widow didn't find the suicide note until two days later, after it had got out into the papers that he was missing. I helped keep it quiet, put out the word that it was an accident. She didn't want a scandal, you see."

"It wasn't the first time you had the papers report a suicide as an accident, was it?"

"No. It wasn't the first time. For some of us, the War lives on in our minds." He shook his head sadly, then checked his watch. "I've some business to finish up at the club tonight. It's taken rather longer than expected to eradicate all traces of the police inquiry, and I'd like to say we are absolutely back to normal tomorrow. I understand you've got an invitation to Aldershott's?"

"Yes. Will I see you there?"

Bradshaw shook his head. "Aldershott and I work well together, Peterkin, and he's a fine fellow in his own way. But on a personal level, we're not at all well suited. His wife, though, is a treasure. I hope you'll convey my best regards to her when you see her."

"I'll do that, never fear."

"Good night, Lieutenant Peterkin, sir." There was a peculiar emphasis on the address, which left Eric wondering. They shook hands, and Bradshaw made his way out of the building.

Back in the auditorium, a stage magician was performing an act of wonder, illusion, and superfluous exclamation points to an appreciative audience. Norris, grinning like a monkey, had got himself up onstage as a volunteer assistant, and was taking full advantage of the attention to play the clown. Penny barely noticed when Eric slid into the seat beside her.

Eric recounted everything to Penny after the show, once they'd parted ways with Norris. She remarked that she had picked a very poor time to visit London. "I don't think you were there at all for any of tonight's show. If it weren't for Patch—"

"Patch?"

"Patrick Norris."

"His closest friends don't call him that!"

"Well, then, I suppose I really am special. What? He's great fun to be around. Don't tell me you've suddenly taken it into your head to disapprove. You seemed quite happy to leave me to him while you were preoccupied with your own thoughts. We've a date tomorrow afternoon to visit the London Zoo, in fact. No one will mind if I arrive in Cambridge on Saturday morning instead of tomorrow."

"What! You're changing your weekend plans for Norris?"

"You'd know all about it if you'd been paying attention. Why, Eric, you look positively murderous! Do you really think I couldn't take care of myself?"

"Famous last words, Penny."

Penny gave him a peck on the cheek and a bright, indulgent smile. "Don't you worry about me, Eric. You just go to your Usual Armchair and finish reading that manuscript . . . or contemplate murder, if you like, as long as it doesn't involve poor old Patch. I'll be fine."

Eric didn't mention, of course, that brief, vivid memory of being lost in the fog in no-man's-land. One sometimes read about ex-servicemen who lost themselves in these memories—who did the most awful things without realising it. Eric had been in the trenches for only a year; others, like Wolfe or Aldershott, had been there for four, and they were as sane as you like. It stung his pride more than any of Wolfe's insults, and Eric, making his way slowly home after dropping Penny off at her friend's, clenched his jaw in determination. This flash of memory had been an aberration, he told himself. It would not happen again.

THE SUSSEX PAPERS

From the Chichester Observer, *dated 23 July 1918:*

WOMAN MISSING FROM WAR HOSPITAL

Police in Chichester are inquiring after the whereabouts of one Emily Siew Pin Ang, aged 26, who disappeared from Chichester some time on Saturday afternoon, the 20th of July. Miss Ang, a native of Hokkien province in China, was employed as a maid at Sotheby Manor. She is described by all as a hardworking, respectable young woman with a bright, cheerful manner.

Sotheby Manor, located near the village of Wexford Crossing, is currently engaged as a war hospital under the direction of Sir Andrew Sotheby. Miss Ang was frequently required to contribute to the nursing work, an addition to her duties that she took on without complaint.

"You could not ask for a better worker," says Sir Andrew Sotheby of Miss Ang. "She was

exceptionally reliable and dependable. All the household staff liked her. It wasn't like her to be late for work, much less fail to appear altogether. When we realised that she hadn't returned to the house after her day off, we knew something had gone terribly wrong."

Miss Ang is known to have left Sotheby Manor on the morning of the 20th and taken the motor coach from Wexford Crossing to Chichester, it being her habit to do so on her days off. The stationmaster, Mr. Reginald Stokes, remembers noting her arrival that day.

"She was the only Chinese lady for miles around," says Mr. Stokes. "I came to recognise her very well."

Miss Ang was last seen in the company of a sinister-looking man driving a green Crossley motor. They had tea at the Hammer and Anvil, a public house near the Chichester train station, where witnesses describe Miss Ang's companion as growing agitated to the point of violence. They departed together in the man's car, after a brief argument in which Miss Ang expressed her reluctance to go with him.

This man is described as being of medium height, between 25 and 35, with dark hair and an unsavoury beard, and dressed very shabbily. Mr. Stokes, the stationmaster, observed that he did not appear to be the sort of person who would own a motorcar, suggesting that the vehicle might have been stolen.

A white feather had been left at the table after Miss Ang and her companion departed the Hammer and Anvil. White feathers are often distributed by our patriotic ladies to those able-bodied men they meet who, in spite of their duty to the Crown, fail to enlist for the War. It is believed that this man had been presented with the feather prior to his arrival in Chichester.

Miss Ang is described as between 5′2″ and 5′4″, weighing approximately 8 or 9 stone, with black hair, dark eyes, and no distinguishing marks aside from race. She was last seen wearing a dark brown dress with white collar and cuffs, a light-brown coat, a wide-brimmed brown bonnet decorated with a white ribbon, and low-heeled black leather shoes.

Any further information that might be of use in locating Miss Emily Ang should be reported to the police in Chichester.

From the Chichester Observer, *dated 16 May 1922:*

UNIDENTIFIED SKELETON FOUND IN BRUTON WOOD

Ramblers in Bruton Wood made a gruesome discovery yesterday of a skeleton in an unmarked, shallow grave several yards from the road.

Mrs. Winifred Jones, 34, and her daughter Clara, 9, of Singleton, Sussex, had been taking a walk through nearby Bruton Wood and had just stopped to eat their packed lunch. It was Clara who first spotted what turned out to be a human skull, half buried in the dirt where it had been shifted from its resting place by a burrowing animal. Mother and daughter immediately abandoned their lunches and made their way back to their village to report their discovery to the authorities.

"Clara's a brave girl," says Mrs. Jones of her daughter, "but I worry about the effect this grisly experience might have on her."

Miss Clara Jones, seemingly

unperturbed, only expresses a desire to one day study archaeology.

The complete skeleton was unearthed near the skull. It bore no identifying marks, nor were any identifiable objects found with it. It is believed to be of a woman in her twenties, no more than 5'4" in height. The case has been referred to the Chichester police, who suspect foul play based on the nature of the burial.

Dr. Timothy Grey, coroner, has been tasked with determining the cause of death, and whether further inquiries should be pursued.

"It's early to say, but I believe we will almost certainly have to proceed with murder inquiries," says Dr. Grey. "The fact that the skeleton was buried at all indicates an outside party, and the lack of personal effects suggests it had been stripped before being buried. I don't see an innocent explanation for any of this."

Dr. Grey assures the public that the Bruton Wood skeleton had almost certainly been in the ground for a significant amount of time, and did not indicate the presence of a homicidal maniac in the area. Any such danger, he says, will have been long gone by now.

Further developments will be reported as they become known.

No further developments were reported. Both stories simply vanished into nothing after those inaugural articles, with no sign of any connection being made between them.

Eric set the two newspapers down in front of him, open to their respective stories, and leaned back in thought. Late-morning light streamed into the Newspaper Reading Room from the windows on Montague Street, and the scent of strong coffee clung to the threadbare jacket of the elderly eccentric at the desk next to him.

He had an idea that the man in the green Crossley might be Saxon. He already knew, from matching Saxon's handwriting to the notepaper scraps taken from Emily Ang's personnel file, that Saxon had been at Sotheby Manor that day. And he remembered from Benson's funeral that Saxon drove a green Crossley. Saxon had to have served to qualify for membership at the Britannia, but the evidence about the white feather could probably be discounted: there were countless soldiers who, being home on leave and in their civvies, had been presented with white feathers on the mistaken assumption that they were contributing nothing to the British war effort. Eric himself never had that trouble, as he looked too much like a foreigner for the white feather brigade to care.

If the man in the green Crossley was, in fact, Saxon, then it was suspicious that he never came forward afterwards.

The Bruton Wood skeleton, meanwhile, was interesting as much for what hadn't been said as for what had. How could there have been no further developments, given the coroner's suspicions? Perhaps the coroner was embarrassed to admit suspecting the worst. But Eric was sensing a pattern of silence and suppressed news here. It wasn't just about these two articles: there was also the story of Joseph Davis, and all those "accidental" shootings that Bradshaw had effectively confessed to keeping quiet. It was suggestive. And one wondered why anyone would want to keep the news around the Bruton Wood skeleton quiet, if it really were innocent.

And what had happened to the Bruton Wood skeleton in the end? It seemed to Eric that a visit to the coroner, Dr. Timothy Grey, might be in order. But first, there was the invitation to dine with the Aldershotts. Eric knew that Bradshaw would not be in attendance, but Saxon might; and it might be worthwhile to see what Saxon thought of the whole matter.

DINNER, I SUSPECT

MARTHA ALDERSHOTT STOOD among the potted ferns of her drawing room in an Egyptian-inspired silk sheath that floated across her curves with subtle flattery. A cluster of red poppies was pinned to one shoulder strap of her gown—real, on closer inspection, though Eric thought poppies would have stopped blooming by this time of the year. She was the one stab of colour in a forest of black ties and evening jackets; the guest list for tonight's dinner party included only the other board officers of the Britannia Club and Eric himself, though Eric knew already that Bradshaw had turned down his invitation.

"My dear Mr. Peterkin," Mrs. Aldershott said, coming forward to welcome Eric, "what a pleasure to see you! I notice you've got yourself one of the Haig Fund poppies for your lapel."

Behind her, Edward Aldershott's stony posture cracked to nod in silent approval, and Eric sent up a prayer of thanks that he'd stopped to ask around about the Aldershotts' dinner party habits. The Aldershotts, he'd been told, were very active supporters of the Haig Fund for ex-servicemen, and had once got Lord Haig himself to speak for the charity at another such dinner. With Armistice Day approaching, it seemed only wise to wear a poppy for the occasion.

As Mrs. Aldershott went to mix him a gin and tonic, Eric took in his surroundings. The drawing room was Victorian in its decor, with green-and-gold wallpaper matching the upholstery on the dark, heavy furniture. The curtains, also dark and heavy, had been drawn against what was promising to be a clammy pea-souper night—the affluence of Mayfair and Marble Arch were no proof against the fog—and the effect was claustrophobic. A highly polished piano stood in one corner, and one of the British Broadcasting Company's wireless receivers was tucked into a corner behind it. A phonograph filled the room with strains of Gershwin's *Rhapsody in Blue*, a modern piece recorded only a few months earlier and quite out of keeping with the generally stifling, staid environment. To Eric, the music was something of a breath of fresh air, much as Mrs. Aldershott's graceful lines were in the midst of all these stiff-suited men.

Wolfe and Saxon were already present, staying as far away from each other as possible. Wolfe was nursing a mixed drink of some sort, and was as impeccably turned out as always. Saxon's suit was unmistakably expensive; but he'd managed to absently tug his bow tie apart, and there was a splash of lemonade on his lapel from the glass in his hand.

Norris arrived right on Eric's heels. He looked around at the distinct lack of feminine presence with an expression of growing disappointment. "This is looking like much less fun than I anticipated," he whispered to Eric. Having spent the afternoon with Penny Peterkin, Norris evidently thought he was now the best of chums with her brother.

"It's something to do with Benson's murder," Eric replied. "That's the only reason I can see to bring us all together outside of the club. I only wonder what Aldershott wants."

"I suppose he expects to settle the matter without involving the authorities. Bradshaw may be rubbing off on him more than I thought."

Bradshaw did seem like the expert at keeping things quiet, didn't he? It made him the perfect accomplice.

"We really should conduct club business here more often," Aldershott said as he brought Norris his aperitif. "It would save me the trouble of leaving the house, and I could kick you all out when things don't go my way."

"I wouldn't have a moment's peace," Mrs. Aldershott said.

"And our meetings wouldn't last five minutes." Norris chuckled. "We all know that would make you miserable."

Before Aldershott could respond to Norris, Saxon interjected. "You're up to something, Aldershott. Is this to do with Bradshaw?"

"Bradshaw wouldn't come." Aldershott pinched the bridge of his nose in irritation. "I was hoping to get together everyone who was involved in this dreadful business—the murder, I mean. Best thing we can do right now is band together, I say."

Had Aldershott just drawn a circle around the possible suspects? This sounded like a declaration that the murderer was likely in the room right now.

"If you're looking for everyone affected by this, then we're also missing Old Faithful," Norris pointed out. "As well as the two night attendants and Inspector Parker."

"Faugh, we don't need them, and we especially don't need Parker. This is not a police inquiry. Nothing said here needs to go any further than this room." Here Aldershott gave everyone a stern look, his gaze settling especially on Eric.

Mrs. Aldershott rolled her eyes. "You men and your games," she muttered.

Eric wondered if she fully understood the implications of what her husband had just done. Saxon had stopped in mid-sip of his lemonade to shoot wary looks all around, and even Norris was looking more sober than usual.

But Wolfe seemed to take it more as a joke. He said, "Are we to be a miniature League of Nations, then, with all sorts of silly rules to keep us from coming to blows? Dibs on Great Britain, and I expect Peterkin here will be Japan. Here, we ought to take some sort of oath." He lifted his cocktail. "As this gin is my witness, I didn't end the poor bugger. Of course, I haven't an alibi, so you'll just have to take my word for it as a gentleman."

"A gentleman!" Norris exclaimed, encouraged by Wolfe's jocularity. "Where does that leave a poor scoundrel like me?"

"On the scene, the suspect who's too obvious to have actually done it." Wolfe rounded on Mrs. Aldershott. "Where were you, madam, on the night of Friday, the twenty-fourth of October?"

"Wolfe!" Aldershott barked, but his wife only laughed.

"I was waiting for my dear husband to get home," she said. "All those papers he ships over to the club for the week have to be shipped back to his actual office sometime, or so he tells me. If he has a better alibi than that, I'll scratch her eyes out."

"I was home alone," Eric said quickly, before Aldershott could protest and derail the explication of alibis. "What about you, Saxon?"

"Home alone too," Saxon grunted. His focus was on Aldershott. "This is all very convenient for you, isn't it? Keys to the place, combination to the vault . . . Benson stabbed with your letter opener. Seems to me you're the one with the most to gain from settling this quietly."

Aldershott's eyes narrowed, and for a moment, Eric thought he was about to throw his drink at Saxon. But Aldershott just drained his glass and said, "That proves nothing. Rather the reverse, in fact: as if I'd use something of my own to commit murder! If I were to attempt such a thing, I'd have the sense to use something that didn't point right back to me."

"There is such a thing as a double bluff," said Norris with a mischievous smile. "In which case, I'd say Wolfe here is our man. Do you remember? Face-to-face with a German patrol, outnumbered and carrying a half-dead mate between us, no less. And you, bold as brass, snarling that we were German stretcher-bearers, wearing British uniforms we'd taken from the English dead because it was the only way to get close enough to the British line to retrieve the German dead. What was it you said? 'If I really were English, would I be coming up to you in an English uniform? Idiot! I would be a spy and I would be wearing a German uniform!'" Norris laughed. "I'm still amazed that they believed you!"

Wolfe said, "Of course they did. My German is flawless, whereas your accent is execrable and your vocabulary somewhere beneath that of a *kleinkind*. Had you tried to speak up, we'd have been gunned down on the spot."

There was a chorus of chuckles, and some of the tension ebbed from the room. Aldershott pounced on the opportunity and said, "I'm not accusing anyone here. Ten to one, it was some burglar Benson surprised—my office was broken into, remember? My point is, this is going to get harder for all of us before it gets easier. Not a single one of us here has a proper alibi. We're each going to come under suspicion, and when that happens, we had better know whom we can count on. Do you understand?"

As the others hesitated, Mrs. Aldershott clapped her hands. "Very well said. Now, gentlemen, we had better sit down to dinner before Cook has my head for letting it go cold."

They finished their cocktails, but Eric noted that Saxon was still darting wary looks at the others. Aldershott's suggestion of an outsider might have been enough for some, but at least one person in the room understood all too well that it wasn't over yet.

The dining room was an equally Victorian chamber even more crowded with potted ferns, with the same heavy green-and-gold drapes to shut out the world. Its only concession to modernity was the electric chandelier. Aldershott took his place at one end of the table, looking for all the world like the chairman of a board meeting, with his wife at the other end. Saxon sat at Mrs. Aldershott's left, and Wolfe at her right. Eric found himself seated next to Wolfe, with Norris directly across from him. That put Saxon diagonally across the table from him, just visible over the top of the overflowing bowl of poppies that was the table centrepiece.

As the soup was served, Norris looked from Mrs. Aldershott to the centrepiece and back. "Poppies!" he exclaimed. "I had no idea you were so fond of poppies, though I fancy our friend Peterkin must have had some inkling. Had I known, I'd have picked up one of the Haig Fund's poppies as well."

"Artificial flowers." Wolfe sniffed. "Hardly the mark of a gentleman." He glanced over at Eric and added, "I understand that in certain cultures, however, the colour red is considered highly auspicious."

"I hope you'll wear one in your lapel for Armistice Day, at least," Aldershott said, his tone sharp. In this matter, he was taking Eric's side over Wolfe's.

Eric, meanwhile, considered his soup. It was a thick cream of mushroom, mildly flavoured. If it were poisoned, he found himself thinking, there would be little to mask the taste.

"I think the poppy is remarkable as a symbol," Mrs. Aldershott was saying. "It started with a Canadian poem, which was answered by an American, which then inspired the French, and ended with Lord Haig adopting it for the Haig Fund. It's as if the whole world were drawn together behind the poppy and what it means to remember."

"That's all very well," said Wolfe, "but some of us would prefer to forget."

This earned a very sharp glare from Aldershott and an exclamation of dismay from his wife. Eric could see that Norris seemed torn—did he, too, prefer to forget?—while Saxon obliviously slurped at his soup.

"I don't say that it's pleasant to remember," Mrs. Aldershott said, drawing herself up. Eric could see that, as a military nurse handling crises on an hourly basis, she must have been a force to be reckoned with. "I mean that remembering the past helps us to recognise where we went wrong and avoid repeating our mistakes. Of course, I don't want to relive any of it! When I think back on it, all those wounded, all those rows of cots filled with men who'd been gassed—"

"Martha!" Aldershott might approve of remembrance as an intellectual concept, but it seemed he had no taste for remembering the gruesome details himself.

"You of all people know how awful it was," said Mrs. Aldershott with an air of understatement. Her husband glared at her.

"We all knew what we were getting into," Wolfe said. His tone was studied nonchalance, but Eric noted that he was carefully avoiding looking anyone in the eye. "No one joins the Army without being aware of the risks."

Norris grinned. "Speak for yourself, Wolfe. I was a conscript, and all I had to go on was Kipling."

Did conscripts get commissions, or was Norris embroidering the truth again?

"Well, that's all over now, at least," said Mrs. Aldershott. "I don't know if any war should be called the Great War. It was the war to end all wars, something so awful that no one can stomach the thought of another. We've paid a high price for our peace, and we'll all work together to preserve it."

"Oh yes," said Wolfe, "the League of Nations, President Wilson's Fourteen Points, all that rot. I seem to recall a couple of Baltic uprisings and a rebellion in Jordan in the years since, so that's going very well. Otherwise, we'll be fine against each other until one of us explodes from the inside with Bolsheviks."

"Wolfe!" barked Aldershott, frowning. "I hope you're not implying that you'd rather subject future generations to what we had to suffer."

"I've no future generations to tell fairy tales to! Besides, think of how the club membership will look after a few decades of this worldwide peace. Unless you're saying we should also change our rules for membership?"

"Oh, what does it matter?" exclaimed Norris, looking around the table with some bewilderment. "We're happy now. Isn't that enough? I never did understand why anyone ever needed to go to war in the first place. All that nationalistic talk just bores me to tears."

"And yet," Wolfe observed, "you sing 'Rule, Britannia!' louder than anyone I know."

Saxon hadn't said a word, so busy was he with his food. He was Eric's prime suspect at the moment, and Eric would have preferred to have him in better view, directly across the table rather than diagonally.

It wasn't until the penultimate course was cleared away in anticipation of pudding that Aldershott stood up and said, "I'd like to get back to what we were talking about earlier: this matter of Benson's death. None of us wants to be put under police scrutiny, I'm sure."

"Oh, you were being serious," muttered Wolfe. Louder, he said, "Hear, hear."

"I daresay some of us have already incriminated ourselves in various ways," Aldershott continued. "All of us have admitted to not having a decent alibi for the night. That's got to stop. I don't believe for a minute that anyone here is capable of murder, and I won't have it blasted across the *News of the World* that we've gone mad and started knifing one another like a pack of savages. We've got to decide on what happened that night, and how each of us in our own little way can support the story. I know we can trust Parker. He's one of us. But we still need a story to give him."

"Decide on what happened" could be a fine thing, and Eric would have clapped had it not been painfully obvious that Aldershott meant "agree on a plausible story" rather than "discern the truth." What did everyone else think? Wolfe looked bored; Norris seemed fascinated; Saxon had picked up his fork again and was fidgeting with it so that it seemed on the point of breaking apart between his fingers.

Mrs. Aldershott simply nodded placidly at her husband's speech. She seemed to have no objections to any of this.

"It was some outsider," Aldershott said. "A burglar. Not one of us. Benson heard a sound, went to investigate, and was killed when he confronted the villain. I believe that to be the most likely story. Are we agreed?"

"I think," Wolfe said, "that you are trying to trivialise my own exploits." He actually looked offended at the suggestion.

"Would you rather be in the dock for murder, Wolfe?"

"Is that a threat, Aldershott?"

"No one's trying to trivialise anything," Mrs. Aldershott said. "Do be sensible, Mr. Wolfe."

"This is for the Britannia," Aldershott said, looking around earnestly, his spectacles flashing under the light of the electric chandelier. His gaze settled on Eric, and he said, "Whatever happens to the Britannia, it reflects back on us. We don't want to tarnish the reputation of the club, do we, boys?"

"I reckon Benson would be something of a hero," Norris piped up, "if he'd caught a burglar in the act." He looked as though he were getting into the spirit of a creative session with his playwright collaborator.

"Exactly!" Aldershott shot Norris a look of pure gratitude. "We owe it to Benson!"

Eric thought Saxon looked as though he'd rather be anywhere but here.

Aldershott caught up a wineglass. "All right, then. Gentlemen? Are we all agreed on what must be done? Then I say we raise a glass to our fallen fellow and drink a toast to Benson and the Britannia."

Norris and Mrs. Aldershott raised their glasses without hesitation. "To Benson and the Britannia!" Saxon, seeming to come to a decision, joined them in raising his glass, but said nothing.

"Yes, yes." Wolfe rolled his eyes and raised his glass as well. "To that which is well worth celebrating. To the Britannia."

That seemed to satisfy Aldershott. Norris, who'd already tossed back half his glass, drained the rest before realising that no one else had actually taken so much as a sip yet. All eyes turned to Eric.

Eric raised his glass. "Yes, to the Britannia—but see here, are we quite sure this story about the burglar is what actually happened?"

"What does it matter?" Aldershott said, looking annoyed. "It's as likely a story as any."

"What I mean is, we'd be giving our words of honour, as gentlemen, that this must be what happened, wouldn't we? What does that mean for us if it turns out to not be true?"

"Oh, for goodness' sake," exclaimed Mrs. Aldershott. "Nobody ever knows a thing with absolute certainty. The point is that you believe it to be true enough to proceed with."

Saxon quietly set down his glass. Eric raised his own again. "Well, to Benson: he was one of us—but look, if he really was one of us, don't we at least owe it to him to make sure his club-related affairs are in order?"

"Of course we do," Aldershott snapped. "What do you think Bradshaw's been up to all week?"

"Those things in Benson's box, Aldershott. They concerned some sort of business involving the Britannia."

"If we knew what that rubbish was all about, then certainly, we might do something about it!"

"You really are milking this for all it's worth, aren't you?" drawled Wolfe.

Mrs. Aldershott sighed and said, "Do hurry up, Mr. Peterkin. I can't hold this glass up forever."

Norris, who'd drained his glass a second time by now, filled it back up.

In the midst of all this, Eric was sure he'd caught a nearly imperceptible nod of the head from Saxon, who had yet to pick up his glass again. Interesting.

"All right," said Eric, raising his glass again. "To the Britannia Club. To Benson." He considered a long moment, and added, "To Emily Ang."

Eric and Wolfe were the only ones to drink. Saxon just stared at Eric; Norris choked on his wine; and Mrs. Aldershott, frozen, had gone as white as her dress. Aldershott slammed his glass down on the table, spilling wine over the tablecloth, and screamed, "What the hell, Peterkin!"

There are moments when one wants to behave as a savage and indulge in strong language—but can't. Such a moment had apparently descended on Aldershott, and he was red with impotent fury.

"Emily was my sister," Mrs. Aldershott said into the charged silence, and Eric looked at her in surprise. Her *sister*? That was more than a step up from what Eric had been led to believe. It was a whole storey. Mrs. Aldershott continued, "What is this about, Mr. Peterkin? How did you hear about her? I don't understand."

Recovering himself, Eric said, "Benson was looking for her, and Parker—"

"Rubbish," said Aldershott. "Benson was doing no such thing, and you are upsetting my wife!"

"Don't get chivalrous now, of all times," snapped Mrs. Aldershott, before turning back to Eric. "Yes, she was my adoptive sister. We grew up together, and we were trained together at Netley. She disappeared, you know, during the War, and nobody knows what happened to her. I know Benson was fond of her—fonder of her than she was of him—but I thought he'd have forgotten her by now. If Benson was looking for her, I'd like to know why nobody ever told me!"

Eric was only half listening. The tension in the room was as thick as the fog outside. Aldershott looked furious, but Eric was focused on Saxon. "Saxon," he said, "did you know Emily Ang?"

Oliver Saxon replied, simply and directly, "Yes."

"Of course Oliver knew Emily," said Mrs. Aldershott. "We were all children together."

Eric kept his eyes on Saxon. "Did you ever visit her at Sotheby Manor?"

"Yes."

Eric had been expecting Saxon to deny it. The notepaper scraps from Emily's file were in his pocket, and he was ready to throw them down on the table in the face of the expected lie, but Saxon's guileless admission rather took the wind out of Eric's sails.

"That's quite enough," Aldershott barked, before Eric could ask another question. "Peterkin, you are not a policeman, and you should stop pretending you are. Solving this murder is not your business."

"You said we should decide what happened that night," Eric pointed out, "and that we owed it to Benson to clear up his club-related business."

Aldershott snarled. "Then I'll speak to you later. For now, you can shut your wretched, half-caste mouth—"

"Edward!" Mrs. Aldershott shut him down with a glare, then turned to Eric. "My apologies, Mr. Peterkin. It's clear we've all had a painfully long week."

"Amateur," Wolfe chuckled. Aldershott just glared at him.

Eric assured Mrs. Aldershott that no offence had been taken. He had more important things on his mind. In any case, Aldershott's little gaffe had served to dispel some of the tension, and the pudding course was saved from a surfeit of awkwardness.

PORT BUT NO CIGAR

ALDERSHOTT PUSHED ERIC into his study and into a chair. He slammed the door shut behind him, locked it, and shoved the key into his pocket. All around, the glassy eyes of taxidermied animal heads stared down at them. An Andean condor spread its wings over the door and cast jagged shadows down the wall. Eric saw a glass-fronted gun cabinet in one corner, housing a trio of well-oiled rifles and a German pistol—a "Red 9" Mauser C96 with the characteristic red 9 burnt into the grip, no doubt a souvenir of the War. He didn't think Aldershott looked like the type who hunted big game or collected firearms, but one never knew.

There was a letter opener on Aldershott's desk. It looked like the twin of the one that had ended up in Benson's neck: a slim-bladed steel dagger with a decorative brass handle. Eric wanted to pick it up for a closer look, but Aldershott strode up to him before he could get up.

"I'll be blunt," said Aldershott, looming over Eric. "What's this business with Emily Ang? She has nothing to do with Benson's murder."

"How did you know her, then?"

"She worked for Sir Andrew Sotheby, who was a close friend of mine. Of course I knew who she was." Aldershott tugged uncomfortably at his collar, then tore off his tie with a snarl of frustration.

His front collar stud flew off, and the stiffly starched collar sprang wide. It would have been comical but for the full exposure of the mustard boil scars underneath: they had the appearance of melting flesh, and they never looked half so awful when his collar was in place.

"Well, Benson was looking for her," Eric said, his attention riveted by the scars melting down Aldershott's neck and under his shirt. "And now Benson is dead. At this point, the two things are looking very much connected."

"Did Benson actually tell you he was looking for her?"

"Not precisely, no." Eric wondered how much to reveal of what he knew. He'd come here tonight thinking that Aldershott had nothing but the most superficial of connections to Emily Ang's disappearance or Benson's murder, but Aldershott's furious reaction seemed to indicate otherwise. "Benson had a photograph of Emily," he said carefully, "and it's now missing. I'd say that means there's a connection."

Aldershott lit a cigarette with shaking fingers and flung the match aside. "Damn it all. It's been years. Ancient history, and I don't like having it raked up again. Martha pretends she's stronger than she really is. She always felt responsible for that Ang girl, and she is not going to take this at all well."

"There was a skeleton found in Bruton Wood—"

"Nothing to do with Emily Ang!" Aldershott leaned down, planting his hands on the arms of Eric's chair and trapping him there. The cigarette clenched between his teeth was inches from Eric's face, and Eric had to lean away to avoid burning his nose on it. Below the line of Aldershott's jaw, boil scars swam with the movement of his throat. "Have you ever considered that she left of her own accord and simply doesn't want to be found? Sir Andrew told me she was with child."

"What!"

"Yes. An unwed mother." Aldershott seemed to relish the words. "He didn't note it in her file, out of respect for whatever poor fool made an honest woman of her later, but he told me about her condition. If she left, it was probably to hide the shame."

Could Benson have been the father? Eric didn't want to say it, out of respect for the woman who'd become Mrs. Benson afterwards, but . . . if what Aldershott said were true, then the identity of her child's father could be vital to finding the murderer.

Aldershott straightened up and sat back against the edge of his desk. Eric's shock seemed to have restored some of his self-assurance, and he said, "Dozens of dashing young soldiers passed through Sotheby Manor. I've no doubt she was a *great comfort* to more than one of them. You know that when the Brighton Pavilion was used as a hospital for Indian soldiers, there were strict rules limiting the interactions between the Indian patients and their English nurses? Perhaps we should have had similar rules about interactions between English patients and foreign nurses."

Eric leapt to his feet, but Aldershott snatched up the letter opener and pointed it at him. "Sit down, Peterkin!" he barked.

Eric dropped back into the chair, eyeing the point of Aldershott's letter opener. Had Benson leapt to Emily's defence, much as Eric had responded to Aldershott's insinuations, and got the knife in his neck as a result?

"She was as much a foreigner as I am," Eric muttered in protest.

"Yes," said Aldershott, looking down at his letter opener. "I daresay she was."

Eric flushed red.

"Martha still thinks of her as some sort of pure, shining angel," Aldershott continued, shaking the letter opener at Eric for emphasis, "but she knew nothing of Emily's condition. You are not to dig further, and you are not to enlighten my wife as to the truth about her friend. Is that understood?"

"But—"

"I'm warning you, Peterkin!"

"Well, then, how is—"

"Leave it alone!"

Eric took a deep breath. "Horatio Parker! How is he connected to all this?"

"He isn't!" Aldershott stood and glared down at Eric.

There was a knock on the door. Aldershott sidled around, not taking his eyes off Eric, to unlock the door and open it a crack. Mrs. Aldershott pushed it open farther and stepped inside.

"I'm done with Peterkin, Martha," Aldershott said, gesturing for Eric to leave. "What is it?"

"Actually, Edward, I was hoping for a few words with Mr. Peterkin. In private, if you please."

Aldershott made an inarticulate, explosive noise, threw his letter opener down on his desk, and swept out of the room, slamming the door behind him. The letter opener skittered across the desk and fell to the floor.

Mrs. Aldershott sighed and bent to retrieve both the letter opener and the lost collar stud. "Such a temper. It appears I shall have to be especially persuasive if you are ever to return here as a dinner guest, Mr. Peterkin."

"I'm sure I'll survive." Aldershott was terrified of something, and the thought gave Eric a small degree of satisfaction. But he remembered, too, that an animal was at its most dangerous when frightened.

Mrs. Aldershott said, "You seem quite certain that Emily's disappearance had something to do with Benson's death. I wish I'd known what he was up to; I'd have liked to help. But then, I never actually saw him until that night before he died, and he left so quickly with Oliver. If you're taking up the torch, as it were, I wish you the best of luck."

She went to open the drapes. Yellow-grey fog obscured the street outside, and she wrinkled her nose in distaste before closing the drapes again. Still, the act seemed to lighten the atmosphere, and Eric felt himself relax.

"You said that Emily was your sister," he said. "How did that happen?"

Mrs. Aldershott was silent for a minute. She sat down in the chair Eric himself had vacated, and said, "My parents were Chinese missionaries, Mr. Peterkin. I spent much of my childhood in a Chinese village in the Hokkien countryside, the only European child in the vicinity." She looked at him shrewdly. "I fancy you must know a little of what that's like."

"My mother was Chinese, but I actually grew up in India."

"I meant being the odd one out, Mr. Peterkin. Anyhow, I shouldn't presume." Getting back to Emily Ang, she continued, "Of course, we were a little better off than the villagers we worked with. When Emily's parents died, my parents took her in and raised her beside me. I think she was meant only to be a playmate for a very lonely English girl, but as time went by, we became as good as sisters. When we came back to England, Emily came with us; and when I went to be a nurse, Emily went with me. The only difference was that I wanted to be a military nurse, while she wanted to stay with the civilian hospitals. Then the War started. I went to Flanders, and Emily went to Sotheby Manor."

Mrs. Aldershott paused wistfully. If there was a party going on outside, Eric didn't hear it: the only sound was the ticking of the clock behind Aldershott's desk. More quietly, she said, "So many of my uncles and cousins were killed in the fighting, but Emily was supposed to remain safe. Her disappearance was . . . well, one more tragedy on top of many. I'm not sure I ever got the chance to think about it. That's the cruel thing about disappearances, Mr. Peterkin: you never really think about them as deaths, so you never grieve over them as such. Then, years later, you realise you really have been thinking of the missing person as dead all along, and by then it's too late to grieve. Looking back now, I just wonder if I should have put more effort into finding out what happened to her."

Eric nodded in sympathy. It looked to him as though Martha Aldershott had survived tragedy simply by not having the luxury of dwelling on it when it happened. "When I was at Sotheby Manor," he said, "there seemed to be some confusion as to whether Emily was a maid or a nurse . . ."

"Oh, that." Mrs. Aldershott made a face and stood up again. "Sir Andrew Sotheby had no right to treat her as he did. I was furious when I realised. I had to read between the lines of Emily's letters, because she was simply too accepting to complain to me about her situation. But her last letter seemed to hint at some sort of distress . . . There wasn't a thing I could do while I was in Flanders, so I wrote to cousin Oliver and had him go look into what was going on. He'd always been fond of Emily, in his own bottled-up way. So he went and he looked and he wrote back that it was exactly as I suspected. But by the time I got back on leave, it was too late. She was gone." She sighed heavily.

"So Saxon was there on your behalf?" That explained why he had been poking around in Emily's file: he'd come to check on her welfare, and part of that involved finding out about Sir Andrew Sotheby's treatment of her. And if Aldershott was telling the truth, then Emily's apparent distress must have been over the matter of her unborn child.

"He was. And it sounds as though he put Sir Andrew Sotheby's back right up, like a flag on a flagpole. When Oliver gets angry, he doesn't care what he says. Mind you, Sir Andrew probably deserved it."

"If Saxon was fond of Emily," Eric said, "he'll probably want to know what happened to her too." Saxon might still have something to hide, but could he turn out to be an ally after all?

But Mrs. Aldershott shook her head. "I get the distinct impression that Oliver would rather drop the inquiry altogether. It isn't like him. He's never cared about the consequences to himself, as long as he's done what he thought was right. Norris seemed to agree, but then Norris always struck me as the sort who doesn't give a fig for yesterday's storm as long as today is sunny. Mr. Peterkin, for all Oliver's faults, he's still my cousin, and I still remember the three of us as children—Oliver, Emily, and myself—tearing about the garden, sharing secrets, discussing our hopes for the future. I don't like to think of Oliver being . . . being complicit in whatever happened to Emily. But I expect the truth will out, as they say."

Head bowed, Mrs. Aldershott hurried out of the study, leaving Eric to meditate on what he'd learnt.

So, there was an innocent explanation for Saxon's presence at Sotheby Manor. Eric had been almost certain that Saxon was his man, but Mrs. Aldershott's explanation changed all that. On the other hand, there was Aldershott. Eric had not been expecting Aldershott's reaction, and it convinced him that Aldershott certainly was hiding something with regards to Emily Ang and, subsequently, Benson's murder. Even as Eric gained confidence in one quarter, he began to lose confidence in another.

This new revelation about Emily's unborn child, though. Who could the father be?

Eric waited a moment or two longer in the study, half expecting either Norris or Saxon, or both of them together, to confront him with a piece of their minds as well. When neither one appeared, Eric finally ventured forth and made his way back to the drawing room.

Aldershott, freshly buttoned up in a new collar and tie, eyed him balefully from a corner. Otherwise, he was motionless, a grey statue watching over the proceedings but holding itself aloof. The fellow was about as much fun as a barrel of your yearly taxes, in Eric's opinion.

Norris was valiantly trying to cheer up the party with a sprightly melody on the piano, and having some marginal success. Eric didn't recognise the tune, though it felt as though he should.

Wolfe, whose mind was on the music and not on any past mysteries, said, "That is a fascinating piece of work, but I know I've heard it before. Just this morning, in fact. It can't be original."

"Impossible," said Norris, stopping abruptly and lowering his hands from the keyboard. "I just finished writing it yesterday. Look!" He held up the crumpled sheet music, with all its attendant ink stains and jottings and notes.

"Well, I think it's lovely," said Mrs. Aldershott firmly. "I can't wait to hear it onstage, with lyrics."

That seemed to soothe Norris's temper. Eric had never seen Norris upset before, but he supposed that Wolfe really did specialise in upsetting people. Norris, for all his happy-go-lucky ways, still had an artist's sensitivity and a craftsman's pride.

Wolfe said, "I can't wait, either. And I should love to meet the composer."

No amount of pleading could induce Norris to play more after that. He shoved his sheet music into his briefcase, barely managed a polite farewell to the Aldershotts, then slammed out of the house.

Even Mortimer Wolfe's urbane charm couldn't salvage the dinner party now—not that he seemed inclined to do so. Given his treatment of Norris, it seemed more likely to Eric that Wolfe was aiming for quite the reverse. When Wolfe made his excuses only a few minutes after Norris's precipitous departure, Eric politely but quickly followed suit.

London was cloaked in a thick greenish-yellow fog when Eric stepped out of the Aldershott residence. Mayfair was an affluent neighbourhood, and when Eric had arrived earlier in the evening, the stately facades of the local terraced townhouses had loomed all around him like canyon walls of expensive red brick. None of that was visible now. The houses were barely discernible, dark shapes beyond the haze, and the pungent odour of sulphur hung in the air. It was indeed a pea-souper, one of those oppressive, isolating fogs that reduced your world to just a few feet in any direction.

Wolfe stood by a lamppost a few houses down, at the corner of a somewhat busier street. He waved Eric over to the island of light around the lamppost, and Eric joined him. The headlamps of a passing motorcar bathed them momentarily in a white glare before disappearing again into the foggy darkness.

"Couldn't stand it much longer, could you? Of course not. I don't know what Aldershott is thinking, gathering all of us so-called suspects together like that. Mutual support indeed! It's more likely the murderer was sitting right there with us at the table."

"Or right here under this lamppost."

Wolfe flashed him a look of scorn and said, "You tell me, Peterkin. You seem to be the one who's been asking all the intelligent questions—surprisingly enough—so tell me what you think."

"If, as Mrs. Aldershott says, Emily Ang was her adoptive sister, that connects her to both Aldershott and Saxon, and leaves me wondering about you and Norris. Did you know her?"

"Only through a haze of morphine. And she was gone by the time I was taken off the stuff."

"So you were there when she disappeared! What about Norris?"

"Malingering his head off to keep himself surrounded with pretty nurses. That man is a menace, Peterkin. I hope you haven't let him within a hundred yards of your sister."

Eric had a suspicion that Wolfe already knew about the previous night's outing to Brolly's. This casual assessment of Norris's popularity with the opposite sex made Eric wonder, though, if Norris might be the father of Emily Ang's unborn child. For Penny's sake, he hoped not. It didn't bear thinking.

A sturdy, snub-nosed Beardmore rolled out of the fog, cautiously slow in the reduced visibility. Its engine did not sound very healthy, but its slowness made it seem almost ghostly. Eric, mistaking it for a taxicab, raised his hand, but it cruised on by without stopping. There was a loud, explosive crack—a backfire—and in that same instant, Eric was thrown flat on the ground with Wolfe's full weight pressed on his back.

Eric didn't have time to be shocked. He reacted instinctively, bucking sharply to kick himself free, then rolling across the mud into a defensive crouch. The other man, he saw, was now in a similarly defensive posture, but, instead of focusing on Eric, his eyes were scanning the fog for the source of the sound. Which was a backfire from a passing motorcar. Of course. The other man—Wolfe, of course it was Wolfe; who did he imagine it was?—had had his back to the street, and must have missed seeing it. Even now, Wolfe's expression was stony, savage, quite unlike the cool, supercilious half sneer he normally presented; and somewhere behind the mask, Eric thought he saw a flicker of blind terror.

Eric straightened up, slowly. "Wolfe," he said soothingly. "Wolfe! It was only a backfire from a motorcar."

Wolfe blinked. He looked at Eric as if seeing him for the first time. Slowly, he stood and brushed himself down. It was plain to Eric that even this action cost him significant effort. Wolfe took a deep breath. He screwed his eyes shut, opened them, and took another deep breath. Then he gave a disapproving glance at Eric's coat, which was rumpled from their brief scuffle, and drawled, "Honestly, Peterkin. One simply cannot take you anywhere."

Eric let Wolfe tweak his coat into shape. He knew a number of the Britannia Club members were jumpy around loud noises, but this was the first time Eric had actually been jumped.

A taxicab, responding to Wolfe's summons, sailed up and came to a stop beside them. "Good night, Peterkin," Wolfe said, climbing inside with every appearance of normality. "I'd wish you good luck in your quest for my peculiar methods of burglary, but I fancy it would be more to my interest to wish you the reverse." The cab door shut, and Wolfe was gone.

Eric watched Wolfe's cab disappear into the fog, then leaned against the lamppost to consider everything he'd learnt this evening. It was enough to make one's head spin. He really ought to write everything down at the first opportunity.

This was odd. There was a sort of scar on the side of the lamppost that he was sure hadn't been there a few minutes ago . . .

That hadn't been a motor backfire.

Eric dived for the pavement again as another bang echoed off the buildings around him. He swore he saw the fog split like the Red Sea around the path of a bullet.

Someone was shooting at him.

Instinct took over. It was the War all over again: caught out alone in no-man's-land, with bullets whizzing overhead and the wet mud sucking at his prone body. His instincts had saved him then, and they saved him again now. Without realising any of his thought processes, he recognised that the shot had come from the direction of the Aldershott house, and discarded any idea of running back that way. Instead, he scrambled to his feet and dashed around the corner of the intersecting street. He was sure he heard another two shots somewhere behind him, and someone shouting in the darkness. The important thing right now was to get away.

The Haig Fund poppy, torn loose from Eric's lapel in the excitement, floated into the gutter and disappeared.

MAYFAIR IN THE DARK

IN HIS WORK, Eric often read romantic passages about the London fog, and the way its soft tendrils twined about the lamp-posts, turning their glare into a soft, glowing halo. One felt alone in the fog, but protected: separated from the world and somehow cocooned against it.

Or so some writers would have it. Eric had stopped feeling that way after the War, and there was certainly nothing romantic about it when one was being shot at.

Eric dodged around the corner of a building about two streets down from Aldershott's home and flattened himself against the wall. The fog had grown thicker. He couldn't see farther than ten feet in any direction. Far from being insulated against the world, he felt separated from the herd—singled out, alone, and vulnerable to whatever dark entity prowled just beyond the limits of his vision.

There had been foggy mornings in Flanders, too, Eric recalled, times when the mist rolled across no-man's-land and hid the enemy from view, reducing one's world to just the trench one was in and the patch of churned-up mud beyond the wire. One of his NCOs had remarked that Londoners, as used as they were to operating in the fog, must be at a natural advantage here. Rubbish. There was no advantage to the fog then, and there was no advantage to it now.

Eric took a deep breath and stifled a cough. Those who roman-ticised the London fog generally forgot that it wasn't just moisture from the Thames but pollution from a million coal fires across the city. That was what gave the fog its yellow tinge and its sometimes pungent odour. When one wanted to take great gulps of air, having just raced down the street to escape being shot at, the effect could be somewhat unpleasant.

Was he still being shot at? Was that cordite he smelled, mixed in with the soot and sulphur?

Eric peered around the corner into the swirling moisture. A shadow loomed in the yellow-green haze . . . the figure of a man? Yes, there was definitely someone moving towards him, a dark shape with a quick but silent tread.

Eric remembered the patrols: meeting strangers in the foggy darkness, not knowing if he'd encountered friend or foe. Norris's story of Wolfe's great bluff seemed a lot more believable just now, as Eric struggled to see if the figure coming towards him was an inno-cent pedestrian or someone out to kill him.

Quietly and cautiously, Eric backed away from the corner until it was just within the bounds of visibility. He ducked behind a nearby pillar box, and waited.

The figure, slouching forward like a hound on a scent, came to the corner and peered around in all directions. This wasn't merely a cautious pedestrian; this was someone actively looking for something—or someone. Dipping into a pocket, Eric's fingers closed around a coin, which he flicked into the opposite direction. It made a light plinking noise as it hit the pavement, and the figure swung around after it, suddenly alert. Eric shrank into the shadow of the pillar box as best he could. It wasn't adequate cover, but the darkness and the fog were his allies now.

The figure passed just two feet away from the pillar box. Eric had just enough time to register his identity—Saxon!—before reaching out with one hand to grasp him by the back of his collar and pull him down. The old infantry training came to the fore as, with his other hand, Eric grabbed for Saxon's right hand and the gun he expected to find there.

Saxon let out a roar of outrage and swung Eric around against the nearby wall. Eric felt the breath driven out of him by the impact. Saxon tore away from his grasp, and Eric dodged to one side just in time to avoid being skewered by a pen-release knife.

A knife. Not a gun.

Eric caught Saxon by the wrist before he could strike out again. The two wrestled for one anxious minute before Eric finally managed to slam Saxon's hand against the wall. The pen-release fell from Saxon's grasp and clattered on the pavement. Eric planted the heel of his shoe on the blade and pushed Saxon violently away. Saxon went sprawling. He threw one arm up in a defensive gesture and shouted, "Don't shoot!"

Eric stood panting, his lungs filling with the unpleasant sulphurous fog. The cowering figure on the pavement had none of the expected manners of an enemy assailant; whoever the would-be assassin was, it wasn't Saxon.

Relaxing, Eric held out a hand. "I'm not going to shoot you, Saxon. Get up."

Saxon got to his feet warily, without Eric's help. His normally rumpled appearance had been rumpled still further by the confrontation, and he looked more like a dockworker poured into a dinner jacket than the lordling he actually was. Eric, still keeping an eye on Saxon, retrieved the pen-release and pushed the slim double-edged blade back into its handle.

"You were following me," Eric said matter-of-factly.

"That's mine," Saxon said, holding his hand out for the pen-release. "Give it back."

Eric held the weapon away. The engraved monogram, Saxon's stylised initial, gleamed dully in the lamplight. "Why were you following me?"

"I heard gunshots." Saxon paused as though thinking this sufficient explanation. When Eric did not return the pen-release, he went on, "I thought I chased off whoever it was, but I couldn't be

sure. This damned fog . . . I heard running footsteps, so I followed."
He paused again. "It was you being shot at, wasn't it?"

Eric held out the pen-release to Saxon. "I reckon you might
have saved my life back there, Saxon, in which case I apologise for
jumping you. But in my defence, I thought you were the one doing
the shooting."

Saxon tucked the pen-release into his pocket and shrugged.
"Don't make a habit of it, Peterkin."

The mud-spattered memories of no-man's-land had faded, and
the fog was beginning to lose some of its sinister edge. That didn't
mean the danger was quite over. Eric looked around and said, with
a studied nonchalance, "I'm headed for Piccadilly."

Saxon nodded and fell into step beside him. They set off at a
brisk pace, then broke into a jog as they rounded the next corner.
Nothing needed to be said: they both saw the wisdom in confusing
the trail for anyone stalking them.

"I notice," Eric said as they paused within (theoretical) sight of
Berkeley Square, "you never asked why anyone might be shooting
at me."

"I bloody well know why you were being shot at, Peterkin. It's
because you were asking questions about Emily Ang. That's why."

Say what you like about Saxon, he was direct. Eric turned to
him, curious. "You know something about it?"

"I know Benson was looking into Emily's death, and now
Benson is dead. You brought Emily up at dinner, and now someone's trying to kill you. What do you think that suggests, Peterkin?"

"Someone in that dining room wants to shut me up in the worst
way possible." While it had occurred to Eric earlier that he might
be sharing a table with a murderer, he'd thought, at the time, the
murderer to be Saxon. The possibilities had expanded since then.

Wolfe had been with him when the first shot was fired; that
probably let him out. Bradshaw hadn't been at dinner, but that
didn't mean Bradshaw couldn't have found out what Eric was up to
and decided to take matters into his own hands.

Saxon's familiarity with the area had put him in the lead. They'd ducked down alleys that were not at first apparent, cut through one private courtyard, circled back around, and roughly doubled the distance they'd have otherwise had to walk had they taken the most direct route. If anyone had been following them, it seemed reasonable to think they'd given him the slip, and they slowed to a walking pace.

Evidently feeling safer now, Saxon stuck his hands in his pockets, hunching his shoulders as he trudged alongside Eric. His head was deeply bowed, and his brow was furrowed enough to plant potatoes in. He said, "I knew exactly what Benson was doing, you know. I'd always wanted to know the truth of what happened to Emily. I . . . I was very fond of her. If cousin Ambrose hadn't been killed in the first year of the War, Father would never have become the Earl of Bufferin, and nobody would have cared two hoots who I married . . ."

Eric looked at Saxon in surprise. The fellow was sunk in a state of melancholy. The last time he'd shaved had been for Benson's funeral the previous day, and the dark stubble had grown quite pronounced. Everyone had got so used to his eccentricity that no one ever questioned his motivations anymore. Any joys and sorrows he had, he'd kept to himself, hidden behind the irascible mask with which he defended his absentminded habits. Confessing his feelings for Emily had stripped the mask away, leaving him raw and vulnerable.

"I didn't think you cared two hoots what people thought," Eric said. He was still trying to digest this revelation that Saxon had been "fond" of Emily Ang.

"Do you have any idea, Peterkin, what it would have done to Emily if I'd presented her to society as Lady Saxon?"

"That would have been her battle, not yours. Her choice to accept, if you asked."

Saxon let out a sigh that was half frustration, half acquiescence. "Too late for that now, isn't it?"

"Saxon." Eric hesitated, then decided that Saxon was a man who appreciated the direct approach. "Your visit to Sotheby Manor . . . that was the day Emily disappeared, wasn't it? She was last seen in the company of a man in a green Crossley, the same sort of motorcar you drive."

"What of it? I drove her back to the house and left her there. I don't know anything else. I didn't even know what had happened until it was too late to do anything about it."

"The story was in the *Chichester Observer*. It said you had some sort of argument."

"I don't read the *Chichester Observer*," Saxon said shortly. He patted himself down in search of an apple and, finding nothing, stuck his hands back into his pockets. "Emily didn't want to put me through the trouble of driving her back to the house, but I had to go and retrieve a briefcase I'd left behind, so it was no trouble at all."

It's more than that, Eric thought. "Mrs. Aldershott said you'd gone to check on Emily, and Aldershott told me she was in the family way—"

"How does Aldershott know?" Saxon demanded, rounding on Eric with a snarl. "Was he responsible?"

"He said Sir Andrew Sotheby told him," Eric replied, taking a step back.

Saxon accepted the explanation only grudgingly. "I expect that's possible," he muttered. "Emily didn't want me to make a scene, on top of the one I'd already made when I confronted Sir Andrew about the unforgivable way he was treating her. I was sure at the time that it was Benson who'd got her in trouble, and I was going to give him as sound a thrashing as I could, but she wouldn't have it. She said it wasn't him, and I wasn't sure if I should believe her. The last thing I said to her was that I'd do everything in my power to see that whoever it was did right by her; or, failing that, that both she and her child would be properly taken care of. I swore it on my word of honour." He spat angrily into the gutter. "I should have just offered to marry her instead, and to hell with English society."

They'd reached Piccadilly by now, and the fog was growing thicker. One knew that the trees of Green Park were just across the way, but one couldn't see them. This southern edge of Mayfair was where Clubland began, with nearly every other building housing one prestigious gentlemen's club or another. Their windows glowed above the haze, and their walls seemed proof against the creeping miasma of fog. Eric shivered and pulled his overcoat closer about him. He'd been sure for some time that the danger had passed, but the unsettling memories lingered still.

Saxon, forgetting that he'd come up empty-handed once before, again searched his pockets for an apple to munch on. This time, he came up with a torn scrap of paper, all covered with sketched diagrams and doodles.

"If you thought Benson was the father of Emily's child," Eric said, "why did you sponsor him to the club? Most people thought you two didn't even know each other."

"Norris introduced us. They came to me about a week before . . . everything happened. Benson said he knew something about what happened to Emily, and he wanted my help to get at the truth. I didn't ask for details. He looked uncomfortable enough as it was, talking to me, and I guessed that he felt guilty."

"Norris was helping Benson too?"

Saxon seemed unimpressed. "For what it's worth. Benson and Norris were friendly, but Benson told me later that Norris was far from helpful. He was a complete outsider when it came to Emily, you see—didn't know what happened, didn't have a thing he could do to help."

Eric was disappointed. "Benson didn't tell you anything? And you weren't curious?"

"I've learnt the hard way, Peterkin, that sometimes it's better if we only know as much as we need to know." Having ascertained that the detritus of his pockets really was detritus, Saxon dropped it into the decorative urn outside one nearby house. "Benson did tell me, the night he died, that he'd found something important. He was worried about this bet he had with Wolfe and Aldershott, though clearly not worried enough to put a stop to it right away. But he was getting more worried by the minute, so I finally told him he should go back to the club and take one of the lodging rooms. That way he'd be on hand if anyone tried anything." Saxon stopped and stared across the street to where Green Park would be if they could see through the yellow-grey haze. He looked up and down the street warily before finally deciding that they were safe. "I sent him to his death, Peterkin. If I hadn't told him to stay at the club, he'd still be alive today."

"It's not your fault, Saxon."

"Isn't it?" Saxon sat down on the steps of one august edifice and looked back up at Eric. "Do you know what I was doing during the War, Peterkin? I was a codebreaker. I spent the War with MI1b, deciphering coded German messages. That kept me here in London, out of the fighting. It was a grand time, Peterkin: we tore the German communications network apart one cypher at a time—some of us without getting out of our pyjamas. But we never actually saw anyone die."

Saxon lapsed into silence, and Eric let him collect his thoughts.

"I always knew, though," Saxon said, more quietly. "Sometimes the news would come back about such and such a failed operation, or so many dead in some futile action; everyone would put on a brave face and just call it jolly bad luck, but I'd look down at the last puzzle I was busy disentangling, connect the dots between the news and the puzzle, and know that if I'd only been faster, or more accurate . . . Everybody looks at people like Field Marshal Haig and blames them for people dying, but what were they supposed to do if people like me didn't give them the information they needed? Now I'm back on civvy street, hawking cider like a common tradesman . . . I thought this business of sending people to die was behind me."

Eric glanced back at the decorative urn where Saxon had absent-mindedly discarded that last scrap of rubbish from his pockets earlier. It occurred to him that Saxon was a walking security risk: to be kept on with MI1b, he had to be bloody brilliant.

"I'm surprised you haven't solved the mystery of Emily's disappearance yourself," Eric said, "or Benson's murder."

"They're not messages written in code, are they? I can't twist the letters into anything that makes sense. No, Peterkin. My job was only to analyse the evidence, not to decide what to do with it afterwards. That's how it was in the War, anyway. You did your part, and you let the boys in the field do theirs. You were at another remove from the violence . . . You were responsible, but you didn't see it actually happen. When Benson came to me, suddenly it was the other way around: he had all the information, and I was in the field. By that logic, I should have been the one to die."

Eric had seen this before, in men who'd come back from disastrous action in which they'd lost friends and comrades. "It should have been me," they said. It took a lot of telling them otherwise to change their minds, sometimes more than was humanly possible. Sometimes it was better to just steer the person in another direction.

"Benson asked you to get him into the Britannia Club, then? Did he ask you to do anything else for him?"

"Yes, he—" Saxon stopped and shook his head. "It's not important."

Eric stood on the pavement and considered Saxon. The untidy fellow, in spite of his dinner jacket, looked a bit like a tramp as he slouched on the bottom step of the Piccadilly clubhouse. They were still enclosed by the surrounding fog, and, without an apple to munch on, he looked lost. But why had Benson gone to Saxon for help, and not to Aldershott, with whom he at least had some sort of existing working relationship? Was it only because they were united in how they'd felt about Emily? What did Benson think Saxon could do that he himself couldn't?

Saxon had money and social influence. He had the proper credentials to impress, and that could go some way towards getting through to certain bureaucratic types.

It was only a guess, but . . . "Was it something to do with the Bruton Wood skeleton?"

Saxon's head jerked up in surprise, and Eric had his answer.

"Yes," Saxon said at last. "Benson said it was Emily. I didn't ask how he knew. He wanted me to quietly claim the body for a proper Christian burial, but I'm afraid it's not so easy as all that. You can't just walk into a coroner's office and demand they hand over a body with no questions asked, especially one found two years ago and already consigned to a pauper's grave. I doubt if even Bradshaw could do it, and Benson didn't want to involve Bradshaw."

It sounded as though Benson had reason to suspect Bradshaw of something unsavoury. After the previous night's encounter at Brolly's music hall, Eric felt just a little bit less inclined to dismiss the idea as fanciful.

Saxon got back to his feet and peered down Piccadilly. The fog made it difficult to see, but Piccadilly was a major thoroughfare, and traffic was to be expected even on a pea-souper night like this. "I'm going to have to ask you to stop asking questions about Emily," Saxon said. He sounded calmer, as though he'd made up his mind. The headlamps of a cruising taxicab glowed in the distance, and Saxon flagged it down. "We all know where asking questions got Benson, and I'd rather not see history repeat itself. Get in, Peterkin."

Eric stood in the open door of the cab and said, "You know I can't just give this up. Not now. Benson may not have been your friend, exactly, but he was your comrade in this matter. Surely you don't want to see his efforts go to waste?"

A look of irritation crossed Saxon's face. "What does it matter? Benson's death means the police are looking into it. Leave the bloody mess to the professionals."

"I don't think Inspector Parker can be trusted. I saw him removing evidence from Benson's room. Even if he didn't kill Benson himself, he's in this up to his neck."

"Benson said Parker was innocent of any wrongdoing."

Did he now? But why mention Parker at all, unless there'd been some question of wrongdoing in the first place? Eric said, "Benson might have been wrong."

"Hey," called the cabbie, "you gentlemen ready to go yet? You want to talk, close the door and talk inside. You're letting the fog get in."

Saxon made a conciliatory gesture in the driver's direction, then turned back to Eric. "Just leave it, Peterkin, or . . . or . . ."

"Or what?"

"Or I'll have you kicked out of the club." Saxon gave a determined nod. "Don't think I won't do it."

As a matter of fact, Eric didn't think for a minute that Saxon would follow through, not unless he were a great deal more deeply invested in suppressing the inquiry, which boded ill for his innocence. "I'll do what's right," he said, getting into the taxi and shifting over to make room for Saxon.

But Saxon just leaned in to thrust half a pound at the driver. "Take my friend here wherever he wants to go," he said before turning back to Eric. "No, I'm not coming with you. I'll walk. But you . . . you were the one getting shot at not half an hour ago, remember?"

"Shot at?" squawked the cabbie, turning in his seat to stare at them. "What d'you mean, shot at?"

"The sooner you drop him off, the less likely you'll get shot at too," Saxon snapped, overriding Eric's attempt to explain the situation. "Good night, Peterkin. And remember what I said." He shut the door firmly before Eric could reply, and withdrew, tendrils of fog swirling to cover his departure.

"Right," said the cabbie. "Where to, guv?"

Eric discarded the idea of home almost immediately. He needed to talk about this with someone, and it seemed likely that Avery would still be haunting the Arabica. "Soho Square," he said, and the taxi tore away into the fog.

CARDS ON THE TABLE

IT WAS NOT quite eleven o'clock when the taxicab dropped Eric off at the Arabica coffeehouse, just a little way off Soho Square. The fog was just as thick, and the night just as dark, but Mayfair felt worlds away from here.

The Arabica was half a flight below street level. It was narrow but very deep, and lined with booths that offered the clientele a touch of welcome privacy. The decor had pretensions of the exotic Near East—India or Arabia or Turkey—and consisted of elaborate geometric patterns next to carvings of elephants and prints taken from the Arabian Nights. It was warm, smoky, and dimly lit; the scent of cinnamon and cloves embraced you as you entered, growing stronger the deeper you went.

The owner and manager was a Chinese fellow named Chiang, who'd been a translator for the Weihaiwei Regiment during the Boxer Rebellion at the turn of the century. He sat behind the front counter with a newspaper and a fez, under a massive picture of Scheherazade gesticulating dramatically by the foot of the Sultan's bed. Eric always got the impression that Chiang disliked him and suffered his presence only because he tipped well and was friendly with Avery, the Arabica's best customer.

Avery, in a shapeless calf-length coat and a knitted scarf long enough for three, fit right in with the Bohemian clientele. As a group, they lingered late into the night over cups of coffee, and their conversation was a self-conscious whisper seeking meaning in both fact and fiction. One saw silk scarves with tassels, startling embroidery, and colours not generally held to be entirely respectable, while the dim lighting glittered on glass beads and hid the worst of the frayed edges.

Eric, with his Clubland-approved dinner jacket and his ramrod-straight soldier's posture, fit in like a fox in a henhouse.

Avery's usual booth—a Usual Booth much like Eric's Usual Armchair—was right at the very back of the room, where the smoke was thickest. Avery was there, as expected, laying out a Tarot reading. It wasn't until Eric drew abreast of the booth that he saw Avery's "seeker" was none other than his own sister, Penny.

"Eric!" Penny cried, leaping out of the booth to give him a sisterly peck on the cheek. "How wonderful! Though if you're out already, I expect this must mean the dinner was a bit of a disaster. Was it?"

"You might say that." Sensible as Penny could be when the situation demanded it, Eric decided it would be best to avoid telling her of the attempt on his life. She'd worry needlessly, he told himself; best keep mum and wait until she's out of earshot before telling Avery. "There've been a few developments," he said, and gave them a summary of what had happened at dinner and after—omitting the gunshots for Penny's benefit. "As you can see, I'm going to have to rethink just about everything."

"Well, my head's swimming," said Penny. "What about you, Avery?"

"I think," said Avery, "it's just a matter of asking the right questions of the right people. I'm sure your father would know exactly—"

"No!" shouted the Peterkin siblings in unison. The Bohemian hubbub elsewhere dropped into a lull as heads peeked out from nearby booths to see what the commotion was.

"We are not holding a séance," Eric said firmly. "Not now, and not ever."

"Have it your way." Avery pouted, stubbed out his clove ciga-rette, and swept up his Tarot cards from the table. "How about a Tarot reading, then? I was just telling Penny how perfectly lovely her future with this Patrick Norris could be. I daresay I could tell you what you need to know to get on with this murder inquiry."

"Oh no," Eric protested, but Avery had already drawn the Knight of Swords from the Tarot deck and laid it faceup in the mid-dle of the table. Eric rolled his eyes. "That's supposed to represent me, is it? Why am I always the Knight of Swords?"

"Because he has such a darling horse," Penny said. "Avery, which cards would you use to represent everyone? I've met Patch, and I remember Mr. Bradshaw from Daddy's funeral. Everyone else is a mystery, and I keep losing track of them. I want pictures to go with the names; it may help us decide who our main suspect is."

Avery glanced at Eric, who sighed and began: "There's Edward Aldershott. He's the club president. He seems like a humorless stick-in-the-mud, but he's strangely anxious that I not ask any ques-tions about Emily Ang. He's the one who told me about Emily's condition. It's curious, though: he was the one who pushed Benson into that bet with Wolfe. It does seem as though he'd engineered that whole mess, now I think about it. His wife, Martha, is the cousin of Oliver Saxon and was apparently brought up right beside Emily, like sisters. They trained as nurses together, but Mrs. Aldershott—Martha Saxon as she was then—went to Flanders as a military nurse while Emily stayed behind to work at Sotheby Manor. I fancy Mrs. Aldershott can be quite the dragon when roused, and if she blamed Benson for what happened to Emily, there's no tell-ing what she'd do. She doesn't care tuppence for the rules of the Britannia Club, either."

"A ruthless woman," Avery murmured, positioning the Queen and King of Wands side by side on the table. "And a husband with something to hide."

"There's Jacob Bradshaw," Eric continued. Avery hesitated over the kings, then settled instead on the white-bearded Emperor. "He's the club secretary, and he's been in that position since very nearly the

dawn of time. He's mixed up in just about anything you could mention, because he's the one who Gets Things Done. Benson was asking questions about him at that music hall, and I got the impression
it had something to do with what sort of influence Bradshaw might
have over the police. And Benson didn't want to involve him, either,
when he wanted to claim the Bruton Wood skeleton as Emily's. It
seems as though Bradshaw might have done a few unsavoury things
behind the scenes to keep things running smoothly for everyone,
and Benson might have found out."

"I remember Daddy talking about him," Penny said. "It seems
impossible to imagine him as the villain of the piece."

"Next is Oliver Saxon—Lord Saxon, actually, but he doesn't use
the title. He said he was fond enough of Emily that he might have
married her if—well, if there weren't the matter of him being next
in line for an earldom, and her being . . . I assume it was because of
her being Chinese."

"Oh, I say!" Penny was indignant. "That's a fine bit of rot!"

"He confirmed what Aldershott told me about Emily's condition. He says he was helping Benson investigate Emily's murder, and
he's horrified by what happened. He wants me to stop before the
same thing happens to me."

Avery looked up from the stern, sullen King of Coins in his
grove of apple trees and said, "Do you believe him?"

"I think so." Eric frowned, uncertain. "I'm not sure, but I think
so. If he's lying . . ." The sort of mind that broke codes for MI1b
might be so given over to puzzles as to be astoundingly simple in
other matters, or it might know nothing but deviousness. "He as
much as admitted that he thought Benson was Emily's lover. He
might have wanted vengeance. Or he might actually have been her
lover and wanted to keep it quiet."

"All right, then." Avery held up the laughing Knight of Cups
and said, "Next up is Patrick Norris, right?"

"Patch!" said Penny. "I don't think that's possible. No one could
be quite as jolly as he was this afternoon after having committed a
cold-blooded murder."

"We have to be fair, Penny. Norris was in the building when the murder took place. They never found any traces of blood on his clothes, as far as I know, but that doesn't mean he couldn't have slipped out in the morning to dispose of his bloodied clothing, and then got in again while no one was looking."

"Well, I don't believe it," Penny said stoutly. "Old Faithful sees all the comings and goings—both you and Daddy have said so often enough."

"And the Knight of Cups is such a romantic figure," Avery added.

Eric gave his sister a stern look. "Norris may be plenty of fun, but he doesn't seem to know the meaning of the word 'truth,' Penny. I honestly think you should have nothing more to do with him."

"Oho, so that's what this is about!" Penny sat up in her seat and glared imperiously at her brother. "You don't trust me at all, do you, Eric?"

"Next suspect!" cried Avery, waving a card—the Magician—between the Peterkin siblings. "Mortimer Wolfe! He's the very smug, superior fellow who found a way to break into the club vault, right?"

Eric gave Penny another hard glare, then looked down at the newest card on the table. "Yes. Mortimer Wolfe. He's an ass, but he's a *competent* ass. On the other hand, that business with the . . . the backfiring motor shows he's not so cool as he pretends. I don't know that it's relevant, but—"

"But you never can tell," Penny said. "Seems to me like there's more to him than meets the eye. Do you think he could be the father of Emily's child?"

"It's possible." Eric considered the fastidious Wolfe, who'd rather die than admit to imperfection. How would he react to learning that he'd fathered a half-caste child out of wedlock? "Emily's condition could be a motive for any of the men here."

Penny nodded. "That really seems to be the big issue, doesn't it? It looks as though everyone's best motive comes down to some variation of a reaction to her being pregnant. Oh for goodness' sake, it's 1924 and I'm allowed to say 'pregnant' in mixed company. What

I mean is that whoever killed Benson must have also *impregnated* Emily. Unless Benson did, in which case Mrs. Aldershott killed him. Who else is there?"

"Just Inspector Parker," said a red-faced Avery as he added the serious, studious Knight of Coins to his spread. "We've heard enough about him, I think. At least, I have. He's the treacherous villain who's supposed to be in charge of the murder inquiry, but is twisting it to his own ends."

"I wouldn't put it quite like that," Eric said. "By all accounts, he's a conscientious fellow. So I don't understand why he'd go tampering with the evidence—unless it's because Bradshaw has some kind of hold on him. Besides, he's a VC."

"Which automatically makes him a paragon of virtue, a hero who can do no wrong. I think your priorities want checking, Eric."

Penny said, "Don't forget, men have had their VCs taken away for things like theft and desertion."

The last man to forfeit his Victoria Cross had died in abject poverty just three years ago. The thought of such a fate for someone who'd been a hero once—whatever mistakes he made afterwards—chilled Eric to the bone.

"And that's the lot," said Avery, sitting back. But Eric shook his head.

"If we're going to be fair, we ought to consider everyone connected to Benson. There's also Helen Benson."

"Her? She was all the way out in the middle of nowhere!" But Avery obligingly laid out the enigmatic High Priestess for Helen Benson, saying, "That woman's a regular horror story, Penny. And she's got her hooks into your brother something awful."

Penny raised her brows at Eric, who suddenly found his collar uncomfortably warm. "She was widowed less than a week ago," he protested. "I would never be so indecent!"

"She has this room full of the most awful paintings—" Avery began, but Eric cleared his throat loudly and cut him off.

"Mrs. Benson," Eric said, adopting a dry, precise tone, "used to be Helen Sotheby, and she was rivals with Emily Ang for Benson's affections. She might have wanted Emily out of the way for that reason, and she almost certainly was angry that Benson still thought of Emily after all these years."

"And there we have it," Avery said. "All the suspects. Speaking of which . . ." He turned and began rummaging around in his satchel.

Eric, meanwhile, counted the cards on the table. Edward and Martha Aldershott, Jacob Bradshaw, Lord Oliver Saxon, Mortimer Wolfe, Patrick Norris, Inspector Horatio Parker, and Helen Benson. Their eight cards—the King and Queen of Wands, the Emperor, the King of Coins, the Magician, the Knight of Cups, the Knight of Coins, and the High Priestess—fanned out around Eric's own Knight of Swords like obsequious courtiers, but Eric knew better. They represented what Benson was up against in his quest. "One of these people killed Albert Benson," he muttered. "I've just got to find out which."

"Well," said Penny, "I think we can eliminate some of them already. I know the Britannia gets locked up tight after nine o'clock, so we can drop everyone who didn't have a key or a way in." She took Mrs. Aldershott's, Inspector Parker's, and Mrs. Benson's cards out of the spread. Then she pulled Norris's out as well. "This isn't me being foolish, Eric. I really think you need to prove he had a way of getting rid of his bloodied clothing—his own way in and out, in other words—before you start warning me away. As things stand, he looks innocent."

That left Aldershott, Saxon, Wolfe, and Bradshaw.

"Here we go!" Avery came up from rummaging in his satchel and dropped a stack of papers on top of the cards. "I've been at Somerset House," he announced, "checking up with the Registry of Births, Marriages, and Deaths. They just love me there. Every time I walk in, they say, 'Oh God, it's Ferrett again,' and toast me with a swig from their pocket flasks." He chuckled. "I hope you appreciate what I go through for you, Eric, because those registry clerks certainly don't."

Avery's papers were neatly typewritten and had all the appearance of serious military intelligence. They were, in fact, astrological reports: Avery had sought out the birth dates of everyone related to the murder, including Benson himself, and compiled an in-depth study of each based on their horoscopes.

Eric and Penny exchanged glances. They never quite knew what to tell Avery when he did something like this. Eric obligingly picked up the first report—Aldershott's—and skimmed through it.

"Aldershott's secretly a very gentle, intuitive soul who will forgive anything and everything?" Eric put down the report and gave Avery a doubtful look. "I'll have to introduce you to him someday."

"Here's Mrs. Benson's," Penny said. "It looks like you've spent more time on her than on any of the others, Avery."

"Well, I had to. The twentieth of July is on the cusp of Leo and Cancer, which means she'll have the characteristics of both—"

"Excuse me, what?" Eric snatched the document from Penny and stared at the heading. "The twentieth of July! Mrs. Benson's birthday is the twentieth of July?"

Penny said, "You're a little late if you want to get her a birthday present, Eric."

"The birthday photograph," Eric whispered, not listening. "This is it. This is why that photograph was important, and why Benson included it in his box. It showed Parker was present at Helen Benson's birthday party, as a patient of the hospital, on the twentieth of July. That's the day Emily Ang disappeared!"

"What?" said Avery. "I thought you said—"

"That Parker was long gone by then? Yes. Because that's what his patient records file said. But records can be faked. That photograph proved that it *was* faked. Parker was still at Sotheby Manor on the twentieth, when Helen celebrated her birthday and when Emily disappeared."

Avery shook his head. "That seems wrong. The papers said she spent the day in Chichester. Why do that, if the other nurses were having a party?"

"Perhaps she hadn't been invited," Penny replied. "Perhaps nobody told her, hoping she wouldn't attend." Both Peterkins knew firsthand how that sort of thing worked. "But, Eric, remember what

I said earlier? It still doesn't mean anything if Parker didn't have a way into the club building."

"There is that," Eric mused. "But if Wolfe did it, then Parker might have done the same. I just have to find out how."

Avery insisted that Eric spend the night at his place once Eric told him, quietly, about the shots in the fog earlier. Together, they accompanied Penny to the house of the friend with whom she was staying while in London, and Eric was half sure that Avery would give the game away at any minute. But Avery managed to hold his tongue, for which Eric was grateful.

To tell the truth, he was beginning to doubt himself. Being shot at in the fog, in the civilised safety of London, seemed like such a thing out of a book that he wondered if he'd imagined the whole thing. In the light of the next day, it seemed utterly absurd.

Penny was bound for Cambridge that morning, and Eric went to see her off. He apologised deeply for not having been the perfect host, but Penny insisted that she'd had a grand time nonetheless. Eric was not entirely sure if he should feel reassured, knowing that she must be referring to the afternoon spent at the London Zoo with Norris.

"Really, Eric. If you're going to be this paranoid of every young bachelor who wants to spend time with me, I wonder why you introduce me to anyone."

"Brothers are rarely rational when it comes to their sisters," Eric admitted, rubbing his head in embarrassment. "I don't want to see you hurt, Penny. I don't want to see what happened to Emily Ang happen to you."

Penny stared off into the distance, thinking. She said, "You know, it's a curse to be thought an exotic. It's worse when you're a woman, because sometimes the most seemingly decent of gentlemen turn into utter cads because of it. They think they can take advantage of you and it won't matter because . . . because you're not properly English, or some nonsense. And you know their intentions aren't honourable, because the last thing they want is to bring a child like us into the world. I wonder if you ever really thought about the sacrifices Mummy and Daddy made for us, Eric."

"Of course, but . . . Penny! You're not speaking from past experience, I hope?"

"Oh, I've been all right. I don't look half so exotic as you do. But I've learnt to spot that sudden glimmer of interest when men realise I'm only half-English, and then I scratch them right off my dance card as sharp as you please. I just don't want you to think any less of this Emily Ang because of what happened to her. Sometimes a woman doesn't have much of a choice."

It took Eric a minute to understand the implications. "Penny, a gentleman does not force himself on a lady—"

"And a gentleman takes responsibility for his actions. But some gentlemen, Eric, aren't really gentlemen at all." Eyes suddenly twinkling with mischief, she gave him a peck on the cheek and said, "Speaking of not-quite-gentlemen, give my love to Patch, and tell him I'll see him the next time I'm in London."

There was nothing to do then but to sputter ineffectually as Penny, laughing at his discomfiture, disappeared into the train car to find a compartment.

As the train chugged out of the station, Eric turned and considered his next move. The previous night's discussions had clarified things only a little, in terms of motive: Benson had been killed because of Emily, and Emily had been killed because of her pregnancy. But this hadn't narrowed things down to a definite, single person. It was time to set aside considerations of who *might* have killed Benson, and consider who *could* have killed Benson. It was time to look at how the deed might have been done.

THE VAULT

THE LAST TIME Eric had a look around the Britannia, the cleaning staff was still trying to get rid of all traces of fingerprint powder, and most members had chosen to cross the street to the Golden Lion rather than dine within sight of the evidence of police activity. The powder was all gone now, and a few brave souls had returned to the dining room; but there was something brittle about the atmosphere, as though the attendants were too conscious of their silence, and the light too anxious to chase away the shadows.

Inside, there was a faint but lingering smell in the air of something unpleasant. The fog had crept in overnight and left its taint.

Wolfe had managed to break into the club without leaving a trace; it was the one thing Eric knew for a fact about the night of Benson's murder. That, then, was where he should start: once he knew how Wolfe had done it, he might begin to see how anyone else could do the same.

Stopping outside on the opposite side of the street, Eric made a critical assessment of the club building.

It had a neoclassical limestone facade, much like the St. James Theatre and most other buildings up and down King Street. Tall windows topped with triangular pediments flanked the entrance. The front doors were very exposed, in spite of the sheltered portico.

They were locked after 9 p.m., though an attendant would let one in if one were to ring the bell.

The ground-floor windows were to the dining room on one side of the doors and a public reception room on the other. These windows were locked up tight at this time of the year. In the summer months, a high transom pane in each might be opened for ventilation. Even if those transoms were open now, getting in through them would require a significant amount of agility. The same went for the windows on the first floor above. And farther up on the second floor were windows to the club lodgings. As Eric knew from his experience last week, these had been painted shut.

Below were the basement windows: frosted glass protected by iron grillwork. Eric had no idea what lay beyond them, but it was clear that no one could have got through them without first tearing off the bars, and no such damage was in evidence.

A number of passages and courts bled off from King Street into the recesses behind and between the buildings, and one such passage ran up one side of the club to a narrow utility court. Once upon a time, the carriage house in the back of the property opened into this court, but today the carriage house was the Britannia Club's gymnasium, and its access to the court had been bricked up. Now, the only entrance to the building from the court was a single door surrounded by dustbins, hidden from the street by a projection of the building. A young sandy-haired attendant, loitering there with a cigarette, was caught by surprise at Eric's approach; he quickly stubbed out his cigarette before disappearing through the door. Eric didn't hear a key being turned, but he found the door locked when he tried it.

This was the back door to the Britannia Club, the one Saxon seemed to favour. Above, a foot or two out of reach, was a row of square windows, which presumably gave light to what servant spaces existed beyond the wall. The mortar was crumbling around the brickwork. Closer to the mouth of the passage were larger windows protected, like the basement windows, with iron grillwork. Eric was able to reach their sills quite easily, and then to pull himself up sufficiently to look inside: through one was Aldershott's office, and through another was Bradshaw's—or, rather, the president's and the club secretary's offices, respectively.

Eric returned to the crowd of dustbins and looked up. He could see a pair of bricked-up windows on the floor above the back door, and higher up still was the single window belonging to the room Benson had occupied.

The door itself seemed quite sturdy, and was fitted with a Bramah lock. Famously, the Bramah lock had been counted unpickable for decades, until the Great Exhibition of 1851, when an American locksmith named Hobbs took up the challenge and picked it—in fifty-one hours. Anyone wanting to pick this lock would have needed a good deal of practice, and would doubtless have made a name for himself as a lockpick before now. Only Wolfe had anything approaching such a reputation.

Eric knocked on the door and waited. It was answered in a moment by the sandy-haired attendant he'd seen earlier.

"I know you," the attendant said. "You're a member, aye? You'll be wanting the front door."

Eric held up a shilling, which disappeared along with the attendant's reservations.

"Then again, what do I know," the attendant said, letting Eric in. The door closed behind him and locked itself with a click.

"Those dustbins outside," Eric said, "do you recall if they'd been moved, the morning that Mr. Benson was found?" He was thinking now of Norris, whose real alibi lay in whether or not he could dispose of any clothes after getting Benson's blood all over them. It occurred to Eric that the simplest way for this would be to drop them into the dustbins and let the dustmen take care of the rest. The back door looked as though it opened easily enough from the inside, though it locked itself on closing; but the dustbins were near enough that one had only to keep the door wedged open for a few seconds. There'd be no risk of the night attendants happening on the wedged-open door and closing it while one was away.

"The dustbins?" said the attendant, raising an incredulous brow. "What d'you care about the dustbins?"

Eric held up another shilling. It disappeared after the first one, and the attendant's lips loosened significantly.

"Ah, service with a smile, says I. That day were a Saturday, weren't it? There's no dustman comes on a Saturday. It's Mondays, Wednesdays, and Fridays, five o'clock in the morning and no earlier."

"No earlier? Why no earlier?"

This time, it was apprehension that stopped the flow of information, and it took half a crown to start it up again.

"They think the court is haunted, that's why. But it ain't the court; it's the room upstairs. That room ain't popular with the gentlemen on account of the alley noise, so old Cully lets people what ain't members spend the night there sometimes. Tramps, mostly—dirty beggars with nowhere to lay their heads, and no wonder. Some of them howl in their sleep like you wouldn't believe, and the things what come out of their mouths when they're dead asleep would wake them as is actually dead. The doors and walls are thick enough so you don't hear them inside, but in the summer, when they sleeps with the window open, you hear it out in the court, and I still get chills though I knows what's really doing it. There's no one dares set foot in there after dark because of the howling."

Old Faithful's service to the Britannia Club was supposedly impeccable, and it surprised Eric that he should do anything to risk incurring the displeasure of the membership.

The attendant said, "You won't let on that it was me what told you, will you? Especially to old Cully. Fellow would have me skinned alive."

"I wouldn't dream of bearing any tales." Eric thanked him with an additional shilling, and the attendant bounded up the half flight of stairs to disappear through the lone door on the landing.

That would be the staff room. Before the door closed, Eric caught a glimpse of plain plaster walls, boards covered with pinned notices, and another attendant lounging about with his collar open. The way into the rest of the club's ground floor would be through that staff room, Eric knew, and there was a narrow stairway from it up to the little flat Old Faithful used. There wasn't much chance of someone slipping through that way on the night in question, not if a pair of attendants had been cooling their heels there the whole time. On the other hand, the stairs also continued down to the basement, and Eric could smell . . . bacon?

Yes, bacon. Bacon and sausages and fried bread. Of course. The kitchen was in the basement, and there was a way up to the dining room from there. Eric followed his nose into the scullery, where the smells were somewhat more pungent and less pleasant. From there, he hurried through to the kitchen proper, where the single cook on duty gave him the evil eye. It looked to be an exceptionally slow day, but Eric was an unexpected interloper in the servants' domain, and the toast had been burnt yet again.

A little lost, Eric tried the nearest door; but this was to the boiler room, and it was locked and bolted. The cook pointed him brusquely to another set of stairs, which took him up to the serving pantry. Here, Eric stopped by the cabinet of silverware and looked around. He was still in the way, to judge by the looks the waiters were giving him, but the dining room was just through the open doorway, and it wasn't the first time a club member had ducked into the pantry for some reason or other.

Eric was sure Wolfe must have found a way through the back door, avoiding the night attendants by taking the detour through the kitchen, pantry, and dining room. There would be nobody in these rooms at that time of night. But there wouldn't be anything to show it: these rooms were used so much and so often, any potential clues would have been cleaned away thrice over by now.

There were just two diners, young bachelors nursing hangovers. They made no comment on Eric's arrival via the pantry; they were still in their evening clothes, and to comment was to invite comment. The usual crowds had yet to return to the Britannia, which explained the reduced staff downstairs—finding themselves useless, the rest must have skived off somewhere for a smoke and a drink.

The white linen finery, unused, gave the dining room an air of having been left at the altar.

Eric passed through to the lobby, where his footsteps seemed to echo more loudly into the emptiness than ever before. There'd be no clues here, either, Eric thought, but did there need to be? Once Wolfe or Benson's murderer had made it up here, it should have been plain sailing but for the door to the vault stairwell and everything that came after.

Someone had broken into Aldershott's office as well, Eric remembered—forced the door with a poker. He'd heard mention that the poker had been taken from the public reception room, and a glance inside showed a brand-new set of andirons in gleaming brass, a shining art deco element in an otherwise Victorian room.

In the dining room, one diner got up to leave, and the other didn't seem intent on staying very much longer. Eric found himself wondering if anyone was in the lounge upstairs.

"Is there something I can help you with, sir?"

Eric looked around. Old Faithful had stepped out from behind the reception desk and seemed anxious to be of service.

"Cully," said Eric, keeping his voice low, "I just heard the oddest rumour, that you were letting in men off the street to spend the night in the club lodgings—"

"Hush! They were one of us, weren't they? They fought, and now they're down on their luck, and here we've got an empty room. A soul or two a night, no harm in that, is there? You can't say they don't deserve better than they've got."

Eric was hard-pressed to disagree. These ex-servicemen plagued with nightmares, and "down on their luck" besides—which was another way of saying that they couldn't get readjusted to life on civvy street . . . None of his men had ended up like this, had they?

He said, "Does Aldershott know about this?"

"That's how it started, sir. Captain Aldershott had a few men from his regiment who needed a place to lay their heads, and he brought them in as guests. That was three years ago, and it's gone on from there."

So Aldershott really wasn't the stiff, unyielding martinet he pretended to be. One had to respect the compassion. It made Eric wonder, once again, about his men, the ones with whom he'd lost touch. Thompson and Clark never seemed to have anything to come home to. Once, waiting in the lull between salvos, Clark had even expressed a wish that the fighting go on forever. It hadn't been bloodthirst, judging by his expression; Eric wondered if he were afraid of what he'd find back home.

Eric shook his head. Better get back to the task at hand. If he was to find out how someone had broken into the vault, it would be useful to know exactly how the vault and its attendant processes worked. And the best way to do that would be to get a box.

Old Faithful seemed relieved that Eric didn't intend to pursue the matter of the lodging room. "Sure," he said, "and there's been a lot of boxes made vacant since last week—"

"Can I get box 13?"

Old Faithful stopped and peered at him. "Well . . . yes and no. That box is supposed to belong to . . . to the officers, but of course Captain Aldershott let that Mr. Benson have it, and—"

"Was it actually Aldershott's, then?"

Old Faithful reluctantly admitted that it was, and that, since the murder, its key had been returned to the key box and was theoretically available to whoever wanted it—Aldershott certainly didn't.

Eric did indeed want it, and Old Faithful accordingly filled out the paperwork.

They made their way down to the vault, where Old Faithful once again turned the wheel of the vault door to unlock it, and let Eric in.

It had been a week since the murder. Benson's body was gone now, of course. The mosaic tiles on the floor gleamed more brightly than Eric remembered; they'd been scrubbed and scoured, and one could smell a strong odour of the sort of disinfectant normally found in hospitals. But under the table, the words *decorum est* seemed to stand out from the rest of the inlaid motto—the grout around those letters was darker than elsewhere.

"We've had a time getting rid of the blood," Old Faithful said. "Almost as if it didn't want to be gone."

Taking his key, Eric went across to the bank of boxes and unlocked the compartment door to box 13. He removed the box and placed it on the table—just as Benson had done one week ago. Eric could almost see the old objects he'd had in the box: Parker's medical report, the pair of surgical scissors, the hypodermic kit, and the photograph of Mrs. Benson. It was still a mystery what they meant, but Eric thought he was getting closer now.

Turning back to the bank of boxes, Eric took out the small electric torch he'd brought for this purpose and shone it into the recesses of the empty compartment. The back of it was a rough brick wall; there was perhaps half an inch between that and the steel frame that held the individual boxes in place. The top and bottom were flat steel sheets, but the sides were open. Only a single steel bar on each side separated one compartment from its neighbour.

Eric reached in and felt around the screws holding the bars in place. He said, "Wolfe had box 12, didn't he?"

Old Faithful stared at him. "He did! Still does. However can you know that?"

"The screws between 13 and 12 have been loosened, and you can feel where someone's been at them with something sharp recently. I'll bet this was how Wolfe got into Benson's box for that wager they had: he unscrewed the bar between 12 and 13, then slid Benson's box out through his own compartment." All he needed now was confirmation that Wolfe knew box 13 to have been Aldershott's.

"Oh! That is clever, sir. But if I may, why this sudden interest in the vault and how Captain Wolfe might have got in?"

"It's to do with the murder, Cully. One of ours was murdered, and I intend to find out how it was done."

Eric pictured in his mind, again, the scene that had greeted them when the vault door was opened the previous Saturday: Benson, crumpled up by the table, with Aldershott's letter opener in his neck, his blood splashed across the words *decorum est.* It seemed like either a pronouncement or a challenge.

"Mr. Benson, you mean." Old Faithful's Irish lilt rang with a clear note of contempt, and it made Eric look up sharply. "Begging your pardon, but as I understand it, Mr. Benson was never properly 'one of us.' He never fought."

Eric had never detected so much as a hint of prejudice in the Britannia Club's faithful porter until now. But it seemed the old man's obsequiousness was reserved for the British warrior caste. That included Eric Peterkin and the down-on-their-luck ex-servicemen of London; everyone else, to use a vulgarity, could go suck eggs.

"But Benson was a stretcher-bearer," he said. "He was in Flanders long enough to be wounded."

"So was the Red Cross, and you don't see us opening our doors to the likes of them. No, sir, it's not the same thing at all."

"Well, even if he wasn't 'one of us,' we still owe it to him to find out what happened. And we owe it to ourselves. The man was killed on our watch."

Old Faithful gave him a queer, wondering look. "A matter of honour, you mean? Yes, I expect so . . . It's what your father would say. He was the one who told me what the Latin words there meant, you know. The *'decorum est'* part means 'it is honourable,' doesn't it?"

Eric raised a questioning brow. The twinkling blue eyes seemed to be regarding him from across a gulf of years. "Cully," Eric said gently, "is there anything you can tell me about the vault boxes? It could be helpful to clearing our names."

Abruptly, the blue eyes looked away, and Old Faithful said, "The board officers all have their own boxes reserved. Mr. Bradshaw's had number 11 since the day they started doing that. The president usually takes number 13, as no one else wants it and he can keep his things in his office if he likes. The rest sort it out among themselves. You know about Captain Wolfe. Lieutenant Saxon is 14, and Lieutenant Norris is 15. Captain Aldershott, as president, also has a master key to all the boxes, and I have another."

Eric was not expecting the sudden volunteering of information. He said, "That seems a bit of a waste, doesn't it? I mean, do the officers actually use their boxes?"

"They do, but . . ." Old Faithful cocked his head to look up the stairwell. "I'm not supposed to be telling you any of this, sir. It's only because . . . well, your father was a great man, and I see him in you. It's more than just the Peterkin eyebrows, sir." Blushing at the show of sentimentality, he cleared his throat and said, "You won't let on that I told you anything, will you? I don't think there's much that'll make or break the Empire, but still."

Eric nodded. It seemed to him that if there were any ghosts about, it would not be Benson's vengeful spirit, but old Colonel Berkeley Peterkin looking on with interest at the proceedings.

They went to box 11 first. Bradshaw's. Old Faithful said, "Mr. Bradshaw uses his from time to time. He usually leaves it to me to handle, so you can check the register to see what he's put in. But once or twice he's done it himself, so we've no records of that."

Touching a finger to his lips, Old Faithful winked and produced his copy of the master key. Bradshaw's box was empty.

Number 12 was Wolfe's, as Eric had guessed. "Captain Wolfe came in twice last month. I don't know what he put in, or if it's still there. He was very secretive about it, and he really didn't want me to see what he had."

The box contained a "Red 9" Mauser just like the one Eric had seen in Aldershott's study the night before. It smelled of gun oil and gleamed in the light of the vault's one light bulb.

"A lot of gentlemen keep their war souvenirs here," Old Faithful commented.

"Has Wolfe come by here since the murder?" Eric was thinking of his mysterious gunman of the night before. Wolfe had been with him for the first shot, but what if that really had been a motorcar backfire? Wolfe could still have fired the subsequent shots.

Old Faithful shook his head, and Eric carefully returned the box to its compartment.

Number 13 was Eric's, but it had been Aldershott's before. "Captain Aldershott had a brown paper package in there from the day he was elected, and I reckon he might have forgotten he had it. He uses his own office for everything."

Number 14, Saxon. "Lieutenant Saxon came in four months ago with a stack of books, and took them out again just three weeks ago. I think they were supposed to be returned to a lending library, only they were months overdue, and Lieutenant Saxon was terribly snappish as a result."

Saxon had been in again almost immediately after the murder, and his box now contained a long cylindrical key that Old Faithful identified as belonging to the back door.

"He roomed here for nearly three years after the War," Old Faithful said, "and he used to keep such odd hours that someone decided it would be easier to let him have his own key. By the time he got his own lodgings, the officers had changed and no one remembered to make him give it back."

"And he still uses it, apparently." Eric remembered Saxon being manhandled up the stairs that last Saturday. "Though perhaps not this week. I gather he doesn't normally keep the key here."

Old Faithful shook his head. "Not until after the murder."

Finally, number 15. Norris. "Lieutenant Norris has never used his. Mind you, he was in Italy for three months right after his election, so maybe he's forgotten he ever had a box here."

Box 15 was indeed empty.

Eric looked thoughtfully at the row of boxes. This might be useful, or it might not. In any case, the next thing to consider was the vault door.

Old Faithful took a moment to run up the stairs and check for witnesses and close the stairwell door. When he returned, he said, "You want to be careful with the vault door, sir: it looks heavy, but it's balanced like the scales of justice, and all it takes is a gentle tap to slam it shut. Mr. Bradshaw changes the combination every time there's a new president. He tells me and the new president with an official memo."

"What happens to that memo?"

"Some presidents keep theirs because they can't remember—I fancy Captain Aldershott is one of those—and others burn the thing immediately. I keep mine just long enough to learn the combination off by heart, and then I burn it."

The last election had been just after Easter, hadn't it? April. So that was the last time the combination had been changed.

"There's a plate in the back of the door that's been removed, so Mr. Bradshaw can change the combination and open it from inside. I don't know how that's done, so if you want to see it, I'll have to stay outside to open the door again. Word of warning, the light goes off when the door's closed—that's to put the fear of God into any would-be burglars. You better have that electric torch of yours ready."

Eric nodded and turned his torch on. As Old Faithful had said, a gentle nudge was all it took to swing the door shut, and then, as promised, the light bulb overhead went out. Eric was left with the beam from his electric torch and an unbidden memory of his father playing the light over a hanging sheet with all the fascination of a small boy.

"Here we go, Dad," he murmured into the stagnant air of the vault.

Turning his torch on the vault door, Eric could see what Old Faithful had meant: in the open panel were three discs on a spindle, and shutting the door had set them spinning randomly. Unlocking the vault door was a matter of turning the wheel outside to different numbers, thus realigning the discs. One might, if one's eye were quick enough, guess at the distance between the three numbers of the combination by following the discs, but the random spin made it all but impossible to guess at the first number.

Or did it? The discs might spin randomly when the door was shut, but the spindle did not. A closer look at the spindle showed a tiny ink mark by which one might orient oneself.

The tumblers in Eric's mind were now not just spinning but beginning to fall into place.

When Old Faithful opened the door again, Eric said, "Has anyone ever locked themselves in here by accident?"

"Yes, sir. That's why there's supposed to be someone who knows the combination outside at all times."

"At least twice?" Once to mark the spindle, and once to watch it spin.

"Yes, sir."

"And was that person Captain Wolfe?"

"Yes, sir. And he gave me a pound note each time to forget about it too." The old man didn't ask how Eric had guessed—he'd already taken it for granted that Eric would.

"Did anyone else? Norris? Saxon?"

But Old Faithful shook his head. Wolfe was the only officer to do so.

Eric stepped out of the vault. The next obstacle to the would-be intruder, working backwards, was the door to the stairwell leading down to the vault's antechamber. It looked like a sturdy, old-fashioned affair. "Who has the key to this, Cully?"

"That door doesn't actually lock, sir," said Old Faithful, puffing up the stairs. "Vault security's in the steel door downstairs and all the boxes, not this door here."

That was unexpected. "But you have all the keys to this place, don't you?"

"Yes, sir. My responsibility, after all."

"And the main door?"

"Only me and Mr. Aldershott, sir."

That, Eric thought, was all he needed from an investigation of the club's security. Who among the people they'd considered last night might have got in and murdered Benson? Standing in the corridor outside the offices, Eric closed his eyes and began to consider them in turn.

Well, Wolfe had a way in, obviously. Eric imagined Wolfe picking the Bramah lock in the middle of the night, after having practiced on it every night for a week; perhaps the bet had just been a happy chance to show off his labours. Benson was anxious about his possessions; he was on the alert for Wolfe, and when he heard Wolfe come in, he followed him down to the vault. He surprised Wolfe . . . Eric remembered the savagery under the mask when they'd been startled by the gunshot the night before, and he pictured the same savagery overtaking the "gentleman thief": Wolfe striking out instinctively, unaware of what he'd done until the blood had soaked into the grout beneath his patent leather shoes.

But why would Wolfe have the letter opener on him? Perhaps Benson had picked it up for self-defence; Wolfe wrestled it away from him and, acting on instinct, stabbed him in the neck. Or perhaps there were more details of which Eric was currently unaware.

Saxon, meanwhile, had his own key. Until last night, Eric would have considered him unlikely to have found the vault's combination on his own, but a man who'd spent four years decoding German cyphers might find it child's play to crack the combination of a vault. He probably wouldn't even need to get "accidentally" locked in to do it. Saxon was the only one to know that Benson was spending the night at the club. If the murder were a carefully planned assault, Saxon would be the only one capable of it. And Eric remembered all too well how Saxon had reacted to a perceived threat by drawing a knife on it.

It would be a cool, calculated, long-headed crime. Could Eric reconcile this image of a crafty, calculating Saxon with the guilt-ridden mess he'd walked with the night before?

And then there was Aldershott. Aldershott had it the easiest: as club president, he had the key to the front doors and the combination to the vault. Eric imagined him watching the club, waiting for Wolfe to leave. Once Wolfe had gone, Aldershott would only have to creep in from the street and wake Benson somehow. Benson would come running down to see what damage Wolfe had done, and Aldershott could then strike him down from behind—a daring raid, decisively and unemotionally executed by a decisive and unemotional officer. Afterwards, he'd break into his own office to set the scene and, giving a deliberate little nod of satisfaction, calmly wait for the murder to be discovered.

It didn't seem badly imagined at all. If Aldershott had been Emily's lover, even if he had nothing to do with her death, the fact could prove disastrous to his marriage. As the one to show Benson how the vault worked, Aldershott presumably had some idea of what Benson wanted to stash away, and might have realised what Benson was up to. It added up to an excellent motive for murder, and Eric had already seen the anger beneath Aldershott's granite exterior. There was a savagery there, as much as there had been with Wolfe; but where Wolfe strove to hide the beast within, Aldershott harnessed it and used it to drive his otherwise unemotional actions.

Eric heard the approach of footsteps and opened his eyes. It was Bradshaw. The older man nodded to Eric, then unlocked his office door and stepped inside, leaving the door slightly ajar behind him. "Mr. Bradshaw comes in for a bit every Saturday," said Old Faithful by way of explanation. "He likes to have a quiet smoke in his office, and maybe a nap, and he likes to read the news."

Bradshaw also had the combination to the vault, being the man who set it in the first place. And after all these years as club secretary, it seemed unlikely that he hadn't been given a key to at least one of the doors to the building by now, if only to make his work easier.

Yes, thought Eric. It was time to beard the Emperor.

THE EMPIRE'S BEST
SERVANT

THE LAST TIME Eric had been in this office, it was to be interviewed by Inspector Parker. There had been a dozen policemen scurrying about then, but not now. Now, he and Bradshaw were alone, in a cosy confidentiality that invited the telling of secrets. An attendant had just gone after filling the chipped teapot; steam wafted from its spout, and the Edward VII coronation teacup stood ready with sugar and milk for tea. Above the desk, the ridiculous children's book illustration of the tortoise on a bicycle made Eric's suspicions of minutes ago seem quite far-fetched. Still, as connected as Bradshaw was reputed to be, the man had to know something.

While waiting for the attendant to leave, Eric had idly picked up a book from Bradshaw's desk and was now peering at its worn-out spine. "*Shell Shock and Its Lessons,*" he read aloud. "Grafton Elliot Smith and Tom Hatherley Pear . . . Smith's the fellow who's been doing all those X-ray studies of the Egyptian mummies in the British Museum, isn't he? I had no idea you had an interest in this sort of thing."

Bradshaw stood, plucked the book out of Eric's hands, and returned it to a drawer. "You didn't come in to discuss my reading material, did you?"

Eric shook his head. "You were a company sergeant major at the training camp near Chichester during the War, weren't you? Did you ever have much to do with the war hospitals there? I mean Sotheby Manor in particular."

"Sotheby Manor? Yes, I remember the place. I dropped by every other week." Bradshaw sat leaning forward over his desk blotter, hands clasped before him. The morning sun caught at his beard and picked out the laugh lines around his warm brown eyes. "I was friendly enough with Sir Andrew Sotheby and most of the doctors and nurses. A lot of the patients were men I'd trained and got to know before sending them off to the War. Of course I visited them. You give a soldier his due when he comes home, whether he's whole, injured, or in a pine box. Why?"

"Benson worked as an orderly there during the War. Did you know him then?"

"I did. I arranged for his transfer there, in fact. But that was a long time ago."

"Benson was murdered just one week ago."

"Yes, but Sotheby Manor can't be relevant now, can it?"

"You know Benson was married to the daughter of the house. She said she'd spoken to you after she got the news of her husband's death. If you were friendly with her father and visited as often as you say, you must have known her before her marriage, too."

"Ah. You've been there, and you've spoken to Mrs. Benson, then. Yes, I knew her well enough. Is that what you've been up to this whole week? You're not actively investigating the murder, are you?" Something of the truth must have shown on Eric's face, because Bradshaw let out a low chuckle and said, "You really are your father's son! But the Colonel always knew better than to waste his efforts. Scotland Yard is handling the case, Peterkin; they don't need our help."

"What if there were extenuating circumstances?"

"Extenuating circumstances? What do you mean?"

The face behind the desk radiated warmth and confidence, and Eric was tempted to simply tell him everything, as he would his own father. But he'd begun to wonder, since the encounter at Brolly's, at what lay behind that fatherly facade.

"Before he died, Benson told me he had to correct an old injustice. I thought it worthwhile to take up the torch, as it were. Discreetly."

"I see." Bradshaw sighed. He had the long-suffering look of a father whose children kept stealing his cufflinks for chess pieces. "And you came to me for help. You'll have to tell me more if I'm to do that."

Eric weighed his words. "It was about the disappearance of a nurse back in 1918."

Bradshaw's eyebrows went up. Eric had been watching for his reaction, and was frustrated that half of it was hidden behind that snow-white beard. For the rest, there had been the expected flash of surprise in Bradshaw's brown eyes, and . . . something else? It was gone as fast as it had appeared, the Father Christmas mask once more in place.

Bradshaw got to his feet. Eric moved to stand, too, but was waved back to his seat. Bradshaw ambled around Eric to the office door, which had been left slightly ajar. He glanced out into the empty corridor—Old Faithful had already gone back to his post at the front desk, and of course no one else was about—and quietly closed the door.

The silence deepened; Eric always forgot how well the walls and doors of the Britannia kept out the sound. The office became its own little world, cut off from everything else.

Eric turned around again. Bradshaw was regarding him with a faintly puzzled expression. "Is something wrong?" Eric asked.

Bradshaw shook his head and returned to his seat. "I know the case you mean. Emily Ang . . . I remember her, yes, but her disappearance is ancient history, or so I thought."

Bradshaw's expression was all fatherly concern.

Eric said, "Not her disappearance. Her murder. There was a skeleton unearthed in Bruton Wood. Benson was sure it was her, and he thought he owed it to her to find the truth. I'm sure he had his reasons for not going to the authorities. Perhaps he didn't have enough yet to make his case to them."

"You got all this from Mrs. Benson?"

Eric shook his head. It occurred to him that the things said in the fog last night had been shared in confidence, and he should not reveal Saxon's part in the matter. "I've learnt a few things since speaking to her," he said. "I know now that whatever happened to Emily Ang must be relevant to Benson's murder. The question is, what exactly did happen?"

Bradshaw didn't answer immediately, and the dark mahogany of his eyes gave nothing away. At last, he said, "That was a long time ago, Peterkin."

"You were in and out of Sotheby Manor quite frequently, you said. I wondered if you might have been there the day she was last seen alive—that was the twentieth of July, Mrs. Benson's birthday. Six years ago, yes, but the nurses had a party that day. That might help to fix events in your mind, if the disappearance doesn't already. Were you there that day?"

Bradshaw nodded slowly. "I can't promise you everything, but what do you need to know?"

Eric started with something simple. "Do you remember if Saxon was there?"

"I don't remember ever seeing him there. I can't think of any cause he'd have to visit."

"Norris?"

"Norris was one of the men I trained. I remember visiting . . . Yes, I think I remember him at the party." A smile played across Bradshaw's face. "He was popular with the nurses, as you can imagine."

"What about Wolfe?"

"I first met him at Sotheby Manor, but I don't think it was at the party." Bradshaw shook his head. "My idea of the timing tells me he should have been there, but I can't say I remember it at all. And he does tend to stand out."

"And Aldershott?"

"He was a friend of Sir Andrew's . . . but I'm sorry. I don't remember."

"Inspector Parker?"

"Parker?" Bradshaw stopped for a long time, his eyes focused on Eric's, then said, "Parker's another of the men I trained, and I know he wasn't there. A little bird told me that he was up for the Victoria Cross, and I remember I brought it up at the birthday party. Everyone wished he was still there so they could congratulate him and maybe raise a toast in his honour. I was quite proud of him."

"Do you remember if any of them were close to Emily Ang?"

"I wouldn't know." Bradshaw gave Eric a long, calculating look. For a moment, Eric was reminded not of Father Christmas but of an ancient reptile regarding the foolishness of mortals. There was, perhaps, a reason Bradshaw seemed to have such an affinity for tortoises. The old man said, "You know, Peterkin, this determination of yours reminds me a lot of your father. He had a keen, questioning mind, but he also had . . . shall we say, a little more experience than you? He knew when to drop a thing and move on. So I'm telling you to drop this and move on—not just because you ought to leave this to the authorities but because you're on the wrong track. It seems clear from your questions that you think the officers of the Britannia are involved. They aren't. I can't tell you how or why I know, but I can swear it to you, on my honour, that none of them had anything to do with this—not with Emily's death and disappearance, and, following your own logic, not with Benson's murder."

There was a steel edge in Bradshaw's tone that Eric had never heard before, and his eyes were stern. It was, he suspected, the old drill sergeant coming to the fore. He said, "You seem very sure—"

"Did you ever think to wonder how Benson knew the Bruton Wood skeleton was Emily? I'll tell you. He knew it was her because he put her there."

"What? Oh come now, you don't expect me to believe that!" The idea was laughable. Wasn't it? But Bradshaw wasn't laughing.

He was, instead, watching Eric's reactions with a strange, reptilian sagacity.

"Benson was the one who buried Emily Ang in Bruton Wood," Bradshaw repeated. "That is the truth. I'll swear to it on my honour."

He said it with an earnestness that was hard to gainsay, and Eric found his initial disbelief giving way to slack-jawed shock. "But," Eric managed to stammer, "how can you possibly know this?"

"I can't tell you that, Peterkin. But you wouldn't have come to speak to me if you didn't think I'd know a few things I shouldn't."

"Benson was looking for Emily's killer!"

"Did he actually say she'd been killed, or are you merely assuming human agency behind her death?"

It was true. Nobody had actually said, yet, that Emily was murdered. "If she wasn't murdered, then why all the secrecy around her death?"

Bradshaw shrugged. "There's a lot of strangeness in this world, Peterkin. If you put it in a book, no one would believe it. And I don't say that Benson killed her, only that he buried her. I assumed he knew all along what had actually happened to her, but perhaps . . . well, perhaps I was mistaken. Or perhaps you are."

Was Bradshaw lying? He had to be. But if he were, how was one to catch him out? And if he weren't, then what did it mean? Eric thought back to the man who'd said, with such conviction, that he was about to right a great wrong. Could that same man have been an active participant in whatever that "great wrong" was? Was it, as Saxon seemed to have assumed, guilt that motivated Benson?

"I gave you my word, Peterkin." Bradshaw waved a hand vaguely around the office. "Listen. How do you imagine I got where I am today? 'Bradshaw Gets Things Done, Bradshaw knows people, Bradshaw pulls a string in Cornwall and half the gentry of Northumberland jump.' That's what they say about me, isn't it? It's all built on favours and promises, Peterkin, and that in turn depends on the integrity of my word as a gentleman. So when I say I give my word, that has to mean something. If not, then all this comes crashing down. My word was good enough for your father; I hope that counts for something more than a hospital orderly's hearsay."

"You lied to the press about Joseph Davis and all those men who'd shot themselves."

"I gave my word to let them have their dignity. That's more important than the truth sometimes, and the War left some men with precious little of it."

Eric thought of the ex-servicemen whom Old Faithful had admitted into the club lodgings. Supposedly, it was Aldershott's idea, but Eric wouldn't be surprised if Bradshaw had had a hand in it as well.

That wasn't the same thing, though. "What if it's a choice between one man's dignity and another man's justice? What then?"

"What do you think, Peterkin?" Bradshaw poured himself a cup of tea and sat back to sip at it. He looked far too comfortable to be plagued much by any moral dilemmas. "Questions like this are far from exceptional in this world, and I'm surprised that you seem to think they are. That's another thing your father understood."

"My father taught me about honour," Eric said. "He taught me that a gentleman does what's right—"

"No. A gentleman does what he *thinks* is right. That may not be the same thing at all. He may do what's right for the wrong reasons, or he may get his hands dirty doing wrong to achieve the right ends. It's never so simple as any code of honour will have you believe. Yes, I lied about Joseph Davis, and a dozen others besides. But I dare you to look their widows and children in the eye and tell them you think I was wrong."

Eric watched Bradshaw, once again thinking of the different masks the man wore. He was beginning to suspect that, if there did exist a sinister side to this personification of Father Christmas, it was not in opposition to the fatherly persona, but an extension of it. Bradshaw would do anything for his men, even if it meant covering up a murder.

Benson, a conscientious objector, had never been one of Bradshaw's men.

"Where were you last Friday night?" Eric asked, turning to simpler topics. "I don't remember seeing you anywhere about."

There was a shift behind Bradshaw's beard that might have been his mouth curling up in triumph. He was willing to keep playing the game, but there wasn't much fatherly favour in it now. "As I told the police, I was at a music hall. Brolly's. Mr. Breuleux will vouch for me, I'm sure."

Of course he would. As Bradshaw would vouch for anyone and everyone.

Eric got up and said, "I know you were lying about Inspector Parker not being at Sotheby Manor, by the way. Benson had a photograph that proved he had been there. If you'd said you didn't remember, that would be one thing; but you said quite definitely that he hadn't been there. And I notice you didn't wonder why I'd think to connect Parker with Sotheby Manor: you knew the question was coming, and you were waiting to feed me the lie. Why? Does someone's dignity depend on Parker being absent that day?"

That got through to Bradshaw, and the Father Christmas facade hardened into that of the rarely seen sergeant major. "That's none of your business, Peterkin. Horatio Parker is a fine man, and I won't have you besmirching his honour for the sake of some long-forgotten story."

"Was he responsible for what happened to Emily Ang?"

"I can't answer that!"

"You seem to be answering for many more people than you'll admit. Not just Davis and all the men in those 'accidental' shootings. I reckon I can understand those. But I wonder where it all ends." In his mind, Eric flipped through images of the various people connected to the murder. Were there any inconsistencies in their pasts that Bradshaw might have had a hand in? Aldershott? Saxon? Norris?

Eric stopped on Norris.

"Norris was supposed to have spent three months in Italy immediately after his election to the board of officers in April," Eric said. "But that's not true, is it? There's a portrait of him in Sotheby Manor dated in May. What's the story there, Bradshaw? What did you do, and why?"

But Bradshaw had settled back again, at ease, laugh lines creasing. "Ah, that's got nothing to do with me. Don't look so surprised, Peterkin. I can't be involved in everything that happens in the British Empire, no matter how the gossip builds me up. I believe Norris was renting the old groundskeeper's cottage from the Bensons. That's all I know. I expect he simply lied about where he'd been to make it all seem that much more romantic."

"But if he was only in Sussex, why would someone else have to cover his duties here for three whole months?"

"I can't answer that. Because I do not know."

Bradshaw was telling the truth this time, Eric thought. He'd been too agitated about Parker for this new ease of manner to be anything but genuine relief.

"Will that be all, Peterkin?" Bradshaw asked, getting to his feet to open the door for Eric.

"For now," said Eric, going to the door. "This isn't over yet."

"Peterkin." Facing him, Bradshaw rested a hand on Eric's shoulder and looked him in the eye. It was a familiar gesture, but not at present a welcome one. "I know it's hard to let things go, but please, take my advice and give this up. Your father would have understood. I give you my word that no one here had anything to do with the murder, and after all, was Benson worth turning the club on its head? If Emily had been murdered, then he's at least an accomplice to murder."

"And what does that make you?"

Bradshaw sighed. "One who's been around for far too long, and who's seen too many good men come and go." He gave Eric's shoulder a friendly squeeze, and there was a sympathetic smile behind the beard; but Eric thought he caught a gleam of something ancient and reptilian in the depths of those eyes.

Eric closed the door on Bradshaw's office with a slight sense of regret. He didn't know if he could really think of fatherly old Bradshaw in quite the same way again.

It wasn't until he was halfway down the corridor that he thought of it: Mrs. Benson had never spoken of any business dealings with Norris. She had, however, spoken of renting the old groundskeeper's cottage to Aldershott. What Aldershott wanted with the groundskeeper's cottage of a deteriorating country house was a mystery, but Eric had the idea that it must have had something to do with Norris.

Of course, he could speak to Norris, but Eric thought Aldershott owed him an explanation for more than just a cottage rental.

THE HOUSE OF WANDS

THE SCAR ON the lamppost where a bullet had narrowly missed its target the night before was still there. Eric could see no sign of a bullet hole in the tarred wood blocks with which the street was paved, however. Unless the whole thing had been his imagination, one of the houses opposite was going to have a bit of a surprise one day when the owners repointed their brickwork.

All around him, residential Mayfair that Saturday morning was awake and oblivious with ladies strolling along to pay calls on close acquaintances. The terraced townhouses stretched down the street on either side, some in limestone but most in brick, and all of them patterned with tall mullioned windows in regular rows and columns. Tiny, narrow basement courts separated the houses from the street, with wrought-iron fences to keep one from falling in.

The memory of the gunshots in the fog seemed more unreal the more he thought about it. The sense of isolation had reminded him of Flanders, and with Flanders had come the memory of gunshots. But Saxon had heard it too, hadn't he? Eric clung to that thought. If someone else had heard the shots, he couldn't have imagined them. Could he?

Meanwhile, the sense of Bradshaw's hand on his shoulder still lingered, much as Mrs. Benson's touch on his jaw had, though Eric took something vastly different from it. It was . . . not unclean, precisely, but similar. Bradshaw didn't offer his support in expectation of anything, but one still felt bound by the obligations of gratitude; and when the time came, Bradshaw was not above appealing to that obligation. It was, Eric realised, integral to his network of favours owed and rendered, and how he Got Things Done.

Eric didn't think he owed Aldershott much. The relationship there was more antagonistic, and therefore simpler. One knew exactly where one stood.

"Morning calls," that ill-named mainstay of social life among the well heeled, generally took place between three and six in the afternoon; at eleven in the morning, one called only on intimate friends—the ones who didn't mind a bit of informality. Eric wasn't so intimate with the Aldershotts as to permit a social call in the actual morning, but the butler recognised him from the previous night's dinner party and, perhaps assuming Eric to be here on business, admitted him into the study without comment.

Little had changed in the study since last night, except that he was seeing it now in the bright light of morning, and he had time to really examine his surroundings. The rosewood bookcase, he saw, was full of dry financial material. The taxidermied animals were more fascinating, though the daylight emphasised their lifelessness and gave them a more eerie, unearthly effect. He remembered the Andean condor over the door, and now he was able to identify several others: a glassy-eyed lemur, a pair of beavers, the heads of animals too big to fit into a small urban study whole.

Eric was still examining the stuffed game when Aldershott walked in. "This had better be good, Peterkin," Aldershott growled as he shut the door. "Put down that stuffed mongoose."

"I couldn't get a good look at it last night," Eric said. "I grew up in India, you know. Well, partly, anyway. Did you know—"

"Peterkin!"

Eric set down the mongoose. "I wanted to know about Norris's visit to Italy earlier this year."

Aldershott was taken aback. "What's that got to do with anything? Why don't you ask him?"

"Well, I doubt he'd care to tell me the truth, and I fancy you know more about it than you let on. I also fancy he was no closer to Italy than I am right now. He was at Sotheby Manor, wasn't he?"

"If you know that—"

"I want to know why."

"You think I have the answer to Norris's business?"

"I think you were paying for it. Mrs. Benson said she was renting the groundskeeper's cottage to you, not to Norris. She also said you were the inspiration behind the plan to turn Sotheby Manor into a rest home for addicts, and I think you were a major investor in that plan. Taken together, it all seems a bit suggestive . . . Nothing definite, of course, but that's what I came here for."

Aldershott stared at Eric. Slowly, he sat down behind his desk.

Eric remained standing. He could practically see the wheels turning in Aldershott's mind. After yesterday's interview, his questions today must seem like a non sequitur, and Aldershott must be wondering just how much goodwill he could extend now—if only to get rid of Eric—and whether it was worth his while.

Eric shrugged. "I expect it doesn't matter. I could ask Mrs. Benson instead; I know she'll tell me. And if not, someone else will know. It's just a question of asking around enough."

"Wait."

Eric waited.

The muscle in Aldershott's jaw twitched as he struggled with a decision.

Eric turned again to exit the study. As his gaze met the dead eyes of a bear, he heard the springs of Aldershott's chair release, and three words rang out.

"The soldier's disease."

Eric turned back around to face Aldershott, meeting a gaze that was more exasperation and sadness than anger.

Aldershott sat down again and said, "You're not the sort of fellow who shuts up easily, are you? All right. I'll tell you about Norris's little holiday, but it doesn't go further than these four walls, is that understood? Your word."

"My word." Eric took a seat.

"The soldier's disease," Aldershott repeated. "Morphine addiction. That was a relic of the American Civil War, when morphine was new and everyone was using it to treat everything. Countless men wound up dependent on it for years afterwards. We never really thought much of it here in Great Britain, though, did we? Until the middle of the War, you could just walk into Harrods and buy a morphine kit off the shelf. Well, the War certainly opened our eyes to what could happen with morphine. You've only to read the newspapers these days to see."

"Are you telling me that Norris was suffering from a morphine addiction?"

Aldershott nodded. "It came to light right after the last elections at the club. I wanted a proper look around the place to know what I was getting into, and there was Norris, in one of the lodging rooms, with all the paraphernalia around him."

Aldershott stood and went to the window. It looked out behind the house to a public garden, and a few children were playing there under the watchful eyes of their nannies. The trees swayed in the breeze. Inside, the air was as still as the stuffed heads on the wall.

"He was just lying there," Aldershott continued, "staring at the ceiling. He'd used his tie as a tourniquet—I'd always wondered before how he kept ruining his ties—and it was hanging off his elbow onto the floor. My first reaction was to scream at him for the mess, but he didn't care. He was just . . . limp, barely breathing, and too far gone to care. I realised I was wasting my breath shouting at him and took action instead. I discarded the empty bottle; everything else I packed up and put away. Then I had him shipped off to Sotheby Manor. Sir Andrew was long gone, but I knew his daughter, and I knew Benson. I knew Norris would be in good hands. And that's all the fellow needed: someone to tell him no. Look at him now, Peterkin. I don't know if you had much contact with him before, but he's a different person."

Eric thought of jolly, bright-eyed Norris, and nodded. Eric had never personally met anyone in the grip of a morphine addiction, but Avery had, and Avery described the poor fellow as a horrific crank when he wasn't limp and lethargic from a fresh dose.

"I reckon you saved his life," Eric said, with feeling. Aldershott nodded and turned from the window. Their eyes met, and there was a mutual understanding in them. Eric had had a corporal very much like Norris: Blake, a fun-loving scoundrel who got the whole platoon to laugh. Less than a month before the Armistice, he'd walked out onto the parapet, looked into the dawn, and blown his brains out. Eric often wondered if he could have done anything to prevent it.

"Norris was my second in command after Wolfe got his promotion to captain," Aldershott said, returning to his chair. "He was a very different prospect from Wolfe, as you can imagine. Morale went up, even if some of the ordinary standards of regimentation went down."

"And you felt responsible for him." As Eric still felt responsible for his men, scattered though they were. He could easily relate.

"It's a very sorry officer who doesn't feel some sort of responsibility for the men below him, Peterkin. As an officer yourself, I hope you understand that much, at least."

"Do you know how he wound up addicted to morphine?"

"I should think that's obvious. Norris loves life and laughter. How much of that did you see in the trenches?"

"I remember that we found ways of carving humour out of the horror," Eric said. "There were plenty of bright spots in between everything else."

"Not enough," Aldershott growled. "And especially not for Norris. He needed to lose himself completely in something, and eventually he found morphine. I think he began stealing it from the Sotheby Manor dispensary when he was warded there."

So it had been going on for years. Eric tried again to imagine Norris with the irritability Avery had described, and decided that an irritable Norris might seem like a more mature, grounded individual than the fun-loving scamp he now was.

Eric stood up. "Thank you, Aldershott," he said soberly. "I think I understand poor Norris a little better now." Norris had escaped Corporal Blake's fate, at least.

"Think nothing of it. I hope you understand what I mean when I say the fellow deserves his privacy." They'd been discussing Norris like a pair of concerned friends, and Aldershott had slipped into that mode with surprising ease. He actually smiled as he stood up to shake Eric's hand.

Eric felt a little bad about demolishing the goodwill that seemed to have arisen between them. But he wasn't quite done yet. He doubted whether all the goodwill in the world could induce Aldershott to give him the answers he wanted. A shock was needed, and Aldershott, relaxed, was primed to receive it.

"Oh, just one more thing," Eric said, turning abruptly from the door. Aldershott's smile vanished. "What did you do with the photograph and the medical report you took from Benson's box?"

Aldershott nearly exploded. "How in hell—"

"From what Wolfe said, it seems plain someone else got to Benson's box before he did. I think that someone was you. Easy enough, since you were given the vault combination when you became club president. No, don't say anything, just listen. You knew exactly which box Benson had because it used to be the box you'd been given as club president. You had the master key, too, so it was easy for you to get into the box. All you had to do was wait. I remembered the lip prints on the brandy glasses in your office, all the cigarettes in the ashtray, and the open transom; someone had been waiting in there after the cleaning staff had gone, and opened the transom to let the stale cigarette smoke air out overnight. This wasn't the same person who'd broken in, or the ashtray wouldn't have been upset on the floor. I think you waited there until you thought it late enough that no one would notice, but not so late that you risked running into Wolfe as he fulfilled his part of the bet. I think you crept down to the vault, used the combination you'd been given back in April, opened Benson's box with your master key, and removed the photograph and medical report from it. Then you left, by the front door, and destroyed the two items."

Aldershott had gone white with anger. He'd been too shocked and angry to interrupt Eric's speech, but he found his tongue now. "I think you should leave now, Peterkin," he said, keeping his voice steady with some effort. "Leave before I have you thrown out."

"Were you wearing gloves that night, Aldershott?"

Aldershott said nothing, but reached for the bell pull that would summon the butler.

"I think you weren't wearing gloves that night. Why should you? You weren't there to commit murder, and you cannot have expected the door would be dusted for fingerprints. But it does mean that your fingerprints are in fact all over the door wheel. Even if the police have identified those prints as yours, they probably haven't attached much importance to the fact. You're the club president, and you have the combination by right. Your fingerprints should be all over the place. But how many people go down to the vault unattended by Old Faithful? Except for Bradshaw, who changes the vault combination from time to time, no one lays a hand on the vault door but Old Faithful himself. Everyone else waits while it's opened for them."

Aldershott gave the bell pull a vicious yank. Eric thought he could hear the bell jangling all the way from the servants' hall.

"I just want to know about those two items," Eric said quickly. "The photograph of Helen Sotheby's birthday party and the medical report for that scar on Inspector Parker's face. What have they to do with each other, and why did you leave the other items—the surgical scissors and the hypodermic kit?"

"We're done here, Peterkin. Or more precisely, you're done. I'm having you thrown out of the Britannia Club so hard, your sorry yellow arse will bounce off the pavement."

The door cracked open to admit the butler, and Eric reflected that this hadn't quite gone as planned. He was sure he'd deduced the truth, but it took a little bit more than that to shock anything out of Aldershott, it seemed.

"That's all right," Eric said, moving away from the butler. "I can find my own way out."

"Good-bye, Peterkin."

Eric didn't protest as the butler took him by the elbow and firmly propelled him out of the study.

He was just being shown the door when Mrs. Aldershott, coming down the stairs, hailed him. In her habitually sober everyday clothes, she looked at first glance like a no-nonsense governess or schoolmistress, but she was smiling in equal parts welcome and amusement.

"You've been speaking with my husband," she said. "Let me guess: it was an unmitigated disaster. Was it about Emily?"

Eric tried to collect himself. "In a way."

Mrs. Aldershott let out an indulgent huff and dismissed the butler. She drew Eric into the drawing room just in time to avoid being seen by Aldershott, who stormed through the hall and slammed out of the house. She said, "I haven't had much opportunity to question him about it since last night, and he's been more obstinate than usual. It makes me almost wonder if he were involved in some fashion."

She said it as though she thought the idea preposterous, but Eric had no doubt whatsoever that Aldershott was involved. "I think it is a little early to be expressing my suspicions, ma'am."

"Because I'm his wife, no doubt, and it might cause irreparable damage to our marriage! I'm made of sterner stuff than that, I hope. Edward likes to kick up a fuss about every little thing, but there's not much bite to him in the end. Underneath that prickly, standoffish facade, he really cares almost too deeply about people."

He did seem to care enough for Norris, and Eric recalled what he'd learnt earlier this morning about the club's secret practice of offering lodging to ex-servicemen on the street. Eric could believe it. "He hides it very well."

"Oh, it's absolutely true. There's not a day goes by without him worrying about what the Britannia Club is doing for its shell-shocked members. All he ever reads is literature by very learned men about

the nature of shell shock, or war neuroses, or whatever they're calling it these days."

They were back in the entrance hall now, and Eric noticed that,
indeed, there were two new books sitting on the hall table. "*Shell
Shock and Its Lessons,*" he read. "Bradshaw has a copy of this. I saw it
in his office Saturday morning."

"That would be Edward's old copy. He's been trying to get
Bradshaw interested."

The second book was *Psycho-Analysis and the War Neuroses.* Eric
flipped it open. "Karl Abraham and Sandor Ferenczi. This one has
an introduction by Sigmund Freud—I've heard of him . . ."

"It's really quite fascinating, this study of the war neuroses, or
however you want to call it. War strain, battle fatigue . . . Edward
prefers to call it shell shock, but, well, leave it to a soldier to define
everything in terms of war—"

"How clinical." So they were calling it a madness now. People
did talk about shell-shocked soldiers going a little mad, but now it
was official. Eric felt his hackles rise.

"Edward says the primary function of the Britannia Club is to
provide a safe place for affected ex-servicemen to gather. He's a firm
believer in the benefits of camaraderie in the face of crisis."

"The gentlemen of the Britannia are perfectly sane," Eric
snapped. "I know a lot of us haven't been able to look at fireworks
the same way since the War, but that's just the way of things. We're
not *mad.*"

"Nobody says you are."

Eric hefted the second book in his hand and brushed a finger
over the title. "You've got doctors who specialise in madmen calling
this a 'neurosis.' How else should I take it?"

His little flashes of unbidden memories were *not* a neurosis.

"But you do admit that something has changed. It doesn't matter what people call it: the fact remains that, since the War, some
people have terrible nightmares, some people have difficulty adjust-
ing to peace, some people react badly to loud, sudden noises . . .

They're sane in all the ways that matter, Mr. Peterkin, but has no one ever jumped on you to protect you from a Christmas cracker?"

"Oh, Wolfe." Of course, last night's slip must have also occurred elsewhere and in other contexts. "Wolfe has things under control. It isn't a . . . a neurosis; it's simply the way he's been trained to handle things. The man holds himself so steady all the time, I reckon he's allowed an odd quirk or two."

Mrs. Aldershott shook her head. "I was thinking of someone else. It doesn't matter whom I meant, but it just goes to show that it's hardly exceptional. And I'm not surprised to hear about Mr. Wolfe. He pretends to be so utterly unflappable, but really he's just doing his best to put a brave face on things. I have it on good authority that once, while he was lodging at the Britannia, he spent half the night cowering under the bed because someone had upset a dustbin under his window."

Eric winced. He really should have been more careful and circumspect. Now he'd gone and given Wolfe away, and the man would hardly thank him for it.

Mrs. Aldershott continued. "He feels this need to keep everything under control at all times. Of course, he was a touch demanding even before the War, but my understanding of it is that the War made him absolutely unbearable. Meanwhile, other men have sought comfort in their excesses—drink, or drugs, or . . . or other vices."

Wolfe's self-control had fooled Eric, at least until last night. Before that, Eric would have called Wolfe one of the sanest men he knew.

Eric tossed the book back onto the hall table. There seemed to be little else to say about it. "'We're all mad here,'" he quoted sarcastically.

"We are."

Eric looked up. Mrs. Aldershott's expression was serious.

"Mr. Peterkin," she said, "did you wonder, at dinner last night, why there's no mustard in our cruet? It's because neither Edward nor I can abide it. It sets us to remembering things we don't care to relive.

You must know that Edward survived a mustard gas attack, and he was lucky to do so. Many of the men who'd been with him died of it, days afterwards, and it haunts him terribly. And I remember those cots, all those men who could bravely endure bullet wounds and shrapnel and broken bones in silence, all of them wailing and crying . . . and me not being able to do anything about it except wash their boils and eyes, and hope . . . One whiff of ordinary table mustard and I'm there all over again. Does this make us mad, Mr. Peterkin?"

Eric laid a hand on her arm, and she shook herself, clearing her head. He didn't want to call it madness, but it wasn't quite normal, either, and Mrs. Aldershott made it sound like the brink of insanity. And it sounded uncomfortably similar to his own unpleasant memories, rising unbidden in moments of stress. They were not a neurosis, he told himself again, but with somewhat less conviction than before.

Perhaps they weren't. That didn't mean they weren't there. And if both the Aldershotts had had the same sort of experience—if Wolfe's reactions to loud noises were the same sort of thing, and if even Norris had had trouble coping—then he was not alone.

He was not alone.

"I had better go," he said quietly. "There's a man I need to see in Chichester before the day is out." He was thinking of Dr. Timothy Grey, the coroner who'd examined the Bruton Wood skeleton. Eric didn't want to interrupt him at work, nor did he want to intrude on him on a Sunday. That left today, Saturday afternoon, as his one chance for a visit.

"Is it about Emily?"

Eric nodded.

"Then you had better go. Tell me whatever you've learnt, when you're done."

Eric returned to the street, giving it a cautious scan for hidden gunmen before heading down in the direction of the parking garage where the family Vauxhall was stashed. He was thinking of his men in the light of what Mrs. Aldershott had said. It was easy to see that one or two had been affected by the War in some way, but most had seemed normal enough. He thought it unlikely that they'd all been affected, but it seemed just as unlikely that none of them had. One maintained a stiff upper lip, and this sangfroid let one carry on while all around were collapsing in hysterics; but that didn't mean one wasn't possessed of human emotion.

Eric was halfway to his destination when a dark grey Austin pulled up beside him.

"Mr. Peterkin!"

"Mrs. Aldershott?"

Mrs. Aldershott was indeed driving the motorcar. She beckoned for him to get in, and he did. "I assume," she said, "if you're going to Chichester that you're headed for Victoria Station. But if so, you're walking in the wrong direction."

Eric shook his head and gave the address of his parking garage. "I'd rather motor down," he said, looking around the Austin. It was a pre-War model, but very well maintained. "Of course, I shan't expect you to take me all the way there. Doesn't this model of motorcar use a hand crank to start?"

"Which makes it therefore an unladylike choice?" The hand crank had a tendency to break its operator's wrist. "I'm not so delicate as that, I assure you. Edward's had this since before the War, and he doesn't like to discard anything. It's still a perfectly decent motor, hand crank or not."

"Well, I thank you for the ride."

"Think nothing of it." She paused to negotiate a corner, then said, "Listen, Mr. Peterkin. I think I've said already how much I want to know about what happened to Emily. I'd always assumed that the police had already done everything possible, and I didn't think an outside inquiry would yield much more. Certainly, the newspapers didn't have anything to say. But it occurred to me, just after you left, that if you've connected her disappearance to Benson's murder, then you've got a lot further than anyone ever did. So, if there's anything I can do to help you along, I'll do it."

"Your husband doesn't seem amenable to that."

"Edward can go jump in the lake. It's not his sister we're talking about." There was that brisk, businesslike ruthlessness that carried Mrs. Aldershott past the attendants at the Britannia and, no doubt, many a blustering general during the War. "I was technically Emily's next of kin, you know, at least as far as the English authorities were concerned. All her things were passed on to me after the police were done with them. I've had a look over them from time to time, but nothing's stood out for me. Perhaps you'll see something there that I've missed."

Eric turned to her and broke into a broad grin. "That would be a godsend, Mrs. Aldershott. I can't thank you enough."

"Oh, I'm just doing this for my own satisfaction, believe me. I'll let you have today for whatever errands you have in Chichester. But tomorrow evening, I'll come find you at the Britannia Club and we'll go over Emily's things together."

"No, not the Britannia." Word would get back to Aldershott if his wife were to seek Eric out at the club; and after their earlier interview, Eric didn't want another confrontation just yet. "Do you know of the Arabica coffeehouse, near Soho Square? Meet me there. I'll be in the booth right at the back."

It was a date. Mrs. Aldershott dropped Eric off in front of his parking garage, then set off for home while Eric turned his sights on Chichester and the Bruton Wood skeleton.

EXIT THE HIGH PRIESTESS

DR. TIMOTHY GREY was a big man, over six feet tall and a solidly built nineteen stone. His craggy features were terraced by a short white beard, and wisps of white hair floated across a mottled pink forehead. He was newly retired, and enjoying the prospect of never having to conduct another inquest again. Eric found him at the Green Elephant inn, right next to the Chichester train station, after having spent an hour trying to look him up at his home address.

Chichester was something of a central hub for the surrounding villages, with an ancient cathedral and a direct line to London. On this Saturday afternoon, the streets swelled with men and women searching the stores for the more specialised items that they couldn't find at home. The Green Elephant's maze of low-ceilinged, half-timbered public rooms was already busy with people looking for a bit of relaxation after a long week, and no doubt the rooms upstairs were full of commercial travellers preparing to either move in or move on.

Dr. Grey was banging out a tune on a standing piano as a gang of rowdy locals joined in song. His own voice was a booming bass that more than carried the room.

"What's the use of worrying?

It never was worthwhile!
Pack up your troubles in your old kit bag;
And smile, smile, smile!"

Eric waited until they were done before cutting in to get the former coroner's attention and drag him from the piano room to a more discreet corner of the inn.

When he wasn't singing, Dr. Grey's voice was a deep rumble. He looked down at Eric's card, then up again. "Peterkin, you say? Of the Peking Peterkins?"

"I'm not aware of any family out that way, but—"

"It's a joke. I meant that you don't look much like the sort of person to be called Peterkin. You look more like a . . . Sheringham."

Eric blinked.

"That's another joke." Dr. Grey chuckled and handed the card back. "What can I do for you?"

Eric signalled for two pints of beer to be brought to their table, then turned to Dr. Grey and said, "I wanted to ask you about the Bruton Wood skeleton. You examined it when it was first unearthed, I believe." When Dr. Grey shook his head in doubt, Eric added, "It was a woman's skeleton, described as under five foot four? Discovered by a mother-and-daughter pair from Singleton? They'd stopped to eat a packed lunch."

Dr. Grey's brow finally cleared. "Oh, that." His sigh was another deep rumble. "There's nothing to tell. I told the *Observer* that it would likely lead to a murder inquiry, but decided in the end that it was not worth pursuing."

"Why not?"

Dr. Grey shrugged. Their beers arrived, and he took a moment to pull at his before wiping his mouth and saying, "There was nothing to identify her, and she'd been in the ground for too long. The medical examiner and I did as much as we could, but there seemed to be no reason to go on. And the papers, thank goodness, didn't seem interested in pursuing it either, or I'd have looked like quite the fool."

"Can you tell me anything more? I mean, could you tell the cause of death? How was she lying? Were there really no personal effects to be found?"

"One thing at a time, Mr. Peterkin!" Dr. Grey chuckled. "My goodness, you really are interested . . . but might I ask why?"

"Oh, it's . . . for a book." Eric took out his other card, which showed his work affiliation rather than his club. "Research, you see."

Dr. Grey examined the card doubtfully. "Looming Press? I've seen some of their books. Whoever picks their literature needs to be shot." He took another pull of his beer as he considered Eric's question. Finally, he shrugged and said, "Well, it's no matter to me. Honestly, it's nice to talk about an unsolved mystery sometimes."

"You must see a lot of those," Eric said.

Dr. Grey let out a booming laugh. "You'd never believe some of the things I've had to deal with! The Bruton Wood skeleton, now, let me tell you . . ." The former coroner's speech took on a more modulated tone as he dropped back into reminiscence. "First of all, there were no personal effects around the body. We did find a few linen scraps that hadn't completely decomposed yet. The distribution seemed to indicate a very large sheet of material—a bedsheet or a tablecloth, perhaps. I think she'd been wrapped in it when she'd been buried. Her legs were straight, her hands were crossed over her chest, and she was lying on her back—the usual attitude of a corpse laid out in a coffin."

"There'd been some gesture towards a respectful burial, you mean?" Eric pictured the scene: A man was digging the grave in the middle of the night. There was no time for a proper six feet, so a shallow scrape would have to do. The man lifted Emily's body in his arms and carefully deposited her into the grave. Her weight and the relative depth of the grave made it awkward . . . No, he lay her flat on the ground at the head of the grave, then took her by the ankles and dragged her in. Or did he have help?

"Odd for a shallow grave in the middle of nowhere, but that's how it looked to me," Dr. Grey said. "She certainly hadn't been carelessly dumped. People dumping bodies generally don't much care how the body is resting—it rolls a bit as it's thrown in, and the limbs splay. I even remember one body that had been curled up into a tight little ball because that meant digging a smaller hole. I began to think the Bruton Wood skeleton might be an impoverished farm-wife whose bereaved husband had decided for whatever reason to bury her himself."

That matched up with what Bradshaw had said about Benson burying her. Benson was heartbroken, and he wanted to give her what respect he could. She was naked but for the sheet, to stymie identification . . . so why go to Saxon later to have him claim the body? Had someone else forced him to bury her there? Eric pictured another person by the grave, perhaps holding a gun on Benson and telling him to hurry up. Bradshaw, perhaps, all drill sergeant with none of his usual bonhomie; or Aldershott, standing still as a statue, spectacles glinting in the moonlight; or even Saxon, growling sav-agely to mask the state of his nerves. Benson, grieving badly, was in no fit state to fight back.

Eric asked, "Could you see how she might have died?"

"Oh yes, there were a pair of skull fractures," Dr. Grey replied, indicating a spot near the base of his skull. He traced a line from the spine to just behind his right ear and another one farther up. "The medical examiner thought each looked consistent with a blow from a long, hard object, quite thin but not sharp. A metal rod of some kind, probably a fireplace poker or a crowbar."

Eric nodded. "Murder, then." Eric pictured a poker swinging at Emily's head. Her assailant would be standing just behind her. The blow would be right-handed, or a somewhat more awkward left-handed backhand.

Could Benson have struck the blow that killed her? Benson had been a big man, almost as tall as Dr. Grey. Emily had been, accord-ing to reports, between five foot two and five foot four. Eric tried to envision Benson swinging at her. How high would he hold his arm? With his height, would the angle be more horizontal? Eric wanted to believe that the angle described by the coroner indicated a shorter man than Benson, but he had to admit that it seemed inconclusive.

"What are you doing, Mr. Peterkin?"

Eric quickly dropped his hands with the sudden realisation that he'd been miming the murder blow. "Sorry. Just . . . trying to picture it, that's all."

Eric emerged from the Green Elephant about an hour later, after having been drawn by Dr. Grey into a series of drinking songs around the piano. This piano, it transpired, had been his own gift to the landlord of the Green Elephant, though it seemed that only Dr. Grey himself ever had the courage to play to an audience. "I'm told that someone quite good came in yesterday morning to play while waiting for his train, but of course I wasn't about to hear it! There's a lesson in that, Mr. Peterkin: you never really see the best fruits of your labours."

Outside the Green Elephant, South Street continued into the heart of Chichester, to an elaborate Gothic pavilion with stone seats facing out from a central core. This was Chichester Cross, and the main streets of the town radiated out from it in the four cardinal directions. The Peterkin Vauxhall had been parked on West Street, where the cathedral formed the whole south side of the street. Looking that way, Eric saw the first golden streaks of sunset forming on the distant clouds. At this time of the year, sunset meant it was late enough to start thinking about tea, but not quite late enough to actually have it.

Eric stopped in the shade of Chichester Cross and considered his options. It might be worthwhile to wait and dine here, he thought. He could motor back to London later. Or he could spend the night at the Green Elephant and attend morning services at the cathedral. It would be All Souls' Day, and time to begin thinking of those he'd lost.

Or, he thought with a twitch of anticipation, he could call on Mrs. Benson and let her know he was ready to let her paint him in oils.

A trio of very small children pulling a Guy in a cart behind them stopped just outside the cross to stare at Eric until the eldest, remembering her manners, requested the customary "penny for the Guy." This Guy was stuffed with straw and dry leaves, and its face was a paper mask. Eric was happy to oblige, and the trio ran off again, the youngest looking back over his shoulder until he nearly tripped over his own feet.

Eric watched them go, then turned back to his seat in the Cross. A furtive movement caught his eye: there was a man watching him from the corner of South and East. He had beady eyes and a bad complexion, and Eric remembered seeing him earlier as he'd come out of the Green Elephant. They'd been walking in opposite directions then; the beady-eyed man's presence here meant he'd turned around to follow Eric.

Eric took the road map from his coat pocket and pretended to study it, but he was on the alert. Ordinarily, he might have approached the beady-eyed man to ask him the issue, but he remembered all too well the attempt on his life just last night. Was this the same person who'd shot at him then? He wasn't anyone Eric recognised, but that didn't rule out the possibility of a hired killer.

A hired killer! Surely, that only happened in books?

Eric shifted his seat around the central core of the Cross to a position just out of view. The beady-eyed man moved to keep Eric in sight. If he wasn't a hired killer, he was at least suspicious enough to warrant caution.

All around, the late-afternoon crowd milled about the shops and chattered among themselves, unaware of what was happening beneath their noses. If any attempt were to be made on Eric's life, it wouldn't occur right here in the shadow of Chichester Cross. But he couldn't wait here forever, and he didn't want to lose what was likely his best lead in the mystery. The police station was back down South Street, beside the train station; if Eric had noticed the beady-eyed man's suspicious behaviour earlier, it might have been an easy matter to wrestle him down and haul him in for questioning. As it was, he couldn't confront him now and drag him all the way down South Street without the good people of Chichester getting quite the wrong idea. If he tried to lead him too close to the police station before making his move, or if he tried to approach a policeman now, he might arouse the beady-eyed man's suspicions.

Eric looked around at the four streets radiating out from the cross. The building that had once been the Butterworth Arms, where Saxon had stayed when he came, was on the corner here. It was now a pub, and it suggested possibilities.

Eric stood up and casually strolled over to the pub. He went inside and made his way to the bar. If the beady-eyed man stayed outside to watch the entrance, Eric could slip out the back way and get help confronting him. If he followed Eric inside . . .

He did.

Eric was counting on there being a fair crowd in the pub. There'd been quite a few people at the Green Elephant, and that was earlier in the afternoon. With the sunset, people would be gathering in the pubs and taverns in preparation for an evening's social entertainment. No one would think it strange if Eric were to order a pint of beer and take it to a table close by the door where the beady-eyed man had just come in. And the scrum of patrons kept the beady-eyed man from slipping away.

Eric tripped over a nonexistent crack in the floorboards and sent his beer flying into the beady-eyed man's face.

"Oh my goodness," Eric cried. "I'm so terribly sorry. Here, let me get that for you . . ." He pulled out a handkerchief—not his good handkerchief, but the turmeric-stained one from his last visit to the Shafi—and began pressing it against the would-be assassin's beer-soaked shirtfront.

Yellow stains on a handkerchief look only slightly less disturbing than blood, and the man had no way of knowing they were only turmeric. He pushed Eric away with an expression of horror and disgust.

Eric's hand closed on the other man's jacket as he stumbled backwards, and they both fell against a beer-laden table. Beer splashed across the floor amid cries of dismay and outrage. Eric was fully prepared for this to turn into an all-out brawl, but there were police-men watching the weekend crowd, and a pair of burly constables began pulling people apart before more than two or three blows could be exchanged.

"Who started this?" one constable bawled. A dozen fingers pointed at Eric and his "friend," and Eric allowed himself a smile of satisfaction. This was certainly one way of getting one's stalker apprehended by the police.

One constable hauled Eric to his feet, and the other helped the beady-eyed man up with somewhat better care. The beady-eyed man glared at Eric, then said to the constables, "That's the Chinaman the maid up at Sotheby Manor told us about—Mr. Eeshahn, she said his name was. Arrest him."

Eric's smile vanished as the two constables—and the third, out of uniform and still wet from the beer that had been thrown in his face—turned on him.

The room was bare but for a table and a pair of chairs, placed facing each other on opposite sides of the table. Eric had been seated in one chair to await interrogation. He'd got up almost immediately to pace. Every passing minute only increased his annoyance. They were probably keeping him waiting on purpose, he thought, to set him on edge. Unfortunately, it was working.

The door began to open, and Eric leapt back into his seat. The light in the corridor outside was much brighter than in the room, and for a moment, all Eric could make out was a trench-coated sil-houette with an unruly shag of hair. It shrugged off the trench coat and slung it over the opposite chair, then turned to face Eric.

It was Detective Inspector Horatio Parker.

What was he doing here? Perhaps he'd come to follow up on Benson's connection to Sotheby Manor. That had to be it. And Eric's own connection to the case must have been the root of the police suspicion that had ended with his current situation. Eric said, "You're a long way from London, Inspector."

"So are you, Mr. Peterkin."

Parker had barely changed since they last saw each other at Benson's funeral. Come to that, he hadn't changed since the day they'd found Benson's body, either. There was a yellow tinge to his collar, and his jacket seemed a touch too big for his thin frame. His face was as haggard as before, and he looked as though he hadn't slept. As when he'd first met the Inspector, Eric's eyes were drawn once more to the scar running across his cheek.

What was he doing here? Chichester and Sussex were surely outside of his jurisdiction.

"Assaulting a police officer," the inspector said, reading from a file. "I thought better of you, Mr. Peterkin."

"It was an accident."

"A likely story."

"He was out of uniform. Why was he following me?"

"You were named as an interested party in a murder case. Constable Fletcher was off duty when he spotted you coming up from the train station. He's . . . quite dedicated to his job."

Choice words, Eric thought bitterly. The same Constable Fletcher had warned his on-duty friends that "these people" were "slippery buggers" who'd "wriggle out of anything if you gave 'em half a chance."

Parker tossed the file onto the table and perched himself sideways on the table edge. It was a casual and informal posture, but it allowed Parker to loom over Eric.

"Not Benson's murder? I wasn't aware that Scotland Yard was enlisting the Chichester police in the inquiry."

"We all help one another," Parker replied with a shrug. "We compare notes. Sometimes we even catch each other's criminals."

"You're wasting your time with me," Eric said, reddening at the implication. "I didn't kill Benson."

"I hear you've made it your business to hunt down Benson's killer on your own. Without help and without support. If I were a suspicious man—and I wouldn't be in this line of work if I weren't—I'd wonder if you weren't looking to cover your tracks after having done the deed yourself."

"Is that an accusation?"

"I merely observe that you seemed rather intimate with the widow Benson. Enough to wonder if you might want her husband out of the way."

Eric had been expecting something like this since he realised that the inspector had been watching them after the funeral. He drew himself up and said, with as much frosty dignity as he could muster, "There is nothing between us, and I have nothing to hide. You know perfectly well that I couldn't have done it."

"Is that so, Mr. Peterkin? And why is that?"

"Because Benson was killed in the vault. That means you want someone who had a way into the vault. I didn't."

A knowing, catlike smile flickered across Parker's face. If Eric didn't know better, he'd have sworn that even his scar turned up at its edges.

"Wolfe told us he'd left the vault door open, and was surprised to find it closed when you lot went down and found the body."

"What?"

"Oh yes." Parker nodded sagely. "Wolfe was quite chagrined about it. He said it spoiled the show he had prepared. He sucked two cigarettes down to nothing as he told us this, which I fancy is the most emotion he's shown in a year."

"But—"

Parker swung down from his perch on the table edge and settled into his chair. "So you'll have to give me something better than the vault door to convince me you're on the up and up, Mr. Peterkin. I'm giving you a chance now. Show me. Convince me that you've been out finding things, not hiding things."

This put Norris right back on the suspect list, and removed all question of whether Saxon could have broken the combination the way he broke German cyphers. Eric was back where he started. He made an effort to pull himself together. He had to turn the tables somehow. "I know the name of the woman in the photograph you removed from Benson's room," he said. "Her name was Emily Ang, and Benson was investigating her death. She was last seen alive here in Chichester. I wonder if that's the reason you were here when they brought me in."

A twitch. It wasn't much, but it was something. "If that's the trail you're following, I wish you the best of luck. It's nothing to do with Benson's death, but you are, of course, free to distract yourself from anything genuinely important."

"Why don't you think it's connected, Inspector?"

"Why do you think it is?"

"You know why."

They sat in silence for a minute, just watching each other. Parker's face had dropped back into its wooden, immobile mask. Eric crossed his arms and said, "I know what I saw, Parker, and I don't understand it. Everyone I've spoken to has talked about your dedication to justice, how you put in the work of three men at the Yard."

"I can't comment on that," Parker replied with a sardonic smile.

"You're supposed to be a hero. They awarded you the Victoria Cross—"

Here Parker gave a bark of laughter. "And that's supposed to mean something, is it? The Victoria Cross recognises bravery, Peterkin, and I can point out bravery in some of the rankest villains of the criminal underworld. Don't deceive yourself that it represents any degree of moral fibre."

"But—"

"If you want the damned thing, stop by my office at the Yard and I'll give it to you. It'll be a load off my chest."

Eric stared at him in silence.

The inspector suddenly stood up and called another constable into the room. Eric thought this meant the end of the interview, but instead he was escorted outside to a motorcar and told to get in. "We're going for a ride," the inspector said.

Five minutes later, they'd pulled up in front of a palatial Georgian building with a wide lawn and a flourishing Chinese wisteria in front. The walls appeared to be smooth plaster, though the ground floor was covered with ivy, and the entrance was centrally located between gracious pilasters under a broad pediment. Parker hadn't said a word on the journey over, and Eric hadn't expected him to. The sign at the driveway's entrance proclaimed this to be the Royal West Sussex Hospital, and Eric wondered if they were here to see a doctor, or perhaps a nurse—someone who'd worked with Emily Ang at Sotheby Manor. A constable accompanied them inside, staying on the other side of Eric from the inspector; Eric might not be in handcuffs, but he wasn't exactly free.

It was well past visiting hours by now. The night shift had come on, and the nursing sisters flitted through the shadows like ghosts. Proceeding quietly down the corridor, Eric heard the whisper of mysterious machines shuffling on the edge of his hearing and blending with the snores and groans of sleeping patients. They did not enter any of the wards, and the glare of a formidable matron extended no invitation. Nor did they stop at any of the office doors. Instead, Parker took them down to the morgue.

It was very still and cold. The scent of hospital disinfectant was stronger here, and mingled with something cloying and sickly sweet.

A figure lay on the table, under a white sheet. It's a second murder, Eric realised, and his blood ran cold. He could think of only one person this could be, for the body to be here in Chichester.

Parker paused to make sure Eric was watching, then whipped back the sheet with a suddenness that nearly made Eric jump. Under the sheet was . . . a total stranger.

This was a man in his sixties, thin and grey, with sunken cheeks and little dents on his nose where spectacles once rested.

Eric felt all the tension simply drop out of his body. He let out the breath he didn't know he was holding, and looked up at Parker. The inspector was watching him intently, though he wasn't sure what for.

"I don't know who this is," Eric said, coming forward for a better view. Now that the tension was gone, his natural curiosity was reasserting itself. He wondered how the man had died; there didn't appear to be any marks on the body.

Eric looked up. "What did you—" And then he froze.

While Eric was busy examining the dead stranger, Parker had surreptitiously peeled back the sheet from the body on the next table. And it was Helen Benson.

All the anxiety and tension that had disappeared with the first body's reveal snapped back like a rubber band and nearly bowled Eric off his feet, and he had to clutch at the table to maintain his balance.

Helen Benson was nearly colourless in death. The bobbed, finger-curled hair was even more incongruous on the table than with the Edwardian crepe dress. Bobbed hair belonged on the heads of women in the prime of life—flappers celebrating their vitality, career women building their own futures, fashionable matrons with their fingers on the pulse of the present—not on the dead. Eric had seen his share of dead people before, but most of those had been soldiers in the War. They had been men who knew what they faced, not the women who were meant to survive them.

Eric's thoughts went, inexplicably, to Glatisant. Who would pursue the Beast now?

He became aware that Inspector Parker was speaking to him. "I'm sorry, what?" said Eric.

"I asked, where were you early yesterday morning?"

"At the British Museum," Eric found himself saying automatically. "The Newspaper Reading Room. I'd asked—" Had that been only yesterday? It felt like ages ago. The last time he'd seen Mrs. Benson had been a day earlier, and *that* felt like only this morning. "Who was this other man? Were they found together?"

"That other man passed from natural causes this afternoon. He's nothing to do with Mrs. Benson. You're a smart man, Mr. Peterkin. You were expecting to see Mrs. Benson as soon as you realised where we were. I had to take that expectation away, to see what your real reaction would be."

Eric glared. "Damn you, Parker. That was a dirty trick."

Parker just shrugged. "We do what we have to do."

"You asked me about yesterday morning," Eric said, focusing on any sort of activity rather than the body in front of him. "Was that when . . . this . . . happened?"

"There was a fire." Parker was watching Eric carefully. "It looks like the result of a lit cigarette meeting a spill of turpentine."

All those paintings, Eric thought. All that canvas covered in oils. Mrs. Benson didn't appear to have suffered any visible burns, but paint fumes could be noxious. "I see. I got the impression that she'd been sleeping in her studio."

"You think the fire took place in the studio."

Eric looked up sharply. "You said there was a turpentine spill."

"I didn't say the spill was in the studio. It was in the office."

"Stop playing with me," Eric snapped. "Tell it to me straight. What the hell happened?"

Parker continued to watch him, his face grim. The stark lighting of the morgue made him seem a decade older. "The dog alerted the house to the fire," he said. "The office door was locked, but a pair of workmen, there for the renovations, broke it down before the fire spread too far."

He stopped, waiting for Eric to respond.

Eric said, "You want me to guess if it might be suicide, don't you? No, I don't believe it for an instant. When last we spoke, she was determined to continue the work she and Benson had started on the house. They had plans to turn it into a rest home for addicts."

Eric remembered again that moment in the lychgate, how her pale, Madonna-like face had stood out from the shadows as she gazed at him. He'd stepped back from her. Why had he done that?

"Yes. The two of you seemed quite intimate, as I recall. I understand you met only very recently?"

"Monday." Eric didn't care to elaborate. He forced himself to look at the body again. He saw no signs of burnt flesh, but then a sheet was drawn up over most of her, and all he could see was a dim silhouette. It made him think of Emily Ang, buried in a shallow grave with only a linen sheet for a shroud. "You say the door was locked. Was there any chance it was locked from the outside? Did Mrs. Benson have her keys on her?"

"No, she didn't." The inspector made a note in his notebook. "What do you think happened?"

"How should I know? I don't know anything about the scene: how she was found, how she died—"

"It was smoke inhalation, eventually. The medical examiner thinks she may have been drugged, and is conducting tests to confirm his suspicions. The maid says she brought the full tea service to Mrs. Benson in the office only an hour before. It suggests a visitor, and the maid certainly thinks so, though she saw no one else."

"What do you know?" Eric demanded. "Do you have a suspect?"

The inspector raised an eyebrow meaningfully at Eric.

"I told you, I was at the British Museum. It wasn't me; it could be anybody." Eric fastened on that one thought to calm and steady himself. "How did this person get by the servants, then? He couldn't have rung the doorbell and hoped for the right person to answer. He must have crept in. If neither Mrs. Benson nor Glatisant raised the alarm on meeting him, that means someone familiar with the household. He'd have to know where to find the turpentine, too."

Someone was going to pay for this. Eric set his jaw as his rage settled into a steady simmer. Parker pulled the sheet back over Mrs. Benson's—Helen's—face, and pulled Eric away.

Nothing had changed in the corridors of the hospital, but all Eric could think of was that Helen had found herself in hospital work—much as her father had—and that the projected Sotheby Manor rest home would now be let go. The silent night-shift nurses reminded him of her in the way they rustled down the deserted corridors, and he wondered if the grimly glaring matron had been a friend.

As the police motorcar started its way back to the station, Eric said, "Who is Mr. Eeshahn?"

Parker turned to look at him, eyes glittering with interest. "Where did you hear that name, Mr. Peterkin?"

"That policeman, Constable Fletcher, mentioned it as his mates were dragging me in. Who is Mr. Eeshahn? What's his connection to all this?"

Parker said nothing.

"Answer me, damn you!"

Parker shot him a glare, and Eric could only seethe.

Eric fumed the rest of the way back to the police station, where Parker led him silently through the corridors to another dank, colourless room. It was getting late in the evening now, and few people were about. The silent constable who'd accompanied them to the hospital stationed himself by the door as the inspector led Eric to a table.

A collection of soot-blackened objects was neatly arranged over it.

"Look at these things, Mr. Peterkin. Is there anything you can say about any of it?"

"Mr. Eeshahn—"

"Look at the table!" The inspector's voice was a harsh bark.

Eric snarled, but turned to examine the objects on the table. "This is the detritus from the fire, I'm guessing? I see the broken teacups. That looks like a piece of the ceiling light. I notice a lot of burnt paper."

"Half the cabinets were pulled open," the inspector said, "and their contents dumped into the middle of the room to make a bonfire."

Eric moved in for a closer look.

"That's the hypodermic kit from Benson's box," he said, pointing to the warped and blackened remains of a rectangular tin. Elsewhere, the metallic parts of the hypodermic needle were identifiable, once one knew what to look for. "It looks like someone tried to tear the thing apart before throwing it on the fire. You can still see the monogram on the lid. It's the same stylised *S* as on the handle of the pen-release knife Saxon carries about."

"Oliver Saxon, eh? Interesting."

As the inspector calmly jotted down his notes, Eric swung around to face him. "All right. I've played your game, Inspector. I've come and I've looked, and I've identified the evidence. Now tell me, who is Mr. Eeshahn?"

The inspector snapped his notebook shut and gave Eric a cool, almost triumphant look. "According to the maid, Mr. Eeshahn was the operator of an opium den in Limehouse who was preying on a certain family friend of the Bensons. Albert Benson went to London to sort the fellow out, and was killed as a result."

What he really meant to say, Eric realised, was that Benson's murder had nothing to do with Emily Ang, after all.

"Let me tell you a theory, Mr. Peterkin. The theory is this: You know exactly who Mr. Eeshahn is. You're one of his agents. You were attracted to Mrs. Benson. Whether because you were ordered to or because you wanted his wife, you engineered Benson's murder at your club. Then you set about insinuating yourself into Mrs. Benson's life. Mr. Eeshahn took exception to that, and had her killed to send you a message. Now, you're playing dumb with me because you want to gauge just how much I know about your boss."

"That's ridiculous!" Not to mention insulting. Eric struggled to rein in his temper. "Why would I have anything to do with this Mr. Eeshahn?"

"A link between you and a Limehouse opium den?" The inspector shrugged. "I should think it's obvious."

The press was filled with horror stories about drug addiction, which they linked to the Chinese communities of Limehouse and the old association between the Chinese and opium. The reins on Eric's temper snapped.

Eric seized the inspector by the lapels and slammed him against the wall. "How dare you," he snarled. "How dare you! You assume, just because I . . . I'll have you know I'm as English as you are!

My mother was a saint, and I won't have you slandering her or her people—"

Eric would have said more, but strong hands fastened on his arms and shoulders and pulled him away.

Inspector Parker straightened his jacket and trench coat. "Take him away," he told the two constables holding Eric down. "A night in the cells should cool his head and teach him a lesson about assaulting police officers."

As the constables began to drag Eric away, Parker flashed him a look that was almost apologetic. "I did tell you," he said, "to stay out of my way."

A KNIGHT IN HIS CUPS

ERIC EMERGED FROM the Chichester police station at dawn, Sunday morning, and blinked in the sunlight. He was stiff from a night on an uncomfortable cell bench, and he was sure he needed a good, long bath to wash the smell away. After the dark and dingy police cell, the world seemed impossibly bright, the colours garish.

Helen Benson was dead. He'd had all night to think about that, but it didn't make things any better. All he could focus on was the intensity of her gaze and the touch of her hand. She was supposed to have been safe—what had she ever done to put herself in danger? The unfairness of it all set his blood boiling, and the rage sparked by Inspector Parker's baseless insinuations simmered in the back of his consciousness.

The anger resolved itself into a name: Eeshahn, the next link in the chain.

Parker hadn't named the "family friend" on whom this Eeshahn character was preying, but it wasn't much of a leap to guess that it was Norris. He'd have to speak to Norris, Eric decided. Then he'd hunt down this Mr. Eeshahn and get some answers.

Norris, however, wasn't at the Britannia when Eric finally got back to London. "I don't know where he's been, sir," Old Faithful told him. "I haven't seen him since Friday afternoon."

Friday afternoon? "You mean, since *before* Aldershott's dinner party?"

"That's right, sir. He came in, went to get dressed, and then left. I knew he'd got the same invitation from Aldershott as you and Lieutenant Saxon. When he didn't ring to be let in, I thought maybe he'd decided to spend the night with a lady friend. He does that sometimes. But he did show up to that dinner, didn't he?"

"He did." Eric felt a sense of dread creeping around his vitals, and it had nothing to do with the idea that Norris might have a "lady friend" while he was ostensibly pursuing Penny. "Has anyone been in his room since?"

"The cleaning staff, sir."

"Bother the cleaning staff. I need a look around in there."

Old Faithful didn't ask any questions. He took Eric up to the lodging room occupied by Norris and let him in.

It was only a little tidier than when Eric last saw it. The cleaning staff had swept and dusted and made the bed, and anything Norris might have dropped onto the floor had been picked up, folded, and put aside. The mess of papers on the armchair hadn't been touched—Norris wouldn't appreciate his work being shuffled around. Likewise the mess on the chest of drawers.

There had to be a clue somewhere as to what might have happened to Norris. He remembered the gunshots in the fog as he left the Aldershotts'. What if Norris had been a victim? But surely the news would have been all over the Britannia by now if he had.

"I'm going to have to check his chest of drawers," Eric said, determination outweighing his sense of propriety.

Old Faithful just nodded.

Eric didn't have to look far. In the top drawer, tossed in with a mess of collars and cravats, was an empty medicine bottle, clearly labelled. Morphine.

Despite Aldershott's best efforts, Norris had fallen back into his old habits.

Eric carefully closed the drawer without touching the bottle. He'd come to find out about Mr. Eeshahn from Norris, but now it looked as though he'd have to find Mr. Eeshahn himself. All he had was the rather vague notion of an opium den in Limehouse, and there had to be dozens of those. But it would have to be enough.

London's Chinese community was gathered along the streets of Limehouse Causeway and Pennyfields. Anyone who'd read one of the popular "yellow peril" thrillers knew what to expect: long shadows and dark alleys, red paper lanterns casting a ruddy glow through the smoke, and fog rolling across one's feet as one stalked past the yawning mouths of shops selling inexplicable oddities. There'd be the pungent scent of exotic spices and the murmur of foreign tongues, inscrutable Oriental gentlemen with their hands tucked into silk sleeves, and now and again the glimpse of a mysterious cat-eyed beauty. And behind all this, gambling, opium, and sin.

Eric remembered with some irony what Avery had said when they'd first interviewed Mrs. Benson: Were they in a Sax Rohmer adventure, and would they then have to infiltrate any Limehouse opium dens? Avery's words had proven prophetic, because if Eric wanted to find Patrick Norris and the mysterious Mr. Eeshahn, it looked as though he might have to do just that.

Eric had no doubt that Parker and his men must have done a thorough canvass of the neighbourhood already, looking for Mr. Eeshahn. Obviously, they hadn't found him. Eric, of course, knew that for once he had an advantage over them.

So here he was on a Sunday afternoon, dressed in what was assuredly not his Sunday best. Armed with a photograph of Patrick Norris and a stout walking stick, he was fully prepared to look Depravity in the eye.

Depravity, however, was not living up to expectations.

In the noonday sun, the colours of Limehouse Causeway were bleak and tired. The doors were scratched and the brickwork was dirty with soot, but this was hardly exceptional. Eric tried to picture the scene after nightfall, and only saw the same dreary brick one might expect anywhere else in the East End. There were, of course, the shopfronts with Chinese names over their doors, but these were fewer than he had expected; they stood side by side with establishments catering to foreign sailors coming off the freighters of the nearby docks. Eric had worried that even his shabbiest coat might mark him as an outsider, English as it was, but most of the Chinese men he saw were wearing similarly English coats. Eric wasn't sure if he should be relieved or disappointed.

A little guiltily, Eric realised that he knew nothing about this world. All he knew of it was his mother. Magdalen Peterkin had been fond of jade and shades of red, and would have nothing to do with gold of less than twenty-four-carat purity. Aside from this, she dressed in European fashions and she encouraged English affectations in her children. The lullabies she knew were Chinese, though, and Eric remembered songs with syllables like water running over cobbles. He'd joined in, once, when Penny was an infant lying peacefully in the nursery cradle: Eric and his mother sharing in the song that soon became less about getting Penny to sleep and more about connecting with generations stretching back to the days of Genghis Khan. He must have understood the words then, but no longer.

It was a different world, and Eric was a stranger. The squalor and poverty were a far cry from the affluence of Mayfair or St. James, and there was none of the dangerous romance promised by the likes of Sax Rohmer. Instead, Eric sensed a sort of curtain-twitching grasp for respectability that sometimes infected poor neighbourhoods. It was a poverty that tended towards law and order because, in the absence of money and power, pride was everything.

Tracking down Mr. Eeshahn meant finding the opium dens of this disconcertingly everyday neighbourhood. To that end, Eric was on the lookout for anything approaching the expected "yellow peril" image. One of these shops had to be hiding an opium den.

Things began to look up again once he stepped inside one of the shops. The decorations, though sparse, were more what he expected: hanging scrolls and an abundance of red. He could smell ginger and spices, and the acrid odour of joss sticks. But the very word *opium* was sufficient to have him chased out by a red-faced proprietor insisting that he ran a respectable business—not that Eric understood a word.

The next shopkeeper only rolled his eyes and shook his head. When Eric was forced to admit that he spoke no Chinese, the shopkeeper's patience ended and Eric was coldly shown the door.

The rest of the shops were closed on account of its being Sunday. Eric was going to have to try a different angle, or come back tomorrow.

"Penny for the Guy, sir?"

The Guy in the little barrow was made of paper, and its insides rustled with crumpled newspaper. Its face was gaily painted, with too-red cheeks and a toothy smile.

On impulse, Eric dropped sixpence into the barrow. The children gasped, thanked him profusely in Chinese, then ran off before he could change his mind. Eric watched them go, and thought to himself: This wasn't a different world at all. It was still England, and the children still loved their fireworks.

He didn't think he had much hope of finding an opium den around here. Perhaps he might have more luck looking for people directly. He'd brought Norris's photograph for that reason, and he had that name, Eeshahn.

He'd reached Pennyfields by now. It had much the same poor-but-respectable appearance as Limehouse Causeway, but the Chinese he heard was a different dialect. It was more clipped and incisive, and Eric reckoned that he might be able to get around his lack of language by pretending to be someone from the other part of Chinatown.

The first shop he entered appeared to be a hardware store, and it was not, technically, open for business. The shopkeeper was a blue-eyed blonde of middle age, and she was instructing her teenaged half-Chinese son on how to manage the inventory.

"Ni yao se me?" the woman asked, switching from English to Cockney-accented Chinese on seeing Eric.

Wordlessly, Eric held up Norris's photograph. Both the woman and her son examined it carefully, but shook their heads. Norris had not been here. Eric made a show of checking for witnesses, then said, in a low voice, "Eeshahn?"

"Eeshahn?" the woman echoed, frowning in perplexity.

Her son frowned, too, and then his brow cleared. He ducked behind the counter and emerged with an umbrella. *"Ni yao de si ba yu san, dui ma?"*

Eric had little choice but to purchase the umbrella and leave the shop. He chucked it into a bin as soon as he decently could, then ambled on to the next store . . . only to emerge five minutes later with another umbrella clutched in his hands.

Was he going to be showered with umbrellas each time he trotted out that name? That was probably what it actually meant, unless he'd mangled the intonation somehow. He'd only ever heard it third-hand from English policemen, after all.

He was about to chuck this second unwanted umbrella and try his luck again when it suddenly dawned on him: This wasn't just an umbrella. It was a *brolly*.

Brolly's was just as Eric remembered from his visit with Penny. It was too early in the day for business, but the custodian who answered the door let Eric in once he'd explained that he wanted to see the manager.

Benson had been here investigating Breuleux's involvement in the drug trade. Eric realised that now, and everything else fell into place, though he wondered just what that meant for Bradshaw. Could it be possible that Bradshaw was protecting the establishment under the impression that it was an unlicensed music hall and nothing else? Wishful thinking—Bradshaw was cannier than that. But if he were involved in the drug trade here, he must have known, long before Aldershott found out, about Norris's problem.

Eric made his way through the empty auditorium and into the corridor beyond. Frye, that great bruiser, was standing at the foot of the stairs at the far end of the corridor, smoking a cigarette. Eric gave him a nod, which he didn't return, and rapped on Breuleux's door.

Breuleux had lost the Chinese whiskers since last they met, though the pink bow tie was still in place. He was surprised to see Eric, and said so.

"I've come about that job you mentioned," Eric said. "The room upstairs?"

"Oh!" Breuleux looked wary. "How much has Bradshaw told you?"

"Not a thing." Eric thought it best to avoid elaborate lies. "He doesn't know I'd thought to take you up on the offer."

Breuleux said, "But you know what it entails?"

"I think I have a good idea that I'm the sort of man you want." When Breuleux still hesitated, Eric added, "You'll remember I'm as good as Frye any time of the day."

"You're a bleeding toff—"

"Even toffs fall into debt." Eric affected a more pleading tone. "Please. I need this, even if only for a little while. I'll be the laughing stock of St. James if I have to let my club membership go just from lack of funds, and I don't want to just borrow it. I know where that can lead. I . . . also know the Chinese word for 'umbrella.'"

"*Yu san.*" Breuleux nodded, and made a decision. "All right. I daresay I need a man who can handle an unruly customer. So come along, and I'll show you what's what."

Frye stepped aside for them as Breuleux led Eric up the stairs to a dingy landing with an unremarkable set of doors. Beyond these doors, however, sweet incense billowed out at them, reminiscent of Oriental spices. It masked an undercurrent of stale sweat. The light was dim, and the air was smoky; the walls were papered in red, and everywhere Eric looked, he saw panels of elaborately carved gypsum, lacquered over to simulate rosewood. It was the heady opulence promised by the "yellow peril" thrillers, and Eric knew exactly what to expect beyond the scarlet curtains.

"We'll have you fitted out in a proper Chinaman costume," Breuleux said. "Unless you've got one of your own? No? Well, that can wait. We shan't have to bother with any makeup in your case. You look perfect for the part already. Almost. You'll have to grow out your moustache: two little tendrils on either side of your mouth, just like in the pictures. Think you could do that?"

"I think so."

"People don't come here just for the opium, you know," Breuleux said as he took hold of the scarlet curtain. "Who needs an opium den when you can smoke the stuff in the privacy of your own home? They come here for the atmosphere. They want to imagine that they really are venturing into a forbidden temptation of the Celestial court, and they want to see it run by a Celestial like you. I've been playing 'Mr. Yu San' long enough." He rubbed his upper lip. "And I'll be honest: gluing those whiskers on every night is a pain I'm happy to leave behind."

They stepped through the curtain into a chamber that was all shadows and smoke. It was lit only by a filthy skylight. Figures huddled in alcoves, and Eric heard the occasional drug-addled sigh. Here were a pair of bright young things, him in a dinner jacket and her in a flapper's party frock, sharing an intimate pipe; and here was a tired, hollow-eyed man with an Army jacket and an attitude of despair. Most were a little better dressed than Eric had expected, but after all, vices cost money.

Breuleux whispered, "They're not all on opium. One or two come just to say they've been, and don't actually take anything at all. But some others are on something stronger."

Eric whispered back, "Something stronger . . . you mean morphine? Cocaine?"

"Whatever they want. They're the serious ones, and they usually take their stuff home to consume at their own leisure. But one or two prefer to stay here."

Eric thought he'd find Patrick Norris here. Along with sizing up the operation itself, he'd been looking out for him, peering at the bright thrill seekers and the despairing addicts alike. The couple sharing a pipe had barely acknowledged him; the girl murmured something about how late it was getting, and her young man responded with an offer to take her home. The hollow-eyed man in the Army jacket didn't look up. A trio of university students—rugby players, by the look of them—offered Eric a rude gesture before slumping back down against one another. An elderly man, probably not actually so elderly as he looked, lay flat on his back and appeared barely alive. Eric began to sense a pattern: the thrill seekers came in groups; the true addicts came alone.

Norris was alone, at the back of the room. He was stretched out on a pallet, a loosened tourniquet dangling from one elbow. He was still in the same dinner clothes he'd had on at Aldershott's dinner party, but his shirt was clammy with sweat. A rank odour clung to him, and it seemed unlikely that any amount of laundering would get it out again. He moaned and sat up when Eric prodded him, but seemed otherwise quite insensible of the world around him.

"Mr. Norris is an old friend," Breuleux told Eric. "I haven't seen him in months. Then, after Thursday's show, he suddenly appeared and demanded a bottle of his usual poison. And now here he is."

After Thursday's show? Eric remembered that Norris had stepped away for a few minutes before meeting him again in the lobby to escort Penny home. Perhaps that was why Norris had suggested Brolly's in the first place. As for Breuleux, the fellow gave no sign of having seen Eric and Norris together that night. Perhaps he simply hadn't looked out into the auditorium.

Eric knelt down to examine Norris more closely. His breathing was shallow, but regular. There was a slight bluish tinge to his lips, and the constricted pupils of his eyes registered nothing. There was no laughter in them.

Eric said, "Has he been here all weekend?"

"Oh yes," Breuleux replied, unconcerned. "He's done that once or twice before."

"He needs to get home."

"I expect he will, eventually, but—"

"No." Eric rounded fiercely on Breuleux. "He needs to get home *now*. And I'm taking him there, like it or not."

"Now see here—"

But Eric had already pulled Norris to his feet. Norris gasped slightly and let out a moan that was more of a whispering sigh. "Sod off, Peterkin," he mumbled. There was a rumbling, deep in his chest, which took Eric a few seconds to recognise as a slow, marching dirge.

"I'm an armless, boneless, chickenless egg,
And I'll have to be put with a bowl out to beg,
Oh, Penny, ye hardly knew me!"

Eric hauled him to his feet. He wasn't quite so far gone that he had to actually be carried, but he still had to be half supported with the aid of one arm. With his free hand, Eric brandished his walking stick at Breuleux, who stepped back in alarm.

"Mr. Breuleux," Eric said, "I'm giving you an option. You can help me get this man to his club—no, to a doctor—and we'll say no more about this. Or we can do this the hard way. What will it be?"

The shock on Breuleux's face hardened into suspicion and fury. "You weren't here about managing the den at all, were you? You were here for him."

Eric was already halfway out of the room with Norris in tow.

"Frye!" Breuleux screamed. "Frye! Get up here!"

Eric dragged Norris out of the opulent antechamber and onto the dingy landing. Frye was already halfway up the stairs. Eric swung around, keeping his back to the wall, so that both the stairs and the entrance to the opium den were in front of him. His grip on the handle of his walking stick tightened. The shaft detached itself and clattered to the floor, revealing a gleaming blade.

Frye paused, then took another step up. Breuleux, white with rage, appeared at the doors.

Eric bared his teeth at them. "I know what you're thinking. You're thinking, sword stick or no, you can best me because I've got to deal with Mr. Patrick Norris here. You're thinking that even if I drop him, all you have to do is back off, then jump me when I go to pick him up again. Don't count on it. If I drop Norris, I know quite well that I can't pick him up again until I've dropped the both of you as well."

The gaze he levelled at Breuleux and Frye belonged not to a gentleman with a sword stick but to someone wielding a carbine, and the point of his blade was that of a bayonet caked in blood.

Somewhere in the back of Eric's mind, a beast born of mist and mud-spattered memory roared out for release.

"Frye," Breuleux said, fighting to keep his voice even, "go down to the street and summon a taxicab. Mr. Norris and Mr. Peterkin are leaving."

UNSEATED

IT WAS CLOSE on six when Eric strode into the Britannia Club after leaving Norris in the capable hands of a medical man he knew: a Dr. Filgrave, whose father and grandfather had practiced almost on the Peterkin family doorstep, but who himself now practiced in the heart of Lambeth, on the south side of the Thames.

Life was slowly coming back to the Britannia. From the dining room came the familiar, subdued clink of silverware, and a pair of elderly bachelors had paused to talk on the stair landing under the painting of the Arthurian Knights. The club wasn't quite up to full strength yet, but it wasn't so dead as it had been since the murder.

Eric noted none of this.

He gave Old Faithful a curt military nod as he marched by. Parker had lit a fire in his belly, and the sight of Norris at Brolly's had fanned it to blazing. Now it carried him forwards the way it carried him through the confrontation with Breuleux, and it sharpened his focus on the present. At the same time, it drew a shade over the images of Helen Benson lying dead in the hospital morgue and Patrick Norris's pinprick pupils. All he saw was his objective: the puppetmaster who pulled the strings, arranged the favours, and Got Things Done. Jacob Bradshaw.

Bradshaw was in his office with a copy of the *Sunday Express*, open to the crossword puzzle that was to be the first of a regular feature. He had the comfortable air of the freshly fed, and a hot cup of tea sat steaming by his elbow. He looked up with some surprise as Eric marched in and kicked the door shut behind him.

"Peterkin, what—"

"Who are you, Bradshaw?"

"I'm not sure I understand."

"Bradshaw knows people. Bradshaw Gets Things Done. Bradshaw pulls a string in Cornwall and half the bloody gentry in Northumberland jump off a bloody bridge. Too bloody right! But who are you really?"

"I don't care for your tone of voice, Peterkin. Now spit it out: What's got your back up?"

"I was at Brolly's an hour ago. Guess who I found there? Norris. And I think you know exactly what the circumstances were."

Bradshaw's brow came together in a frown. "Be quiet, Peterkin. You don't know what you're on about."

"And you do!" Eric said. "So explain it to me, Bradshaw. Norris was half dead when I found him. I think if I'd left it to tomorrow, he *would* be dead. But that would just go down in the papers as another 'accidental shooting,' wouldn't it?"

"Shut up, Peterkin!"

Bradshaw was standing now. His face was red, and Eric thought the man ready to explode. Eric clenched his jaw, ready to weather the storm. But in that moment, Bradshaw's face slackened and a sad warmth poured back into his brown eyes.

"Peterkin," Bradshaw said, "you know better than I do what the Great War was like. I wasn't there, but I heard it all from the boys I'd put into uniform and shipped over. My war was the Second Boer War. The men who came home from that . . . some of them turned to drink, and you understood that they'd seen and done things they wanted to forget but couldn't. But that was nothing like the trenches, was it? Did what you see match up in any way with anything your father ever told you about what to expect on the battlefield? Did it sound at all like Kipling?"

Bradshaw stared across the desk at Eric. The conflicting emotions continued to resolve themselves into an expression of sorrow and regret.

"I made him," the man who Got Things Done said. "I trained him and I taught him to hold a rifle and then I sent him out there. You're responsible for the things you make, Peterkin, and I made him—like a toymaker painting a set of toy soldiers, hoping against hope that they're sturdy enough to withstand a bit of punishment, that they don't get crushed underfoot or left out in the rain to rust. You find a broken soldier, and your heart breaks along with it."

"So you set him up to kill himself on morphine?"

"I kept him alive! You can't take all the rust off a toy soldier, but you can clean it up and paint it over, and you can set it aside where it'll be safe, and you can give it the special care it needs. As a boy, you'd only ever played at toy soldiers; you don't know what it is to make one, to build something up and see it destroyed in ways you never thought possible."

It was a frightening image: Father Christmas in his workshop, churning out toy soldiers for Flanders. What child reenact Ypres or Verdun with toy soldiers? Eric imagined a shell landing among the tidy formations of his childhood, and the gaily painted red-coated figures scattering in broken shards.

Bradshaw said, "I set Norris up with Breuleux because I know Breuleux and Breuleux knows me. Norris was still alive when you found him, wasn't he? Breuleux knows to take care of my men, and I depend on him for that. If a man's going to lose himself in a vice, better he do it where I can keep an eye on him."

The effort of explanation seemed to have drained Bradshaw of all energy. The old man dropped back into his chair, and Eric dared to venture forward. Age had put grey rings around the brown eyes looking back at Eric; they looked alien, as though Bradshaw had pupils within his pupils.

"The world was a different place when I was your age, Peterkin. Mustard gas! Chlorine! That's not how things used to work. This wasn't the war I set those boys up for." Bradshaw looked at Eric, and for the first time, Eric saw—not Father Christmas, not a stern drill sergeant, and not even an ancient reptile—just a tired old man. The white beard trembled, and a voice behind it whispered, "I just didn't want to see another old boy swinging from a rope or bleeding out over a pavement."

No. Nobody did. But Eric remembered the squalid mattress where he'd found Norris, and the rank odour of two-day-old sweat. He thought of the bright-eyed laughter dying behind the stultifying haze of morphine. He thought of his own men. The rage blazed up again.

"That is not how you handle an ex-serviceman's distress! Wrap them up in comforting vice? You'd given up on them!"

Bradshaw's eyes narrowed dangerously as his fury returned. "Peterkin—"

"You didn't 'set them aside'; you decided they were worthless and turned your back on them!"

"Peterkin!"

"And it's clear Norris wasn't the only one you ruined—"

"Lieutenant!"

Bradshaw had leapt to his feet. It was his turn to raise his voice, and he raised it in true drill sergeant fashion. It rang out like a gunshot and rattled the window. A porcelain tortoise, displaced by the excitement, finally fell off the edge and shattered on the floor. Eric, like countless soldiers before him, started back in silence.

"Bloody subalterns," Bradshaw growled. "You get a pip on your shoulder and you think you know everything. I've been doing this since before you were born. Don't you dare question my decisions."

"Aldershott cured Norris."

"He doesn't sound cured to me."

"No thanks to you! He'd have been fine, but you abandoned him to the likes of Breuleux, and look what happened!"

A second emotion joined the fury on Bradshaw's face. Resolution.

"Get out. Get out of my office and get out of this building. I brought you in, and I can take you out. Did you know that Aldershott stormed in here yesterday demanding to have you expelled?" Bradshaw swept his newspaper aside to reveal a letter of dismissal, already signed by Aldershott. The Britannia liked to be thorough about its membership records, and this document, once approved by the board, would be clipped to Eric's original application and the file closed forever. All it wanted was a second signature, which Bradshaw applied now with vicious strokes of his pen, and acknowledgment initials from the rest of the officers.

Eric stood frozen as Bradshaw waved the document in the air to dry the ink. "I think Saxon and Wolfe are in the dining room," Bradshaw said. "We can make this official tonight, and you can go home with all ties to your father's club cut and done with. You'd like that, wouldn't you?"

Eric's mouth felt suddenly dry. The rage that had carried him this far began to ebb. He said, "You need Norris's initials too."

"The purpose of acknowledgment is to say the motion won't be challenged. Just two out of the remaining three officers are needed for that, and even then it's more formality than necessity." Bradshaw strode around Eric, yanked open the door, and marched on out.

Following Bradshaw, Eric paused in the lobby to glance up the stairs to the painting on the landing of the Arthurian Knights. King Pellinore was still modelled on a Peterkin ancestor, and Sir Palomides was still a reminder that any man could be a knight. Eric's rage had been dampened. All he could think of was what his father would say.

Saxon and Wolfe were indeed in the dining room. Saxon was lounging in one corner with his feet up on the next chair, an apple in one hand and a Latin text open in his lap. Wolfe had just sent his dinner back for being overcooked and was waiting to be served again. He came over at Bradshaw's beckoning, eyes dancing at the prospect of drama. Saxon, engrossed in his book, didn't notice.

Wolfe took one look at the dismissal letter and turned to Eric. "My goodness, Peterkin. Ever the charmer, aren't you? What can you possibly have done to get Bradshaw, of all people, to second a motion of dismissal against you?"

Eric had too much pride to plead with either man, especially with everyone watching. He adopted a gruff attitude and said, "Do what you have to do, Wolfe. I don't care anymore."

"Don't you really?" Wolfe took the letter from Bradshaw, looked it over again, then handed it back. "No, I don't think I will. Spoil my fun? You must be joking."

"Are you challenging the motion, Wolfe?" Bradshaw barked.

"Don't be a bore, Bradshaw. Sunday evenings weren't made for official club business. Now, Peterkin, why don't you join me for dinner? They've overcooked the portions, but you'd eat anything, wouldn't you?" Wolfe grinned at Eric, pulled him close with an arm around the shoulder, and ruffled his hair.

There was a bang from the entry vestibule as someone slammed open the front doors. Inspector Horatio Parker strode into the Britannia and planted himself in the lobby, feet apart, face grim. He was flanked by a pair of burly constables who took a step forward as Eric and the others emerged from the dining room.

"Mr. Mortimer Wolfe," Parker said, "your presence is requested at the Yard. If you please?" Even as he spoke, Parker's eyes darted to the stairs and to the dining room doorway, where other members were trying and failing to hide their curiosity. Nobody wanted the indignity of being dragged away in handcuffs in front of everyone, but that, Parker intimated, was always an option.

The constables fell in on either side of Wolfe, who lit a cigarette with exaggerated calm, nodded to Parker, and strode out half a pace ahead of them. He paused at the doors to look back and give Eric and Bradshaw a mocking salute. His eyes rested on Eric. "It appears we're both hors de combat, eh, Peterkin? I wonder if you'd care to duplicate my exit."

Then the doors closed, and they were gone.

EMILY'S EFFECTS

A SLOW, WEAK DRIZZLE started just as Eric descended the steps to the Arabica. Looking back, he could see reflections beginning to form on the dark pavement, and the pinprick raindrops glittering around the haloes of the streetlamps. Above, the night sky was a solid charcoal grey, and the moon could not be seen.

Eric ducked inside the Arabica and shut the door, sealing himself in the too-warm, smoky atmosphere. It was thankfully quiet. Most of the usual Bohemian crowd had gone home to their Sunday roasts, but Avery, of course, was still ensconced in the back booth. Eric nodded to him in greeting and slid into the bench opposite, sideways with his feet up on the seat. He missed the side wings of his Usual Armchair.

"You look like something the cat would refuse to drag in," Avery commented. "Has the weekend really been that bad?"

Eric sighed. He lit up a cigarette. And then he poured out everything that had happened since they last spoke. Avery listened, wide-eyed, and began laying out a new reading around the Knight of Swords. Eric glared at it. Avery meant well, but Eric was growing heartily sick of the Knight of Swords.

"Parker told me," Eric said, "that Wolfe spent Thursday night—after Benson's funeral—at the Green Elephant inn in Chichester. That makes him the only suspect from Benson's murder to be on hand for the Sotheby Manor fire on Friday morning. I can imagine Wolfe wanting to kill Benson if he were Emily's secret lover and the father of her child, but I don't understand what any of that could have to do with Mrs. Benson's death. And now I'm getting the boot from the club. It's just a matter of time and paperwork."

"Ah, that's not so bad," said Avery. "You don't need those asses at the Britannia. You never have, and you never will. Bloodthirsty thugs in tailcoats! Personally, I'd be flattered by the rejection—"

Eric practically spat his cigarette across the table. "That's a damned shameful thing to say, Avery. Good or bad, the Empire still owes a debt to each and every man in the Britannia. That hasn't changed." The last inch of ash from his cigarette scattered over the Knight of Swords, and Eric flicked the spent stub aside. "And anyway, this isn't about *them*. This is about the Britannia and what it represents. It's about recognising generations of service to the Empire. It's about South Africa and Afghanistan and Crimea and Napoleon and 1812 and a dozen other skirmishes people never hear about." He paused, then continued, more quietly, "And *my* war. Ypres, the Somme, Gallipoli . . . there was a Peterkin at every single one of those. And always a Peterkin at the Britannia. Now that ends with me, and for what? I'm no closer to getting justice for anyone!"

Avery just gave him an incredulous look.

A shadow fell across the table. "Am I interrupting?"

Eric looked up to see Mrs. Aldershott standing outside the booth with a large carpetbag in her hands. He'd completely forgotten about their arrangement to meet here tonight. Seeing her reminded him unpleasantly of his last conversation with Aldershott, and everything that had come as a result. Then his eye fell on the carpetbag.

He hastened out of his seat to let Mrs. Aldershott in, introduced Avery to her, and went to join Avery on his side of the table.

"So you're Mrs. Aldershott," Avery said, gathering up his cards and searching for the Queen of Wands. "You're not quite what I expected. Would you like a reading?"

"A reading! Don't be ridiculous." She hauled the carpetbag onto the table, landing it right where Avery had just set down the Queen of Wands. "We haven't the time for games, Mr. Ferrett."

Avery reddened. "On second thought," he murmured, "you might be exactly what I expected."

Eric's world had narrowed to the bag, any clues within it now his sole hope for finding the killer—or killers.

"Edward kicked up a tremendous fuss when he found out what I was doing," Mrs. Aldershott said. "He forbade me to leave the house! Can you imagine? I told him we were not living in the Dark Ages and he had no business stopping me from going anywhere. I suppose he imagines this sort of thing would offend my delicate feminine sensibilities. What utter rot. I was a nurse, and nurses do not have 'delicate sensibilities,' feminine or otherwise. We have them surgically removed the day we get our certification."

She snapped open the carpetbag and began extracting its contents. A pair of notebooks tumbled onto the table: cheap, with cardboard covers, such as you might find at any stationer's anywhere. The first was filled with pages of writing, and the second, considerably more battered and dog-eared, seemed to contain the more practical, day-to-day matters of Emily's nursing duties. Avery picked up the first while Eric picked up the second, and both began browsing through.

Eric went right to the last written page of the notebook. This was actually from the nineteenth of July, the day before her disappearance. Emily's handwriting was neatly rounded and very upright: a mission school hand with no nonsense about it. There was a note there about meeting Saxon at the Hammer and Anvil for tea the next day; she'd fixed a medical appointment for the following week in Horsham; she'd found her lost hypodermic syringe again, and planned to keep it on her person in the future.

The next page had been torn out.

Meanwhile, Mrs. Aldershott had drawn an old portable camera and a thick envelope out of the bag. Eric raised his brows. Cameras were somewhat cheaper these days, and every Tom, Dick, and Harry seemed to have one to record the more ridiculous moments of their lives. But this model predated the War, and it seemed unlikely that Emily Ang, given her position, should have owned such a thing.

"It used to be my father's," Mrs. Aldershott explained. "He used it to take some really lovely shots of the Hokkien countryside where we lived before coming back to England. He gave it to me, and I gave it to Emily and told her to take pictures of life in England while I was gone, because I would miss it all dreadfully. She was as good as her word, too. The police took and developed all the film still in it when they investigated her disappearance. The pictures are in this envelope."

Eric abandoned the notebook in favour of the photographs. They slid smoothly out of the envelope and across the table, like Avery's Tarot cards in black-and-white. The photographs were almost universally of the patients and staff of the Sotheby Manor war hospital. There were a few of the dispensary, surgery, nursing offices, and patient rooms. There was one of Helen, radiant in a fresh VAD uniform, and Eric felt his heart constrict. She was posing in the dispensary with all her nursing paraphernalia, and looking very proud of herself. He wondered if the setting, emphasising Helen's occupation as a nurse, had been Emily's suggestion or Helen's.

Eric carefully set this photograph down on top of the envelope, where he could still see it as he shuffled through the others.

Here was a photograph of Jacob Bradshaw, seated by the bed of a soldier Eric didn't recognise. Bradshaw's beard was cut very short, but there was no mistaking the bonhomie radiating out from him. In one upper corner, Eric could see one of the chandeliers from the Sotheby Manor dining room; a desk was right underneath it, and other beds lined the walls. Bradshaw was smiling, but the focus was on how he held the hand of the patient, wrapped protectively in both his own. Emily approved of his visits, Eric thought, and Bradshaw's smile was as much for her as for the camera.

There was a series of unrelated photographs before Eric came to one of Patrick Norris, smiling as he leaned against the frame of an upstairs window. Was he already in the grip of his morphine addiction when this photograph was taken? The smile he presented to the camera was bright and joyful. Ivy curled at the edges of the window behind him, framing a panoramic view of Sotheby Manor spread out from wing to wing, a well-tended corner of a well-tended world. One would never have guessed the context of war and recovery from this—it was too much about the rightness of things.

The photographic paper used had been the cheapest available, but Eric realised that, despite being kept loose in an envelope, the images showed little sign of having been handled. He glanced up at Mrs. Aldershott. She seemed perfectly calm as she watched him, but something Helen had said sprang to mind, that "Some scars aren't visible."

Eric lowered his eyes to the next photograph. This was Mortimer Wolfe sitting up in bed, head held high with hands neatly folded on his lap. He had a corner bed. A wide mullioned window was behind him, and there was another on the adjacent wall: a pleasant situation with a lot of sunlight and a lovely view of the lawn behind the house. But his eyes seemed unusually pale, and his posture seemed stiff. This was more of a posed portrait, something taken only out of obligation. Was there some resentment or bad blood between Emily and Wolfe? Had Wolfe demanded the photograph, since she'd taken everyone else's? Wolfe's expression was grim; it had none of the supercilious urbanity with which Eric associated him. Perhaps this was Wolfe the killer.

The final photograph was of another familiar face: Inspector Horatio Parker, unscarred, sitting in a wicker garden chair out on the lawn. Edward Aldershott and Sir Andrew Sotheby stood behind him, along with a third man whom Eric deduced, from prior appearances among the photographs, to be an attending doctor. The focus was on Parker, who looked back as sternly as he would at an uncooperative suspect. Aldershott, above, was smiling a little smugly, but he was assuredly not the subject of Emily's photograph. Eric guessed that Parker had been a subject of interest to Emily, but that Aldershott was someone she could well do without.

Mrs. Aldershott drew a stationery case and large bundle of papers out of the bag next. "Now, here's her correspondence. I went through it all this morning; there doesn't seem to be much out of the ordinary. There are my own letters to her, and a couple from Oliver as well. The Army censors have been all over them."

Something in Mrs. Aldershott's voice made Eric look up. She was fingering the last of the letters with a sad, wistful look, no doubt reminiscing about happier times with her sister. Leaving her to her reverie, Eric put the photographs aside and began leafing through the letters.

Avery, who'd been quietly reading Emily's notebook all this while, began to chuckle. "I say, Eric, here's that story you told me about, the one involving Wolfe and the German patrol, that Norris told you over dinner. I don't think you ever mentioned that Parker was part of it."

"What? I didn't know he was. Let me see it."

Aldershott had talked about Norris taking over from Wolfe as his second in command—they were in the same regiment. But Parker's connection to them was news.

This notebook was filled with the same mission school handwriting Eric had seen in the other. Eric glanced through the pages and found detailed passages from war stories gathered from the soldiers passing through the hospital. He wondered what her interest in them had been, and for what purpose she had sought to so precisely record them.

The names that stared back at him on the page Avery marked were all too familiar. The story had been pieced together from accounts told to Emily by Norris, Parker, Aldershott, and Wolfe. According to the preceding note, Bradshaw had told her a rumour that Parker was being considered for the Victoria Cross, but she thought the others deserved just as much recognition for getting him out of no-man's-land after what he'd done.

Eric remembered no-man's-land, and could easily picture the scene: the smoke and the devastated landscape, the mud, the smell of falling ash, of rot, and of something burning. It stretched out in all directions. You could get turned around easy as anything out there, and wind up walking right into the enemy line.

The story began in the aftermath of a disastrous mission, though it was not so disastrous as it could have been. One soldier stood out head and shoulders above the rest in bravery, breaking up the onslaught with no concern for his own life. That was Sergeant Horatio Parker, and without him, the two companies attempting this stretch of no-man's-land might never have returned. They'd been beaten back from the ridge that was their objective by a superior defence, but they did have a few prisoners. Sergeant Parker was among the wounded, with at least three bullets in him, a gash from a bayonet, and a concussion.

They regrouped in the inadequate shelter of a muddy dip of the landscape, but everyone knew it was death to wait. Captain Aldershott took charge, sending the remnants of the company ahead with the prisoners they'd taken and the other wounded. He was to follow with Lieutenant Norris, supporting Sergeant Parker between them. They were out of ammunition, and the German rounds they'd recovered didn't fit their personal sidearms. Captain Wolfe armed each of them with a pistol taken from the German prisoners and began leading them back.

It wasn't long before the group had lost track of the men they'd sent ahead, and were stumbling through no-man's-land in what they could only hope was the right direction. Eric could imagine: desolation in every direction that wasn't obscured by smoke, and a distant shadow that may or may not have been the parapet of the British line. He himself had been lost in no-man's-land before; he wouldn't wish the experience on anyone.

Norris's account of Wolfe bluffing his way through a German patrol was there, albeit with the understanding that this wasn't so much a patrol as a detail of men sent to recover survivors from the battlefield. Norris had embellished the story with his version of Wolfe's bluff. Wolfe's own version was much longer and tenser, if less amusing.

Unfortunately, the next encounter did not go quite so well.

Aldershott, Norris, and Parker didn't speak German. They were trusting in Wolfe to get them through, and it was getting abundantly clear that it wasn't working. The three Germans of this recovery detail were moving to surround Wolfe, who began discreetly signalling to the others to leave him and save themselves.

That was when Norris, the only one with his right hand free, shot one of the Germans in the back. He got another in the head before the first had quite crumpled to the muddy ground. Wolfe tackled the third, eventually overpowering him.

Eric could smell the cordite from Norris's gun. He wondered about the face behind it. Had Norris been white with shock? Triumphant? Cocky? Had he simply been anxious to get moving again?

Parker had completely lost consciousness by now. They had to make haste. The British line became much more clearly discernible just as rifle fire began behind them. Wolfe scrambled over the parapet and helped to lift Parker in, and then Aldershott and Norris tumbled over to join him.

"That's how Parker got his Victoria Cross," Mrs. Aldershott said, her voice breaking through Eric's visions of barbed wire and sandbags. She'd been watching him read, and she knew the story. "That's also the first thing I learned about Edward, before I ever met him. He was the only one to come out of that unscathed, and he set the recommendation process in motion as soon as he had pen and paper to write it down. Norris was shot as he came over the parapet, and Wolfe collapsed on top of him. I don't know what the others did with their German pistols, but Edward has his mounted in his study like another trophy. You must have seen it."

"Why didn't you tell me Parker was in your husband's regiment?"

Mrs. Aldershott looked at him in surprise. "I thought you knew."

On the table, the photograph of Horatio Parker stared back up at them. At the time the picture had been taken, the recommendation for his Victoria Cross was probably winging its way up the ladder from the regiment's commanding officer to the king.

Aldershott's expression suggested that he knew exactly where it stood, but Parker himself, all unwitting, just stared at the camera, his expression wooden. Thinking back now to the dinner party, Eric understood that when Aldershott described Parker as "one of us," he hadn't simply meant that Parker was an ex-serviceman like them; he was referring to their shared experiences in the same regiment, and this one in particular.

Why hadn't anyone mentioned their connection to Parker? Could it really be that it had simply never come up in conversation? The alternative was that they were trying to keep Parker at arm's length. Could something have happened after this to estrange him from the rest?

Or perhaps they were hoping for special treatment, and didn't want anyone to realise the potential conflict of interest.

Frowning, Eric spread the photographs out again on the table. He stared at them for a minute. Then he gathered up the photographs and stared at them some more.

"I know that look," Avery said. "You've thought of something. You know who killed all those people, don't you?"

"No, not yet, not exactly, but I have an idea." Eric paused to shuffle through the photographs a third time. "Mrs. Aldershott, would it be all right if I held on to these four photographs? And this notebook, too?" He was tempted to ask for Helen's photograph as well, but perhaps it was better not to.

"Certainly. Just be careful not to damage them."

"This is all part of your great plan, isn't it?" asked Avery, watching avidly. "What's your next step?"

Eric smiled. He was, in fact, looking forward to reading the rest of Emily's collection of war stories. "I'll need to talk to Wolfe," he said at last. "And I'll need to talk to Parker. And I'll also need to talk to Saxon, who was the last person to see Emily alive . . . but I don't know if he'll want to speak to me." Saxon had made it quite clear on their last meeting that he did not want Eric pursuing the matter any further.

"Oh, is Oliver being contrary?" Mrs. Aldershott's lips twitched up into a determined smile. Somewhere, a recalcitrant patient was about to take his medicine. "Leave him to me. It's too late now to know where to find him, but first thing in the morning, we'll beard him in his office, and I'll teach him the meaning of gratitude."

Eric stood to help Mrs. Aldershott return Emily's belongings to the carpetbag. He said, "Gratitude? What do you mean?"

"I mean that it was your father who got him out of trouble when he came a hair's breadth away from a court martial. Didn't you know? Oliver spent the War breaking code for military intelligence, and bless him, he thought nothing of taking his work home to puzzle over in bed. All that top secret material lying around, and someone discovered that he also kept the key to his flat under his doormat. He claims he'd lose it otherwise."

Mrs. Aldershott snapped the carpetbag shut, shook Eric briskly by the hand, and departed.

THE KING OF COINS

"WE WERE THE POOR RELATIONS," Mrs. Aldershott told Eric as they made their way in the Peterkin Vauxhall the next morning to the grim industrial neighbourhood where Saxon's Hard Cider had its London office. "My particular branch of the family tree was quite prepared to fade away and be forgotten; we'd half forgotten that we were related to an earl already. I mean to say, it is generally not acceptable for the cousin of an earl to sully her hands with a career as a military nurse. The cousin of an earl should spend her life in idleness and, in the event of a war, join the VAD." Sarcasm dripped from her voice as she said this.

The warehouse was a soot-blackened brick building with wide, dirty windows, a corrugated tin roof, and nothing to recommend it architecturally. Lorries trundled into a walled work yard, laden down with crates of hard cider from the distillery in Somerset. More lorries trundled out again to take the cider, by land or by sea, to public houses across the country and some outside of it. A faded wooden sign over the door bore the name "Saxon's Hard Cider" in the same decorative script that graced the individual bottles.

The door to the administrative side, Eric noticed, had a combination lock instead of the more usual lock-and-key system.

Saxon's office looked out over the crowded warehouse. His desk was enormous, with a glass top somewhere underneath messy stacks of papers and a green blotter heavily stained with apple juice and ink. A cabinet in a corner contained bottles of cider, probably more for show than for use; a cabinet in the opposite corner contained various alternative specimens of alcohol and a pitcher of lemonade. Saxon himself was standing at his window with a half-eaten apple in one hand, and his brow darkened when he realised his cousin Mrs. Aldershott had brought Eric with her on the visit.

"Martha," he said, not taking his eyes from Eric, "what is the meaning of this?"

"Mr. Peterkin has some questions, Oliver, and you need to answer them."

"The hell I will!"

"The hell you won't!"

Eric suddenly had a mental image of Oliver Saxon and Mrs. Aldershott as children, the latter dragging the former along by the ear. It really looked as if that scene would play out again with them as adults. Saxon moved to put his desk between himself and his cousin, then growled at Eric, "Make it quick, Peterkin. As you can see, I'm a busy man. And put that bottle down."

Eric had been examining a display bottle commemorating the coronation of George V while waiting for the cousins to conclude their spat. Getting down to business, he said, "The day you met Emily in Chichester, Saxon, you drove her back to Sotheby Manor. I need to know exactly what happened afterwards."

"I drove her back, dropped her off, and drove back to London. I've already told you this."

"And we need to finish that conversation, Saxon. You told me that you'd had to go back to Sotheby Manor to retrieve a briefcase you'd left behind. That didn't happen to contain sensitive MI1b work, did it?"

Saxon's expression grew more sullen. "So what if it did?"

"I know some of it, but what else did you talk about? Did you meet anyone on the way back? Did you, perhaps, have cause to use that pen-release of yours on someone?"

"Tell him, Oliver." Mrs. Aldershott stood by the side of the desk, glaring down at Saxon.

Saxon looked mutinous.

"You'd just had tea at the Hammer and Anvil," Eric prompted. "You were talking about—"

"No!" Saxon shot a look of alarm at Mrs. Aldershott, who wasn't so dense as to miss it.

"What?" she said, looking from Saxon to Eric and back. "What aren't you telling me, Oliver?"

Saxon, sinking sullenly into his seat, mumbled something inaudible. Another prod from Mrs. Aldershott set him off: "She was pregnant, Martha. That's what we wound up discussing over tea, and what we fought about before making our way back. She was all set to . . . to get rid of it, and I told her not to even think about it."

Mrs. Aldershott sat down, more from surprise than shock. "So that was why she seemed so distressed in her last letter. Oh, Emily!" She stopped for a full minute to collect herself. "Oliver, why didn't you tell me? My feminine nerves, I suppose! I've been covered in someone else's blood while shells went off all around me, and you worry about my nerves! I can't believe . . ." She shook her head, her normal briskness returning. "Of course, we'd all have stood by her. That should go without saying. But if that's how you put it to her, I'm not surprised you fought. Did she tell you who the father was?"

Saxon shook his head. "I thought it was Benson. I don't know."

"It wasn't you, was it?"

"Martha!" Saxon looked both pained and scandalised.

"I know how much you liked her, and that's all I'm saying."

Eric cleared his throat. "Saxon, you were telling me about your return to Sotheby Manor with Emily."

Saxon glared, evidently holding Eric entirely responsible for his situation with his cousin. "Yes," he said with bad grace. "We didn't say much on the motor back. I was angry, and I wanted to cool off; and she needed to think. I remember escorting her to the side entrance. We talked about it again, with cooler heads this time. Emily was afraid of what would happen to her if she kept the child, and I assured her that the family would stand by her—I'd see to that. And I'd see to it that the cad who did this to her would pay for what he'd done."

Saxon clenched his jaw with remembered determination, and Mrs. Aldershott nodded. Eric almost felt sorry for anyone unlucky enough to be caught between the two of them.

"And that," Saxon continued, "was when Horatio Parker jumped out at us. He had my briefcase, and he accused us both of being German spies."

"Oliver!" Mrs. Aldershott exclaimed. "I never heard any of this!"

"What was there to tell? The man was clearly delusional. He had this mad look in his eyes, and he was baring his teeth at us like a dog. Emily was terrified. He called us spies, traitors, saboteurs . . . other words I wouldn't repeat in private, never mind in mixed company. When he started swinging a fireplace poker at us, I pushed Emily back and . . . and defended her." Saxon nodded, taking some grim pleasure in the memory. "We struggled, and I got the better of him in the end. We put him in the bed in the next room. Emily gave him a sedative and said she'd sit up with him until he could be moved back to his own bed."

"You cut him with your pen-release, didn't you?" Eric said. "That's how he got his scar. The photographs show that he came to Sotheby Manor without a scar, but the medical report Benson had suggests he did have one when he left."

"You knew that already, or you wouldn't have suggested it earlier. Fine. Yes. It was only a scratch, and Emily didn't think he'd need stitches. But he attacked me first. Getting him with the knife was what put him out, really. Shock, I expect. The last I saw of them, they were in that little room beside the vestibule, and she was patching him up with bandages."

"And you left her there?" Mrs. Aldershott's eyes were narrowed as she stalked to the side of the desk.

"He seemed peaceful," Saxon said obstinately.

"You left her alone with her killer!"

"She threw me out!" It was almost a shout, and Saxon had half risen from his seat. He looked at Eric. "I told you I should have offered to marry her. That was only half the truth: I did offer. I asked her there in the vestibule—I said I'd raise her child as my own. She thanked me very nicely, but she'd have none of it. She looked annoyed when I insisted. Annoyed! And then she told me to leave. She actually pushed me out the door and shut it in my face. All I could do was bang on it and . . . I don't know what I said. All sorts of things. I must have repeated the offer, or I must have demanded to know who the other man was. Maybe I did both. But the door stayed shut and there was nothing for it then but to turn around and go back to London like a beaten dog with my tail between my legs."

Mrs. Aldershott stared at him.

Saxon buried his head in his hands. "When I found out she'd gone, I never bothered to look for her because I thought she'd run off with . . . whoever it was. I assumed she didn't want to be found, and I respected that. It wasn't until Benson came to me about the Bruton Wood skeleton that I even thought things might have turned out differently after I left that day."

Mrs. Aldershott must surely have wanted to know what he meant by the Bruton Wood skeleton, but she went around the desk instead to kneel beside the chair and put her arm around him. Saxon melted into the embrace for a moment, then extricated himself, stood up, and went to look out the window. His pride would allow no tears to be shed. Mrs. Aldershott, wordlessly, went to stand at the window, watching him.

"You'd think," Saxon said softly, "she'd want to be rescued."

"She was her own woman," Mrs. Aldershott replied gently. "She might have needed help, but she didn't need rescuing."

"This isn't the world I signed up for, Martha. None of this is."

On the warehouse floor, workers scurried to organise the shipments of cider. They came and went at Saxon's direction, crates stacked in enigmatic patterns.

Eric let them be. His thoughts returned to the little room at Sotheby Manor with the cot and the desk. He imagined Emily Ang

there, putting bandages on Parker. Would Parker have willingly submitted to that, if he'd just accused her of espionage? Eric didn't think
so. Perhaps he really had succumbed to the sedative by the time
Saxon left . . . or perhaps he was in shock and only appeared peaceful. Eric imagined Parker starting to his feet in a blind rage, seizing
Emily and swinging her around at the metal bedstead. There was
the crunch of bone on metal, and she slipped to the floor, dead.

And then what? Might Parker have been fired up with enough
passion to overcome the effects of the sedative he'd just taken? He'd
have to be. The accepted history was that Benson buried the body
in Bruton Wood. This meant that Parker had had to enlist Benson's
help and transport the body there. In Eric's envisioning, the red rage
cleared from Parker's eyes as he realised what he'd done. He sat down
on the bed with blood still pouring down the side of his face, his
expression turning from horror to determination. He looked around
the scene, analysing it with a policeman's eye, noting the details that
would have to be changed to effect a proper misdirection. Then he
got up, pressed a bandage to his face, and went to find the people he
needed. After what he'd done in Flanders, there were at least three
men in the hospital who would lay down their lives for him.

It wasn't badly imagined, but Eric shook his head. He said to
Saxon, "Did you explain to Parker about your military intelligence
work?"

"I might have said something about it before I left. I don't quite
remember." Saxon frowned in thought. "He accused me of being a
German spy. I'd have told him I was nothing of the sort and to sod
off. I might have told him exactly what I was, but I don't remember."

"He must have seen all the cryptic work you had in your
briefcase."

"And understood it?" Saxon turned from the window to face
Eric and shrugged. "Maybe he did. Most of it was in German, which
might be enough for some, but I think a trained policeman would
want to be sure. What does it matter now?"

Eric thought he was beginning to see his way to a narrative without any holes. "Saxon," he said, "I'm going to want a little get-together with all the officers of the club—"

Saxon looked at him incredulously. "You do remember we're having you booted, don't you?"

"Oliver!" Mrs. Aldershott cried. "You've got to challenge the motion!"

"It's too late for that, Martha."

"Not if I have anything to say about it!"

But Eric put out a restraining hand. "Don't worry about me, Mrs. Aldershott. In fact, this might actually work to our advantage." He lifted his chin to face Saxon. "I want a chance to defend myself before the board makes their decision."

"You mean you want to beg." Saxon was unimpressed. "No Peterkin has begged for anything before, not even his life, or so I've been told. But I suppose there's a first time for everything."

"Oh," said Eric with a smile, "I don't plan to be the one doing the begging."

RECOVERY

LAMBETH, ON THE south side of the Thames, was a working-class neighbourhood much like Limehouse. Dr. Filgrave, with whom Eric had left Norris the night before, had an unremarkable though well-kept house in one of the more prosperous corners. The brick might be blackened from the factory soot, but the curtains in the windows were spotless. All around, housewives bustled about with the shopping and housework, while their children stayed out of their way. Here and there, an upstairs curtain twitched as elderly matrons watched the street with better care than a squad of policemen.

Eric stood a long while on Filgrave's doorstep, his eyes on the activity as a possible scenario for the crime played out in his mind. In it, Benson, wanting to find out more about Aldershott's doings, crept out of his room to break into the office. Norris heard him and followed him down. They met in the office, where Norris pocketed the letter opener as the nearest thing at hand, placated Benson with his natural charm, and lured him over to the vault. They were surprised to find the vault door open, and when Benson turned to see what damage Wolfe had done, Norris plunged the letter opener into his neck. Blood sprayed across the floor and the words *decorum est* as Benson crumpled.

Eric tore his mind away. No refuge: he pictured Saxon instead. Saxon slowed his motor as he reached Wexford Crossing, shame turning to fury on his face, then wrenched the wheel around and raced back to the manor. He marched back to the west wing entry, gravel scattering from under his shoes, to find the door still locked. His fury doubled; he fetched a crowbar, or some other tool from his motorcar, and waited for Emily to finish her chores and head back to the cottage where she'd been billeted. The moment she emerged, he lashed out at her. The crowbar met her skull with strangely little sound, and she fell, her body sliding across the gravel. With no witnesses, Saxon quickly gathered her up and carried her back to his motorcar to take her to a suitable hiding spot in Bruton Wood.

The door opened suddenly behind Eric, snapping him out of his reverie. He turned and nearly fell over a rotund little Roman Catholic priest, who peered up at him as though thoroughly befuddled by the encounter.

"My apologies," Eric said, moving to let the cleric pass. "My fault for lingering in doorways!"

"We often dwell too much on our perceived faults, I find," the priest said, before offering his own apologies and wandering off down the street.

Eric went inside. For some reason, he found himself thinking of Parker kneeling in his pew while the congregation at Benson's funeral trooped down for Communion.

Norris had been installed in the upstairs front room, in a comfortable armchair by the window overlooking the street. Filgrave had wrapped him up in a tartan blanket so that only his head and right hand were visible. His natural buoyancy hadn't quite returned; he looked barely animate—a broken toy soldier, Eric thought, remembering Bradshaw's words. Norris looked up and attempted a smile that quickly resolved back into a tired, irritable pout.

"I've you to thank for my present predicament," he said. "I ought to be grateful, or so I'm told. I hope you won't mind waiting for my thanks."

"How are you feeling, Norris?" Eric asked politely.

"Lousy. You know that perfectly well." Norris blew his nose on a sodden handkerchief and scowled at it. "Come back tomorrow. Or next week. I'm no fun right now."

If Emily's photograph of Norris was a picture of the rightness of things, the reality now was of the wrongness. Norris looked defeated. His shoulders slumped under the blanket, and his nose was red. He was barely recognisable as the cheerful rogue of one week ago who'd accosted Eric in the corridor wearing only a towel.

As he had with Bradshaw, Eric tried to picture the other faces of Norris. Norris the soldier, firing a pistol—the "Red 9" he remembered from Aldershott's study—into an enemy back. Norris the soldier was a bold fellow, swift to seize opportunities as they arose. Pragmatic, too, not shying from making an attack from behind. Eric imagined Benson sliding to the floor to reveal Norris standing behind him with the letter opener, blood splashed like the mud of Flanders across his sleeve and face. His expression was both grim and regretful: he'd only done what he had to do.

"What on earth are you looking at?" Norris said. "I'll bet there's something on my nose. There's always something on my nose." He blew it again. "You don't have to be so rude about it."

"I'm sorry," Eric said, blinking away the bloodied letter opener and the smoking Mauser. Norris, still bundled up with one hand tucked under the blanket, stared at him unhappily. "I was just wondering—" Eric began.

"What your sister sees in me? I wonder that myself."

Eric pulled up another chair and sat down, facing Norris with the light from the window spilling out between them. "We need to talk."

Norris rolled his eyes. "All right, Peterkin. If you really must. But get me a glass of something strong first. Your doctor friend must have a bottle of whisky stashed around here somewhere."

"I don't think that's wise, Norris."

"At this point, I'd drink rubbing alcohol," Norris muttered. He frowned at Eric, and then the words poured out. "I expect you must know the whole story by now—my so-called Italian tour and everything. But you do also know I never really intended to get back on the dope, don't you? I don't know why I suggested going to Brolly's that night. Tempting fate, I suppose. I wound up spending all the next morning on one of Breuleux's mattresses getting . . . reacquainted, and almost missed the appointment to meet Penny that afternoon. I wonder that she never noticed."

Eric stared at him, then sighed. "I was afraid of that," he murmured.

"That was the whole morning wasted," Norris continued earnestly. "I practically ran back to the Britannia to splash some water on myself and put on something decent for Penny. Old Faithful must have thought I'd spent the night with some lady friend—"

Eric held up a hand. He didn't want to hear any more.

"I realise I'm not much of a catch."

Eric turned his back on Norris's pitiful expression and leaned against the window, staring out into the street, where the schoolchildren of Lambeth were trooping back into their houses after a day of lessons. One or two had already been ejected again, to spend the last remaining hour or two of daylight out from under their mothers' feet.

"So what happens now?" Eric asked.

"Aldershott will probably think of something," Norris replied. "He always does. A sanatorium in the Swiss Alps, perhaps. That would be fun. Or look for a miracle at Lourdes—less fun, but for the French food and French 'demoiselles. It won't be the same, though. Strangers. Foreigners. I'll miss Benson, no doubt about it. I wonder if you understand what his murder did to me, Peterkin."

Eric looked around at Norris, who had his face buried in his handkerchief again. He hadn't shown much distress at Benson's death when it was first discovered, Eric thought. But then Eric himself had been dry-eyed at his father's funeral. Each in their own way was as much a master of the stiff upper lip as Wolfe.

"Tell me something, Norris," Eric said, pushing himself away from the window. "Saxon said you were helping Benson look into the matter of Emily Ang. What happened there? What do you know about his investigation?"

Norris made a face. "Straight to business, is it? You really are a bore. I can't imagine how a girl like Penny could be your sister. One of you must be adopted."

"Norris. I've had a rough few days. Don't make me take it out on you."

"Your doctor friend's whisky," Norris said firmly. "Or whatever else he's got that's like it. Get it. Now."

"Fine."

Eric felt Norris's eyes burning into his back as he left, and he pictured the Mauser beneath the tartan blanket. But no shots came, and Norris's eyes lit up with unholy delight as Eric returned with the bottle and a pair of glasses. Eric poured out a measure for Norris and thrust it into his hand.

"Ah," sighed Norris after a sip. "It's the cheap stuff, but that's where you get the heartbeat of the street, eh? The drink of the common people, Peterkin—sometimes it's sweeter than champagne."

"I didn't think you were a socialist, Norris."

"God, no. I just love the poetry of the idea." Norris swallowed the rest of his glass and held it up for more.

Eric held back the bottle and said, "You were going to tell me what you knew about Benson's investigation."

"Was I? There's actually not much to tell. Benson spoke to me first because we'd just spent three months under the same roof, and he thought he knew me best. He had an idea about claiming a skeleton somewhere that he thought was Emily. He didn't want Bradshaw's help, so I introduced him to Saxon instead and left them to it."

Eric poured another measure. "Why Saxon?"

"Why not?" A mischievous smile broke across Norris's face, and he almost looked his old self again. "Saxon's got all sorts of advantages he never thinks about, and he was Emily's cousin, besides. I thought it would be funny to take him out of himself for a bit. Give him something to think about that wasn't a dusty old thing by Cicero and an apple core."

"I begged this bottle off old Filgrave for that?"

Norris shrugged. "On the bright side, now you have whisky."

Eric poured out a measure for himself and knocked it back. When Norris held out his glass again, Eric shook his head. "You still owe me, Norris. So tell me something else: Why hasn't anyone mentioned that Parker was a sergeant in the same regiment where you, Aldershott, and Wolfe were officers?"

"How would I know? It just hasn't come up in conversation. Isn't that enough?"

"No."

"I don't know why Aldershott and Wolfe would keep mum. Now give."

"Bother Aldershott and Wolfe. Why haven't *you* mentioned it? He was a major part of that story you told at Aldershott's dinner party—"

"The hell he was!" Norris snapped. "I just wanted to show you all what a brilliant liar Wolfe can be when he puts his mind to it. Parker didn't come into it at all. Life's too short to remember the miserable pieces of the past, Peterkin. I choose to remember the happy, funny parts, and Parker wasn't one of them."

It didn't look as though Norris was remembering anything happy right now. Eric poured him another tot of whisky, and the momentary irritability faded again. The whisky brought colour back to his cheeks. He'd been popular with the nurses, Eric remembered.

Eric imagined Norris by the window again, this time meeting Emily Ang—a dashing soldier and an angelic nurse—and their hands clasping as they smiled into each other's eyes. Then later, Norris slipping into the dispensary to help himself to the morphine, overhearing the conversation between Saxon and Emily, realising that a pregnant Emily couldn't be so easily discarded—not with the Saxons of Bufferin behind her—and seizing the opportunity to be rid of her, just as he'd seized the opportunity to be rid of the German soldiers barring his way back to the British line.

"One last question, Norris. Were you and Emily Ang lovers?"

Norris choked on his whisky and fell into a coughing fit. Eric started forward to catch Norris's expression, but his eyes were screwed shut with the effort of recovery. Eric wondered if the fit was real or just a helpful prelude to further prevarication.

"Good heavens, Eric! Are you trying to murder him?"

Penny's voice cut through Norris's coughs with the clarity of a church bell, and Eric looked up in surprise. She was the last person he'd expected to see, but there she was in the doorway: pink cloche hat, red cardigan, grey pleated skirt, as neat as any military nurse. She kicked the door shut behind her and marched over with a sense of purpose that reminded Eric of Mrs. Aldershott brushing past the Britannia Club attendants, and began rubbing Norris's back.

"What are you doing here?" Eric asked her. "I thought you were going straight home after the Cambridge weekend party!"

"Filgrave sent me a wire. It got to me this morning just as I was about to set out for the station."

Norris, mostly recovered by now, said, "Thank goodness you're here, Penny. It's been just awful. Your brother's a monster. He's tried to shoot me in the head three times already. Thankfully, I have no brains to speak of."

"You are a ridiculous man," Penny told him. Their hands clasped as they smiled into each other's eyes. Then Penny straightened up, took off her cloche hat, and shook out her curls. "All right," she said. "I'm here. Now, what's the problem exactly? The message just said that Patch was here and I should come."

"Filgrave's blown things out of proportion," Eric said quickly. He glanced back at Norris, and his eye fell on the sodden handkerchief in his hand. "Norris has a nasty case of the flu, that's all."

"Ah, your brother's being a gentleman," Norris said, before Penny could express her disbelief. "In fact, he's just rescued me from a ghastly opium den. I'm damaged goods, I'm afraid—a slave to dope. You have no idea."

Norris met Eric's gaze with the sure but hollow eyes of an old roué. Then the whole story of his trouble with morphine came pouring out, and Penny's disbelief slowly gave way to astonishment and then to pity. Yes, Norris knew exactly what he was doing, thought Eric.

"You poor dear," Penny murmured as she gave Norris a sympathetic hug. Over her shoulder, Norris shot Eric a knowing wink. He certainly didn't seem to mind remembering the miserable bits if it meant wringing some feminine sympathy out of Penny.

"I did think you seemed strangely anxious that day at the zoo," Penny said, settling on the arm of Norris's armchair instead of in the seat Eric had vacated for her. "Now I know. And, Eric, how wonderful of you! Daddy would be proud. But this business about the morphine does sound serious."

"Unfortunately so," Norris replied. "You don't hate me for it, do you?"

"What a ridiculous, melodramatic thing to say! Of course not. You said you'd got over this once before, so I know you can do it again. This one little slip barely even counts. You just want someone to hold your hand through it all."

As the conversation turned back to an intimate exchange about Norris's trials and tribulations, Eric found himself more and more shunted into the position of a glowering chaperone.

"Eric," said Penny suddenly, "I don't suppose you could give Patch and me a few minutes of privacy? Only it's rather difficult to be as affectionate as one likes when one's brother is looming behind like a portent of doom."

Eric crossed his arms. "I don't think that's such a good idea."

"You see what I have to put up with," Norris told Penny, who let out a little huff of annoyance and got up to push Eric over to the door.

"I hope you're not suggesting that poor old Patch is a danger to me," she whispered. "He's just been through hell."

"We've all been through hell. And it's turned some of us into monsters."

"Well, if Patch turns out to be the monster you seem to think he is, he'll find that I can be a bit of a monster too. Don't worry about me, Eric. Go home." Behind Penny, Norris waited in his armchair, the jagged, broken edges of the toy soldier wrapped up in the tartan blanket.

"I need a few words with Filgrave," Eric lied. "I assume you're staying with Dottie Moffat as usual? I'll drive you there afterwards."

Penny rolled her eyes. "Fine," she said. Firmly, she pushed Eric out the door.

"Peterkin," Norris's voice rang out.

Eric stopped and looked back.

"I meant what I said about Benson," Norris told him. "I miss him."

THE MAGICIAN
BEHIND BARS

EVEN IN POLICE CUSTODY, Wolfe contrived to look impeccably groomed. He took his seat in the visitation room with the air of a royal dignitary granting an audience. The police constable watching from the corner seemed more his servant than his guard.

Wolfe arched one brow as Eric took a seat across from him. He drawled, "I wasn't expecting a visit from you, Peterkin. If you expect me to challenge the motion to expel you from the Britannia, you're clearly quite desperate. I am, to put it mildly, indisposed."

Eric remembered the austerity of the interview room in the Chichester police station. It was much the same here, and sitting on the other side of the table didn't make it any less so. The walls were drab and the lighting was stark; the one real spot of colour was the wine red of Wolfe's cravat.

"You don't seem remotely concerned," Eric remarked.

"I expect to be out of here soon enough. The case against me is preposterous."

"I wouldn't be so sure of that, Wolfe. Did I ever tell you why I started looking into Benson's murder in the first place? It's because I saw Parker pocketing a photograph of Emily Ang from Benson's room at the Britannia. He's not an impartial outsider—not that he ever was, but I don't think you can depend on any old regimental connections to tip the scales in your favour."

"Don't insult me, Peterkin." Wolfe put on an expression of exaggerated boredom. He made no note one way or another on Eric's reference to Parker's regimental connections; perhaps he really did think Eric had always known. "I don't depend on anyone. Unless it's a valet. I don't suppose you'd consider throwing a fist at my esteemed guard over there, would you?"

"And get myself thrown in a cell for assaulting a police officer? I've already done that." The policeman, who must have overheard Wolfe's suggestion, nevertheless remained motionless at his post.

"Have you, now?" Wolfe smiled, interested. "One generally avoids employing a valet with a police record, but these are difficult times."

"I didn't come here to interview for a position as your valet, Wolfe."

"Oh no? What did you come for, then?"

"Let me put this to you, Wolfe. Benson was killed because he was getting too close to the truth about Emily Ang's disappearance, and very likely Mrs. Benson was killed for the same reason. Emily Ang didn't just disappear—she was murdered. Her body was found buried in Bruton Wood two years ago. Parker was a patient of the hospital at the time of her murder, but his records have been doctored to show that he'd actually left a week earlier. I happen to know that Emily Ang was last seen in his company. What do you think that means?"

"It means you ought to be speaking to the counsel for my defence. I haven't had one appointed yet, so you'll simply have to wait." He smiled again. "Oh, this will be entertaining, Peterkin. I can't wait to see you in the witness stand, telling old Parker to sod off. Do me a favour and avoid mentioning this to Bradshaw, won't you? He'll just pull a string to have Parker reassigned, and there's no fun in that."

"I already have. And Bradshaw's chosen to throw his lot in with Parker."

"What?" Wolfe actually looked annoyed. "Because Parker's a VC, no doubt. How inconvenient. Aldershott—"

"You remember his reaction when I brought up Emily Ang at dinner that night. And consider this: If Emily Ang was murdered, someone had to have moved the body. Someone with a motorcar, like Aldershott, who's had his Austin since before the War." Eric paused to let this sink in. "I hope you're not expecting Saxon or Norris to come to your aid."

Wolfe was silent, frowning.

Eric leaned across the table towards him. "That's three people with everything to lose unless someone were put away for the murder before the truth can come out. I don't think I have to explain to you where you stand in this scheme."

Wolfe grimaced. He sat for a long time, thinking, and Eric let him. Finally, he said, "And you want to tell me you're my last hope, do you?"

"Yes, as a matter of fact." Taking a page from Wolfe's book, Eric cleaned and inspected his nails, as if this assertion were of no particular consequence to himself. When Wolfe snorted in derision, he glanced up and said, "Who are you, Wolfe? You're not *Lord* Oliver Saxon. You're not the president of the Britannia Club. You haven't got Parker's Victoria Cross, and you haven't a web of connections spanning the Empire. You're not one of Bradshaw's precious broken toy soldiers. You're . . . expendable."

Wolfe reddened. "And you're not?"

"Oh, I absolutely am. We're in the same boat, you and I. But you see, I'm on *this* side of the table."

"Do you expect me to beg, Peterkin?"

"No, Wolfe. I expect you to be sensible."

"Be a good boy and tell you everything I know, is that it? I could do that, but . . . I don't know." Wolfe watched Eric with narrowed eyes for a moment, then whispered, "You want me to help you, fine. But I want you to tell me why. Why do you care, Peterkin? What was Benson to you? I fought to keep him out of the Britannia, in case you've forgotten."

"Benson may not have fought, per se, but he saved a lot of lives as a stretcher-bearer. He deserved a lot better than a knife in his neck."

"And Emily Ang? Oh, I don't have to ask, do I? She was one of your people."

Eric kept his face impassive. "You don't strike down a lady and have her buried in a shallow, unmarked grave in the middle of the woods. That goes against all common decency, Wolfe. You don't sweep people under the carpet, whoever they are."

"How very high-minded of you!"

Eric sat up and placed his hands flat on the table. He said, "I'm safe where I am, Wolfe. And I could go on being safe, but I don't see anyone else here sticking their necks out for the Bensons or for Emily Ang. Or, come to that, for you."

Wolfe stared at him some more, then let out a low, appreciative chuckle. "Maybe so, Peterkin. Maybe so. In any case, only a fool turns away reinforcements." The smug, superior look faded away, leaving a focused earnestness in its place. This was Wolfe preparing for a new exploit, and his voice when he spoke was as crisp as if he were discussing battle plans. "All right, Peterkin. What do you need to know?"

"I need to know about the day Emily died. I think you were in the quarantine ward when it happened; I recognised it from the windows by your bed in a photograph Emily took. You were there for illness, not injury . . . something treated with morphine."

"Pneumonia. It put quite a damper on my social life, let me tell you. But this was all six years ago. What makes you think I'd remember a single blessed thing?"

"Did someone come to you at some point with a briefcase full of cryptic little notes, asking for your expertise in translating them?"

Wolfe's brow went up a fraction of an inch to show his unmitigated surprise. Something almost like admiration sparked in his eyes as well, and he said, "Clever, Peterkin! You really are surprisingly good at this. Yes. Parker did. But I thought you said Parker couldn't be trusted?"

"I want to know what happened."

Wolfe closed his eyes, remembering. "I recall being bored out of my mind. Parker showing up was a godsend, and even more so when I understood what he wanted help with. Very little of it was intelligible; most of it was nonsense. There were two documents that looked like German military orders—troop movements, attack plans, that sort of thing. Parker was sure he'd found a spy. That's when the beams of a motorcar's headlamps flashed through the window, and Parker got this look of alarm. He said, 'They're back,' and then he stuffed all the papers back into the briefcase. He caught up a fireplace poker and marched out as though he were preparing to confront the kaiser himself."

"What happened after that?"

Wolfe opened his eyes. "I don't know. Parker didn't come back."

Eric remembered the door to what had once been the quarantine ward, and later Helen's studio. It was thick enough to have shut out most of the confrontation between Saxon and Parker.

"I'd copied down one of the more puzzling bits from the briefcase," Wolfe continued. "I'd only just worked out that the numbers referred to Bible passages when the nurse came in to give me my morphine shot." He frowned. "Did you say it was the same day when that Ang woman disappeared? Because she was the nurse who came in. I remember that. She was in her civvies. I told her to give me an hour before the shot, and asked if there were a German Bible in the house."

"A German Bible?"

"Of course a German Bible, Peterkin. If these passages were part of a German message, it stands to reason that the key would be in a German Bible, wouldn't it? I remember twisting Matthew 10:39 into every permutation of German I could—"

Eric gave a start of recognition. Matthew 10:39 was the Bible reference inscribed on his father's gravestone, and Eric belatedly remembered that he'd meant to look it up. Avery would have called it an omen.

"'He that findeth his life shall lose it: and he that loseth his life for my sake shall find it,'" quoted Wolfe. "Don't look so surprised, Peterkin. My mother was a clergyman's daughter, with all the pious priggishness that entails. She made sure I and my siblings could rattle off reams of the Bible at the drop of a hat."

"I'm sorry. Did she come back? Emily, I mean."

"No. I was quite peeved about it. I didn't get my morphine shot until the next morning, and it's a good thing I didn't cough myself to death in the middle of the night."

Eric sat back, thinking. The story was getting clearer, and he could see the part played by each of the men involved. Each of them had contributed, some unwittingly, to the final tragedy, and each of them was reflected in the details surrounding it.

"Do you remember," Eric said, "anything about Emily's manner that evening?"

Wolfe shook his head. "I remember nothing out of the ordinary. She had that calm, brisk manner all nurses have—it's drilled into them, I swear. We spoke a bit about the Bible references I'd deciphered. She'd been raised by missionaries, apparently, and knew the faith better than most Englishwomen I know. She was even able to correct me on some of the passages I'd pulled up from memory."

Their eyes met across the table: just two men watching each other's back as they searched for a way out of no-man's-land.

"What do you plan to do with this information, Peterkin?"

"I'll want all the concerned parties in the same room when I put forth my idea of the truth," Eric said. "I've already told Saxon I want a hearing about this motion to expel me from the Britannia; that'll be as good a time as any."

Wolfe smirked. "Still on about that, are you? I don't blame you. But I'm still here behind bars, in case you've forgotten."

"Oh, I wouldn't worry about that. Bradshaw isn't the only one with a string or two he can pull."

DENOUEMENT

THE FIFTH OF NOVEMBER, Wednesday, was Bonfire Night. In 1605, Guy Fawkes was arrested for his part in a plot to blow up the Houses of Parliament; since then, he'd been burnt in effigy in an annual remembrance of the event.

Piles of wood and junk were going up everywhere for the bonfires. The hulking heaps loomed in the darkness, something primal and barbaric in their promise of festive destruction. There was one in the park not far from Eric's flat, and the Guys that had haunted the local streets over the past week were now converging there in their various carts and wagons, their hollow-eyed masks grinning emptily at their funeral pyres.

Gunpowder, treason, and plot. Only the first was figurative in his case, Eric thought as he set his jaw and climbed the front steps of the Britannia. Like Fawkes, there was no turning back for him.

The Britannia Club was nearly empty. Most members gave the excuse that they wished to spend Bonfire Night with their families, but in truth, they simply didn't care to brave the streets while fireworks were going off like shells and gunfire overhead. The staff had been reduced as well. Everyone knew it would be a slow night.

Eric nodded to Old Faithful, glanced up to the Arthurian Knights painting on the landing, saluted King Pellinore and Sir Palomides, then made his way to the back of the dining room.

There was a room here for private parties. It had a bow window looking out to the back of the building and was separated from the rest of the dining room by a pair of sliding doors. Eric had asked that the dining table be moved to one side, leaving the middle of the floor open. Chairs had been arranged here, in a semicircle under the chandelier, and Eric paced the parquet flooring before them.

The first to arrive was Bradshaw. He looked, unsmiling, at Eric's empty hands and said, "Not subjecting the silverware to idle scrutiny, Peterkin? You must be taking this seriously. I just hope you don't expect this to actually amount to anything."

"All I ask is your word that I be allowed to finish saying my piece."

Bradshaw peered at him suspiciously. "My word, is it?"

"For my father's sake."

Bradshaw considered, then shrugged. "As you wish. I give you my word. But there'll be no second chances, so don't waste it."

Aldershott arrived soon after. Mrs. Aldershott was with him— an irregularity, but Eric had asked her and she'd insisted, and Aldershott had submitted with bad grace. He simply sat down now and folded his arms in the attitude of one who has no intention of changing his mind. Mrs. Aldershott, meanwhile, gave Eric a sympathetic look before joining her husband.

Saxon was right behind them. He dropped an apple core into a nearby urn, wiped his mouth on his sleeve, and came up to Eric to say, in a low voice so the others didn't hear, "I hope you know what you're doing, Peterkin. This isn't really about your membership, is it?"

Eric shook his head.

"I didn't think so. Don't disgrace yourself." Saxon gave him a curt nod and went to sit beside Mrs. Aldershott.

Norris stumbled in a few minutes later. He'd been cleaned up and dressed, and brought to the doorstep of the Britannia in a taxicab. Thanks to Dr. Filgrave, he looked very much his old self again, and no one would have guessed he'd been anything else.

Looking with some disappointment at the bare dining table, Norris said, "This really is a sad state of affairs, Peterkin. I'll challenge this motion if you like—for Penny's sake, if nothing else—but I really thought you'd at least bring out the good wine to thank me for it."

"I still might, Norris."

Norris brightened up at that and sat down near the door to the serving pantry.

There was one empty chair left. "Are you expecting Wolfe?" Bradshaw asked. "You know he's in police custody at the moment."

The sliding doors parted with a whistle of oiled rollers, and Wolfe strode in. He lit a cigarette—milking the moment for all its dramatic potential—and said, "Honestly, Bradshaw, how long have I ever been detained in anyone's custody? It took a little longer this time, but these were *British* policemen."

Wolfe settled into his seat and gave Eric a regal nod. "All right, Peterkin," he said. "We're all here. Tell us why we shouldn't boot you like a public school football." He had to be aware of the curiosity his presence aroused, and he was revelling in it.

"Actually," Eric said, eyeing his audience, "I think I'd much rather solve a murder."

"Oh, for Christ's sake—" Aldershott sprang to his feet, only to be pulled down again by his wife.

"Language, Edward," she warned him. She was straight-backed and stern, like one of the formidable night-shift matrons Eric had seen at the Royal West Sussex Hospital. "And sit. I want to hear this."

"Martha, I don't even know why you insisted on being here." He looked around. "Are the rest of you going to stand for this?"

"I gave Peterkin my word I'd hear him out," Bradshaw said.

"I'd like to hear Peterkin out too," Saxon said, peering owlishly back at Aldershott.

"Yes," said Wolfe. "Do sit down, Aldershott. I didn't waste money on the cab fare here just to see you walk out."

"Fine, then." Aldershott sat down again, surlier than before. "Let's get this farce over with."

The doors were closed. The chandelier cast a circle of light around Eric, with the others sitting around its edge. It was time, thought Eric.

He cleared his throat. "Just under two weeks ago, Albert Benson walked into the Britannia Club as a new member. Up in the club lounge, he entered into a bet that Wolfe couldn't liberate the contents of his vault box. The next day, he was dead. Perhaps I'm being presumptuous, but after having it drilled into me that there have always been Peterkins at the Britannia, I got to feeling a certain responsibility for what goes on around here. And when I saw the investigating officer, Horatio Parker, removing key evidence from Benson's room, let us just say it did not fill me with the greatest confidence in the likelihood of our fellow member getting the justice and respect due to him as a human being."

Nobody leapt up to ask why he didn't report Parker to the authorities. They were all familiar enough with the story already.

"This is not a case of one murder, but three," Eric said. "Aside from Albert Benson, his wife, whom most of you might remember as Helen Sotheby, died of smoke inhalation last Friday when someone drugged her and left her in a burning room. And six years ago, a nurse by the name of Emily Ang was killed at Sotheby Manor, her body buried some distance away in Bruton Wood. The three are related. Benson was struck down because he was searching for the truth behind Emily's murder, and Mrs. Benson was killed because it was thought that her husband might have revealed something to her before he came here. So the real question is, who killed Emily?"

Saxon and Mrs. Aldershott exchanged glances. They knew this was coming, though it was hard to see if they were sitting up with trepidation or anticipation. Norris appeared a little bemused by developments; the others wore the stony expressions of men marching into battle.

"Benson knew that Emily hadn't simply disappeared; she'd died. And he knew that she'd been buried in a shallow grave in Bruton Wood. He knew this because he'd been the one to bury her."

"What?" exclaimed Mrs. Aldershott. "Impossible. If he'd done that, then why was he asking questions at all? Shouldn't he have known what happened?"

"I thought he might have felt guilty about something," Saxon said, "but . . . I don't understand."

Had Eric not been watching Aldershott, he would have missed the near-imperceptible frown Aldershott directed at Bradshaw. Eric nodded to Saxon and said, "He *thought* he knew, but then he found something to challenge his assumptions. So, what were his assumptions? What did he find that day six years ago, the day Emily Ang was last seen alive, having missed Helen Sotheby's party and vanished into thin air? Picture this: the nurses' station at Sotheby Manor. There's a small cot with a metal bedstead, and a desk against the wall. Emily Ang is lying on the floor, dead from two strong blows to the head, fracturing her skull in two places. And lying half out of the cot is Horatio Parker, unconscious and bleeding from a facial wound. The conclusion seems obvious: Parker attacked Emily, perhaps in a raging fit induced by shell shock, and was wounded in the face when she defended herself. He killed her, then lost consciousness. As for what caused that facial wound, there was a pair of surgical scissors nearby. Clearly, that had been Emily's weapon in her self-defence."

"That's utter rubbish," Saxon declared. "I told you—"

Eric waved him down. "We'll get to that, Saxon. Don't worry." He continued, "Benson did not make this discovery alone. Others were with him—others who decided they had to save Parker from the hangman's noose. Emily had been hit twice in the head; they couldn't disguise that as an accident. They had to make her disappear." He paused, and added, more conversationally, "Mrs. Aldershott said something quite interesting to me about this once. She said that the cruel thing about disappearances is that you never get to grieve until it's too late. That's how it's been for Emily's loved ones. And Emily herself? Benson went to Saxon in hopes that Saxon's social position might help in reclaiming her remains for a proper burial, but that's not such an easy thing to accomplish, is it?"

"Hundreds of thousands of soldiers were lost in the War," Aldershott said, sitting absolutely still. "Tens of thousands were never given the appropriate rites."

"That doesn't make it right."

Aldershott's mouth tightened into a hard, thin line. Beside him, Mrs. Aldershott wiped away a tear. Saxon, meanwhile, seemed ready to burst.

"Emily was dead," Eric said. "Nothing could bring her back. But Parker was alive. Parker was a hero in line for the Victoria Cross. He was a good man. This wasn't a conscious choice, and he couldn't be held responsible. Was it right that he should hang? The men who'd discovered the scene with Benson made a decision, and I think it was a difficult one. They chose the living." He looked at Aldershott. "You chose the living."

Aldershott looked back at him. His eyes were slits that gave away nothing, and his jaw remained bonded in place.

"You were there that day. You were friendly with Sir Andrew Sotheby and could obtain access to Parker's files. You had a motor-car with which to transport the body to Bruton Wood. And you owed Parker your life."

It was not an accusation. It was a statement of debts paid and of a choice between two evils. Aldershott met Eric's eyes, and remorse flickered behind the granite facade.

"Aldershott?" thundered Saxon.

"Edward?" Martha Aldershott's hoarse choke carried over Saxon's angry bellow.

"I owed Parker my life," Aldershott replied stiffly.

"What would you have done?" Bradshaw erupted. "He couldn't see Parker hang—*we* couldn't see Parker hang. Parker wasn't respon-sible, and he'd saved too many other lives to be doomed for the loss of one. Yes, I was there, and you're not to blame Aldershott for what we did. It was my idea." He was looking at Mrs. Aldershott as he said this; his words were for her benefit. Mrs. Aldershott looked away from her husband and set her eyes steadily forwards, at Eric.

"I know," said Eric. "But I also know what Benson had discovered: that the scene you found was staged. Parker didn't kill Emily. Covering up her murder has resulted in two things. First, Parker's lived for the past six years believing himself guilty, and paying his own price for a crime he didn't actually commit. Second, the actual killer got away free and has done two more murders."

Bradshaw said, "That's not possible. I know what I saw that day."

Eric turned to Saxon for the answer, and Saxon said, "Emily never stabbed anyone with those scissors, least of all Parker, and Parker never attacked her. He came at me with a poker, and I defended myself with this." He flicked open his pen-release. "I gave him that scar he's got now. Emily gave him a sedative, and the last I saw of them, she was getting ready to apply bandages."

Wolfe stared, fascinated, at Saxon. "So you were the spy! Parker showed me—"

"I was not a spy!" Saxon shouted, rounding angrily on Wolfe. "I was working for British military intelligence!"

Wolfe just smirked, and Saxon finally settled down, grumbling to himself.

Eric continued, "Benson had been sorting through Sir Andrew Sotheby's old files, and he realised that the report did not match what he thought he knew about it. The long, slim single blade of a knife leaves a very different sort of cut from the short, thick double blades of a pair of scissors. You wouldn't have thought he'd been wounded with the scissors unless there was blood on them, so how did that blood get there? It had to have been put there deliberately by someone intending to frame Parker. Was there supporting evidence for Parker's innocence? Had Benson continued in his investigations, he might have learnt that Emily made the rounds of the quarantine ward afterwards, and that she even stayed to discuss Bible passages with Wolfe." He turned to Mrs. Aldershott. "I ask you, would Emily, a trained nurse, leave Parker alone after he'd been violent, unless she were certain he was no longer a threat to himself or others?"

Mrs. Aldershott said, "She might, if it were absolutely unavoidable, but she'd stay on the alert. I certainly don't see her sitting down for a friendly chat with anyone." Her answer was almost mechanical, coolness prevailing over sentiment.

Eric nodded. "Exactly. So Parker was no longer a threat. The sedative had taken effect, and he was fast asleep. But he believed what he was told about Emily. He believed he'd killed her in a blackout induced by shell shock. When Benson came to the Britannia, it was not to expose Parker, but to clear his name—to save him from his burden of unwarranted guilt. That's why he collected the evidence he did and put it together in his vault box: the photograph showing Parker at Sotheby Manor on the day of Emily's disappearance; the medical report explaining the nature of his facial wound; the surgical scissors which were supposed to have inflicted that wound but were ill-designed to do so; and the hypodermic kit, whose significance we'll come to later. That's why he was hesitant about entering into the bet. That's why he decided at the last minute to spend the night in the club. And that's why he was murdered."

Eric looked around. The others were silent. He'd been worried about Aldershott and Bradshaw, but the prospect of clearing Parker's name seemed to have glued them to their seats.

"Benson's murder was less than a fortnight ago," Eric continued. "You know what happened. On Friday night, Wolfe made a bet that he'd be able to break into the vault and extract something from Benson's box. The next day, we found Benson in the vault with Aldershott's letter opener in his neck. Aldershott's office had been broken into and ransacked. I went up with Old Faithful to secure Benson's room, and here's what I found inside: the window open, and the covers thrown up on the near side of the bed. Benson had leapt out of bed on the far side, which is a narrow space of about a foot, to look out the window. He'd been concerned about the bet, and I think he left the window open, in spite of the temperature, because he guessed that Wolfe would attempt to enter via the back entrance, and he hoped to catch him at it. But, Wolfe, you'd been perfectly silent, hadn't you?"

"Of course. I'm insulted that you should even question it."

"I wondered, What could have awakened Benson and brought him down from his room? Then I remembered the open transom in Aldershott's office. Whoever broke open Aldershott's office door would have made some noise, and sound carries in the passage outside. It woke Benson up, and he hurried down, expecting to find Wolfe in the vault. He didn't happen to look into Aldershott's office as he passed, as that wasn't his objective, but whoever was in there saw Benson hurry past. This person snatched up the letter opener, followed Benson down to the vault, and stabbed him."

"So it was a burglar," Aldershott said. "Just as I surmised." He almost looked as though he approved.

"A burglar wouldn't have seen the need to follow Benson anywhere, Aldershott. This was someone who had a reason to want Benson dead, and a reason to break into your office. So the question is, what do you have in your office that someone would want to break in there for?"

"My papers, obviously." The near approval on Aldershott's face disappeared and was replaced by irritation. "They represent the investments of half the Britannia Club."

"Then why didn't this burglar make off with them once Benson was dead? When all is said and done, he made off with only one item: the hypodermic kit from Benson's box. Perhaps this was what he was after all along. If so, then the thing he wanted from your office was the memo containing the combination to the vault. As for the hypodermic kit, it was found later at Sotheby Manor, where it had been mangled and chucked into the heart of a fire. It was badly damaged, but not destroyed. Whatever its reason for being there, it ties the murders together: if Benson's killer had taken the kit from the vault, then Benson's killer was present at Sotheby Manor at the time of the fire, and was almost certainly responsible for Mrs. Benson's death. This person was therefore someone familiar with both the Britannia Club and with Sotheby Manor—familiar enough to know how to bypass the servants and convince Mrs. Benson to join them for a nice cup of tea in the office."

"That's nearly everyone in this room," Wolfe said, looking around. "I'd have washed Saxon out, but he's just admitted to having visited once with no one the wiser. Mrs. Aldershott?"

"I've never been to Sotheby Manor," Mrs. Aldershott said. "Emily always found some excuse when I visited Chichester."

"We need to consider the significance of that hypodermic kit," Eric said. "Unlike the other items in Benson's vault box, it doesn't seem to have ties to Parker. Instead, it's characterised by a distinctive monogram: a stylised S, like the one on Saxon's pen-release."

Two—at least two—chairs scraped back as their occupants stifled their reactions. Eric turned to one of them. "Mrs. Aldershott, your maiden name was Saxon. You passed a great many of your belongings on to Emily over the years, including, you mentioned, the tools of your trade. That hypodermic kit used to be yours."

"And I gave it to Emily, yes." Mrs. Aldershott grew pale. "I don't know how it wound up in Benson's possession, or in the fire at Sotheby Manor. The last time I saw it was before I went to Flanders for the War. That was nearly ten years ago."

"Those who worked with Emily at Sotheby Manor recognised it well enough. Benson must have. But others wouldn't have. Your husband certainly didn't; he'd kept it in his vault box for the last six months without realising what it was."

Aldershott frowned. "What are you talking about, Peterkin?"

"Old Faithful told me about a package wrapped in brown paper that you put in your vault box the day after you were elected club president, and which you never took out. That was the hypodermic kit, wasn't it? You'd forgotten about it until you decided to give your box to Benson, and then you gave the kit to him as well."

"Yes. So? It was a perfectly good hypodermic kit, and Benson had ideas of setting up Sotheby Manor as a rest home for addicts. He would have found it useful."

"Where did you get it?"

"I took it . . . I got it from Norris."

Norris, who'd been ignored up to now, sat up in the sudden attention.

"You confiscated it from Norris," Eric said, "six months ago, when you discovered he was in the grip of a morphine addiction. You said you discarded the empty morphine bottle and put the rest away—meaning the kit. Then you shipped Norris off to the Bensons at Sotheby Manor for a rest cure."

"The so-called Italian tour!" Wolfe exclaimed. "I knew there was something fishy about that story. Not much of the Neapolitan sun at Sotheby, is there?"

"We all make mistakes," Norris protested, embarrassed. "That's in the past, Peterkin. Honest. There's no need to go into it, is there?" His tone was pleading, and it was for more than just the story of his past addiction.

Eric said, "But if whoever killed Albert and Helen Benson had also killed Emily Ang, then the question before us is this: Why would anyone want Emily Ang dead? The only secret she had seems to have been a love affair, a secret lover who'd left her in the family way."

Of the people in the room with whom Eric had yet to discuss Emily's pregnancy, only Bradshaw showed surprise at the news. Wolfe, of course, would never allow himself to express something so gauche as surprise.

"Who was Emily's secret lover?" Eric held up a photograph. "This photograph shows Norris in an upstairs window, with Sotheby Manor spread out in the background. Not in the house itself, then, but on the grounds. The groundskeeper's cottage, in other words, which was reserved for nurses at the time, 'women only.' For Norris to have been there, he had to be let in by the person taking the photograph: Emily Ang. You were intimate with her, Norris."

"I get on quite well with most women," Norris said. "That's really no secret. Look, this isn't because I'm getting sweet on your sister, is it? Whatever happened with Emily happened a long time ago. It's not fair to hold these old mistakes against me."

"How did you come to possess Emily's hypodermic kit, Norris?"

"I . . . well, all right. I stole it. I'd got into the morphine, hadn't I? Having my own hypodermic was more useful than you can imagine."

"Oh, I've no doubt that you did. She did lose it for a time, but she wrote in her notebook the day before her death that she'd found it again. And it wasn't just a tool: it was a gift from her sister, and she had no plans to let it out of her sight again."

Norris stood up. "This is ridiculous! If Benson got the kit from Aldershott, why aren't you looking at him? He could have taken it from Emily himself."

"Norris! How dare you!" Aldershott's spectacles flashed angrily in the light of the chandelier. He turned back to Eric. "I took that kit from Norris. That is God's own truth, and I will swear to it on any number of Bibles."

Norris hesitated between sitting and running, and finally dropped into his seat again as Saxon moved to place himself in front of the sliding doors.

"I believe you, Aldershott," Eric said, "because Benson believed you. He knew you had no reason to lie. You could have taken anything from Emily after her death, and your possession of her kit would have been meaningless. Besides, I know you removed the photograph and the medical report from Benson's vault box before Wolfe got there that night. As far as you were concerned, that saved Parker from inquiry, and you'd got what you wanted. You had no reason to kill Benson after that."

Saxon was glaring at Norris, and Mrs. Aldershott had risen to do the same. Bradshaw was leaning forwards in his chair, massaging his forehead with one hand as he stared down at the herringbone parquet.

Eric turned to Norris and said, "The kit places you at the murder of Emily Ang. We all know you were right here in the Britannia when Benson was murdered. You were there for Mrs. Benson's murder too. While waiting for your train back, you popped into the Green Elephant, beside the Chichester station, and passed the time playing your own composition on the standing piano there. Wolfe heard it, and recognised it later when you played it at Aldershott's dinner party.

"I told you I'd heard it before," Wolfe said. But his face bore none of its usual smugness. It was as dead serious as everyone else's.

"You told me, quite insistently as I recall, that you'd spent that morning lost in a morphine-induced stupor at Brolly's. Why would you lie about where you were that morning," Eric asked Norris, "unless there were a worse reason for you to be in Chichester? Why bring it up at all?"

Norris shook his head wordlessly.

"You obtained a bottle of morphine after the music hall show we both attended on Thursday night, then made your way to Sotheby Manor by the earliest train you could. You called on Mrs. Benson, bypassing the servants by using the west wing entry. She didn't suspect a thing. You got her into the office on some pretext, drugged her tea with the morphine, then jumbled out anything you thought might incriminate you and set it on fire. When Penny remarked on your anxiety that afternoon, it was because you'd just done a murder, not because you were coming out of a morphine stupor."

"No," Norris said, finally finding his voice. It was hoarse, as though he'd never used it before. "I'm not a killer, Peterkin. You know me. Even if Emily and I were lovers—"

"I think you were afraid of being tied down by this new responsibility. It's no fun worrying about a family, is it? Or perhaps you may even have been afraid of what it could mean for you socially. People talk about how brave my parents were to cross the racial divide, but my father was a colonel with enough social status that gossip and calumny couldn't touch them. You didn't have that. And while artists and musicians often manage unconventional lifestyles, you still had your name to make at the time. You urged Emily to get rid of the baby, but she came back from her outing that Saturday determined to keep it after all. So you fought. When she turned away, you snatched up the poker and struck her in a rage. Twice. I think you regretted it immediately, but now you had a dead woman on your hands. What to do? There was Parker, asleep and dead to the world. All you had to do was drag him out of bed, remove his bandages, and tear out the final page of Emily's notebook where she'd noted down the administration of Parker's sedative. Now it looked as though he'd killed Emily in a fit of shell shock."

Norris said, "I did no such thing. The only people there were Benson, Aldershott, and Bradshaw. Look at them, not me."

Aldershott grew even colder towards him. He turned to Eric. "Go on, Peterkin. Let's hear the rest of it." Mrs. Aldershott nodded her agreement, her face as grim as her husband's.

"Norris knew Benson was looking into the matter of Emily's death, but he thought he was safe. Benson was focused, at the time, on clearing Parker. But on Friday night, Aldershott sat up late in his office, and he had company. There were two used glasses there the next morning. Aldershott, you were up with Norris, weren't you?"

"Aldershott—"

"If you're innocent, you'll have nothing to hide," roared Aldershott before turning to Eric. "Yes, Peterkin. I was up with Norris."

Eric asked, "And you talked about Benson and the bet?"

"Yes."

"Did you tell Norris about giving the hypodermic kit to Benson?"

"Yes. I didn't think anything of it."

Eric nodded. "And from that moment, Norris knew he had to get the kit out of Benson's vault box. A poker might be sufficient to pry open the box compartment, or so he hoped, but he needed the combination to the vault door. After Aldershott left the office, Norris waited a bit to be sure no one was about, then broke in to find it. And the rest we already know."

The silence was absolute. Norris straightened up in his seat. The look he gave Eric was calm and devoid of his usual humour. He stood up, straighter than Eric had seen before, and said, "That's all very entertaining, provided you're not the one being accused of murder here. And what have you got, really? Words! Wild conjecture!"

"It's enough to get the police to start looking in the right places," Eric said, "once I speak to them in the morning and show them what I have." He held up an envelope that bulged in the middle with something hard and metallic. "This is Saxon's key, which he used to keep hidden behind a loose brick over a window by the back door."

"My key." Saxon started forward, his eyes blazing. Eric took a step back from him, but his rage was directed at Norris. "My key? You used my key to do all this?"

Wolfe stood up. "Steady on, old man, you don't want—"

Saxon launched himself at Norris, and Wolfe was only just able to pull him back in time. Bradshaw stood up as well, and helped Wolfe wrestle Saxon down into a chair. Saxon glared, then spat on the carpet. "I'll see him hanged," he muttered. "Hanged!"

Norris returned his gaze steadily, his eyes bright.

Eric said to him, "Norris, you told me once about being awakened by someone rattling the dustbins outside the window at the Britannia. I think you looked out and saw it was Saxon retrieving or returning his key. Wolfe did exactly the same. That came in useful when you had to leave in secret to dispose of your bloodied clothing and the hypodermic kit. I wonder, though, if you remembered to wipe it off, or if you even thought it might be considered evidence."

Norris turned to face him. His face was pale and his jaw was clenched.

"I don't think you were really thinking straight that night, Norris. You left the letter opener behind; I think the vault door closed before you could think to retrieve it or clean it, and the only reason the police haven't arrested you already was because, as a board officer, there was every possibility that you might have handled it quite innocently before. But there are dozens of other little points you may have overlooked, and the police, once they know to focus on you, are sure to find them."

Norris said, "You hope! You have nothing. The only thing we've really learnt here tonight is that Aldershott and Bradshaw conspired to hide a murder. Martha, my dear, I'd look for a good solicitor if I were you. I can't imagine that being married to our Captain Aldershott was ever much fun to begin with. And now? Well, I wasn't the one who took your sister away from you. I'm not the villain of this story—that much is certain. Bradshaw . . . I'd ask if you really believed all this nonsense, but given your part in this, I expect the point is moot." He turned to Wolfe, who avoided his gaze, and Saxon, who met it fiercely. There was no sympathy either way, and he sniffed in disdain. "You lot should be ashamed of yourselves. Good luck, Peterkin. Maybe if you had a policeman in charge who wasn't the likely killer, he'd tell you to go to hell. I thought you were my friend, but I guess I was mistaken."

He opened the doors and stalked out.

THE FINAL JOUST

IT WAS ALMOST an hour's walk from the Britannia Club to the flat that Eric called home. He usually enjoyed the journey for the exertion and the sights, but tonight it was fraught with anxiety and unease. Little of the Bonfire Night festivities could be seen along the majority of his route; the pyres were far off in the distance, hidden behind the dark, towering walls that rose up on either side of the street. They sent up sparks into the black night, and columns of smoke, and they cast an orange glow on the low clouds above. From Eric's vantage point, this evidence of distant fires reminded him of Flanders, and it would not surprise him if the silent buildings around him could be peeled back, like the veneers of civility he knew them to be, to reveal the devastation of no-man's-land behind.

The streets were empty now. Most people had gone to take part in the festivities, and Eric was alone. He walked slowly. He had no idea where Norris had gone after leaving the Britannia Club, but he was well aware that he'd made a target of himself. If Norris were of a mind to stop him, now would be the time.

At the boundary of St. James, Eric stopped to peer back down the street behind him. Eric thought he saw an elusive shadow that may or may not have been a figure following behind. It was hard to be sure in the hazy, blurry night.

Eric turned and kept walking. The fog was getting thick. Tendrils of moisture chased about his ankles as he swept onwards. The murkiness muffled his footsteps and those of anyone behind him. His unease grew as he began to wonder if he was marked by friend or by foe.

The first firework went off as Eric drew within sight of home. A Roman candle, the opening shot in what would soon become a barrage of back-and-forth, soared over Battersea Park and scattered shards of gold on the Thames. It was answered by a salvo of rockets from somewhere near Notting Hill, and another from Ealing Common. Victoria Park sent up a burst of glitter that shot across the night before floating softly back to earth.

Eric hadn't expected to make it this far back unmolested, but here he was. The figure he thought had been following him since he left St. James was nowhere in sight. Eric waited and listened, but could hear only distant merrymaking and, now, faraway explosions. He heaved a sigh, opened the door, and went up to his flat.

Something was wrong.

A flickering glow spilled forth from the sitting room doorway onto the entry hall floor. It was accompanied by the crackle of a fire, and the metallic scrape of a poker working the wood into a blaze. Eric quietly shut the door behind him, then trod silently towards the sitting room.

This was a square room overlooking the street. Eric had a pair of armchairs drawn up to the fireplace, a cosy mirror of his usual corner at the Britannia. Penny was bending over the fireplace, poking at a freshly made fire, and Eric breathed a sigh of relief when he saw it was her. "Penny," he said. "I wasn't expecting—"

The words died on his lips as she gave a start and turned, white-faced and wide-eyed, to face him. Her eyes were dry, but a faint redness about them suggested that they hadn't been dry for long.

"You've been taking your time, Peterkin."

The voice, uneven, came from the armchairs. Norris was sitting in the far chair, just out of sight until one actually entered the room. The light from the fireplace cast an unsteady ruddy glow on his features. It made an island of wavering light around the scene, cut through with long shadows that melted into the shadows on the peripheries. Beyond, the window onto the dark street reflected the similarly wavering glow of fireworks as they blossomed and faded in the night. Norris held the "Red 9" Mauser in his lap, the firelight playing over the flat square of the built-in box magazine. The broom handle, with the characteristic red 9 burnt into it, was obscured in Norris's hand, and the long, slender barrel seemed almost too delicate for its purposes. The earlier indignation had faded from Norris's face, leaving only regret and sorrow.

Norris gestured at Penny with the Mauser, and she sat down quickly in the opposite armchair. "Patch came by Dottie's not half an hour ago," she said, her voice trembling. "He told me it was urgent, that we needed to find you. I brought him here, and then—"

"And then I took out the gun and told her to make a fire and wait." Norris smiled, and for the first time since Eric had known him, the smile didn't reach his eyes. "The miracle of motorcars, Peterkin! I was able to get back to Brolly's to retrieve my briefcase—and this pistol—then look up Penny, and then make it here, all in the time it took you to walk. That's the modern age for you. One of these days, half the families in England will have their own motorcar, and I wonder what that will do to our beloved English country roads."

"Why are you here, Norris?" Eric asked, though he thought he already knew.

Their eyes met. "I had to tie up a loose end or two," Norris replied.

The slender barrel remained trained on Penny. "Penny isn't part of this," Eric said. "Let her go."

Norris ignored him. He glanced at the window and said, "I'm not a complete idiot. I know what they say about me at the Britannia: Norris only knows how to have fun; Norris can't hold an idea for more than two minutes unless it involves wine, women, and song in some combination or other. And I don't mind. I rather enjoy the reputation, in fact. I'm not a great planner—never have been—but I am capable of putting two and two together when the need arises. For instance, I'm pretty certain you've already spoken to Parker and told him exactly what you told us. That's why Wolfe was released. Which means that Parker and his men have been watching you from the moment you left the Britannia Club. You never really expected to find my prints on Saxon's key, did you? It was a ploy to get me to make some sort of move against you and seal the case against me."

"Eric!" Penny exclaimed. "Were you asking to be killed?"

"Your brother's an uncommonly brave little soldier, Penny. Why do you think I've been pointing this gun at you and not at him? He'd charge me the minute he thought the only life at stake was his own. He remembered that I'd tried to shoot him once before, and he thought I'd try again."

"Once before! When?"

"Last Friday night," Norris said, his tone as light as though he were discussing a summer holiday. Penny's knuckles whitened on the arms of her chair. "The fog made it hard to see, and then Saxon interfered. I could have pursued you, though, Peterkin. Dodged around Mayfair, finally caught up with you on Piccadilly . . . or maybe made a second attempt the next day. Do you know why I didn't?"

Eric shook his head.

"I don't like to remember the miserable bits. And I realised I was reliving one of the more miserable bits right then and there, and why? What had my life become, that I was dodging around in the fog with a gun while all the normal people were at home with their after-dinner drinks, or playing darts in the pub, or singing along with a music hall act? That's not who I am, Peterkin. That's not who I wanted to be."

Outside, a quick succession of Roman candles rattled the window like a machine-gun salvo and cast a ruddy glow on the sill. Both Peterkins flinched, but the Mauser remained silent.

"After I'd got well and truly lost in the fog," Norris said, "I sat down and coughed my lungs out. The London fog is like poison gas, Peterkin. I wonder that more of the Britannia gentlemen don't remark on it. I went straight back to Breuleux, and you know the rest. Almost. I woke up in your doctor friend's bed on Monday realising that nothing had changed at all. It's just got worse. I was trapped in one of Helen Benson's infernal paintings, and there was no way out."

"Norris—"

"You saw how the others looked at me. I'm finished at the Britannia. Even if the police don't get me, you've won. Do you understand? You've won . . . You'd already won six years ago."

Eric said, "In that case, then why—?"

Norris shrugged. "I told you. I had to tie up a loose end or two." His eyes slid sadly to Penny, who shifted nervously. Norris considered her for a minute, then said, "You're a bit like Emily, you know. I don't mean the Chinese blood; it looks like your brother's had the lion's share of it, and I wouldn't have known that about you but for him. I mean that you have this fascination with the world that's simply irrepressible. Did you know Emily used to collect the stories of the soldiers who passed through the hospital? In spite of how she was treated there, as long as she had that interest in others, nothing could get her down."

Penny was staring at the pistol. She asked, more for the sake of talking than anything else, "What happened to Emily?"

"It was an accident," Norris replied. "I'd overheard Saxon's promises to her, and I was afraid. I was fond of her, but not so fond that I wanted to be tied down just yet. I thought we'd be able to go our own separate ways afterwards—I certainly had no intention of ever seeing Sotheby Manor again. I . . . I pulled her to me in the heat of the moment, and she fell and hit her head. I panicked." He looked at Penny and added, "I'm sorry."

"She fell and hit her head," Eric echoed. "Twice."

Norris winced. "I thought this made a better story. All right. I panicked first, and then I . . . You know what, I don't want to think about it. I went a little mad, and let's leave it at that. It was awful. And then I saw Parker lying there, and I thought, there's a way out of this mess. I didn't realise then that I was only getting deeper into it."

"But you took her hypodermic kit."

"It was just sitting there, on the little desk. I thought it would be useful. I had a habit to feed, as you might recall. Or maybe it was sentiment." Norris paused, thinking—remembering. "I wish I'd never taken it. When Benson started asking questions . . ." The Mauser began to lower, as if the massive box magazine were growing too heavy to lift, but sprang up again as Eric took a step forwards. Norris shook his head at him, and continued, "Benson was a loose end. I couldn't have him talking to Aldershott and Bradshaw about what he thought had happened to Emily. I was worried enough when he spoke to me about his belief that Parker was innocent after all, but I told myself not to worry. Nothing would come of it. I tried to get away. I pointed him at Saxon and washed my hands of his so-called investigation. Then Saxon got the bright idea of bringing him into the Britannia. You know what happened after that: Aldershott wanted company while he waited. I didn't know why, at the time. He told me about giving the hypodermic kit to Benson, and I knew I had to do something."

Norris scowled into the fire, and the light flickered across his face. The barrel of the Mauser blended in and out of the shadows.

"That damned kit," he growled. "I knew Benson must have recognised it. I went as soon as I was sure it was safe, but Wolfe beat me there. I was lucky that he'd chosen to take the scissors instead of the kit. He'd left the vault door open, and if I'd known that, I'd never have bothered trying to get into Aldershott's office . . . and I wouldn't have had the letter opener on me when I saw Benson hurrying to the vault."

An especially loud explosion of fireworks went off outside, amid the cheers of the Bonfire Night revellers. Eric winced.

Norris glanced down at the Mauser and chuckled. "Nearly thought I'd pulled the trigger there." He waited for the noise to die down before continuing. "I actually rather liked Benson, you know. But it was him or me, just as it was with Parker six years ago.

Maybe I was a bit mad. Maybe I'd had too much of Aldershott's brandy while sitting up with him. I don't know. I remember creeping down to the vault after Benson. I found him peering into the empty compartment as though he expected to find Wolfe in there, and he didn't hear me until I got to the vault door. The look he gave me, Peterkin. He knew. He came at me, but I dodged quite easily. Conscientious objectors! No one ever teaches them how to fight. I caught him by the hair as he hurtled past, and—" Norris made a gesture, the barrel of his Mauser sweeping the room. "And then I ran."

Eric cleared his throat. It felt unusually dry. "I expect it was the same with Mrs. Benson, wasn't it? I hold myself responsible there. If I hadn't gone on about having talked to her, and the possibility she might know more about what Benson had been doing, you might not have thought of her as a threat. She might still be alive."

A scowl flitted through Norris's sadness. "It wasn't difficult to decide she was another loose end to be got out of the way, you know. Oh, I liked her well enough at first; but as the years passed by and this . . . slavery to morphine dogged me wherever I went, I began to understand. It was her fault. Hers and her father's and . . . and Emily's, too. If Emily had lived, I'm sure I'd have grown to loathe her for what she'd done. All that morphine to kill the pain of surgery, and then more morphine to kill the pain of not having morphine. The only thing keeping me going was the company at the Britannia Club—that and regular visits to the upstairs room at Brolly's. When Aldershott sent me back to Sotheby Manor, I was surprised at my anger. I told myself it was the morphine. It made me irritable. Well, Benson got me off the stuff, but the anger didn't go away. I was never made to hate people, Peterkin, and I think she knew that. The War did that to me. Morphine did that to me. She did that to me."

"That's not fair—"

"Don't tell me what's fair!" Norris snapped. The Mauser trembled in his hands, and Penny shrank back into her armchair, afraid. Eric bit his tongue. Norris's feelings ran even deeper than his words suggested. "Angels of mercy? Angels of death! They murdered me, Peterkin. Bradshaw may have started it by putting me in a uniform and sending me out there to shoot men in the back, but they—Helen and Emily and the rest—they murdered me. I think I may have just begun to realise that when I killed Emily, in my heart if not in my head, and that's how I was able to do it at all. And later, when it was Helen Benson's turn, knowing it made things so much easier."

"When you drugged her and left her to burn, you mean?" Eric felt a surge of anger at the thought, but he suppressed it. He did not want to startle Norris into doing anything he might regret. Penny already looked sick to her stomach.

"You were wrong there, you know. At least, you were wrong in pretending that I drugged her surreptitiously, without her knowledge. No. I held this gun to her head and made her drink the morphine straight out of the bottle. If she had to go for knowing too much, she might as well go in poetic style." He stopped, then said, "I was about to leave when I felt the case of that hypodermic kit in my pocket, and I realised it was . . . it was the chorus of the song. Do you understand what I mean? I got it when I killed Emily, I killed Benson because of it, and for the song to end, I had to get rid of it along with Helen Benson. I smashed the syringe and threw the case on the fire. I thought it would free me, but there was nothing left to free."

Penny looked away.

Norris looked at her, a genuine smile softening his eyes. "Ah, Penny. You don't hate me for this, do you?"

"I—" Penny's eyes flickered to the Mauser. "Of course not."

Norris chuckled. He got up, moved to the window, and sat on the sill. "Liar. Well, it's no matter to me. I'm done with being angry and fearful. There's still a lot that's beautiful in this world. I wish I could enjoy it." He looked at Penny. "I hope you do enjoy it. It's yours now, the world your brother and I fought and died for."

"Died for?" Penny echoed, glancing at Eric. "What do you mean, died for?"

"I'm not the Norris you should have met," Norris said. "That Norris died somewhere between Flanders and Sotheby Manor. I just needed you to understand that, the last loose end in this tangle. Think of what might have been! But that's done now. What's the use of worrying?" Norris opened the window, and the cold November air blew in, carrying with it the smoke of the bonfires. A gang of local youths was singing.

"Pack up your troubles in your old kit bag;
And smile, smile, smile . . ."

"Ah, there's Parker watching the flat from the pavement opposite," Norris remarked. "I'm sorry, Parker! For everything!"

"While you've a lucifer to light your fag,
Smile, boys, that's the style!"

Norris joined in with a ringing tenor: *"What's the use of worrying?*
It never was worthwhile!

So! Pack up your troubles in your old kit bag—"

He raised the slender barrel of his pistol. *"And smile—"*

"Norris! Don't!"

"Smile—"

A glittering waterfall exploded overhead, drowning out the final word. Scarlet and gold cascaded down the sky, and Penny leapt to her feet with a shriek that silenced the singers outside. Eric leapt forward to catch her in his arms. Norris toppled out the window and fell to the street below.

Penny struggled to go to the window, and Eric held her back. "Don't," he told her. "It won't be pretty." He remembered the suicide of another fine, funny fellow, brains and blood soaking into the parapet sandbags.

"I have to see," Penny sobbed. "Let me go, damn it! I need to see!"

Reluctantly, Eric went to the window with her. Coloured light showered down from above onto the dark woodblock street where Lieutenant Patrick Norris lay in a crumpled heap. The impact had blown an island in the low fog, and it swirled around him where he lay. The fog parted as Detective Inspector Horatio Parker swept through, misty tendrils sliding off his trench coat, to kneel beside the body. Parker checked quickly for a pulse, though both he and Eric knew full well there would be none. He looked up and met Eric's eyes, his face as grim as the day they'd met.

AFTERMATH

ARMISTICE DAY, the eleventh of November, began with rain in the early morning that darkened the pavements, but the clouds cleared before midmorning. A magnificent cornflower-blue sky arched above and was reflected in the puddles below.

Eric joined the sombre crowds at the Cenotaph on Whitehall for the service in remembrance of the War at eleven o'clock—the eleventh hour of the eleventh day of the eleventh month. It began with two minutes of silence: one for the fallen, and one for the survivors. After that would come wreaths and remembrances and men marching by with grim salutes . . . boots on rain-glossed pavements, artificial poppies blooming blood red on black lapels, tears in the eyes of men who never cried. But first, there were two solemn minutes of silence. England held her breath.

London, the heart of an empire, was still for two minutes.

A minute for the fallen.

Benson hadn't been a soldier, technically. His convictions opposed the War, but he hadn't run away. He hadn't taken the easy way out, and that, in Eric's opinion, was true courage. As much as any gentleman at the Britannia Club and perhaps more than most, Benson had earned his spurs doing what he believed to be right in spite of the cost to himself. Twice.

He could have sat back and let things be, when he realised he held evidence of Parker's innocence in his hands. But he stood up for a man he barely knew, and paid the price with his life.

And what of Emily Ang and Helen Benson? They'd served too, in their own way, but their lives weren't supposed to be on the line. Nobody expected tragedy to befall them on the home front. They were, in many ways, the civilian casualties of war, and their stories were all the more tragic as a result. As Mrs. Aldershott said, Emily was supposed to have been safe. Helen Benson was supposed to have been safe.

In spite of himself, Eric found his thoughts turning next to Patrick Norris. Norris had murdered three people and tried to pin the killings on a fourth. There was a part of Eric that revolted against the idea of including him in this solemnity after that, but Eric also remembered the jolly fellow who loved life, who laughed, who just wanted to be your friend. That hadn't been a mask, but a shadow. As Norris himself had said, he'd actually died in the War. Some scars weren't visible. And some deaths weren't physical.

Eric bowed his head, not for the Norris who'd tumbled out of his window on Bonfire Night, but for the Norris who'd gone off to Flanders knowing nothing of the Army apart from what he'd read in Kipling.

A minute for the survivors.

Frost dusted the ground at St. Tobias, crisp white over the green. Winter was coming. The church, grey and immutable, caught the stark morning sun on its stones and stained glass; its steeple gleamed like a beacon. In the churchyard, Eric picked his way through the colonies of monuments and gravestones to the two he loved best: the one with the phoenix, and the plain rectangular slab. He sat down beside them. His warmth melted the frost so the damp soaked his trousers, but he didn't much care about that.

"Hi, Mum. Hi, Dad. I've missed you."

He drew a pair of Haig Fund poppies from his pocket and placed them, one each, on his parents' graves.

"I missed All Souls'," he said. "Sorry about that. A lot's happened since we last spoke." And then the whole story came pouring out.

The Colonel, of course, listened quietly. Eric imagined him in a sunny room, feet up on an ottoman, shaggy brows shifting in response to each new revelation.

"Penny will be all right, I think," Eric concluded. "As long as she has her horses. She spends nearly every day on horseback, scouting the countryside and visiting the farms. It's made her quite popular with the rural community. I wouldn't be surprised if they made her a Member of Parliament now, like Lady Astor."

A gust of wind ruffled the petals of the Haig Fund poppies. Eric traced the gravestone inscriptions with his finger. *Him that cometh to me I will in no wise cast out,* and Matthew 10:39—*He that findeth his life shall lose it: and he that loseth his life for my sake shall find it.* He thought them strangely appropriate.

"Well, I'm still at the Britannia. Saxon tore up that letter of dismissal before I could touch it and declared they'd expel me over his dead body. The Britannia . . . it's not quite what I'd always imagined as a boy. It's less the company of heroes and more the company of survivors, I think. There are times when I'm still there, Dad. I wonder if your experience was very much different."

Eric looked up from the stone and took a moment to drink in the blue sky with its wintry-grey edging, and the green yews spreading over the churchyard monuments.

"Norris was right about one thing, at least: the world is still a beautiful place."

The nearest stained-glass window gleamed as the sunlight hit it. It was made to be seen from the inside; from the outside, one saw only the lead-lined shapes of Tobias and Raphael journeying to Media.

"I was thinking about escaping for a while. It turns out that Wolfe was serious about that antique collector in Churston who wanted someone to go to China for him. Unfortunately, he's already given the job to his brother, which might be just as well. I don't know that it would be much fun going about in a place where they expect you to speak Chinese because of how you look, only you don't know a single word aside from 'umbrella.' Eh, Mum? Getting from Limehouse Causeway to Pennyfields was harrowing enough; this would be mortifying. So, I'll carry on as I have before."

Eric leaned back against the cold marble of the gravestone. The sun was in a position now to fall directly on his face, a shaft of warmth through the seasonal cold. Just a few minutes more, he thought. Then he'd get back home, and return to his normal life. His employers were quite peeved at him for taking as long as he did on the last manuscript; the author had accepted an offer from another publisher in the meantime. But Eric had a new assignment to read and review, and he'd do a better job of it this time. The document was sitting in the passenger seat of the Vauxhall right now. So far, Eric had seen only the title: *The Menacing Mandarin*.

Eric really, really hoped it was about oranges.

The thirtieth of November was the first Sunday of Advent. Eric had been excited to spot a few flakes of snow as he left his flat in the morning, but by the time he reached the Britannia Club, it had turned to a bleak, freezing rain. The skies were dull and overcast; but for the bright lights of modern London, the world was painted in a palette of drab greys.

The posters had come down from outside the St. James Theatre. Eric didn't miss the leering yellow face of the play's Oriental villain, but he did miss the colour it lent to the street. Posters for the Christmas pantomime would be going up soon, though. Eric was looking forward to that.

Eric was greeted by a blast of warmth as he passed through the door of the Britannia Club. Avery, coming in with him, stopped in the vestibule to look around in wonder.

"So this is the Britannia," Avery said, eyeing the roster of fallen soldiers. "It certainly isn't anything I'm used to. I'll bet the ladies here have never even heard of patchouli."

"It's gentlemen only, Avery. And no, it isn't always like this. We're setting up for Christmas, you see." Eric scanned the roster for his Peterkin cousins, then paused at the *N*s. He imagined Patrick Norris listed there, and wondered how much longer the roster would be if it were to include the walking dead.

The grey was left outside the door, and the lobby was bathed in warm light. The marble floors glowed, and the walnut panelling was polished to a high shine. Looking straight up from the middle of the lobby, one could see the rain splashing harmlessly against the glass barrier of the skylight. Wreaths of holly had already been woven around the balustrade of the first-floor gallery and the stairs.

"Morning, Lieutenant Peterkin, sir," said Old Faithful from behind the front desk. "Got a guest with you today, have you?"

"Oh yes," said Eric as he signed the register. "Avery Ferrett's an old friend."

Avery had wandered to the foot of the stairs and was peering curiously up at the Arthurian Knights painting on the landing. Eric had told him often enough about how King Pellinore was modelled on a Peterkin ancestor, and about the sense of kinship he felt with Sir Palomides, the one dark face among the pale Britons.

Old Faithful called out to him, "Sir, upstairs is members only."

"Oh, don't worry about Avery," Eric said quickly. "Pretend he's a prospective member, and I'm showing him the amenities."

Old Faithful looked doubtful as Avery flashed him his most ingratiating smile. "Oh, all right," the old retainer said at last, "but only because it's you, sir. You've got mail, by the way. Rather a lot of it." He set a stack of letters on the desk, and Eric was delighted to recognise the handwriting and return addresses of his men in the War. Reaching out to them had been the right thing to do. It would be good to know how they were getting along on civvy street.

"And Mr. Bradshaw wants to speak with you," Old Faithful added. "At your earliest convenience."

"Oh." Eric didn't know what this could be about, but he preferred to get it over with as quickly as possible. On the other hand, there was Avery to consider.

The front door opened, and the familiar figure of Horatio Parker strode in, shaking the rain from his hat and trench coat. Eric waved Parker over.

"Avery, you remember Inspector Parker from Patrick Norris's inquest? He's our newest member. Parker, this is my friend Avery Ferrett."

Parker reached out to shake Avery's hand. "A friend of Peterkin's is a friend of mine," he declared. He was smiling and quite without his old haggardness. The last time Eric visited him at his Scotland Yard office, he'd had his Victoria Cross polished and proudly mounted in a display case on his desk.

"Really?" Avery replied. "Some of the friends Eric makes scare me to pieces."

"I've got to see Bradshaw about something," Eric told them. "If you're not doing anything else, Parker, I wonder if you'd show Avery the members' lounge and try to keep him out of trouble until I get back."

"It's no bother at all. Come along, Mr. Ferrett. The bar there is quite excellent, and Peterkin tells me that the dent in the woodwork comes from his grandfather having once tossed the club president over it in a brawl."

Eric watched the pair climb the stairs as Old Faithful pretended to be too busy with something else to notice any trespassing non-members. Then Eric made his way to Bradshaw's office.

The porcelain tortoises were all gone. Only the children's book print of the tortoise on a bicycle remained. Bradshaw was in the act of tidying as Eric came in.

They hadn't spoken since the night of Eric's so-called "hearing."

"I'll be brief," Bradshaw said, once Eric had seated himself. "There's been something of a coup on the board of officers. Aldershott has been kindly encouraged to step down both as club president and as an officer of the board. I'm sure you can guess why. Wolfe will be taking his place. And I'm stepping down as well."

"I'm sorry to hear that," Eric said.

"Don't be." Bradshaw put down his papers and stared out the window. There was nothing to see there but the rain falling into a dark brick-walled side passage. "The world's begun to move too quickly for an old soldier like me, Peterkin. It's time I moved on before I get turned onto my back."

"Moved on? Are you going somewhere?"

"I don't think I could stay here and not be club secretary. Those duties have been so much a part of my membership that I don't know how to separate them now." His beard twitched as he continued, "Bradshaw has friends across the Empire, doesn't he? It's time to see if that's still true. I'll be travelling . . . looking for a place that's still a bit like yesterday, where an old soldier like me still knows what's what. South Africa, perhaps. It'll be good to see the grass growing over the old battlefields of my youth." He looked back at Eric. "Perhaps one day you'll look at Flanders in much the same way."

Eric thought of the blood-red muck of no-man's-land. He knew better.

Bradshaw said, "I've asked for you to take over as club secretary, if you're willing. I'll be around until the New Year to show you the ropes."

"Me?"

"Yes, you," said Bradshaw with a gruff nod. He seemed to have regained his equilibrium as the wise old man of the Britannia: his dark eyes were calm, if more sombre than before, and not a hair was out of place on his beard. He sat down, at ease despite the absence of tortoises, and picked up his newspaper. Then he looked at the sheaf of envelopes in Eric's hands and asked, "What've you got there, Peterkin?"

"This? Letters from the men I used to have under me. I thought I'd check in on them, see that they're doing all right."

"Berkeley would be proud. Now get out. This is still my office, and I have the paper to read."

,

The holly wreaths had only just begun to make themselves known in the club lounge. As the Advent season progressed towards Christmas, the staff would drape more over the fireplace mantels and the windowsills. Already, the red berries offered a touch of festive contrast to the grey misery outside the windows. Saxon was sitting at one end of the bar, like a black blot on the escutcheon, with a dusty tome on his lap and an apple core floating in someone else's beer. He glanced up briefly to nod a greeting to Eric before turning back to his reading. Some things, Eric thought, didn't change. And he wouldn't want them to.

A cheery fire crackled in each of the fireplaces, including the one beside Eric's Usual Armchair. Parker and Avery were there, as Eric expected. Wolfe had joined them, and was looking with some doubt at the Tarot cards Avery had spread over the low table between them. Eric waved to them and went to sit down in his spot, only to find it occupied.

"Hullo, Eric." Penny was sitting in his Usual Armchair and smiling mischievously up at him. Her pleated plaid skirt and matching jacket were as much a sharp contrast with the solid greys and blacks of the gentlemen around her as the holly berries against the rain-spattered windowpanes.

"Penny. You're not supposed to be here."

"If your new club president doesn't mind, I don't see why you should."

Eric shot a look at Wolfe, who smiled playfully and said, "There have always been Peterkins at the Britannia, after all."

"If we weren't in mixed company," Eric replied with equal good humour, "there's another Peterkin legacy, involving the bar and the reigning club president, that I'd be happy to uphold. Congratulations, by the way. Bradshaw told me what happened."

"Thank you. I assume you're taking him up on his offer? Halpern and Merridew have threatened their resignations if you do."

Eric couldn't pick those two members out of a crowd if his life depended on it. They'd evidently been avoiding him all this time.

"What offer?" asked Avery, looking up from his cards.

"Bradshaw wants me to take over as club secretary," Eric told him.

"Oh, I say," Penny exclaimed, leaping out of the armchair to give him a hug. "They'll never be rid of you now!"

Avery and Parker congratulated him as well. Parker said, "Of course, if I were a suspicious man—and you know I am—I'd wonder if you orchestrated this whole thing to get rid of him so you could take his job."

Eric opened his mouth to protest, but Parker was grinning humorously at him. The police inspector seemed very fond of putting people off balance, and now he was free to inflict his humour on the innocent.

Wolfe grinned. "Wonderful! You'll be my secretary. I've been wanting a new batman."

"Pshaw," said Penny with a laugh. "Everyone knows it's the secretary who holds all the power around here."

Wolfe's grin vanished. "Miss Peterkin, I believe the club lounge is gentlemen only."

Penny said, "All right, then. I just came for Horsie, anyway. They were going to send an attendant to fetch him, but I told them I could do it myself."

Eric was puzzled. "Horsie? Who's—"

Horatio Parker stood up and linked his arm with Penny's. "If you mention that name within a hundred yards of a policeman," he told the group, "remember that there exists such a thing as the Yanks call 'police brutality.'"

As the pair left the lounge, Parker glanced back at Eric and winked.

Openmouthed, Eric sat down and dumped his collection of letters on the table, scattering Avery's careful Tarot layout. Wolfe's lips curled up in amusement as Eric, fumbling for something to do, picked up the first envelope and tore it open.

"I do think you could be more careful," Avery grumbled, collecting his cards from under the mess of correspondence. "That's ruined the reading, and the spirits never answer the same way twice."

Wolfe turned to him. "Still on about that rubbish? I suspect most spirits will have better things to do than associate with a clutch of mawkish spiritualists. I wouldn't be caught dead in their company."

"Mawkish spiritualists! Some very respectable people are spiritualists. Just today, somebody showed me a newspaper story about Sir Arthur Conan Doyle getting an apology from Lord Northcliffe, who's been dead for two years."

Avery had been full of that account in *The People* about Doyle's séance all morning, and Eric began to tune him out in favour of his correspondence. Ah, it appeared that Private Clark was now managing a pub in the East End. That was good to know. Eric assumed that Parker wouldn't be taking Penny to any East End pubs, though.

"The séance will turn out to be just another parlour trick," Wolfe told Avery. "I've yet to meet a spirit medium who wasn't a charlatan."

"You don't honestly expect a fellow of Doyle's calibre to be taken in, do you?"

"I think he needs to be taken in. He's clearly had too much sun."

Corporal Butler was a partner now in a motorcar repair shop in the Midlands. Eric made a note to motor out there one of these days.

"I know several mediums I'd stake my reputation on," Avery declared.

"Your reputation!" Wolfe scoffed. "I'll tell you what: ten shillings says that any spirit medium you care to bring into the Britannia, I can—"

"Don't do it, Avery," Eric said, without looking up from his next letter. Private Collins had gone back into the Army and was now a sergeant.

But Avery, rather rashly, had already put ten shillings on the wager, and Wolfe's eyes were gleaming wickedly.

"We'll want someone to act as referee," Wolfe said. "Ordinarily, I'd ask Peterkin here, as he never seems to have anything better to do with his life, but he seems a bit preoccupied at the moment."

The next nearest person was Saxon, still sitting at the end of the bar with an apple in his mouth. His eyes met Wolfe's, and Eric didn't have to look up to note the standoffish glare in them. Besides, here was a letter from Sergeant Forrester, who'd cut off his correspondence so abruptly some years before.

Eric read it once through, then a second time with a frown.

"This isn't Forrester's handwriting," he said, interrupting the discussion between Wolfe and Avery. The two turned to look curiously at him, and he went on, "It says he's very well, and he's got a job on a ship, which means he'll be hard to reach . . . Forrester's useless on water. He gets more violently seasick than anyone else I know. Something's wrong, Avery."

"Already? But . . . what about this bet?"

"Bother the bet. Forrester was one of my men, and I'm responsible for him. We've got to see what's going on."

"The more things change," Wolfe murmured, smirking as Eric hurriedly shoved the rest of the correspondence into his pocket. "Bon voyage, Peterkin! Maybe we'll have some sport when you get back."

But Eric had already marched out of the lounge, his stride swift and purposeful, and Avery had to trot to catch up.

AUTHOR'S NOTE

My relationship with detective fiction began when I picked up a copy of *The Mystery of the Flying Express*, a Hardy Boys mystery, at a school book fair. I was eight years old. From there, I went to Encyclopedia Brown, McGurk, and onwards. By the time I was fourteen, I was stalking Brother Cadfael in the local library and trading Christies with classmates. I got interested enough to make a study of the genre for a school project—at which point I expanded my exposure to include Raymond Chandler, Dashiell Hammett, and Ellery Queen. It was Ellery Queen who first articulated to me to the fundamental principle of the genre: that it was a game played with the reader, and that the reader ought to be given every clue and opportunity to solve the mystery for themselves before the detective delivers the solution. And then, everything made sense.

Edgar Allan Poe's "The Murders in the Rue Morgue," 1841, is credited as the first modern detective story, but this understanding of the detective story as a game seems to have only really taken off around the period between the two world wars—the Golden Age of detective fiction. Ronald Knox compiled his decalogue of rules, and the Detection Club had its initiation oath. All of it was directed at how the game should be played. Detective fiction wasn't just literature; it was interactive entertainment. There is no Encyclopedia Brown equivalent in any other genre.

But even as I was discovering the joys of Golden Age detective fiction, the efficiency of modern forensics made me uneasy. It was fascinating to see a killer brought to heel by the DNA analysis of a single speck of spit, but I got the sense that the resources available to modern police put the amateur sleuth increasingly out of their league. Aunt Charity might have a keen eye for human nature, but what are the chances that she'd know enough to put her ahead of Inspector Dogsworth and his team? What are the chances that Inspector Dogsworth would share any clues with Aunt Charity?

And I wanted an amateur sleuth. I wanted someone who could be a stand-in for the reader, someone who could bring the entire detection process within the realm of possibility for the ordinary civilian. It seemed to me that there was a greater scope for such things in the world of the 1920s and 1930s, when things like police protocol were, perhaps, a little less set in stone, and the investigative procedures a little less dependent on specialised training and equipment.

Mind you, there are dozens of writers out there with amateur sleuths in the modern age. They've managed it, and I congratulate them; I just wonder if I could do it convincingly myself.

In any case, the 1920s were a delicious time to consider. It was an age of transition, and such times are always exciting. We still had many of the manners and mores of the Victorian era, but also the birth of much of the modern world. Telephones, radio, cars, electricity . . . some of this technology was new; some of it had been around for a while but was only just now becoming freely available to the masses. Someone coming out of the Victorian or Edwardian eras would have been bowled over by this explosion of modern innovation.

Some things that we take for granted today were exceptional in that era, or simply didn't exist. Searching the newspaper archives, for one thing—nowadays, Eric and Avery might have accomplished all they did with under an hour of internet research. And cars then were rare enough that simply having one could be enough to constitute a clue.

Looking at behaviour, much seemed the same as it is today; but then little things crop up, like whether or not one addresses someone by their first or last name, and what it means either way. One of my most treasured possessions is an etiquette book from 1915—just nine years off—which provides me with such gems as how you always introduce men to women and never the other way around. Looking at the literature of the time, one finds certain words and phrases that have fallen out of fashion but are still perfectly understandable. Take the word *ghastly*, for instance: We know what it means, but who says it nowadays without an eye to effect? And then there are the other words and phrases whose meanings have shifted, but whose older meanings are still recognised. The world was just similar enough to our modern day to be familiar, but just different enough to be remarkable. Curious. *Exotic.*

As fantastic as it looked, the 1920s was also an era shadowed by the devastation of the First World War. A great deal of the joie de vivre stemmed from a rejection of the horrors of the war. It did occur to me to wonder why this didn't seem to figure more prominently in the works I was reading. I mean, it was certainly acknowledged to have happened, but the long-lasting effects seemed only barely touched. Perhaps I wasn't reading the right books . . . or perhaps it was, on some level, so much a normal part of everyday life that nobody thought to remark on it. But it really did seem to me that, to understand the era, I had to understand the war that gave birth to it—all the first principles that added up to this exotic creature they called the Roaring Twenties.

We did cover some of the First World War in school, as I recall. In history class, we saw the tangle of ententes and alliances that resulted in a conflagration that few people on the ground could adequately explain. That was all very cerebral for me. More visceral was literature class, where we compared Rupert Brooke's "The Soldier" to Wilfred Owen's "Anthem for Doomed Youth." This was in Singapore, though; we had less at stake there. In Canada, where I live now, I find that nearly everyone knows John McCrae's "In Flanders Fields" by heart. It seems to be part of the national mythology that

Canada really became truly itself—not an appendage of the United Kingdom—on Vimy Ridge, and I think Australia and New Zealand have a similar relationship with Gallipoli. Whether or not you understand why it happened, this was a war with an impact.

The devastation was greater than ever before, inflicted with technology for which the old tactics were ill-prepared to handle. Poison gas—chlorine, mustard, and phosgene—was a new thing in this war; the military uses of aviation had only just begun to be explored in 1911; and the guns, of course, grew more powerful with each passing year. The war was fought on more fronts than just the trenches across Flanders, but Flanders remains in the popular imagination for its four long, frustrating years of stalemate: a standing target against which everything could be thrown. This was the war for which Bradshaw trained his men but the nature of which he could not himself conceive.

As to the human cost, the numbers vary. The British death toll is estimated at between 700,000 and 800,000: roughly 500 a day over a four-year period. When the War first broke out, before volunteer recruitment and conscription, the British Army had a manpower strength of 733,514. Let that sink in for a moment, and note that many other world powers had it worse. In total, some ten million soldiers were killed in the service of the War to End All Wars.

Statistics are dry. Could I relate to any of this on a more human level? My own personal experience with the military came in my two years of National Service with the Singapore Army, but this was in peacetime and I'd never been thrust into any armed conflicts.

I was able to pick up a battered copy of J. C. Dunn's *The War the Infantry Knew, 1914–1919* back in 2012. It's compiled from the journals of multiple soldiers, including Dunn himself, and I learned from it that life in the trenches was not an unrelenting misery. There were bright moments. One of the most fantastic sections comes in an entry for the twentieth of June 1916, in which the officers, after a dinner welcoming a few new faces into their ranks, engage in a spirited romp across the devastated countryside, playing follow-my-leader like a bunch of six-year-olds. I imagine they must have been drunk, though if not—well, more power to them.

The next entry mentions taking one of those new faces out for his first look at the trenches, and the lines, "He was thrilled . . . Poor boy! three hours later he was dead." And the entry after that is a hair-raising account of being trapped in no-man's-land with one dead private and another whose legs had both been broken.

As I write this, it is seven months short of the centennial anniversary of the armistice, not something I thought about when writing the first draft of this book seven years ago. There is no one left who actually remembers the First World War as a personal experience. All we have is documentation and the things they left behind. One hopes, at least, that these preserved memories will function as a great "USE WITH CAUTION" stamp on the war machine, and that nothing ever escalates to the same levels of devastation as was seen then. As Siegfried Sassoon wrote, "Look down, and swear by the slain of the War that you'll never forget."

In the midst of those dark memories, though, I should like to hold on to that image of a group of grown men, experienced warriors, playing follow-my-leader through a war zone. I think it is a testament to the human spirit, this ability to carve a little humour out of the horror and thereby maintain one's sanity. And perhaps it is also a precursor to that postwar impulse to make a game out of murder.

One of the things to come out of the Great War was the term *shell shock*, and it wasn't a stretch to recognise it as an older name for what we call PTSD today. Many of the men I encountered in my reading ought to be at least familiar with it, if not suffering from some mild form of it themselves. But it turns out that not only was shell shock a much narrower definition of the phenomenon, the entire concept of post-traumatic stress was barely understood at all. It had once been believed, for instance, that actual exposure to enemy artillery fire was required for shell shock to occur, but the evidence of symptoms among unexposed soldiers soon proved otherwise.

I have no doubt that many soldiers over the centuries, in countless wars since Cain first raised a rock at Abel, have experienced some form of PTSD, but nobody ever really thought of it as anything unusual. Because of the increased scope and intensity of its devastation, though, the First World War brought out the affected soldiers in greater quantities than ever before, and with greater severity of symptoms. The phenomenon became impossible to ignore.

The first use of the term *shell shock* in a medical journal was by Charles Myers in 1915, though he claimed not to have invented it. He was frustrated by the military's unwillingness to recognise the dimensions of the problem, and it appears he was dissatisfied with the implied limited scope of its name. Other medical professionals joined him, though. After the War, hospitals like Craiglockhart and Seale Hayne took on the rehabilitation of shell-shocked survivors, some with notable success. The two texts mentioned in the story are real; and in one case, the choice of *war neurosis* as a better name certainly comes from a desire to expand the definition to include more of the behavioural anomalies that arise as a result of traumatic experiences.

I don't think it takes much to imagine what the attitudes of the time might have been like. Already, a soldier who folded under bombardment was called a coward. Once shell shock was recognised as a mental issue, it was probably not a large step to decide that sufferers must be "mad," and no one wants to think of themselves as "mad." Psychoanalysis was still in its infancy, and it wasn't so long ago that mental illness meant straitjackets, dirty cells, and a complete loss of human dignity. And to fall was to admit weakness—or worse, cowardice. No one wants to do that, either. It's only natural that many soldiers, those who could hide it, tried to keep their distance from any suggestion that they might have been adversely affected by their experiences—to remain in denial that there was ever anything wrong. And of course, public perception was limited to whatever extreme cases made the news.

It's tempting to say we know better now, but I think that human understanding will never quite attain the truth of anything. We still have a lot to learn, and we always will.

As prominent as PTSD is in military circles, I was surprised to discover that "the soldier's disease" actually referred to morphine addiction. As Aldershott says in the story, it was a term coined in the American Civil War, when rampant use of the drug resulted in widespread addiction. North America had more serious troubles with addiction than the United Kingdom did, apparently. It was such a nonissue in the UK that, until 1916, anyone could buy morphine over the counter there. When the issue of morphine addiction began to appear on English soil, it was seen as a Canadian problem, as the addicts causing trouble were mostly Canadian soldiers. A law was passed imposing a fine on anyone selling morphine (among other drugs) to soldiers—though regular civilians were still free to do as they pleased. It wasn't until after the war, in 1920, that the law was extended to include civilians in the ban. Even with the press now harping on the dangers of drug use, I suspect that many of the older generation still saw drug addiction as essentially the same thing as alcoholism. Remember that when Conan Doyle gave Sherlock Holmes a cocaine addiction, it was more with a view to giving him an interesting personal quirk than to imply any depravity on the part of the character.

So, just as the fashions and the technology were changing, the old attitudes to drug use were changing as well. And meanwhile, among the soldiers . . . a generation of them, already traumatised, came home to a prewar attitude to medication and a postwar fear of addiction. Perhaps the medical professionals were more careful after the lessons of the American Civil War, but morphine was still used to treat, for example, pneumonia. People would still self-medicate. Given the trauma to which these soldiers had just been subjected, it is hardly surprising if they were more susceptible than most to the addiction of painkiller drugs. Norris was hardly alone here.

One unfortunate side effect of the rising awareness of drug use as a criminal issue seems to have been a vilification of the Chinese community. The Chinese had long been associated with opium, and when it disappeared from the ordinary English chemist's shelf, it was assumed that anyone with opium—or the related opiate drugs—must have got it through the Chinese. There evolved myths of far-reaching criminal empires headed by Chinese masterminds, and Sax Rohmer's Fu Manchu, though his first appearance predated the ban on hard drugs by seven years, was the quintessential example of this: sophisticated, educated, intelligent, and utterly immoral.

Perhaps there was an element of blame shifting involved, a desire for a scapegoat who wasn't "one of us." Certainly, there was an element of romantic exoticism mixed in. My decision to make the opium den here an Orientalist pastiche is far from merely humorous. It's about the lure of the exotic when limited to only its trappings—something empty and exploitative.

And this brings us back to the rules of the game: specifically, Ronald Knox's decalogue and the infamous fifth rule, that "no Chinaman must figure in the story." It's a much misunderstood rule, I think. Anytime I bring it up, people assume that Knox was speaking against the appearance of Asians in general. In fact, he was speaking against the then-prevalent trope of the malevolent Chinese arch-criminal, and pointing out the unfairness of the stereotype. People today assume the opposite because they don't know the context in which the rule was made. We're not surrounded today by "yellow peril" stories, the very sort of thing Knox found so noxious—and thank goodness for that.

I've been very lucky. Even as a first-generation immigrant, I've never felt that my race was held against me in any way. I'm tickled that the offensive racist stereotype attached to me and mine should be a sophisticated supervillain—tomorrow, I shall take over the world—but the idea that I might once have been associated with a depraved "other" still comes as something of a shock.

As I researched the experience, I found accounts of race riots in Britain over a perceived loss of seaman jobs to the Chinese. In

Liverpool, at least, there appears to have been a curfew for "alien seamen" after the 1919 riots—and officials who applied the rules to non-seamen as well. Many of the Chinese men married British wives, and these wives were automatically considered aliens upon their marriage. The "yellow peril" stories seem quaint today, and I have no doubt that many were written only because the Oriental mastermind sold books faster than a sexy vampire; but they were hardly innocent.

These things all came together in the Limehouse opium den: drugs, exoticism, and Oriental villainy. Fu Manchu's secret lair was invariably here. In reality, any opium dens that may have been there had died out by the turn of the century. Drug dealers did exist, but probably no more than anywhere else. The Limehouse opium den itself was largely a myth by the 1920s, perpetuated by the aforementioned "yellow peril" stories and a press anxious for any news that would support the ongoing narrative of the sinister Asiatic corrupting the morals of innocent white women.

I knew none of this when I decided to make Eric Peterkin half-Chinese.

I hadn't done it with any thought of responding to the "yellow peril." That ship had not only sailed; it had come back and been dry-docked. Rohmer's Fu Manchu already had his answer in Earl Derr Biggers's Charlie Chan, and time has reduced the old supervillain to little more than an amusing relic.

I'd done it, perhaps, with an idea of putting more of myself into my creation, without excluding him from all the sorts of stories I want to tell. I'm not half-Chinese; I'm all Chinese. But when I fell in love with the Golden Age detective story, perhaps I also fell in love with the setting and the milieu. I want to send Eric Peterkin off to a succession of country house murders, which could get difficult for a fully Chinese immigrant, given the racial climate of the time.

Singapore is, in many ways, very British. Modern Singapore was founded as a British port in 1819, and remained under British control until 1963. Life is conducted primarily in English, and a great deal of the political and commercial infrastructure dates back to the old colonial days. At the same time, Singapore is also firmly Asian, with the Chinese forming a powerful majority. The relationship is, perhaps, a little complicated. On the one hand, no one can deny that without the British, Singapore as a political entity simply would not exist; on the other hand, the British were a recognisable "other," a foreign colonial master. Looking into the mirror, we feared losing ourselves, and the result was a backlash against becoming too westernised. Meanwhile, we spooned Bovril onto our rice congee, and we drank bird's nest soup in hopes it would help with our GCSEs. We traded oranges at Chinese New Year over dishes of Indian curry and Malay desserts while Duncan Watt read us the English news.

(On a weeklong visit to the UK in 2017, one of the first things I did was pick up a jar of Bovril—the real stuff, thick and black and gooey—which I proceeded to make into beef tea every night. Dear Canada, Bovril is *not* beef stock: it's a liquefied cow, and that sloshing bottle on your grocery store shelf is not the same thing at all.)

Growing up in that milieu, I felt a little caught out between the two cultural identities. I'd developed a certain Anglophilia, even as I was encouraged to embrace my ethnically Chinese heritage. Perhaps Eric Peterkin's biracial status is as much a reflection of this culture clash as it is a pragmatic attempt to project myself into one of the Golden Age's country house parties. Whatever the case, it's made him a permanent "other," an outsider whether he's in London or Hong Kong. His world is somewhat less welcoming than the one I've been blessed with, and one can only hope that he, like Poirot, will in time be able to turn his otherness to his advantage.

In other respects, I like to think that Eric Peterkin follows in the footsteps of the fictional detectives I've always admired. I've always favoured the puzzle-type mysteries of the Golden Age, as I think this discourse should have made clear already. These tended to have quirky detectives who relied on their brains far more than their brawn, so it goes without saying that Eric Peterkin's chief asset should be his intellect. But . . . I will admit that I wanted to move away a little bit from that intellectual infallibility as well. I made

Eric young, brash, and impulsive—qualities more generally associated with the Watson than the Holmes in any detective–sidekick pairing.

He's far from infallible, but he'll always know exactly who the murderer is when he begins his summation. That is a promise.

So there's my detective. And there's the world I'm throwing him into: a world streaked by the shadows of the war that separated it from the age before, and determined to *live* in rejection of the darkness. It's more than just art deco architecture (which technically doesn't exist until 1925, a year after the story) and drop-waisted flapper frocks. It's the passing of an age, and life in the aftermath. It's a rising awareness and a need to deal with things that had never been problems before. I don't think exoticism and the romanticisation of the foreign is new, but it's there . . . and always will be.

This is not an era I've ever lived in, and it fascinates like a sailor's first foreign port. The unexpected details surprise and delight. I don't think I can ever fully understand everything about it without a time machine, but I like to think that I've come some way closer to understanding a part of it—gotten a bit closer to the heart of the era, beyond the trappings thereof . . . made of it more than mere exoticism.

At the heart of any mystery, I think, is a desire to understand . . . to get to the heart, from which all the trappings flow. And that is more than just a game.

HISTORICAL NOTES

The Britannia Club is, of course, a fictional establishment, as is the Arabica coffeehouse. Sotheby Manor, the Butterworth Arms, the Hammer and Anvil, the Green Elephant inn, the churches of St. Tobias and St. Julian, Brolly's music hall, and the village of Wexford Crossing are also fictional. The town of Barchester and the county of Barsetshire are an homage to Anthony Trollope.

I don't actually know if the town of Chichester had a motor coach service to the surrounding villages during the First World War and the years following. This was a necessary fabrication for plot-related purposes. The hospitals mentioned—Graylingwell and the Royal West Sussex—did indeed exist, but are no longer. Graylingwell's last psychiatric inpatients were moved out in 2001, and its buildings were sold to developers in 2010. The Royal West Sussex was closed in 1972 following the commissioning of the new St. Richard's Hospital, and its building became part of a housing development. I will admit that the presence of a morgue in the Royal West Sussex is only a guess on my part, but I believe it to be a reasonable assumption.

I continue to be fascinated by the architecture of Chichester Cross.

Netley Hospital, also known as the Royal Victoria Hospital, fell into gradual decline after the Second World War. It was damaged by fire in 1963 and demolished in 1966.

The Golden Lion pub still operates on King Street. However, the St. James Theatre was pulled down in 1957, despite organised protests and campaigns led by Laurence Olivier and Vivien Leigh. A modern office building, without a neoclassical facade, now stands in its place.

A new facility for the newspaper archives in Colindale was completed in 1932, allowing people to consult them directly without the papers' having to be delivered to the British Museum. Until then, these deliveries were made just once a week. I have taken liberties with just exactly when in the week the deliveries might have been made, allowing Eric Peterkin the convenience of consulting the Sussex newspapers within a day or two of his wanting them. Today, the archives are digitised, and what might once have taken weeks to discover can now be found after a few minutes of an internet search.

I'm only guessing, based on a plan of the British Museum from the 1930s, that public access to the Newspaper Reading Room was from the side entrance on Montague Street.

The Shafi was a real Indian restaurant, opening its doors in 1920. It was not the first of its kind, though by the 1940s it had become something of a social hub for London's Indian community.

While opium dens did exist in Limehouse in the 1870s, they'd been stamped out by the turn of the century. By 1924, Chinatown's reputation for drugs and gambling would have been largely unfounded, perpetuated only by the romantic imaginations of the press and a general suspicion of the Chinese. Following the bombings of the Second World War, London's Chinatown moved out of Limehouse and westward to the area around Gerrard Street. The reputation for opium dens does not appear to have followed it.

The British Broadcasting Company was a commercial venture, unlike the British Broadcasting Corporation we know today. The Company was dissolved in 1926, and its assets transferred to the Corporation.

MI1b was merged with the Navy's Room 40 team in 1919 to form the Government Code and Cypher School. The GCCS would be housed at Bletchley Park during the Second World War, where its crypto-analytical work would once again prove invaluable. One presumes that the upgraded accommodations helped as well.

Mention is made of the art deco aesthetic. In fact, the name would not come into use until the Exposition Internationale des Arts Décoratifs et Industriels Modernes, held in Paris in 1925, one year after the events of this novel.

Both *Shell Shock and Its Lessons* and *Psycho-Analysis and the War Neuroses* are real texts, representing the birth of studies into what we now call PTSD, or post-traumatic stress disorder. At the time, it was unlikely to have been understood at all by the ordinary civilian. While many soldiers might have recognised something different about themselves or their mates—common tendencies towards certain behaviours, for instance—I doubt if they'd have really understood it either.

It should go without saying that all the weather effects are entirely my invention, with no regard either to how weather patterns work or to what the weather actually was in the various places described at the dates and times mentioned.

It should also go without saying that all the characters of the story are fictional. Mention has been made of certain real-life figures, however: John Archer, Philip Bowden-Smith, Sax Rohmer, Wilfred Owen, Field Marshall Douglas Haig, Rudyard Kipling, Alfred Hobbs, Sigmund Freud, Lady Astor, Sir Arthur Conan Doyle, and, of course, King George V.

King George V felt very strongly that the Victoria Cross, once given, should never be taken away. While the mechanism for its forfeiture remains in place, no Victoria Cross has been forfeited since 1908.